MW01002668

SECONDS TO LIVE

DISCARD

ALSO BY MELINDA LEIGH

SCARLET FALLS NOVELS
Hour of Need
Minutes to Kill

SHE CAN SERIES
She Can Run
She Can Tell
She Can Scream
She Can Hide
He Can Fall (A Short Story)
She Can Kill

MIDNIGHT NOVELS
Midnight Exposure
Midnight Sacrifice
Midnight Betrayal

ROGUE RIVER NOVELLAS
Gone to Her Grave
Walking on Her Grave

ROGUE WINTER NOVELLAS
Tracks of Her Tears

SECONDS TO LIVE

A SCARLET FALLS NOVEL

MELINDA LEIGH

Montlake
Romance

This is a work of fiction. Names, characters, organizations, places, events, and incidents are either products of the author's imagination or are used fictitiously.

Text copyright © 2016 Melinda Leigh
All rights reserved.

No part of this book may be reproduced, or stored in a retrieval system, or transmitted in any form or by any means, electronic, mechanical, photocopying, recording, or otherwise, without express written permission of the publisher.

Published by Montlake Romance, Seattle

www.apub.com

Amazon, the Amazon logo, and Montlake Romance are trademarks of Amazon.com, Inc., or its affiliates.

ISBN-13: 9781503935020
ISBN-10: 1503935027

Cover design by Jason Blackburn

Printed in the United States of America

For the man who taught me happily-ever-after isn't a dream
Twenty-two years and still going strong
Love you, Babe.

Chapter One

Saturday, June 18, five p.m.

"Please let me go." Missy spoke to the tiny green LED light in the corner of the ceiling. The light blinked like a buoy beacon in the darkness, letting her know that the camera was working.

That *he* was watching.

The only other light in the room was a red LED mounted by the door. A bottle of water sat on the cement next to it. The light's reflection glowed red on the clear plastic. As thirsty as she was, she couldn't drink that water. After all, that must have been how he'd abducted her. He must have slipped something into her coffee. Not that she remembered.

Licking her dry lips, she shifted her position, drawing her knees up and hugging her legs. In the corner of her cell, water puddled on the concrete, and the cinder block walls dripped. Her body ached from sitting on damp cement—and from what he'd done to her.

How long would it take for her to die of dehydration? Though Scarlet Falls was in the middle of a heat wave, her prison was cool. The darkness, the damp, and the misery in her bones suggested she was below ground.

She could possibly survive for a few days without water.

A few days . . .

How would she bear it?

"You have a choice to make." The disembodied voice sounded from a speaker mounted next to the camera.

He'd made her an offer. This whole ordeal could be over quickly. There would be no more pain. The thought of ending her nightmare sounded as peaceful as sunlight on her skin.

She wasn't even sure how long she'd been there. What seemed like forever was probably a couple of days. What was he planning next?

Fear drove her to her feet. The cement scraped under her shoes. She stretched her arms over her head, her fingertips just brushing the heavy wooden beams of the ceiling. She paced the length of her prison, five strides forward, five strides back. She reached her hands out at her sides, and her fingertips brushed the rough cinder blocks on both sides.

At the end of her cell, she stopped and flattened her palms against the wooden door. She knew from experience that it was heavy and thick. It would not give to her pushes or kicks, not that she had any energy left for such efforts.

The camera blinked. Watching. Always watching.

So far, he'd been true to his word. He'd kept every promise he'd made. The first thing he'd said to her was that if she resisted, he would hurt her. And so he had. The memory sent a chill straight through her bowels. A sob rose into her throat and bubbled from her mouth. Her bones trembled.

Sinking back to the concrete, she crossed her legs and breathed, seeking calm, but it was no use. Her skin itched with the need to escape.

No matter what it cost.

This could all be over. Release was just a word away.

Hope died inside her. She had no illusions. She would never return to the life she'd worked so hard to rebuild. But in a way, knowing that there would be no more struggle, no more resisting temptation every single moment of every single day, was liberating.

Freeing.

Just as he'd promised.

She was tired of fighting. Even before this, every day had been a battle. He'd made her see that so clearly. But it could end here and now. Could she finally find real peace?

I always keep my promises.

She swallowed, her throat raw from unanswered screams. The hours of darkness were more than she could bear. Her willpower was ebbing, seeping from her pores like sweat.

Her mother would be devastated, but Mom's happiness wasn't enough. Missy was a coward. Selfish. Only concerned with herself. He was right. She didn't deserve forgiveness or redemption. Silence pressed in on her, blanketing her with fear of the darkness. Of the sound of the door unlocking. Of the terror of what might happen. Of the horror of what had already happened.

But once she answered, there would be no going back. Her escape would be a one-way journey. Who was she kidding? She'd gone to a place from which there was no return. She might as well finish it.

Nausea rose. She bent forward, her body folding at the waist. She rested her forehead against the cold, hard floor. She was done.

Her neck muscles ached as she lifted her head. Her voice sounded raspy, foreign as she said, "Yes."

"I didn't hear you. Have you decided?" the voice asked.

"Yes!" she shouted, weeping.

"All right." The sadness, the sheer disappointment that emanated from the speaker, surprised her.

"I thought this was what you wanted," she said.

"It's not about what I want," he answered. "You need to be sure. No mulligans."

Anger and hopelessness swamped her fear. After all he'd done to her . . .

"What do you want from me?" she screamed. Then her voice dropped to a frightened whimper. "I can't take any more. I'll do whatever you want. I just want it to be over."

Nothing mattered except that it be over.

Watching her in the monitor, her eyes and face tinted alien-green in the low-light surveillance camera feed, he ignored her display of temper.

Her voice weakened like the dying embers of a fire. "Please."

He'd known this was going to happen today. Her predictability was underwhelming. Maybe if she'd resisted longer, he would have been interested. But she'd failed him in so many ways.

She hadn't lasted two full days. Her breakdown had been mental rather than physical.

He liked the dark, but it terrified her. He'd discovered that immediately. Left with only her imagination to entertain her, and encouraged by the welcome reception in the room down the hall, she was drowning in her own fear. Endless hours of complete darkness, a ration of pain, and isolation had brought her will to live to its knees.

Even though he'd expected it, Missy's failure weighed on him. The disappointment was crushing. How would he continue?

How could he not?

He had a mission. She'd had her chance to prove herself, but she hadn't been able to stay the course. Somewhere out there was The One who could pass the test, handle the punishment earned. But it wasn't Missy.

She deserved her end as much as the pain he'd inflicted as her penance. She occupied the bottom of the humanity barrel. He was doing the world a great service by ridding it of her and others of her kind.

"You can't leave me in here any longer." She lurched to her feet, lunged across the room, and slapped the door. "You promised. You said that if I cooperated, if I did what you wanted, that it would be over."

He froze. She was right. This wasn't her fault. She couldn't change her nature, couldn't make herself more than she was. He should have known when she hadn't fought him. He should have known then she wasn't special. That she would fail his test.

That she wasn't The One.

He glanced back at the dark screen, the green-tinted eyes that stared into the lens. Unlike her stay, her death would be painless. A promise was a promise, and he was a man of his word, even if a more violent death was completely justified.

It didn't matter. He was done with her. Unlike her abduction, which had been filled with hope and promise, her disposal was simply a chore. But did it have to be? Could the end be just as fulfilling as the beginning?

She could still be of use to him. Though her trial had been a failure, her death needn't be in vain. Her last act on this earth could serve a purpose.

His purpose.

She could relay his message. But how?

He continued on his way, his step quicker, his mood lighter.

This one might not have been The One, but that special someone was still out there, waiting.

Chapter Two

Detective Stella Dane could smell the body from the street.

Just a faint whiff, but the presence of it told her the corpse wasn't fresh. Even in a heat wave like the freakish one currently suffocating upstate New York, it took a day or so for a corpse to reek.

She closed the driver's side door of the dark blue, dented sedan assigned to her when she'd been promoted to detective six months before.

The senior detective on the SFPD, Brody McNamara, climbed out of the passenger seat. He sniffed, and a frown creased his lean, tanned face. "This is when I miss winter."

The afternoon sun beat down on the top of her head as they walked past a line of emergency vehicles toward the baseball diamond. Three patrol officers secured the scene. Behind the medical examiner's van, Dr. Frank Jenkins and his assistant donned personal protective equipment: coveralls, boots, gloves. Next to the CSI van, a three-member county forensics team suited up in their own PPEs. A local news crew cruised onto the street and parked at the curb.

Wonderful. The vultures had already found the carcass.

"Detective Dane!"

Stella ignored the reporter's shout. What could she tell him? She hadn't even seen the body yet.

In the small parking lot, a middle-aged man sat on the rear bumper of a minivan. He leaned forward, forearms propped on his thighs, his face hanging over his splayed legs. Sweat beaded on his bald spot. Squatting in front of him, an EMT offered him a bottle of water. Without straightening, the man shook his head. The EMT placed the bottle at his feet.

A uniformed officer approached Stella and Brody. He nodded toward the minivan. "Body was found by Ron Taggert. He's a Little League coach. He arrived at the field to set up for his team's practice, saw the dead woman in the dugout, and called nine-one-one."

"You want to see the body first or talk to the coach?" Stella asked Brody.

The officer lowered his voice. "Mr. Taggert's pretty shook up. The puddle of vomit next to the dugout is his. The EMTs wanted to take him to the hospital, but he declined."

Brody cast the man a sympathetic glance. "Normally I'd like to see the body first, but this heat is brutal. Let's get the poor man out of here."

They skirted a puddle and crossed the asphalt.

"You take the lead on this one," Brody said. "You're ready, and with Hannah's father barely hanging on, I'll probably be taking some personal leave in the next week or so." Brody checked his phone.

"I'm sorry to hear about Hannah's dad." Stella thoroughly approved of Brody's girlfriend, Hannah Barrett, and the thought of her losing her father brought back a wave of sorrow. Fifteen years after her own dad's death, sudden reminders could still make Stella's grief feel impossibly raw.

Brody nodded. "Thanks. He's been sick a long time, but his death will still be hard on her."

"I'm sure it will."

The death of Hannah's father would surely bring her younger brother back to town. The last Stella had heard, Mac Barrett was in Brazil. Not that she was keeping track of him. OK. She was. But thoughts of Mac, his lean body, and the clear blue eyes that spoke more than he did had no business at a death scene. Why couldn't she be distracted by a man who didn't spend half his time in South America?

The first time they'd met, back in November, the Scarlet Falls PD had been in the middle of a desperate search for a killer—a killer Stella could have stopped if her aim had been truer in a shootout earlier that day. But he'd escaped and embarked on a terrible spree of violence. Brody and Hannah had nearly lost their lives, and two cops had died. Two families had opened their doors to uniformed chaplains on their doorsteps. Stella's stomach cringed at the memory of her own mother opening their front door fifteen years before and collapsing the instant she'd seen the chief and chaplain standing on the stoop. Her mother had known her father was dead before either man had said a word.

Stella put the past away and focused on Mac.

Last fall, he'd been invaluable in tracking down the killer. He'd saved lives. So when others were quick to write him off as scattered, Stella knew better. There was more to Mac Barrett than a handsome face. Much more.

"Earth to Stella." Brody's voice pulled her back to the job at hand. "I was asking how you felt about taking the lead."

"Good," she said, faking confidence while nerves gathered in her belly. Their small police force had only two detectives to work everything from burglary to homicide. Since her promotion, she'd worked plenty of cases alongside Brody, but this would be the first time she'd be lead on a major crime. The responsibility weighed on her. All she'd wanted for her whole life was to be a good cop.

Brody stopped and caught her gaze. "You can handle this."

"I know," she said without hesitation. She was meant to be a detective. It was in her genes. Her father had been killed in the line of duty, her grandfather was a retired NYPD detective, and her siblings were all involved in law enforcement.

Mr. Taggert looked up as Stella and Brody stopped in front of him. The man was in his mid-fifties. His face was pasty, and the hands clenched between his knees trembled.

"I'm Detective Dane and this is Detective McNamara," Stella said. "Are you sure you don't need to go to the hospital?"

Mr. Taggert swallowed. His eyes flickered to the dugout and back. "I just want to go home."

"We'll get you out of here shortly." Stella began, "Can you tell us what happened?"

"We're supposed to have practice in a couple of hours. But after yesterday's thunderstorms, I wanted to check the field and make sure it wasn't too muddy. That's when I smelled it. At first I thought an animal had gotten into the dugout and died. But when I looked inside . . ." His eyes closed, his lips flattened, and he breathed through his nose for a few seconds. "Well, I could tell right away that she was dead."

"Do you recognize her?" Stella asked.

He shook his head.

"Did you touch the body?"

He closed his eyes and swallowed. "God. No."

"Where are the rest of the kids?" she asked. The only nonemergency vehicle in view was Taggert's minivan.

"I called everyone and canceled tonight's practice right after I called nine-one-one." He drank from the water bottle.

Stella scanned the empty fields. "Do you know when this field was used last?"

"Games usually run until nine or ten Saturday night. Yesterday was a washout." Taggert screwed the cap back on.

But the facility wasn't fenced. Anyone could have wandered in.

"Did you see any other people or vehicles in the area?" Stella asked.

"No."

Stella considered the wet ground. "We'll need to borrow your shoes."

Mr. Taggert followed her gaze and began unlacing his muddy cleats. "Sure. I have my work boots in the car."

"Thanks for your help. We'll call you if we have any further questions." Stella led the way toward the ball field. Brody followed.

A tall chain-link fence ran behind home plate and angled off toward first and third bases. Bleachers fanned out on either side. They turned toward the yellow crime scene tape that fluttered around one of the dugouts. Mud sucked at their shoes as they walked across ten feet of sopping grass.

Stella studied the spongy ground between the parking area and the field. "Two sets of footprints. Forensics will have to match the treads, but let's assume those are Taggert's." She pointed to a line of footprints that ended next to the vomit. The second set stopped a few feet earlier. "And those belong to the uniform."

Brody studied the ground. "If the victim or anyone else walked back here after yesterday's storms, we'd definitely see footprints."

"So she's been here since before the rain," Stella said. "But probably not until late Saturday night, after the games were finished."

The thick, humid air intensified the odor as they neared the entrance to the dugout. The almost sweet, metallic scent seeped past Stella's sinuses and penetrated her taste buds. She clamped her mouth closed and breathed through her nose. Didn't help much. Next to her, Brody exhaled as they faced the body.

In damp jeans and a long-sleeved blouse, a woman was sprawled on the aluminum bench. Long hair spilled across her face in a brown curtain, and a pale blue silk scarf was knotted loosely around her neck. Flies buzzed around her head. One hand trailed off into a mud puddle, and animals had found the corpse. Stella spotted a hypodermic needle in the mud under the bench and a brown leather purse on the bench.

She turned in a circle. "The back of the dugout shielded her from view of the street or parking lot."

Frank came around the dugout and stood next to Stella. He put on gloves as he scanned the scene. "What do we know?"

"Little League coach found her about an hour ago." Stella gave him a summary while the forensic photographer snapped long-range, medium, and close-up shots from varying angles. When the photographs were complete, Frank moved closer. He lifted the victim's hair. Bruises trailed down the left side of her face. "Insects have been busy, and it looks like someone used her as a punching bag."

Stella's legs weakened as she studied the woman's face.

It couldn't be.

Brody touched her arm. "What's wrong?"

Even with the bruising and insect activity, the woman looked familiar. Too familiar.

Stella's stomach did a slow tumble. "I think I know her."

Frank raised an eyebrow.

Hoping she was wrong, Stella moved toward the woman's purse. With unsteady, gloved hands, she drew the zipper, pulled out a wallet, and opened it to view the woman's driver's license. Shock slid over her in a clammy wave. "Her name is Missy Green. We graduated high school together."

"She was a friend?" Brody asked.

"Yes, but I haven't seen her in a long time." Stella noted her address was not the house where her parents had lived, but then, not many people still lived at home at thirty. Except Stella. "There's thirty dollars cash in here, so she wasn't robbed."

"Is there a cell phone in her purse?" Brody asked.

Stella looked past the usual tissues, tampons, and lipstick and found a cheap cell. "Yes. Battery's dead."

"No obvious cause of death on initial inspection." Frank lifted the woman's arm. The limb moved with no resistance. "Rigor's come and gone." His gaze moved over the dugout. "The heat and moisture would have accelerated decomposition." He frowned at the body. "She's been dead *at least* thirty-six hours." Frank tapped his assistant on the arm. "I doubt she's been dead longer than three days, but I want live and dead maggots just in case."

Stella breathed. The bugs always got to her.

Brody leaned close to her ear. "You can step away if you need to."

She shook her head. "This is a small town. It isn't the first time I've encountered someone I know." Sadness clogged her throat as she corrected herself. "Knew."

"Considering the hypodermic, overdose is a definite possibility," Frank said.

"Did you look for track marks?" Stella asked.

"Her sleeves are snug. I don't want to disturb her hands until after I've scraped under her nails." Frank stepped back. "Not sure when I'll get to her autopsy. We're tied up with multiple victims from that residential house fire. I'll call you." Frank stood and signaled to his assistant.

"What do you think?" Brody asked, stepping back as the morgue assistant wheeled a gurney to the dugout. Arranging a white evidence sheet inside the black body bag, he and Frank transferred the body. Stella flinched as the bag closed over Missy's face with a final *zip*.

Poor Missy.

"The needle indicates drugs, but someone beat her." Stella turned back toward her car.

Brody fell into step beside her. "Drugs and violence often go hand-in-hand."

"They do."

Reporters swarmed her as she ducked under the crime scene tape. She raised a hand to block the microphone shoved in her face.

"Detective Dane, are you handling this case?"

She breathed through her first instinct, which was to tell the reporter to go away. Police Chief Horner was adamant about polite press-police relations. As long as Stella worked for the Scarlet Falls PD, she had to give the press her attention and company manners. "I'll be working on this case, along with the rest of the Scarlet Falls Police Department."

"What can you tell us about the victim?" Another reporter waved his mic at her. "How did she die?"

Stella leaned closer to a mic. "Cause of death will be determined by the medical examiner."

"Can you identify the body?"

"The deceased's identity will be publicized after next of kin are notified," Stella said.

The shouts continued. "What can you tell us about the death? Was it murder?"

Stella held up her hand. "We're just beginning our investigation. It's too early for any assumptions. We'll issue updates as information becomes available. Now you'll have to excuse me." Stella threaded her way through the throng to her vehicle. But the reporters' questions hit home. She knew nothing about Missy's adult life.

Stella and Brody got into the car, and she drove to the address listed on Missy's driver's license. Parking at the curb, she surveyed the one-story, gray house. "A 2004 blue Toyota Corolla is registered to Missy Green. I don't see it here."

"It wasn't at the baseball field either." Brody climbed out of the car.

"So how did she get there?" Stella followed him to the sidewalk.

Missy had lived in an apartment behind the house. Painted to match the house in front, the small unit appeared to be a converted workshop or storage building. A single cement step led to a tiny stoop and front door. They climbed the step, and Stella knocked. No one answered. Covering her eyes, she peered through the glass panes in the door.

"Can I help you?"

Stella turned. An elderly woman stood on the walkway. Her black polyester slacks swished as she pushed her four-wheeled walker forward.

"Yes, ma'am." Stella moved her blazer to show the badge on her belt and introduced herself and Brody. "Could I have your name please?"

Under a poof of dyed brown hair, the woman's penciled-on eyebrows rose in surprise. "I'm Mrs. Sterling. I own this property."

"Missy is your tenant?"

"She is." Mrs. Sterling's wrinkled lips pressed flat. "Did something happen to her?"

"We'd like to ask you a few questions." Stella evaded the question. Missy's family deserved to hear the news first.

Mrs. Sterling splayed a hand above her saggy bosom. "She was that woman found at the baseball field, wasn't she? I just saw it on the news. They didn't give her name, but why else would two detectives be here?"

"Yes, ma'am," Stella admitted.

"I knew there was a reason I hadn't seen her for a few days." Mrs. Sterling turned and sat on the padded seat of her walker. "I was hoping maybe she'd met someone." Taking a tissue from the pocket of her sweater, she blotted her eyes. "Missy was a nice girl."

"No trouble with her as a tenant?"

"No. None. Missy kept to herself. She worked two jobs, day shift as a cashier at the grocery store on Elm Street, and she cleaned offices at night. Didn't leave her much time for trouble."

"I guess not," Stella said. "How long has she lived here?"

"Just a few months."

"Do you know if she has any friends?"

"I've never seen any around, but I know her mother lives nearby. If you want to look in her apartment, I can get my key." She rocked back and forth twice to gain enough momentum to shift to her feet.

"Did she live alone?" Stella asked.

"Of course. I specified no roommates when she signed the lease, and she was too busy working for any entertaining. My last tenant was a college student. *He* was a problem. Loud music and girls coming and going at all hours." Mrs. Sterling's mouth puckered. "But there were no parties or other shenanigans with Missy."

"When was the last time you saw her?"

"Let's see." Stuffing the tissue back in her pocket, she pressed a forefinger to the corner of her mouth. "I don't remember exactly. A few days at least. Missy works a lot. Sometimes she's gone before I get up and not home yet when I go to bed." She shuffled up a cement path toward the house. "Let me get that key."

"Mind if I look around?" Brody asked.

"Not at all," Mrs. Sterling said over her shoulder. "How did she die?"

"We're not sure," Stella said.

Stella followed Mrs. Sterling to the back door and retrieved the key. Missy's apartment was small and Spartan, but a skylight in the center of the living room admitted plenty of light. A kitchen was visible through an archway, and a short hallway led to the bedroom and single bath. Missy's furniture was limited to the basics. Stella walked down the corridor and peered into the bedroom. A full size mattress and box spring rested on the carpet. An overturned shipping crate served for a nightstand and a floor lamp was positioned next to the bed.

"This won't take long," Brody said.

Stella opened kitchen drawers and found the usual contents. Magnets affixed a few recent snapshots of Missy and her mom to the fridge. Below them, a paper listed phone numbers: two places of work, Mrs. Sterling, and a number labeled "Mom."

"Do you know where her mother lives?" Brody asked.

"I know where she used to live." And going there was the very last thing that Stella wanted to do. They didn't find a laptop, but a calendar hung on the kitchen wall. The majority of the notations appeared to be work shifts, but a few abbreviations caught Stella's eye. She took down the calendar, slid it into a yellow clasp envelope, and filled out the Evidence label.

They left the apartment and drove across town to a mature neighborhood. Tall oak trees lined the street. One-level box homes squatted on tiny lots defined by chain-link fences. Stella parked in front of a yellow house that seemed unchanged from high school. Peeling gold letters spelled *Green* in block print on the mailbox.

None of the scripts Stella had rehearsed in her head seemed to work. How did you tell a woman her daughter was dead?

"When I gave you this case, we didn't know you'd been friends with the victim. It's all right if you need to pass it back." Brody put a hand on her shoulder. "Notifying next of kin is hard enough when it's strangers."

It was tempting to hand off the duty, but Stella shook her head and headed for the front gate. "It'll be easier on Mrs. Green coming from me. That's what's important."

Her hand lingered on the gate. How many times had she opened and closed it during her teen years? Mrs. Green had had a yappy little dog that had liked to chase cars, and she'd been vigilant about keeping the gate closed.

The air had gone still, and her blazer was stifling. Sweat broke out under her arms. She took a shaky breath and pressed the doorbell, half hoping that no one was home. But footsteps approached, and the door swung open. In her late-fifties, Mrs. Green was tall like her daughter had been. Her hair was cut in a chin-length bob and dyed medium brown. Her cheekbones and jawline had softened, but she'd aged well.

Mrs. Green tilted her head. "Stella? Stella Dane. I haven't seen you in ages." Smiling, she stepped back. "Come in."

"Thank you, Mrs. Green." Stella gestured to Brody. "This is Detective McNamara."

"I heard you were a policewoman." Mrs. Green's smiled faded, as if she suddenly wondered why two police officers were standing on her doorstep.

Stella crossed the threshold. "Yes, ma'am."

"What can I do for you?" Mrs. Green's voice lifted with apprehension.

"Can we sit down?" Stella felt Brody's steady presence behind her as Mrs. Green led them into the kitchen.

Mrs. Green's eyes were worried as she eased into a chair.

Stella turned a chair to face her. "Did you see the news today?"

"No." Mrs. Green's smile was weak. "I just got home from work."

Stella breathed. "The body of a woman was found at one of the township baseball fields today."

Mrs. Green gasped. One hand covered her mouth then dropped into her lap.

Stella reached out to take her hands. "It's Missy."

"No." Mrs. Green shook her head as if she was trying to shake out the thought. "That can't be. I just saw her Thursday. I took her to lunch. She was fine."

Stella squeezed her fingers. "I'm sorry."

"No." Mrs. Green wrenched them away. She jumped to her feet, knocking the chair over and backing up until she was trapped against the kitchen counter. "No." She slid down the front of the cabinet to the floor. She pressed a fist to her mouth and rocked. In her eyes, shock and denial warred with the truth. "It has to be a mistake."

Stella went to her. She dropped onto her knees beside Missy's mother and wrapped her arms around her shoulders. The older woman's grief seemed to flow into her.

A long minute later, Mrs. Green pushed away. "How?"

"We don't know yet," Stella said in a gentle tone. "I need to ask you a few questions."

Nodding, Mrs. Green wiped tears from her face with her fingertips.

"Did Missy use drugs?"

Mrs. Green nodded. "Alcohol, too. When she was living in Los Angeles. She had some success writing screenplays, but threw away

17

all her money on drugs. I warned her about that lifestyle. Too much money. Too many wild parties. It took me three years to convince her to come home and get straightened out." She looked up, her gaze sharpening. "How did you know?"

"We found a needle at the scene," Stella said gently.

Mrs. Green shuddered. A trembling breath left her body. "I can't believe it. She promised me she'd never use again, and you know how stubborn she is."

Stella thought of the bruises on Missy's face. "Was there a man or other friends in her life?"

"I don't think so."

"Did she have any contact with her friends in California?" Stella asked.

"Not that I know of. She was determined to stay far away from everything that reminded her of that life. She wouldn't even consider writing again." Mrs. Green hugged her own waist. "What happened to her?"

"We'll do everything we can to find out," Stella reassured her. "How did she get clean?"

Mrs. Green sniffed and blotted her eyes with a tissue. "I borrowed money from my sister to put her in rehab." Fresh tears overflowed Mrs. Green's eyes. "She was doing so well, working two jobs to earn the money to pay back my sister. I was so proud of her."

Sorrow filled Stella's heart until she couldn't draw a deep breath.

"Tell me you'll find out what happened to my baby," Mrs. Green pleaded. "I know she didn't do this to herself. Missy wouldn't lie to me."

Stella put a hand on her forearm. "I'll do my best."

Images of a youthful Missy spun through her mind: sitting on the floor of Stella's bedroom painting her toenails, floating in an inner tube on the river behind Stella's house, tossing her cap at high school graduation.

And now she was dead.

Chapter Three

He pushed the Record button on his cable box as a Breaking News Report banner scrolled across the screen. A reporter stood in front of the baseball field, as close as she could get to the dugout without crossing the crime scene tape barrier.

Finally! They'd found her. He never thought it would take so long.

The reporters intercepted a beautiful brunette in a serious suit. He turned up the volume just in time to catch her name. *She* was a police detective?

"It's too early to make assumptions," Detective Dane said before she ducked the reporters.

Too early? Assumptions? How did they not understand? They just didn't get it. No one appreciated the irony. His sigh was long, deep, and full of disappointment.

He'd left Missy at a baseball field with a hypodermic needle at her side, a junkie in the middle of America's symbol of wholesomeness. He'd thought the contrast was interesting, even artistic. He'd positioned her carefully. Hell, he'd even wrapped a fucking bow around her neck. But apparently he'd been too subtle. Maybe if he'd left an apple pie in her lap, the police would have gotten the message.

He opened his folder. Eight-by-ten color glossies of Missy lying on the bench, arms folded across her midsection Sleeping Beauty-style, hypodermic needle tucked beneath her overlapping fingers. He'd positioned her late Saturday night. Since then, an entire day of severe storms had raged through the area. Maybe the weather or time had affected the precise positioning of Missy's body.

Next time he'd be more careful. He'd make sure his message was delivered on time.

On the TV, behind the reporters, two men in coveralls rolled a gurney toward a white and red van. Missy had been zipped into a black body bag.

Too bad.

The public should see what happened to the fallen. She'd deserved what she'd gotten. He'd performed a public service: judgment, punishment, and execution of the depraved.

Missy had claimed to be redeemed, but none of them were. She'd been dirty. Weak. Pathetic. And now she was gone, plucked from society like a dandelion ripped from a lush, green lawn. The grass would fill in, healthier, stronger without her tainted roots.

The news segued to a traffic report. He stopped recording.

How could he make his message clear? Some people were unworthy of life. There were consequences for bad decisions. People should be punished for their sins. What would it take for the world to understand?

He replayed the news clip. When Detective Dane entered the frame, he paused the recording. She was in charge. Therefore, she was the one he needed to convince.

Chapter Four

Monday, June 20, near Tabatinga, Brazil

The booming growl of a howler monkey echoed across the forest. Mac froze. He lowered his binoculars, his survival instincts quivering as the rain forest around him went on alert. Something was wrong.

June was past the official rainy season, but this part of the jungle didn't really have a dry one. The Amazon River flowed fat and fast past him, sunlight glimmering on its rippled surface. Twenty yards away, a male giant river otter poked its head above the water and stared downstream. Mac followed the weasel's focus, looking for the snout of the black caiman that had been hanging around the day before.

A pair of scarlet macaws burst from the forest and winged out over the river. Mac shifted his binoculars from the water to the canopy. A hundred feet above, the reddish brown body of a howler monkey poised on a thick branch. The air smelled like rain was coming, but torrential downpours were daily events and wouldn't bother the monkeys. The big male sounded another throaty warning. Something—or someone—was invading the primate's territory.

Mac lowered his binoculars. His three-member team had been camped near a small village ten miles from Tabatinga, Brazil, for weeks. The monkeys had become accustomed to their presence. Another group of primates could be encroaching on the home turf of the resident troop. Or it could be something else entirely, maybe a jaguar. The monkeys scattered, the canopy shifting, branches and foliage swaying, as the creatures took flight. If another group of primates were muscling in on their territory, the howlers would have stood their ground, at least for a time. There would have been a vocal protest, posturing, possibly even a physical altercation. The animals' quick abandonment of their domain meant one thing: predator.

He scanned the river. The young otters had stopped playing and had scurried into the shallows. Three adults swam in circles, agitation evident in their tense posture. Their cute, cuddly appearance and playful antics camouflaged their place at the top of the Amazon food chain. Nearly six feet long, giant river otters had few natural predators except black caimans or jaguars. If the otters were on alert, the threat was likely unnatural.

In the jungle, unnatural equaled human.

Sweat dripped into his eye. He yanked a bandana from the back pocket of his nylon cargo pants and tied it around his head.

"Mac!" Behind him, Cheryl bulldozed through the rain forest. *How could a woman that small make that much noise?* She moved with the grace of a miniature bison. Sweat soaked the armpits of her long-sleeve safari shirt and a camera bounced around her neck.

"Shh." Mac raised a hand, tilted his head, and listened.

Cheryl stopped and waited. Her gaze roaming the riverbanks. "I don't hear anything."

Mac didn't hear as much as *feel* the tension in the jungle. It rippled along his skin like a swarm of ants.

Cheryl tightened the band on her ponytail. "We've been here for weeks. The locals are friendly. All we've seen are fishing boats and ecotours."

She'd worked in São Paulo. She didn't know jack about life in the jungle. Mac didn't have the details, but her assignment to his team had been punishment for some infraction.

"Maybe." He had his doubts about some of the fishing boats they'd seen. The occupants hadn't looked all that interested in the water.

Cheryl swatted at a mosquito the size of a kitten. "The biggest danger here is the bugs. Why don't they ever bite you?"

Ignoring her complaints, Mac glanced back at the water. The otters had disappeared. Bad sign. He held up a hand to quiet his companion. "The animals know something's up."

"Great," Cheryl muttered. "I had to pull the *Dances With Otters* assignment."

"I *am* a wildlife biologist," Mac whispered. "Now shut up so I can listen."

The faint sputter of a motor drifted over the water. Most of the local fishing boats were man-powered. Engines were faster, but they were also expensive and required fuel. Most locals didn't have the resources for such luxury.

An ecotour maybe?

This was a particularly dangerous region in South America, where the borders of Peru, Brazil, and Colombia converged. Drug traffickers, both large cartels and small-scale operations run by families tired of hardscrabble, subsistence living, used the river as a key method of transportation.

Cheryl went still. They both knew their university credentials satisfied villagers and officials but garnered no respect from drug traffickers.

The nose of a boat appeared around the bend in the river. The craft was a long, dilapidated vessel with a rectangular cabin and a pair of rusted outboard motors that looked like they belonged in a salvage yard. A man in the bow, wearing only a pair of frayed denim cutoffs, lifted a hand in greeting. His skin was brown, his hair black, his body slim and hard in a way that suggested a lifetime of manual labor and minimal nourishment. A second man sat in the stern, one hand on the tiller to steer the boat.

"See. Fishermen." Cheryl gestured toward the boat. She raised the camera. The lens whirred and clicked as she snapped pictures.

He pushed the camera's nose down. "I know most of the villagers, and these guys don't look familiar. That boat could be full of coca paste instead of fish." Not to mention men with machetes and machine guns. Mac's gaze swept the riverbanks.

"Sorry." She snapped on the lens cap.

Not her fault, he reminded himself. She hadn't asked for this assignment. She didn't have the necessary experience. With his eyes focused on the waterway, he asked, "What brought you out here anyway?"

Cheryl and the third member of their team, a guide named Juan, had just returned to the camp for an afternoon siesta. Napping was the only part of South American life she embraced. "You got a call from the States. Your brother."

An instant ache tightened behind Mac's sternum, and guilt washed through him with the force of the river. His brother Grant would not have called unless it was an emergency. "Did he leave a message?"

"Yes." Cheryl waved her hand at a swarm of insects buzzing around her face. "It's your dad." Sympathy softened her voice. "Your brother said, 'This is it, Mac,' and that you should hurry if you want to get there before . . ."

"Oh. OK. Thanks." Mac lowered his binoculars, his emotions going into limbo. Their father had been actively dying for the past fifteen months. A paraplegic war hero, the Colonel had been robbed of his mental faculties by dementia in recent years. Mac had thought he'd come to terms with his father's imminent death, but the scratching sensation inside his chest said otherwise.

"You should go home, Mac." Cheryl nodded toward the river. She might be a disaster in the jungle, but she was a decent soul. "This will keep."

"You're right." Mac turned toward their camp, dread slowing his movements. Home. A small word with big meaning. He'd spent most of his childhood watching his father suffer. Just thinking about returning to his hometown made the ground feel unstable under his feet. But after his brother Lee's murder last year and his sister's close brush with death last November, Mac had sworn he wouldn't leave his family high and dry again. He'd be there for them this time, no matter what the cost.

"I'll drive you into the village," Cheryl said. The team had only one vehicle, and no one wanted to be stranded in the jungle without transportation. The mile to the nearest village would feel like twenty in sweltering temperatures and jungle humidity.

"Thanks. From there I should be able to bum a ride into Tabatinga." The border city's airport had limited flights. He'd be lucky to get on a plane in the next twenty-four hours. Once he got to Manaus, catching a flight to New York would be easier. If he got lucky, he could be home in two days. But transportation in the South American jungle was highly unreliable.

In all likelihood, whatever was going to happen at home would happen without him.

"You shouldn't stay out here by yourself," Mac said.

"Because I'm a woman?" She crossed her arms over her chest.

"Because your jungle survival skills suck." And because she was a woman. As much as he believed in equality, the dangerous men who trafficked drugs on the Amazon didn't.

"You have a point," she admitted. "Let's pack up. I'll stay in Tabatinga until you come back. How long do you think you'll be gone?"

"Couple of weeks." Long enough to bury the Colonel and help his siblings deal with the fallout. Hopefully not long enough for his troubled youth to catch up with him. The gang he'd been in back then was still active. And still dangerous.

Pushing aside the poke of guilt, Mac turned toward the rough path that led to their campsite just as rain began to fall. Grant wouldn't have called unless there was a chance that Mac could get there in time to say good-bye. He quickened his steps.

On the bright side, in Scarlet Falls there was the possibility he'd run into Stella Dane, the only police officer he'd ever wanted to see in his life. Since he'd met her last November, dreams of her all buttoned up in her uniform had made some hot South American nights swelter. The chances of anything happening between them were slim. She'd helped find his sister and stop a killer. She was totally out of his league, and since his past wasn't exactly a secret, he was pretty sure she didn't trust him. But a man could fantasize.

"Wait." Cheryl was looking out over the water. Rain speckled its surface. "Where's the boat?"

Mac pivoted. The river was empty and silent. Even if the boat had rounded the bend, the motor should still be audible. Despite the intense and steamy heat of the jungle, his insides went cold. He shoved at her. "Move. Back to camp."

She nodded. The rain increased to its usual afternoon torrent. A gunshot rang out, and Cheryl's body jerked.

He dove for cover, one arm catching Cheryl around the middle and taking her to the ground.

Cheryl. Mac rolled her to her back. She blinked at the canopy, raindrops beating on her face as blood spread across the chest of her soaked safari shirt.

Another bullet zinged past. Mac draped his body across her torso, shielding her as best he could.

"Hold tight." Mac lurched to his feet.

He grabbed her under the armpits and dragged her into a patch of underbrush. Then Mac pulled a clean bandana from his back pocket, folded it, and pressed it to the wound high on her chest. He took her hand, put it over the square, and whispered, "Pressure."

Eyes wide and shivering, Cheryl pleaded in a whisper, "Don't leave me."

Another shot rang out. Mac got to his feet and hesitated. He needed to do something about the men with the guns. "I'll be right back. I promise."

"No." She shook her head. Rain slicked her hair and face as blood darkened the entire front of her shirt. She reached out for him.

Backing out of the foliage, Mac put a finger over his lips. She needed to be quiet. If they found her, she was dead.

A voice yelled, "Get them!" in Portuguese.

He sprinted down the trail toward camp. He needed the satellite phone, and the SUV was their best hope for escape. If these men had come from the boat, they wouldn't have land transportation. He also had to warn Juan, although their guide certainly would have heard the gunshots.

Vegetation sliced at Mac's arms and face as he raced down the rough path. Behind him, over the echo of his thundering heartbeat, men shouted and foliage snapped as bodies crashed through the jungle. He broke into the clearing. No Juan. Odds were he had run. Money could buy interpretive and guide services, but not loyalty. Had Juan sold them out? Mac ran behind the supply tent and skidded to a stop.

The spot where the four-wheeler should have been parked was empty. The SUV was gone.

A figure burst into the clearing. It was the man from the bow of the boat. Brown skin glistened with sweat as he slashed a machete toward Mac's head. He ducked. The blade kissed his hair.

Mac lunged forward and grabbed his assailant's right wrist with both hands. A solid front kick drove the ball of his foot into the man's solar plexus. The machete fell to the ground. Mac kicked out again, this time striking him in the side of the knee. The man's leg buckled, and he swung out with his left hand. Light glimmered on a short blade. Mac yanked hard on his right arm, throwing him further off balance.

A twig snapped. In his peripheral vision, Mac saw the second man enter the clearing, an AK-47 in his hands.

The bastard who'd shot Cheryl.

Anger surged hot through Mac's veins. The muzzle of the AK arced toward him. He whirled around, swinging Machete Man between him and the gunman as a shield. Shots burst from the rifle muzzle with orange flashes. The man in Mac's grip flailed as the bullets cut across his middle. Something hot stung Mac in the side.

The trigger clicked on an empty cartridge. The gunman snapped the magazine off the bottom of the rifle and reached for his pocket. Mac tossed Machete Man's dead body aside and lunged toward the machete on the ground. He snatched it off the dirt as the gunman shoved a new magazine into the AK.

The muzzle lifted. Jumping forward, Mac swung the blade. The razor-thin tip sliced the gunman's forearm to the bone. Mac jumped closer, too close for the man's AK to be of any use. Turning the long blade, he brought the tool up and across the gunman's body, slicing him open from thigh to shoulder. The AK dropped to the ground. The gunman fell on top of it.

Mac wiped the blood from the machete on the ground.

He'd always wished he hadn't grown up with a borderline psychotic and highly trained military father obsessed with turning his four offspring into a tiny paramilitary force. But the Colonel—and all the batshit-crazy survival weekends, weapons training, and combat drills he'd forced on his children—had just saved his youngest son's life.

Mac rolled the gunman to his back to make sure he was dead. No worries. Mac's conditioning had ensured his strike would be deadly.

The surge of relief was cut short as a sudden wave of agony sliced through his side. He put a hand just below his ribs. Hot blood seeped red through his T-shirt.

Not good. He was Cheryl's only hope of getting help.

He ducked into the supply tent. The sat phone was gone, and the first aid kit was in the missing SUV. Son-of-a-bitch Juan. He hadn't taken everything, just the essentials.

The village was a mile-long hike through the jungle, the day was getting shorter, and Mac was leaking. He found a bottle of Juan's tequila, opened his shirt, and assessed the wound. The bullet had grazed the fleshy part of his side. Hoping it hadn't hit any vital organs on its journey, he dumped alcohol on the wound. Pain burst through him as bright as a flashbang, blinding him and buckling his legs. Panting, he dropped to his knees and waited for the dizziness to pass.

When his vision cleared, he made a makeshift bandage from a bandana, filled his canteen with water, and fashioned a litter from a camp cot. The daily downpour continued. In the driving rain, it took him a few minutes to find Cheryl.

But only a second to realize she was dead.

No!

He dropped to his knees beside her body. He didn't give a damn if the caiman ate those two drug traffickers, but he couldn't leave Cheryl here.

Don't leave me!

But he had, and she'd died alone.

White hot pain sliced him in two as he secured her to the cot. Dragging the litter behind him, he stumbled down the rutted trail. Each step sent sharp agony through his body. *Good.* Mac held on to the pain like a lifeline. Maybe it would keep him conscious long enough to make it to the village before he bled out. He pressed a hand to his side. At the moment, his survival seemed like a big maybe.

As he staggered through the jungle, he sent his family a mental apology. It didn't seem likely that he'd make it home after all. The irony wasn't lost on him. He'd been prepared to go home to see his father pass. Now it looked like Mac might be the first one to die.

Chapter Five

Stella walked into the firing range. The muffled crack of gunshots bled through her earplugs.

And sweat pooled between her breasts.

This shouldn't be hard. She was a good shot. Before November, her weekly practice session had been no more exciting than a trip to the gym, just one more thing she did to stay in shape as a cop. But now, every time she stared down the sights on her pistol, she thought of the shot she'd missed and the two cops who'd died as a result.

She set her bag on the wooden platform at the front of her assigned stall and removed her safety glasses and a box of bullets. Her heartbeat thudded over the steady *pop pop* of gunfire as she readied her stance. Discomfort flooded her body as she lined up her sights with the paper target. Her position felt all wrong, as if she'd never shot a gun before. She rolled a shoulder, cracked her neck, and stretched her arm, but there was no convincing her body that she'd done this a million times.

Her phone buzzed on her hip. She welcomed the distraction, until she read Frank's name on her phone screen. She read his text: Done. Get over here.

She holstered her weapon, returned her gear to her bag, and drove to the medical examiner's office. Stella took a deep breath of fresh air in the parking lot, as if it were her last, and pushed inside. In the antechamber, she donned a gown, cap, and plastic face shield. Bracing herself, she tugged on a pair of gloves and went into the autopsy suite. Frank was leaning over a sink, his back to Stella.

The metallic, sweet smell of blood and cold decay hit her through the face shield. The rubber-edged doors swished shut behind her as she focused on shallow breaths.

Frank glanced over his shoulder. "Stella, perfect timing."

Perfect timing would be accidentally missing the whole thing.

"You said it was urgent," Stella said, her face mask fogging up.

With a snort, Frank turned back to the sink. "We both know I wasn't that polite."

Frank stepped away from the sink. His face mask was tilted up onto his head. "You can come closer. I've finished with her."

The sight of Missy, naked on the table, assaulted Stella's senses, but she refused to turn away. The small surge of relief she'd felt that Frank had completed the autopsy faded almost as quickly as it hit.

"Oh, my God."

Dozens of cuts lined Missy's arms and legs. The lines were arranged in groups of five. Each had four vertical lines and one cross-wise cut, like tally marks.

Frank crossed his arms over his chest. "Each of these wounds is approximately two inches long and a quarter-inch deep."

"How many are there?" Stella stared at the bloodless, raw-looking wounds.

"Forty." Frank looked grim. "Plus this single stroke in the center of her belly."

"Have you seen anything like this before?" Stella asked.

"Not quite. I've run into cutters before but nothing quite like this," Frank said.

"Missy was a cutter?"

Frank pointed to a thin scar below the new wounds. "She has old scars on her forearms, so she probably cut herself at some point in the past."

Stella could see healed track marks on Missy's arms as well. All those old scars explained why she'd been wearing long sleeves in the heat of summer.

"But she didn't do this to herself. Not this time." Frank waved a hand over the body. "The directions and angles of the cuts aren't consistent with self-inflicted wounds." He pointed to a cluster of five lines. "A cut is deeper in the beginning or head of a knife wound because that's where the pressure is the greatest. Toward the end or tail of the wound, the pressure is lighter and the cut becomes increasingly shallow. If she made these cuts herself, she would have cut toward herself. Instead the cuts run the opposite direction."

"Someone was standing next to her," Stella said.

"Also, she was restrained." Frank pointed to deep bruises around Missy's wrists and ankles.

"She was tied up and tortured." Stunned and sickened, Stella scanned the body for other evidence. "Can you tell if the old cutting scars were self-inflicted?"

"No, but I doubt they were as deep." Frank shook his head. "Are you thinking someone did this to her before?"

"I don't know what to think. What else can you tell me?"

"She didn't die at the scene. Estimated time of death is Saturday between four p.m. and midnight. There's no sign of sexual assault. She presents as an overdose, and the syringe found at the scene contained traces of heroin, but I'll need the toxicology report to confirm cause of death. I'll let you know when that comes in. Even without the results,

I'm calling this a homicide based on the use of restraints, the torture, and the fact that she was dumped at the scene. This was clearly not an accidental death or a suicide."

"Thanks." Stella bolted from the ME's office and into the fresh air of the parking lot. As she walked to the crime scene investigators' offices in the same complex, she dug a mint from her purse and chewed it to obliterate the smell of death from her nostrils. She stopped at the forensic lab in the same complex and signed Missy's now-charged cell phone out on the evidence log. There were only a few recent calls and no texts. Missy likely kept the phone for emergency use only. Stella had already requested the call detail records from Missy's cell service provider.

Neither of Missy's employers had been surprised to hear of her death. The fact that she hadn't shown up for work Friday or Saturday had been enough to worry them. She'd been a hard-working, exemplary employee. Stella hadn't found so much as a single disgruntled coworker. Missy paid her bills on time and managed to save a small portion of her pay each week. Her background check was equally unremarkable. No arrests either here or in California.

A call from Brody interrupted her thoughts. "We have a possible break-in and missing woman. Can you pick me up at the station?"

Brody was waiting outside when she pulled up. He slid into the passenger seat and gave her the address.

As she drove, she updated him with Missy's autopsy results. "She was tortured and killed. Either we have a sadistic killer roaming Scarlet Falls or Missy made someone very angry."

"So our simple overdose is a murder investigation." Brody's voice rang with surprise. "This is a good reminder not to make assumptions about a case."

A few minutes later, Stella parked at the curb in front of a white bungalow on a quiet street on the outskirts of town. The houses on both sides sat close, but mature trees and a line of tall hedges created privacy. A potential intruder would be shielded from any neighbor's sight.

They climbed out of the car and headed toward the front porch. In addition to the patrol car at the curb, two vehicles occupied the driveway: a powder-blue Prius and a red Infiniti sedan. The front door stood open. Stella went up the three steps onto the stoop. Cool air chilled her skin as she stepped over the threshold.

Patrol Officer Lance Kruger met them in the foyer. This was Lance's first week back on the job after taking a bullet in the November shootout. Stella would never forget the sound of the bullet hitting his flesh or the sight of him pale, shaking, and bleeding out on the grass. She shuddered and blocked the memory to give him a quick once-over. He was a little leaner and buffer. She saw no sign of a limp as he crossed the foyer and gestured toward the stairs. Lots of physical therapy, he'd said.

"The mess is in the master bath. The missing woman's name is Dena Miller, age thirty-two." Lance lowered his voice as he offered them the crime scene log. "The husband called it in. Says he came home from the golf course and found the master bathroom trashed and his wife missing."

Stella took the clipboard. The call had come into the 911 dispatcher at two fifty-six p.m. She checked her watch. It was now three forty-five.

"Where is the husband?" Stella signed the log and handed the clipboard to Brody.

"Adam Miller is in the kitchen." Lance showed her a snapshot of a painfully thin woman with a head of short, dark curls. "Dena Miller. Five-six. Brown hair and eyes."

In the photo, she was sitting behind a birthday cake, candles ablaze. The smile on her face was robotic, as if her birthday hadn't been a happy one.

"Do you want to talk to him or check out the scene first?" Lance asked.

"We'll have a look upstairs." She pulled gloves from her pocket and headed for the stairway. She wanted to see the scene before any conversation with the husband affected her initial impressions. Brody followed her up the steps.

A floorboard creaked underfoot as they stepped onto the second-floor landing. The master bedroom was mid-sized, with off-white carpeting and a queen-size bed. A jewelry box occupied the center of a dark wood dresser. With a gloved fingertip, Brody lifted the lid. Metal and stones sparkled against navy-blue velvet.

"There's an iPad on the nightstand, too." Stella peered over his shoulder. "I'm no jeweler, but it looks like she has a few nice pieces. Those studs look like diamonds."

"Definitely not a robbery." Brody eased the lid closed.

Stella crossed the carpet to the entrance of the master bath. Blood spattered the tiles and walls. Gold-colored glass shards littered the tile floor, and the room reeked of perfume. The glass door to the shower was open. The hamper was overturned, and the bathmat shoved against the wall. But Stella's gaze lingered on the crimson trail on the white tile.

"The blood drops are dry, but they look fresh." The drops would darken as they aged due to oxidation of iron in the blood. "It couldn't have happened too long before the husband called it in. Maybe she was showering when someone surprised her." Stella let her gaze sweep the room. She suppressed a shudder as she imagined standing in the shower, naked, vulnerable. The shower door opening. Terror washing over her as she saw the stranger in her bathroom. She envisioned her wet feet slipping on the tile, perhaps gaining her footing for a few seconds and reaching for the vanity. A man grabbing her, dragging her toward the door.

"You ready to talk to the husband?" Brody asked.

"Yes." Shivering, Stella headed for the stairs with Brody on her heels.

At the foot of the steps, they walked down a short hall and into a living room open to the kitchen. The downstairs appeared undisturbed. There was the normal amount of daily living clutter: some mail on the hall table, a pair of athletic shoes half tucked under the sofa, two glasses in the sink, but nothing that indicated a struggle.

Adam Miller sat at the kitchen table. In his early thirties, he was clean-cut and dressed in my-daddy's-a-lawyer attire: basic salmon-colored shorts and a white polo shirt. He blinked up at them as they walked into the room. His eyes were empty and stunned.

Stella turned a chair to face the husband, sat, and then introduced herself and Brody. "Mr. Miller, can you tell us what happened?"

His gaze dropped to his clenched hands. "I came home from the golf course to change. The door was open. It's never open. Dena always keeps the doors locked when she's home alone."

"Was the door wide open?" Stella nudged him back on track.

"No. Less than an inch. Not enough for me to notice until I tried to put my key in the lock."

"What did you do?"

"I went into the kitchen." He rubbed the back of his hand under his nose. "She wasn't there, but her phone was on the counter where she usually leaves it to charge." Adam nodded toward a flat expanse of counter where a cell phone was plugged into the wall. "I thought she must be upstairs. Maybe her hands had been full and she'd forgotten to shut the door. But when I got up there and saw the mess . . ." He paused, squeezing the bridge of his nose between his thumb and forefinger.

"Do you recognize the broken glass?" Stella asked.

"Yes. Dena keeps several bottles of perfume on the vanity." Adam's chest heaved. "I can't believe it. Everything was finally going good for her. For us."

"Does Dena work?"

"No. She's on disability," he said. "She fell down the stairs four years ago and broke a bone in her neck."

"Is she able to walk and drive?"

He nodded. "She's doing really well lately. She found a good physical therapist and is making progress."

"What do you do for a living?" Stella asked.

"I'm an accountant." Miller clenched his fist, uncurled the fingers, and tightened them again.

"You were playing golf today?"

He nodded. "I've been trying to land this new client. A round of golf guarantees four solid hours to make a subtle pitch."

"What time did you get home?" Stella prompted.

"I left the course about two thirty, after a long lunch." Adam's voice was quiet and unsteady. "I wanted to drop off my clubs, shower, and change before heading back to the office." He dropped his hand, raised his chin, and met Stella's gaze. His brown eyes radiated pain and confusion. "Where is my wife?" His voice broke.

"That's what we want to find out," Stella said.

He sniffed, a ragged breath shaking him.

Stella gave him a few seconds to compose himself. "Does she have any close family or friends?"

He shook his head. "No. Since her accident, she doesn't go out much. She's an only child and her parents are dead."

"Do you know what your wife's plans were for today?"

"She was scheduled to see her physical therapist this morning and then get a massage at one o'clock. I *expected* her to be home when I got here."

"Do you know if she made it to either appointment?" Stella took a small notebook from her jacket pocket.

Adam jumped to his feet, his hand patting his pocket and pulling out a cell phone. "No. I was so upset when I saw the broken glass and the blood in the bathroom, I wasn't thinking. Let me call them now."

"We'll call." Stella made a note of the phone numbers as he read them to her. "Did she mention anything unusual this week? Was she upset or did she display any odd behavior?"

"No." His chin snapped up. "You're not going to write her off as not worth your time, are you? Or make me wait forty-eight hours before you start looking for her?"

"No, Mr. Miller. We want to start looking for your wife right away," Stella assured him. The forty-eight hour rule only applied to TV shows. The sooner they started looking for Dena, the better. "Which golf course did you say you played this morning?"

Adam shot her a sharp glance.

"Routine." Stella smiled. "The more information you give us, the better."

"I'll give you anything you want if it'll help you find her," Adam said.

"Financial records would be helpful as well," Brody added from where he'd been leaning on the wall.

Adam's head whipped around. "Why would you need those?"

Brody didn't miss a beat. "Credit card statements are very helpful in tracking a person's movements."

"Oh." But Adam's eyes narrowed in distrust.

Stella scanned the countertops. "Have you seen your wife's purse?"

He shook his head, confusion knotting his brows. "No. It's usually on the dresser."

Stella would look again, but she didn't remember seeing it in the bedroom. "What about her calendar and contact information?"

"In her cell phone." Adam gave Stella the passcode and the phone. "Take anything else you need."

"A current picture of your wife would be helpful," Brody added.

"Of course." Adam crossed the room to a unit of shelves and selected a framed photo.

Stella pictured the broken glass and the blood in the bedroom. The absence of Dena's purse was odd. "Is it possible she cut herself and called a friend to take her to the ER?"

"No." Adam lifted his chin. "She would have called me. There's no one in her life closer to her." With a stifled sob, he closed his eyes and pressed his fingertips to his forehead.

Brody called for additional support, and two more patrol officers arrived to help knock on doors and question neighbors. Hours later, they had little information. None of the neighbors had seen any unusual activity. A search of the grounds and neighborhood turned up nothing. No one by the name of Dena Miller had been admitted to the local hospital, and the morgue didn't have any unclaimed bodies meeting her description. Dena didn't use social media, and she had no chronic health conditions other than her neck injury.

Standing on the covered front porch, Stella stared out at the rain. Thunder boomed across the quiet neighborhood. On the porch, purple petunias rioted in hanging pots, and a pair of wicker rocking chairs invited guests to have a glass of iced tea. Small but cheerful, it was the sort of house young married couples purchased as a starter home. While it wasn't a ritzy area, the neighborhood was mature and solid. People took care of their homes. Kids played in the street. Homeowners mowed their lawns on Saturday mornings.

Brody came out of the house, pulling the door closed behind him. "I'm catching a ride with Lance to the nursing home. Hannah called. She needs me there. Can you handle things here?"

"Sure." Stella was waiting for the forensics techs to finish collecting evidence. "Do you think it's coincidental that we have one woman kidnapped, tortured, and killed and another gone missing just a few days apart?"

Brody shook his head. "I don't like coincidences, but it's too early for assumptions. Missy Green's apartment showed no signs of a struggle."

"True, but we don't know where or how she was abducted." Stella took a step back, out of the rain's reach. "But both women have dark hair. They're close in age."

"Maybe we'll find a link." Brody nodded. "Go home and get a few hours of sleep."

Stella had called the physical therapist and the spa. Dena had attended both appointments, and had left the spa at one p.m. "I'll go through her calendar and contacts and get background checks on Mr. and Mrs. Miller."

"What did you think of the husband?" Brody asked.

"I don't know." Stella glanced back at the house. "The spouse is always the first suspect."

"I'll take their financial statements home with me, and I'll focus on Adam. We could get a call tonight that she turned up safe and sound. That's what usually happens."

Most missing people turned up within a day or two. But Stella didn't think that was going to be the case. Too much blood was splattered all over the Millers' bathroom. No matter how Stella tried to explain it away, she knew deep in her gut that Dena Miller didn't leave her house under her own steam.

Someone took her.

Chapter Six

Mac pulled into the lot of the nursing home and parked his beat-up Jeep. A glance in the rearview mirror told him he looked ragged. He heaved his battered body out of the vehicle. Every inch of him ached. He ran a hand through his rain-dampened hair but knew he still could pass for a guy who lived in a cardboard box under the bridge.

But what could he do? He'd concentrated on not dying and getting home as quickly as possible.

Two villagers had driven him—and Cheryl's body—to the hospital in Tabatinga. Returning her remains to her family was small consolation. She shouldn't have died.

Mac had been lucky. The bullet had merely grazed him, and the wound had been shallow. Thirty stitches and a truckload of antibiotics had been followed by a painful discussion with Mac's boss and a grueling session with the local *policía*. As far as they were concerned, Americans should stay out of the jungle, the traffickers were dead, and justice had been served.

After he'd been patched up, he'd embarked on a series of planes, trains, and automobiles. A three-hour layover in Manaus provided enough time to shower and change, and he'd managed to doze off a few times on the flight to LaGuardia. But sleeping in economy class with a bullet wound in his side had proved challenging, and he felt like he'd been dragged behind the train from New York City to Albany instead of riding in the business-class car.

The sliding glass doors of the nursing home opened with a *whoosh*. After the intense heat and humidity of the jungle, the air-conditioning felt like a refrigerator. He fought his instant claustrophobia. His feet wanted to turn and run out of the building. He'd take the Adirondacks, the jungle, the frigging Arctic Circle, anything to avoid being trapped in a medical facility. With every breath, the scents of disinfectant and human waste flooded his nose. The olfactory representation of human misery—and his childhood—closed in on him.

He signed in at the registration desk just as a young nurse locked the main door. She rounded the desk and sat down, her blond ponytail bobbing as she glanced up at him. "Visiting hours just ended."

"I know. I'm here to see Colonel Barrett." Official hours didn't matter when death was imminent.

"Of course," she said with sympathy. "Do you need me to show you to his room?"

"No. I know the way." And Mac didn't want any company.

At least he was still alive.

In the hallway, commercial gray carpet silenced his trail runners. Open doors along the corridor made him feel as if he was intruding on the patients' privacy, so he kept his eyes forward as he walked. Next to his father's room, he stopped for a breath before poking his head through the doorway.

Grant and Hannah were on either side of the bed, each holding one of the Colonel's hands. At the foot of the bed, Grant's fiancée, Ellie, and Hannah's cop boyfriend, Brody, stood in silent support.

"I'm sorry, Mac. He passed about ten minutes ago." Grant gently placed the Colonel's thin, veiny hand on the white sheet. Then he moved toward his brother.

Emotions steamrolled Mac. They hit him hard and fast and in such great variety he couldn't distinguish disappointment from sorrow from relief. He backed out of the room. What did it matter? He hadn't been here very often for the Colonel during his two-year stay at the nursing home.

Grant followed him into the hallway. "We'll give you some privacy if you want to say good-bye."

"No point now, is there?"

"Mac, don't beat yourself up," Grant said. "He's been unconscious for days. He didn't know who was here and who wasn't."

"But I do."

"Just go in and see him. You'll be sorry if you don't."

Mac knew his brother was right. He nodded.

Grant herded him into the room and cleared everyone else out.

Hannah gave him a quick hug on her way to the door. Her blond cap of hair was longer and softer-looking than he remembered. A stray lock fell across her eye, and she shook it off her forehead. "We'll be in the hall if you need us." Before she left the room, Brody had an arm around her shoulders. Ellie held Grant's hand.

And Mac stood alone.

He gathered his courage and approached the bed. His father didn't even look like the Colonel he remembered. His face was gaunt and gray, his body withered. Mac had no memories of his father before he'd been paralyzed, but mental images from his childhood still evoked strength. At his core, the Colonel was a warrior. When his legs had failed him, he'd specially rigged an ATV into a four-wheeled warhorse to charge through the woods with his kids. Nothing could stop the Colonel from battling his way through, over, or around the obstacles in his path. But

Fate had battered him with relentless determination. The bitch hadn't been satisfied until she'd shattered not just his body but his soul.

Mac reached out to touch his father's hand. The physical contact felt alien. Nerve damage had left the Colonel in constant pain, a cruel irony considering his paralyzed state. Even if he'd been a demonstrative person, which he hadn't, physical displays of affection had been impossible.

"I'm sorry, Dad," Mac whispered, his eyes traveling over his father's sunken face and body. The Colonel would have hated people seeing him like this. Mac had no doubt that the Colonel would have preferred the roadside bomb had blown him to the grave in Operation Desert Storm rather than left him in bits and pieces. But it hadn't been in his nature to quit, no matter how much misery he'd had to endure.

"I never quite measured up, did I? Maybe someday . . ." Mac's next breath sliced his lungs like shards of glass. Ripping them to shreds from the inside out.

This was one of the reasons he avoided his hometown. It was easier to leave the trappings of his childhood behind than to relive them. Every time he returned to Scarlet Falls, he drowned in memories.

Mac turned toward the door. The quick movement sent a dizzying wave of agony through his injured side, but he plowed forward, using the white-hot pain as an anchor. Physical discomfort he could handle, which made him frighteningly like his father.

"Mac!" Grant came after him, grabbing hold of his shoulder.

"I'm OK. I just need some air." Mac shrugged off his brother's grip and bolted for the exit. Luckily, the door was only locked from the outside and it opened automatically to let him out. Rain drummed onto the pavement. The smell of death was embedded in his nostrils. Mac turned his face to the storm and breathed in its cleansing scent. His heart rate slowed, and his lungs relaxed. He looked back at the nursing home. Through the rain-streaked glass doors, he could see Grant waiting for him in the brightly lit lobby.

Like the Colonel, Grant was an imposing figure, and it wasn't his size that intimidated Mac. Grant was as honorable as a man could be. Fifteen months ago, after their brother Lee had been murdered, Grant had left his military career to raise Lee's two young children. Grant had also inherited their father's determination, and it was damned hard to refuse him any request. Grant wanted to fold his wayward brother back into the family, but Mac wasn't ready to make any commitments.

His chest constricted and panic clawed at his throat like a beast at a cage door. He couldn't go back in there. Grant would never let him go if he did.

Lightning blazed across the sky as he strode across the wet pavement toward his Jeep. He was failing his family one more time. Running away from his responsibilities. He tossed his cell phone on the passenger seat, started the engine, and roared out of the lot. He'd call Grant tomorrow.

The downpour—and the tightness in Mac's chest—eased as he put a few miles between him and the nursing home. He turned onto the narrow road that led toward his home in the woods. Thick forest lined the rural route and cast dark shadows over the shiny blacktop. Mac slowed his wipers as the rainstorm subsided. Approaching a curve, he eased off the gas. A dark shadow lying in the road sent Mac's foot to the brake pedal. His headlights swept across a person. A woman.

Cheryl?

Impossible. Shock jammed his foot to the floorboards, and he yanked the wheel hard to the right. There was nowhere for the vehicle to go but into the trees, but Mac didn't care. He couldn't run over her.

His tires skidded. The Jeep lurched though the sharp turn and slammed nose-first into a thicket of trees. The air bag punched Mac in the face and chest, knocking the air from his lungs. His vision went black.

With a vicious gasp, he lifted his head. Dust swirled in the damp air. The deflated air bag blanketed the steering wheel. Beyond the spider-webbed windshield, pine boughs covered the front end of the Jeep. He'd driven into a stand of evergreens.

Had he blacked out? For how long?

His face and chest ached, but the new pain was no competition for the roaring agony that burst through his side. Darkness encroached on his vision. *No.* He couldn't pass out again. He needed to get the woman off the road before someone ran over her.

Closing his eyes, he breathed through it. He needed help. *She* needed help.

But she'd looked dead . . .

Dead like Cheryl.

He shook off the doubt that sprouted like an invasive species.

Cell phone.

Mac turned on the dome light and scanned the inside of the vehicle. The phone had been on the passenger seat. Who knew where it was now? Both the passenger seat and the floor were empty. The phone's battery was probably dead anyway. He hadn't charged it since his layover in Manaus.

He reached for the door handle. The door stuck. He shoved at it. It gave suddenly, and he fell halfway out of the Jeep. Pain sent him to his knees for a minute. Then he took a breath and wobbled to his feet. Wiping the rain out of his eyes, he squinted into the darkness. Rain fell in a steady downpour. Thunder rumbled and a few flashes of lightning illuminated the trees like a strobe light before the woods returned to pitch black.

Right. Flashlight.

He leaned into the Jeep and fished in the center console for his Maglite. With a click of his thumb, he pointed the beam at the ground and stumbled toward the road. He swept the light back and forth. Rain sluiced across the slanted blacktop, puddling on the gravel and dirt shoulder of the road.

Where was she?

She'd been lying near the bend. Mac backtracked. Each step felt like a knife was slicing him in two. He reached the curve and shone his light on the road. No woman. Nothing.

What the hell?

He blinked hard, but his vision was clear. He could clearly see the raindrops bouncing off the empty street.

She was gone.

Chapter Seven

Stella had stayed at the Miller home longer than she'd planned. It was nearly nine-thirty before she'd left. Halfway to her home out on the Scarlet River, the rain increased to a torrent. Squinting through the windshield, she slowed the car to a crawl on the rural highway. A light in the trees just beyond the shoulder of the road caught her attention. It was the dome light of a car. Someone had run off the road and hit the trees. She didn't see an occupant in the vehicle, but she needed to make sure no one was injured inside. She pulled over onto the shoulder, reported the vehicle's location, and requested a backup unit.

There was no sense calling an ambulance if the driver had walked away.

Taking a flashlight from her glove compartment, she left her phone in the car to keep it dry. Hunching against the driving rain, she made her way to the other vehicle. By the time she jogged across thirty feet of muddy ground, her hair was plastered to her head and water ran into her eyes. She wiped at her face. The vehicle was an older model Jeep. Once bright yellow, the SUV was covered with scratches and dings that attested to many miles of four-wheeling.

And it looked familiar in a way that made her more uncomfortable than her soaked clothes.

The door was unlocked. She opened it. No driver, and the backseat was empty as well. The driver had probably walked away or called someone to be picked up.

Stella shined the light around the interior. Shiny drops of blood glistened on the gearshift, the driver's seat, and the deflated air bag. More blood was smeared on the door handle. She rounded the Jeep and took note of the license number. Once back in her cruiser, she'd have the owner's name and contact information in a few seconds.

But as Stella pointed her light at the wet ground, her discomfort grew. Something was wrong. Instinct—and raindrops—pricked the hairs on the back of her neck. She turned in a circle, slowly moving her beam across the ground. Her light fell on a boot sticking out of the tall weeds halfway between the road and the car.

She crossed the muddy ground and crouched beside him. Shock paralyzed her for a second. It was Mac Barrett. She knew that face even soaking wet and in the dark. Especially in the dark. She'd thought of him often during her middle-of-the-night bouts of insomnia.

He lay on his side in the mud. She placed her fingers on his neck. His pulse rapped against her fingertips, and relief swept through her. She straightened and turned back toward her car. Her phone was inside, and she kept an emergency blanket and first-aid kit in the trunk.

"Wait," he croaked, his voice barely audible over the storm.

"I'm not leaving. I'm going to call for help," she shouted.

"I'm OK," he said.

"Let me call for an ambulance. Then you can tell me what happened." She leaned over him and put a hand on his unshaven cheek. "Don't move. I'll be right back."

He grabbed her wrist. "No. I'm fine. There was a woman lying in the road. I swerved into the trees to avoid hitting her."

Had someone been hit by a car? Stella turned her head and scanned the road. "I don't see a woman."

"She was there." He struggled to sit up as the rain slowed to a drizzle.

Stella stopped him with a hand on his chest. "Slow it down. You were unconscious."

"No." He shook his head. "I just tripped."

Bullshit rang in Stella's head, but she held her tongue. She and Mac had met the previous November and numerous times since. In addition to being hotter than a solar flare, he was frustratingly closed off. An intense person, he elevated self-control to an art form.

"I *need* to find her." Tonight, his eyes were wild, and his self-control looked tenuous.

"Easy. Stay put. I'll go double check the road." She raced back to the bend. Sweeping her light across the wet pavement, she saw nothing that indicated a person had lain there. She checked the weedy area on both sides of the road in case a wounded person had crawled off the pavement. But there was nothing.

"She was there."

Stella turned. Mac stood behind her, scanning the ground, one hand pressed against his side. "At the bend."

How had he sneaked up behind her without making any noise? She shined the flashlight on him. Its beam highlighted the sharp planes of his face. With his control back in place, he'd returned to his usual countenance: lean and lethal.

"I already looked there." Stella lowered her light to his body. A large, dark splotch stained the side of his light-colored T-shirt. "Are you bleeding?"

He glanced down, irritation crossing his face. "It's nothing. The woman . . ."

She put a hand on the center of his chest. "There's no one here, Mac."

"But how . . . ?"

Maybe he had a concussion.

"No one is hurt in the road. I'm going to call an ambulance. Come sit in my car where it's dry, and I'll have a look at that wound."

His head swung back and forth. "No. I'm fine."

Stella headed for her car, one hand firmly under his elbow to steer him in the right direction. The rain tapered off until only the trees were dripping.

He pulled his arm away. "You can't make me go in an ambulance. I have to look for her."

She whirled, temper heating her face as she studied him. His square jaw was set in defiance.

Stella channeled some of her partner's calm. "My backup should be here any minute. How about I have patrol sweep the area for her? Then will you agree to go to the ER?"

He gave her a curt nod. "But it'll be faster if *you* drive me."

She hesitated. He was right. It would likely take an ambulance twenty minutes just to drive out here. She could have him at the hospital in that amount of time. Her gaze dropped to the spreading patch on his shirt. How badly was he injured?

The red-white-and-blue strobe lights of a patrol car cut through the darkness. Stella briefed the responding officer and herded Mac to her car. He got into the passenger seat gingerly, and she bet he was hurt much worse than he would admit.

She leaned into the car. "I should put a pressure bandage on that wound."

"It's not that bad. Do you have a first-aid kit?" Mac lifted the hem of his shirt.

Stella got the kit from her trunk and slid behind the wheel. "Let me take a look at that."

Mac waved her off and opened a stack of gauze pads. "Honest, I'll be fine."

Suddenly Stella remembered that Brody was with Hannah because her father was dying. *Mac's father!*

She touched his hand. "Were you at the nursing home tonight?"

Mac deflated as a deep sigh eased from his chest. "My father passed away a short while ago."

"I'm so sorry."

He answered with a sharp nod, then turned to the window and studied the darkness. Had he been so upset by his father's death that he hadn't been thinking straight and had crashed his car? Visibility had been poor. He could have mistaken an animal in the road for a human. She hated to think of other possible causes of hallucinations.

She reached for his shirt and lifted it. Bandages already covered the side of Mac's torso. Blood had soaked through the white gauze. His shirt and the bandages were soaking wet, and the tape was peeling off in places. His injury wasn't new.

"What is this?" Stella's anger flared again. She bit it back. *Patience.* But really, couldn't this man be up-front rather than make her drag every bit of information out of him?

"Gunshot."

Shock and concern bloomed fresh. "When were you shot?"

"Long story."

So much for keeping her anger in check. What was Mac into?

She studied his profile. Despite his annoying habit of not telling her anything, she liked him. She'd found him smart, determined, and if she was totally honest, too damned good-looking for his—or her— own good. But as a cop, and maybe a loose friend, she needed to play hardball. His behavior was too odd, and his family had alluded to a past that included a teenage stint in a rehab facility.

She shoved the gear stick into drive. "I want you to submit to drug and alcohol testing."

"OK." No hesitation or surprise in his voice. Just pure resignation, as if her request was exactly what he'd expected. He went quiet for the rest of the drive.

Was that because he was innocent? Or guilty?

Fifteen minutes later, she parked in the ER lot. He opened the car door and stepped out into the humid night.

Stella got out of the car. "Eventually you're going to tell me how you got that gunshot wound." Among other things . . .

He shut the car door and walked away.

"Hold on." Stella locked her vehicle and hurried to catch up. "I'm coming with you."

And she wasn't leaving him until she had some answers.

Chapter Eight

The ER was Wednesday-night slow, and Mac didn't have to wait. An hour later, the doctor had finished restitching Mac's wound.

He eased back onto the pillow in his hospital bed, his side blissfully numb from the local anesthetic. For the first time since he'd been shot two days before, Mac wasn't split in two with pain. The downside of less physical discomfort was that the empty space left plenty of room for grief over the deaths of his father and Cheryl.

And the image of the woman lying in the rain was seared into his optic nerve. He couldn't get it out of his head. Had he actually seen a woman, or had his mind summoned an image of Cheryl dying in the rain forest?

He was sure of one thing: he'd seen too much death in the past few days.

Sorrow came rushing back with a vengeance. Tension in his chest clamped around his lungs.

"Hello?" Stella's voice sounded from the other side of the curtain.

Relieved at the distraction, Mac said, "Come in."

The curtain shifted as she stepped up to the side of the gurney.

Stella Dane.

Her black slacks and blazer were damp and wrinkled. The downpour had destroyed her uptight bun. He knew instantly why she wore it up. Wet tendrils fell past her shoulders, framing her face and highlighting her gorgeous blue eyes. The shiny wave of black made a man want to plunge his fingers into it, cup the back of her head with both hands, take control of that serious mouth and kiss her until the cop in her eyes melted.

As far as distractions went, it didn't get much better than Stella. The first time he'd seen her, she'd been in full uniform. No cop had ever made a uniform look like she had, but body armor had concealed her shape. The new look definitely did not.

"Your new job suits you." His comment surprised them both.

Where did that come from? Usually he was better at keeping his mouth shut, a great life-preserving quality in the circles in which he traveled. But his raw emotions were affecting his self-control. His filter was on the fritz.

She flushed.

Silence filled the space. What was there to say? She was waiting for the drug tests to come back. He didn't blame her for the request. He had a bad track record, and no one knew the truth. But her direct questions had told him Detective Dane wasn't going to settle for his usual bullshit. She was kind and sympathetic, but she was no pushover.

Last November he'd discovered she was smart and loyal. Tonight she'd listened to his crazy story. Instead of telling him he was nuts, she'd reacted with common sense and empathy. To a man who couldn't connect to a goldfish, sincere compassion impressed him.

As if he needed another reason to have her stuck in his head.

"Mr. Barrett." The doctor came in and opened a wall-mounted laptop. He glanced at Stella, then Mac. "Is it all right to discuss your medical care and history in her presence?"

"It's fine." Mac was tired of secrets, and he suddenly didn't want to keep anything from Stella. What kind of luck had brought her back into his life? He'd known he was in trouble with the pretty cop last fall, and she'd been one of the reasons he'd stayed far away since.

"I'll send you home with some prescription pain meds."

"I already told you I won't take any narcotics," Mac said without breaking eye contact with Stella.

The doctor typed on the computer. "You did, which is why I injected a long-acting local anesthetic into the site. That should alleviate your pain for up to four days. The medication I'm dispensing is a non-narcotic, anti-inflammatory pain reliever. It's not habit forming." He closed the laptop. "I know we talked about your reluctance to take any medications, but there's no need for you to be in agony. We have good non-opioid options for pain relief."

The doctor turned to Stella. "His drug and alcohol tests came back negative. Frankly, I can't believe anyone could be walking around with that injury and not taking anything for the pain. I'd be crying like a baby." He refocused on Mac. "How do you handle it?"

"I had a drug problem in my teens. I won't go there again."

"And I respect you for it." The doctor closed the laptop.

"Seriously I find the best method for controlling pain is to accept it and find a distraction." Mac's gaze found Stella's.

"OK. Well, you won't have to live with it this time. The nurse will be in with paperwork." The doctor disappeared through the break in the curtain.

Stella propped a hand on a curvy hip. "So you want to tell me how you were shot?"

Voices hummed in the three-bed ER triage room. This was not the place for confessions. Mac lowered his voice. "Not here."

Stella's eyes narrowed, and that gorgeous mouth flattened out into a suspicious line. "Are you sure I can't call your brother or sister for you?"

"No." Mac sat up and reached for his shirt. "They have enough to deal with right now."

Her eyes softened. "Again, I'm sorry for your loss. Isn't your family going to be angry that you didn't call them?"

"Maybe." *Definitely.* "But I'm not ready to deal with them." Mac almost wished for the pain in his side to return.

"I can't keep this from Brody, and you know he'll tell Hannah."

Mac sighed. Relationships interfered with subterfuge. "He will."

"They care about you."

"I know." The tightness returned to Mac's chest. "This isn't about them. I'm the one with the problem. Our family history is complicated."

"Aren't they all?"

Mac hated the sadness that clouded her eyes, but every family had its issues. "I'll talk to them tomorrow. I'm just not up for it tonight."

"Fair enough."

He reached for his stained shirt. Stella's gaze drifted down over his torso. Female appreciation lit her eyes, and a lick of heat warmed Mac's belly. As much as he wasn't ready for an interrogation session with his siblings, for the first time in his memory, he didn't want to be alone. "Give me a ride home, and I'll tell you everything."

A wry smile turned up the corners of her mouth. "Deal."

What would she think when he told her the truth?

Chapter Nine

Stella blinked and turned away as Mac tugged his shirt over his head. Staring at the man's bare chest, no matter how fine, was beyond inappropriate.

It was, however, perfectly professional to be excited about the prospect of a real conversation with the mysterious Mac Barrett, one in which he did not spend every second evading her questions. She'd been exhausted when she'd left the Millers' house, but the prospect of getting to know Mac better had energized her. A little caffeine would keep her going for a couple of hours, long enough to satisfy her curiosity. His family seemed to think he was scatterbrained, but Stella knew there was more to Mac than he allowed to show on the surface.

A nurse came in with discharge papers and a small prescription bottle. Mac ignored the bottle and shoved the folded papers in the back pocket of his cargo pants. As he headed for the door, Stella picked up the medicine.

"I won't need those," he said over his shoulder.

Stubborn man.

"But you'll have them if you do." She slipped the bottle into her pocket.

He was in front of her, so she felt rather than saw his amusement.

They left through the sliding doors. The rain had stopped, but humidity hung in the air. Crickets chirped as they crossed the parking lot and climbed into her cruiser.

Stella started the engine. "When did you get in from Brazil?"

"Left Manaus yesterday. Flew into New York today."

In the course of two days, he'd been shot, traveled from one hemisphere to another, lost his father, and crashed his car. How was he still conscious? Exhaustion was fuzzing Stella's brain. She checked the dashboard clock. Nearly midnight. With Missy's case turning into a homicide investigation and Dena Miller's strange disappearance, Stella's day had been long *before* she'd run into Mac.

"Do you have coffee at your place?" she asked.

"I don't know. I haven't been home yet." He eased the seat belt across his torso and clicked the latch. "Do you know where my Jeep was towed?"

"Probably to Thompson's Garage. I'll call in the morning."

"Thanks. My phone and bags are still in it."

At the edge of town, Stella pulled into a strip mall and went thru the drive-thru of a Dunkin' Donuts. "Coffee?"

"Coffee would be great."

Stella's stomach rumbled, and she assumed Mac hadn't eaten recently. "Food?"

"I'm OK."

She added three sandwiches and a dozen donuts to the order. Even if he wasn't hungry right this minute, she bet he would be soon. "Well, I'm starving."

"Sounds like it."

The cashier handed Stella the food, and she passed the bags and box to Mac. Back on the road, he directed her to the rural highway where he'd crashed. The only sign of his accident was a muddy path of bent weeds and a few broken pine trees.

She drove a mile farther and pointed to a turnoff on the right-hand side of the road. "I live down there, on the river."

"We're practically neighbors, though you live on the developed side of the road," said Mac.

"I live with my grandfather. My sister and her three kids live there, too."

"Sounds crowded."

"I don't mind. They're family." Stella took the coffee cup he handed her. "Morgan's husband was killed in Iraq. She and the kids need us."

"I'm sorry." From a military family, Mac would understand.

"I wish I could help more, but I can't grieve for them." Sadness spread through Stella's limbs, weighting them down.

"No, you can't." The news quieted Mac. He didn't speak again until they'd driven another two miles. "Take the next left. Watch the mud. My lot is a little more rustic than yours."

Stella had neighbors around the lake. Mac had no one close to him. *She* might be his closest neighbor.

She slowed the car. Her cruiser splashed and lurched down the rutted dirt lane. "Some road."

"Keeps out the riffraff. I like it quiet."

"You must." Stella's teeth snapped together as the car lurched through a lake-size puddle.

The narrow lane ended in a small clearing. Her headlights swept over a log cabin. Except for the beams of her headlights, the clearing was black as pitch. She could see the dark outline of a small outbuilding behind the cabin. "You really like your solitude."

"I do."

She fished her flashlight from her glove box, but Mac was already out of the car and striding into the darkness. Clicking on the flashlight, she followed him up onto a wooden porch. He dug keys out of the front pocket of his pants and opened the door.

The overhead light went on, illuminating a cozy but dusty combined kitchen and living area. The air was stuffy and hot. The scents of must and mildew tickled Stella's nose. She sneezed.

"Sorry." Setting the food on the kitchen table, he went to the kitchen window and wrestled it open. The wood groaned. "The place has been closed up for weeks."

"No air-conditioning?"

"Nah." He opened three windows in the living area. "I spend a lot of time in the jungle. I'm used to serious heat, and I like the sounds of the forest at night."

Warm and humid air flooded the cabin, and the scent of pine freshened the room. Something moved in her peripheral vision. A gigantic brown spider skittered across the floor. Stella jumped sideways.

"There are always a few squatters when I get home from a trip." Mac laughed. "Relax, he won't hurt you. He's probably terrified."

"You could saddle that thing and ride it." Stella didn't take her eyes off the spider for fear that it would move out of sight, and then she wouldn't know where it was. Somehow that would be worse than having it right in front of her. Goose bumps rose on her arms.

"Wolf spiders only bite if they feel threatened, and they eat a lot of other insects." He picked up a magazine, scooped up the spider, and released it on the porch.

"They can balance the ecosystem *outside*."

Mac contemplated the food. "Would you mind if I took a quick shower?"

Stella gestured toward the discharge papers he'd tossed onto the table. "You should read those. The doctor said you're not supposed to get your stitches wet for forty-eight hours."

He sighed. "I *need* a shower."

"Do you have plastic wrap?"

"Probably." He opened a kitchen drawer and seemed surprised to find some. He handed her the box.

"Take off your shirt." She probably should have phrased that differently.

"Yes, ma'am." Humor glinted in Mac's clear blue eyes, but his movements were slow and careful as he eased the shirt over his head.

Stella refused to admire his impressive physique as she began to wind clear plastic around his ribs. Not one bit. Except maybe the hard ridges of his tanned twelve-pack. *Eyes up.*

"You're pretty good at that."

"My mother was an ER nurse, and my brother was a regular customer. He didn't grasp the concepts of gravity or mortality until our dad died." She walked around him, keeping the wrap snug and her gaze *off* his muscles. Mostly.

"When was that?"

"He's been gone fifteen years."

"Must have been hard."

"Yes. I still miss him every day. Dad was a great guy. He was an NYPD detective. Killed in the line of duty." Stella swallowed the grapefruit in her throat.

Mac tilted his head. "I bet he'd be proud of you."

How did he know the exact question she'd asked herself every day since the shooting? Would her dad be disappointed that she'd missed the opportunity to stop a killer before he hurt more innocents?

"I hope so." She tore off the plastic, smoothed it against his hard belly, and tucked in the tail. "That should keep the stitches dry if you're careful."

"I'm not a very careful man." Mischief lit his eyes again.

"No kidding." She stepped back and pointed to his bandage. "Keep the spray on your other side."

He reached forward. Stella froze. Part of her wanted him to touch her very, very much. But her sanity questioned her judgment. This man had too many secrets.

He tucked a lock of hair behind her ear, draped his bloodstained T-shirt over his shoulder, and sauntered down a hallway. A minute later, she heard more windows opening, then the rush of water through pipes. She definitely needed air-conditioning.

Keeping one wary eye on the shadows, she popped the top off her coffee cup and sipped with gratitude. Her day had been long, and it didn't appear as if she'd see her bed any time soon. The thought of bed brought Mac's ripped body to mind, but the only things she would be eliciting from him tonight were answers.

Dust coated every surface in Mac's little cabin. Stella unwrapped a chicken sandwich and ate it while she snooped. His fridge was empty except for condiments, and the cupboards contained only canned goods. Wildlife magazines were stacked on the counter. She picked up the latest issue, *not* the one covered in spider cooties. The mailing label read Dr. McClellan Barrett.

"Find anything interesting?"

Stella turned. Mac stood in the doorway, dressed in a soft blue shirt, unbuttoned over a pair of low-slung jeans. His damp, shaggy blond hair hung well past his ears, and he obviously hadn't shaved for weeks. Holy hell, the man could work ruggedly handsome like nobody's business.

She raised the magazine in her hand. "I didn't know you were a doctor."

"I'm not."

"You have a PhD."

"Yes." The admission seemed to embarrass him.

"Considering you had a troubled youth and likely didn't spend much time on schoolwork in high school, your PhD is pretty impressive," Stella said. "Is your real name really McClellan?"

He crossed the room. "It is. My father was a Civil War buff."

"Hence your brothers, Grant and Lee." Stella sipped her coffee. The caffeine was working its magic on her brain.

"Exactly." He reached for a sandwich and ate it in three bites. "Where does Stella come from? That's not a name you hear very often."

"I was named after my grandmother." She handed him another without a word. When he'd finished it, he went to work on three glazed donuts and downed half a cup of coffee. Once she was satisfied he wasn't dying of hunger, Stella got down to business. "Now tell me about the woman you saw tonight."

Mac wiped his mouth with a napkin, balled it up, and tossed it into a trash can in the corner. "I only saw her for a couple of seconds as my headlights hit her. The road was wet, and I couldn't stop. I didn't have any option but to swerve into the trees."

"Anything you can remember will help."

Mac rested his forearms on the table and closed his eyes. "She was naked and sprawled on her back." He opened his eyes. "I wasn't close enough to see her face, but her body was thin. Her hair was short. Don't know what color since it was wet. She wasn't moving. At the time, I thought she was dead. But I suppose she wasn't." Confusion lowered his brow. "Unconscious maybe?"

A thin woman with short hair . . .

Dena Miller?

It couldn't be.

"If she was dead or unconscious, how did she disappear?" Stella asked.

"That's the important question, isn't it?"

Dena Miller went missing after a violent altercation. Why would she be lying across a rural road, miles from her house? And if she was, how did she get there? Mac's story was plain crazy, but what were the chances a thin woman with short hair disappeared and he saw another thin woman with short hair under equally strange circumstances the same night?

Stella shifted gears. "How did you get shot?"

He closed the donut box and sat back in his chair. "I spent the last few weeks in the Amazon on assignment. My partner took some photos of coca dealers. They didn't appreciate it."

"But you study river otters."

He studied her face for a few seconds. "Not exactly." He set his coffee down, and his eyes turned serious. "Do you trust me, Stella?"

"In what way?" A vague sense of discomfort tossed the sandwich in Stella's belly. What had Mac gotten himself into?

"You're going to find my story a little hard to believe, but I need your assistance."

She planted both palms on the table and held his gaze. "If you're in some sort of trouble, you need to be straight with me. I can't help you if you're holding back important information."

Mac leaned his forearms on the table and leveled his eyes with hers. "I'm a DEA agent."

Chapter Ten

Mac needed her help to find that woman and prove he hadn't imagined her.

If he was really going to be honest with himself, he wanted Stella to know he was one of the good guys. Since he was a teenager, he'd been unable to shake his reputation. He'd been clean and sober for twelve years, and his family still doubted him.

Tonight it felt suddenly and inexplicably important that Stella believed his story.

"I thought the DEA had a strict policy of not hiring anyone with prior drug experience."

"I didn't ask for the job. They came to me." Mac knew the DEA's policies. "I had a particular skill set they needed." Lately, he'd wondered if he was listed as a disposable asset. His former boss had sought Mac's help, but the region was under new management. Mac's new boss didn't want to give up a valuable source of information, but he didn't seem to mind putting Mac into dangerous situations. A few years ago, Mac hadn't cared, but Lee's death had changed his perspective.

Her lips pursed. "Dangerous job."

His hand strayed to his bandage. He probably shouldn't have told her, but he couldn't take back his admission now. Maybe that was the point.

Stella frowned, deepening a vertical line between her brows. "How long?"

"Three years."

"Three years of hanging out in the jungle, snooping on drug traffickers, and pretending to be studying otters?"

"Well, I actually do observe the otters. I've published several papers on family group behavior. Local kids are always wandering into camp. It's important that my cover be well-established." Mac sank back into his chair. "And I like otters."

She deadpanned.

"What?" He raised a hand, palm up. "Otters are badass."

"Seriously?" Stella shook her head in disbelief.

"They eat piranha. Once, I saw four adults kill a young caiman that showed too much interest in their den."

"That's not what I meant." She stabbed the table with a forefinger. "When I first met you, everyone treated you as if you were a space cadet, but I knew it was an act. You're smart, and you were too good at planning that search last November. Now it all makes perfect sense."

Mac felt heat rise into his face.

"Do your brother and sister know about the job with the DEA?"

"No." He shook his head. "I didn't want them to worry."

Her head tilted. "Why did you tell me?"

Good question. The first time he'd met her, Stella Dane had left an impression on him that he hadn't been able to shake. But he could hardly tell her that. "You're a good cop, and I want you to take this disappearing woman seriously."

Her face turned solemn. "I would have anyway. I only asked for a drug test because your story was so strange, and I was concerned."

She'd been worried about him. The idea pleased him. Most people simply assumed the worst, but Stella was different, which brought on a whole other set of concerns. Mac would be heading back to Brazil in eight weeks. He was spread thin trying to establish a connection with his family. But Stella . . .

She made him think about things he'd never considered before, like not coming home to an empty house. Like having someone to share a late-night meal.

Or his bed.

"So that's what you were doing when you were shot? Investigating drug traffickers."

"I've been working in that region studying wildlife since I was an undergraduate. I know many of the villagers. Until I went to work for the DEA, I was a simple wildlife biologist studying the effects of deforestation and pollution on giant river otters. Now my expeditions are funded by a fake university that's actually a front for the DEA. Before this trip, I always worked alone, but my new boss wanted me to have a team." In reality, his new boss hadn't trusted him. "So this time I was paired with a special agent and a guide. We were only supposed to observe," he said. "There's been an increase in traffic on the Amazon River from Peru and Colombia into Brazil. Our job was to report who was moving what."

"How did you end up with the DEA?"

"I *am* a wildlife biologist, but three years ago, I accidentally ran into drug traffickers who'd captured two agents. They were in the process of torturing them. I couldn't walk away."

"You saved them?" Stella slid her cardboard cup back and forth between her hands.

"I set the place on fire. When the traffickers left the men inside to burn, I went in after them."

"Interesting tactic."

"I was outnumbered twelve machine guns to my machete. Not good odds." Mac traced a scar in his oak table. Even if he'd failed and the agents had burned, a quick death by fire would have been better than an entire night of having their bits and pieces lopped off one by one. Mac had known from personal experience that drug traffickers were the bane of humanity, but seeing them in action had flipped a switch inside him. Before that night, he'd never taken a life. But he'd killed three men, easily, almost automatically, as the Colonel's training and Mac's muscle memory had taken over his body.

Respect crossed Stella's face, and maybe a little shock, as if the true risk of his job was just sinking in. Was that why he'd told her? To impress a pretty girl? She wasn't just a pretty girl, he reasoned. She was a cop. They were on the same side. Maybe it was time he gave up being the Lone Ranger.

"So the DEA recruited you?"

"It felt good to strike back at the people who flood our country with the poison that ruins lives."

"Like yours?"

"Yes. Like mine." And everyone else in his family who'd been affected by his bad choices.

Stella nodded. "What happened to the rest of your team?"

"My guide conveniently disappeared, and my partner was killed." In his mind's eye, Cheryl reached out to him through the rain. He blinked it away. In his heart, he knew the bureaucrat who'd assigned an inexperienced field agent to his team was to blame, but that knowledge didn't ease his conscience.

"I'm sorry." She digested that tidbit for a minute. "Was your cover compromised?"

"I don't know."

"If it was, going back there would be suicide."

And it wouldn't be a pleasant way to go. The drug cartels liked to make examples of people who crossed them. Mac was attached to all his bits and pieces. "I haven't decided yet. But I'm pretty tough. Thanks to the Colonel, I could probably survive a zombie apocalypse."

But his joke didn't erase her worried frown.

"I don't want anything to happen to you," she said.

Mac tapped his bandaged side with his fingertips. "I have at least eight weeks to think about it."

"Don't take any stupid risks. No job is worth that."

Three years ago, Mac had thought making a dent in the drug trade was worth his life. But two things had changed since then. His efforts had very little effect on drug trafficking, and Lee's death had made him feel new connections with his remaining family.

"You could always go back to being a biologist—a badass biologist," she corrected, her eyes teasing.

Had a woman ever made him blush? No. Stella was definitely an original.

But Mac couldn't think about his future. Not yet. "So you'll look for the woman?"

"I told you I was already looking for her." Irritation sharpened her voice. She clasped her hands on the table. "Earlier today I caught the case of a missing woman. Thin. Short dark hair. Possibly taken from her house while she was showering. We've had a BOLO alert out since this afternoon."

The relief that swept over Mac was staggering. He *hadn't* imagined Cheryl's body was lying across a dark, rainy road. He *hadn't* gone crazy. The woman he'd seen was real. "I want to help." The offer was out of his mouth before his brain had a chance to consider it. "Please. I need to."

"I don't know. I'll have to clear it with my boss. In order to do that, I'll have to tell him everything. Brody, too. And I'm sure he'll tell Hannah . . ."

Hannah would tell Grant. The only question remaining was how early all the fan-hitting would happen and could he get out of bed and escape into the forest before the family drama ensued. And there he went again, trying to avoid the people in his life who cared about him. No more running. Tomorrow he was going to be straight with his siblings. He owed that to Lee. He owed it to all of them.

"I'm tired of secrets," he said. "You know I'm going to look for this woman with or without your help."

"I wouldn't expect anything else. You are a Barrett." She yawned. "I'll call you in the morning."

"My cell is in my Jeep, and I don't have a landline." He ducked back into the kitchen for a notepad but settled for the back of an envelope. "If you give me your number, I'll call you when I get my phone back."

"You'll be stranded here." She wrote down her number.

"I have a bike in the shed. I can ride into town. But I plan to be unconscious for the next eight hours." He rolled his shoulder. His body ached from the accident and everything else he'd put it through over the last two days.

Stella reached into her pocket and pulled out the vial of pills from the hospital. She set it on the table. "In case you want a decent night's sleep."

The woman could read his mind. Her gaze lingered on his face. Would it be too rude to ask her to come and wrap him in plastic again tomorrow? Probably.

"Get some rest," she said.

Walking out onto the porch, he watched her get into her car and then drive away. The forest loomed deep and dark around his cabin. An owl hooted. A few seconds later, the high-pitched death squeal of a small creature pierced the humid air. Isolation closed around him. Usually, he considered solitude his best friend, but not tonight.

His back ached, and he studied the prescription bottle. Maybe he should stop punishing himself. He filled a glass with water and swallowed one tablet. Then he put fresh sheets on his bed and checked under the bed and behind the headboard in case any brown recluses had decided to make a new home. He respected spiders, but he didn't want to sleep with one. Stripping off his clothes, he stretched out on the cool sheets. Warm night air and forest sounds drifted over him.

He must have fallen asleep because when he opened his eyes, pale gray light brightened the room. A scratching sound in the front of his cabin sent a burst of adrenaline into his veins. He raised his head, reaching for the knife he kept in his nightstand, just as his bedroom door squeaked open and a hulking figure shadowed the doorway.

Chapter Eleven

The smell of rubber—and the balled up piece of cloth he'd shoved into her mouth—gagged her. Pain roared through her neck, hot and sharp, blotting out the minor aches in the rest of her body and the sting of the glass cuts on her hands and feet. Not even the adrenaline of terror could dull its force.

Running away had been a very bad idea.

With her hands bound behind her back, Dena curled on her side in the trunk of a car, her shoulder pressed into the thin carpet that covered the spare tire well. She breathed through her nose, the thin fabric of the hood he'd fastened around her neck flattening against her face. It was soft and smelled of fabric softener. A pillowcase?

The trunk was hot, nearly suffocating, but a full-body shiver quaked her bones. She breathed through a wave of terror, but fear seized her by the lungs. Despair cut off her next breath. Lightheaded, her mind spun.

Why?

The car lurched, and Dena bounced. The delicate skin of her breast rubbed as her body slid on the scratchy carpet. The sudden movement jarred her out of her paralysis. Her lungs expelled stale air in a *whoosh*, and she gasped around her gag to refill them. Tears leaked from her eyes and ran hot over her skin.

She couldn't give up. But fighting wasn't an option; she was trussed like a suckling pig. She had to survive. Bide her time. Wait for an opportunity.

An opportunity to do what? Escape again? She was naked, blindfolded, gagged, and bound in the trunk of a car. How the hell could she possibly save herself?

He couldn't keep her in here forever. Eventually, he'd need to stop. Of course, he'd be more careful this time. She'd lost the element of surprise when she'd leaped from the trunk at a stop sign. He'd removed the trunk release lever, but she'd had a lucky find of the cable. Unfortunately, she'd been in the middle of nowhere and hadn't been fast or clever enough to get away. But running barefoot through the woods in the driving rain for hours had been hopeless. With clothes and boots and a flashlight, he'd tracked her down like an animal.

Like prey.

Surely, after all he'd gone through to kidnap and keep her, he wouldn't just kill her quickly. He must have a plan. She'd have time.

Please, let there be time.

Irony nearly made her giddy. Laughter that bordered on insanity stirred in her chest.

She should have left last week. She'd been planning for months, hiding money, researching bus and train schedules, recruiting a trusted friend to help her disappear, friends Adam didn't even know existed. But she'd waited too long. If she had left when she'd originally planned, she'd be in the Keys by now, sipping a margarita and digging her toes into the sand.

Alone. Free. At peace.

Now she would never be free.

The trunk opened, and through the thin fabric over her eyes, she saw a shadow lean over her. She recoiled, instinct driving her to squirm as far away as possible. But the space didn't allow for much movement. Her bare back hit the carpeted rear of the trunk.

His hands closed around her arms. He pulled her forward and scooped her under her knees and back. Grunting, he hoisted her over the lip of the trunk and dropped her into a container of some kind. The skin of her side and arm hit wet, cold metal. The pain in her neck exploded. Her vision dimmed and her body went limp. Her legs dangled over the side, the rim digging into the back of her knees. A wheel squeaked as she lurched into motion.

A wheelbarrow?

They stopped. A door opened and closed. She jolted as they moved forward again. Terror drove her heart to pound faster, as if she were still running away. As if she still had a chance.

Where was she?

She strained to hear anything above the slamming echo of her own pulse. Her fear and pain were deafening.

She held her breath for a few seconds, then forced her lungs to expand slowly, drawing air deep into her belly. If she meditated long enough, she could make her muscles relax and chase the pain into a corner. But there was no relaxing in the face of her current situation.

The wheelbarrow squeaked onward, tipping forward as if descending a ramp. They went down and down, seemingly into the bowels of the Earth.

Another door opened. Rough hands lifted her from the wheelbarrow and deposited her on what felt like cold tile. Fingers at her throat loosened the tie, and he yanked the pillowcase hood from her head.

An overhead light blinded her.

A quiet voice sent fresh horror sliding through her veins. "We've been over this before, but I'll repeat myself. If you resist, I will hurt you. As you know, I am a man who keeps my word."

He stared at the woman on the tile. Her naked body was covered in mud, bits of wet grass, and dead leaves. Tears ran in clean streaks down her filthy face. Mucus leaked from her nose.

Disgust curled inside him. "You are a dirty, dirty girl."

She'd been clean when he'd taken her from the shower. Well, she could just as easily be clean again. With a gloved hand, he turned on the faucet. Old pipes groaned. Water rained down on her, and mud sluiced from her bony frame. A few droplets bounced off the tile and onto the legs of his coveralls.

She was pale and thin-skinned. Makeup and clothes usually gave her an attractive outward appearance, but without the commercial beauty trappings, her true ugliness shone through her facade. She had no fat over her bones. Blue veins streaked across her body and the outline of her ribs was clearly visible. If he hadn't known better, he'd think she was a corpse.

This was the real Dena.

Pathetic. Weak. Deceptive. She was no better than the rest.

How would she handle the test he'd designed for her?

A sob seeped out from behind the gag in her mouth. Her eyes pleaded.

"I told you what would happen if you didn't cooperate. You've given me no choice. It's all your own fault." Grabbing the showerhead, he lifted it from its hook to better direct the spray. Sturdy nylon rope bound her ankles and wrists, making it difficult for her to worm away from the cold water.

He'd learned his lesson tonight. Missy had been more compliant, but then she'd broken quickly. Perhaps Dena would be harder to crack. Excitement hummed in his blood. Would she be The One? So far, his efforts had provided nothing but disappointment. But he'd known from the first time he'd seen Dena that she was strong.

He chased her with the spray until she hit the corner and curled into a fetal position. Goose bumps erupted over her skin as the freezing water beat down on her.

"You should have thought of the consequences before you escaped, but you never think of the consequences of your actions, do you?"

She would learn all about repercussions now.

Pale pink colored the water as some dried blood washed from her nose. She closed her eyes as he rinsed blood and dirt from her face. He returned the showerhead to its hook and wheeled a janitor's mop and rolling bucket onto the tile. Soapy water churned as he loaded the mop. He brought it around and began to wash her.

"This is going to take all day," he chastised.

But there was no help for it. He would have none of that filth under his roof, and with the resilience she'd shown, she might be here for a while.

"I can't believe you made me chase you through the storm. What if I hadn't found you?" But he supposed that had been her intention, hadn't it?

Seemingly resigned to her fate, she lay still, shivering.

She deserved no pity. She was the one who refused to comply with his polite requests. He hoped she hadn't run out of fight. She'd need to be tough for what he had planned.

"Why is 'If you don't cooperate, I'll hurt you' so hard to understand?" His voice rose with his temper.

Some people never fucking learned.

He moved down her body, suds gathering around her on the tiles.

"Turn over."

She didn't move.

"I said turn over."

When she didn't respond, he set down his cleaning implements, grabbed her feet, and flipped her body. She flopped and twitched as she resumed her fetal position on the opposite side.

The bottoms of her feet were stained dark greenish brown. He applied more pressure to the mop. The grass and mud stains refused to yield. He traded the mop for a scrubbing brush. She whimpered as he leaned into the strokes. Anger leant strength to his arm, and the stains slowly faded, revealing small cuts she must have sustained during her flight though the woods.

She deserved every wound.

He turned his attention to her hands, making sure to clean thoroughly under her nails. She'd managed to scratch his back when he'd put her in a fireman carry. He'd have to clip her nails tomorrow just to be sure none of his DNA remained.

A final rinse sent the suds scurrying down the drain. Satisfied that she was clean, he turned off the water and moved her to a tarp. Leaving her to air-dry, he dumped his bucket and used the mop to scour the tiles until no trace of her presence remained. Then he sprayed the shower down with bleach and rinsed it again.

Finished, he turned to her. She was curled on her side. Her body was still, but her gaze followed him. He breathed deeply, welcoming calm into his lungs and exhaling his anger. Such a wasteful emotion. Its energy was better spent on action.

"I really wish you'd behaved," he sighed.

She inched away from him as best she could, but her bound arms at the base of her spine limited her mobility, just as he'd planned. He reached for her. Her chest heaved, and her eyes widened.

He yawned. It was almost dawn. He hadn't gotten any sleep last night, and today would be a busy day as well. He and Dena had work to do.

Her body shifted from shivering to trembling. Fear paled her skin to the color of bleached grout. She sobbed.

An ounce of pity trickled through him. Yes, she was worse than worthless, but was that really her fault? Perhaps her weakness had been determined from her birth. Was it her gender that encouraged sin? No, he refused to believe that Eve's original disobedience predestined all women to sin. But then what made one person strong and another weak?

That was the million-dollar question, wasn't it?

"As I promised in the very beginning, if you don't cooperate, I will hurt you. And if you've only learned one thing from last night's experience, it's that I never break my promises. I am a man of my word."

She turned away.

He grabbed her jaw and forced her to face him. "There will be no more running away. You and I have work to do. It's going to be a busy day."

How long would it take to find her weaknesses and exploit them? He cleaned the wheelbarrow and then carted her to the cell Missy had vacated. Hopefully Dena would be a guest for much longer. Excitement energized him as he formulated a plan. What would they do first? He'd let her rest a while before he began her first challenge. It was only fair that she go into the test fresh. He had to give her every opportunity to prove she was worthy. That she was The One he sought.

That she didn't need to die.

Chapter Twelve

Mac's hand gripped the knife as his bedroom door opened fully and a man stepped into the dim light. Grant. Mac's lungs expelled the breath he'd been holding.

"Shit, Grant. Don't surprise me like that." He dropped his knife back into his nightstand drawer. "I was ready to spear you."

His brother filled the doorway. Grant might have left the military for civilian life, but good food and the manual labor in his new contracting business had added muscle to his frame. He crossed his arms over his chest and glared down at Mac.

"How about answering your cell? I called six times." Grant's gaze dropped to the bandage on Mac's side. "And what the hell happened to you?" His voice rose.

Mac rubbed his face. "We need to talk."

"You bet we do." Grant walked closer, his blue eyes full of frustration.

Mac held up a hand in surrender. "I got in late, and it's not even dawn. I need a shower and some coffee before I'm up for any damned sharing session."

Stopping, Grant gave him a serious nod. "All right. But you'd better hurry. Hannah's in the kitchen, and she's pissed."

"Shit." Mac's sister was much scarier than his brother.

Grant's gaze swept over his torso. Concern tightened his mouth. "Do you need help?"

"Plastic wrap."

"Got it." Grant was back in a minute.

Having his brother wrap him in plastic took all the fun out of the process, but Grant did a thorough job before retreating to the kitchen.

Mac stepped into the shower. The blast of cold water cleared his head and soothed the new bruises that mottled his chest and ribs, courtesy of the accident the night before.

As he dried off, he geared up to face his siblings. Then he stepped into a pair of jeans and reached for a T-shirt. The local anesthetic was still going strong, but his stitches pulled under the bandage. His entire torso had stiffened during the night. He took care putting his arms into the sleeves and headed for the kitchen. The smell of coffee perked him up even more.

Grant leaned against the kitchen counter. But it was the sight of Hannah sitting at the table, her hands folded neatly in front of her, that drew Mac up short. The former corporate attorney pinned him with her boardroom face.

Feigning indifference, Mac said in a flippant voice. "What is this, an intervention?"

Hannah leaned forward. Her sense of humor wasn't up yet. "Do you need an intervention?"

Walked right into that one.

"I didn't even know I had coffee." Mac poured a huge mug and sipped, welcoming the burn as he swallowed. Last night he'd decided to tell his family everything, but in the harsh kitchen light, the truth didn't seem so appealing. They were going to be angry.

"Look, Mac," Grant started. "We care about you. Your behavior has been growing more erratic over the past few years." His voice grew rough. "None of us have recovered from Lee's death, and last night was hard. Really hard." He breathed. "But we're not going to let you walk away this time."

"No one will understand what you're going through better than us." Hannah gestured between the three of them.

"We're here for you," said Grant.

"Whether you like it or not." Hannah paused. "We don't want you to get so overwhelmed that you—"

"It's been more than a decade. Eventually, you both have to trust me." Irritation flared in Mac.

But had he ever given them reason to have faith? He'd kept his entire life a secret. Trust went both ways.

Hannah raised a single brow. "I was going to say hop on the next flight to South America."

"Oh." Mac went back to his coffee. "Sorry. I guess I'm defensive."

"We all need to try harder." Grant raised his hands. "We haven't communicated well in a long time, but I remember when we operated like a junior commando team. We could practically read each other's thoughts."

"That was a long time ago, Grant." But deep inside, Mac longed for the connection he'd once had with his siblings.

"Where's your Jeep?" Hannah asked.

Mac scalded his throat with another gulp. "I crashed it into a tree last night."

Hannah straightened. "Do you need my help?"

"No." Mac shook his head. "It's not like that. I wasn't under the influence of anything. I swear."

Hannah's response was uncharacteristically gentle. "I'm sorry. That's not what I meant."

He glanced from his sister to his brother. Exhaustion lined both their faces. Less than twelve hours ago, they'd watched their father die, and they'd likely spent the rest of the night frantic about Mac. The last year had been hell on all of them. While the Colonel's death was difficult, none of them had fully recovered from Lee's murder. It was their brother's murder they were all still processing.

Guilt and grief rocked Mac. Hannah and Grant had suffered enough. No more adding to their pain. He owed them the truth.

"I work for the DEA." Mac gave them the same speech he'd given Stella the night before.

"How long?" Hannah asked.

"The last three years," Mac admitted.

"I don't know whether to be relieved or pissed off," Grant said.

"I'm both." Hannah leaned back in her chair and tapped a finger on her chin. "Why all the lies?"

"Undercover assignments are dangerous. More lives than mine depend on complete secrecy." Mac sighed.

"I'm insulted you didn't trust us," she said.

Mac nodded. "I know, and I'm sorry."

"It's not that simple." Grant dropped into a chair. Both hands scrubbed down his face. "I went on plenty of missions I couldn't share with either of you." His blue eyes pierced Mac like twin bayonets. "Why are you telling us now?"

"My last assignment went FUBAR." He summed up the incident in Brazil. "I'm going to be home, lying low, for a while."

"You're not going back?" Grant's tone was more statement than question.

Mac kept to his pledge to be honest. "I haven't decided what I'm going to do."

His brother folded his arms over his chest, clearly unhappy with his answer.

Mac added, "Part of the reason I kept my job a secret was that I didn't want you to try and talk me out of it. I screwed up my life. I screwed up everyone's lives. I finally have a chance to make up for all my mistakes."

"You don't have to make up for anything," Grant said.

But Mac felt like he did.

Hannah's eyes went misty. "But you're all right?"

"Yes. To be totally clichéd, it's just a flesh wound," Mac said.

"So what happened last night?" Hannah asked.

With a deep breath, Mac told them everything, from leaving the nursing home to his conversation with Stella.

"Strange . . ." Grant said. "And I'm not a big fan of weird events, not after everything that's happened over the last year."

"I'm going to find her." Mac set down his empty cup. "I *need* to find her."

He couldn't have another woman he couldn't save haunting his sleep.

"Does Brody know about this?" Hannah's mouth pursed.

"I imagine Stella will tell him this morning." Mac spun his empty coffee mug on the table.

"Is there anything we can do?" Grant asked.

Mac stretched. "Let me borrow your cell phone. I need to call the auto shop."

"OK." Grant held his phone toward him. "On one condition."

Wary, Mac froze. "What?"

"You have dinner at my house tonight. We can talk about all of this. Plus, we have funeral and estate issues to discuss. Ellie has been worried sick, and the kids miss you." Grant had proposed to Ellie on Christmas Day. They'd bought and renovated a home. They were raising Carson and Faith and building a family together. They were happy. Was that envy crawling around in Mac's chest? Since when did hearth and home have any appeal to him?

"Deal." For once in his life, Mac wanted to be part of his family. Now he had to figure out how to make that happen. He'd been alone so long, anything else took thought and effort.

Hannah reached across the table and opened her hand. Mac took it. Grant placed a hand on each of their shoulders. The three of them were connected now in a way they hadn't been since they'd faced all those survival challenges their father had set up for them. They were bound by their shared experiences.

But once there had been four of them.

Grief welled in Mac's chest. Raw and sharp, it nearly choked him. Grant's hand squeezed his shoulder. Mac swallowed hard. Lee had been gone for fifteen months, but the wound his murder left was still wide open, and the Colonel's death had been a handful of salt.

Mac needed to deal with his pain before the scar it left was permanent.

Chapter Thirteen

Stella jerked awake. Her heart hammered. Her breaths bellowed in and out of her lungs as if she'd just run the academy obstacle course.

Trembling, she pushed her sweaty hair off her forehead. The nightmare had been vivid enough she could smell gunpowder, feel the stock of her AR-15 against her shoulder, and hear Lance groaning as she fired at the armed and fleeing suspect. But winging him hadn't been enough. He'd gotten away. He'd gone on to kill two cops. Hannah and Brody had nearly died.

Swallowing the sickness rising in her throat, she got out of bed and stumbled to the shower. Not even the scalding water could completely wash away the nightmare. Dawn had not made an appearance yet when Stella tiptoed into the dark kitchen. The remnants of her nightmare lingered. Gunshots, blood, the sharp scent of gunpowder. A quick burst of panic kicked her adrenals into overdrive. Breathing deeply, she leaned on the counter, her fingers gripping the edge until she got her pulse under control. She hadn't had a flashback in a long time. She'd thought she was over them.

But would she ever truly get over what had happened? Failure was tough to accept.

She turned on the overhead light and lifted the coffeepot, grateful that it was already full. Pouring herself a mugful, she drank half its contents standing over the sink. The caffeine hit her system and eased her lack-of-sleep headache. Three restless nights were beginning to take their toll.

The front door opened and her grandfather entered, fully dressed and carrying a camera rigged with a telephoto lens.

"You were working so late, I didn't expect you to be up this early." He kissed her cheek. Worried eyes scanned her face. It was impossible to hide anything from the retired NYPD homicide detective.

"I need to get to the station." Stella had reviewed her case notes until she'd fallen asleep over the files.

"If you're not going to sleep, you need to eat. Let me make you some breakfast." Setting down his camera, Grandpa ignited a burner and set a frying pan on the stove. On cue, nails pattered on the tile as her sister's French bulldog trotted into the room and sat at Grandpa's feet, his oversize head cocked in expectation.

"What were you doing outside with the camera at this hour?" Stella leaned a hip on the counter. "Obviously you weren't walking the dog."

Snoozer wasn't an early riser, unless there was food.

Grandpa added butter to the pan and retrieved a carton of eggs from the fridge. "Someone has been letting their dog crap on our lawn during the night. I'm going to find out who it is."

Stella covered her grin by sipping from her mug.

"What? I still know how to conduct an investigation." He pointed to the camera. "People should take responsibility. I'm tired of cleaning the kids' shoes."

"It's probably a loose dog."

"Then people should keep their dogs on leashes." Grandpa cracked eggs into the pan one-handed. "I *will* find out who it is."

"I don't doubt you for a second." Stella knew her grandfather would hunt their errant pooper like a bloodhound.

"You'd think three-acre lots would give people enough room for their animals on their own property." He slid four slices of bread into the toaster. "You were late last night and now up early this morning. Tough case?"

"Several. Do you remember Missy Green?"

"Didn't you hang around with her in high school?" He took two plates from the cabinet and poured Stella a glass of orange juice.

"Yes. She turned up dead on Monday."

Grandpa paused, the carton in one veiny hand. "I'm sorry to hear that. She was a good kid."

"She was tortured and killed. Then her body was dumped." How many people could share that kind of information with a grandparent?

"It must be hard to work on a case when you knew the victim." Grandpa loaded the toast and eggs onto two plates and carried them to the table. Snoozer followed, his bulgy eyes sticking with the plates.

Only at the Dane house was homicide a topic of breakfast conversation.

"I was lucky." He tucked his napkin into the front of his shirt. "I worked in a big city department. I rarely ran into a homicide that wasn't a stranger. Maybe I'd have to investigate the death of an informant or someone I'd arrested previously, but never a friend. If your former relationship with Missy prevents you from doing your job, there's no shame in stepping away from the case."

"You're right, of course." Stella sampled her breakfast. Heavy on the butter as usual but tasty. "But I get this feeling that something is off with the case, and I don't know if I have enough experience to trust my gut."

"Are you investigating all possible leads?"

"I am. I'm waiting for forensics and a toxicology report. Until then, I'm digging into her life."

Grandpa dug into his breakfast. "That's all you can do. Keep picking away. Everyone has secrets."

"I also caught a missing persons case yesterday that I have a very bad feeling about. I have no evidence that the cases are linked, but something tells me they are. Is that ridiculous?"

"Not at all." Grandpa put his hand over hers. "You might not have a lot of experience yet, but that doesn't mean you should ignore your gut. Good instincts are genetic. You come from a long line of crack detectives." He grinned.

"I do." Stella smiled. "Thanks."

"Anytime." He salted his eggs, stopping with a frown when she caught his eye. "My blood pressure is fine."

"Because you take a pill."

Sighing, he set the saltshaker aside. "Do you think you can borrow a nighttime surveillance camera from the department?"

Stella laughed. "No. I don't think I could get that requisition signed."

"Damn." He buttered a piece of toast, tore off a corner, and flipped it to the dog. Snoozer watched the food hit the floor, then shuffled over to eat it. "I might have to get creative."

Stella finished her eggs and transferred her coffee into a travel mug. "I have to go. Thanks for the breakfast and the advice."

"I love you." He kissed her on the cheek. "Be careful."

Grandpa carried the empty dishes to the sink. The dog took his cue that no more food was available and trotted to his bed in the corner. He rested his head on his paws, and his eyelids drooped instantly.

"You, too." She grabbed her briefcase. "Don't do anything I wouldn't do."

Grandpa snorted. "I make no promises."

Stella left the house bolstered by food and love. The roads were dark and empty on her way to the station. The sky was barely gray when she parked in front of the municipal building. With blue clapboard and red shutters, the structure was quaint-pretty on the outside, industrial-ugly on the inside. The police station occupied the entire first floor. Upstairs housed the various township tax and zoning offices.

In her cubicle, she draped her blazer over her chair, sat, and booted up the computer. She typed up her reports from the day before as the station bustled through shift change. Chief Horner was in his office by seven, and the administrative staff started at eight.

She'd barely finished her reports when Brody came in. All typical cop. Boring tie. Nondescript suit. Sharp brown eyes.

"I have something to tell you," Stella said.

"It'll have to wait. The chief wants to see us in his office," he gestured to the door at the other end of the room.

Stella hurried to catch up. "I've been here for hours. He didn't say anything to me."

"He called me at home an hour ago." Brody frowned as if the chief's personal summons had been an unwelcome intrusion.

"How is Hannah?" Stella asked.

"It was a rough night. She didn't sleep. Between losing her father and worrying about Mac . . ."

Obviously Brody hadn't slept either.

"Please tell her . . ." She couldn't articulate her empathy. "I lost my dad when I was fifteen. Tell her I'm sorry."

"I will. Thanks." Brody knocked on the chief's door.

"Come in." The command reverberated through the wood.

Brody opened the door and they went inside. Chief Dave Horner sat behind his tidy desk. As usual, his dark blue uniform was heavy on the starch. His hair was perfect.

Staring at Stella, the chief jabbed a finger on a closed file on his desk. "You were due at the range for pistol qualification yesterday."

"Sorry. I've been tied up with cases, and it totally slipped my mind," she lied.

"You've missed your appointment twice." The chief studied her face. "You're an excellent shot, so why are you putting it off?"

Wishing she was better at concealing her emotions, Stella schooled her face. A muscle in her cheek twitched. Could the chief see that? "No reason. I'm focused on the investigations we're running. I hate to take the time out so some administrator can check a box."

Had she fooled him?

Damn it. She couldn't tell. Unlike her, Horner had a great poker face, which was helpful in the frequent press conferences he favored. Just thinking about the firing range sent her blood pressure spiking and a bead of sweat running into her bra. She'd like to blame it on this morning's flashback, but she hadn't been able to perform well at the range since the shooting.

"It's part of the job. Get it done." He opened the file.

"Yes, sir. I will." *Somehow.*

The chief waved a printout in his hand. "Now, what happened last night after you left the Miller's house? I have a report of a one-vehicle accident and a vanishing body in the road?"

Stella swallowed a curse. She'd wanted to tell Brody privately. She gave a rundown of her evening with Mac, including the news about Mac's involvement with the DEA.

"Hannah's brother was a huge help last November," Brody added.

"I remember." The chief tapped a finger on his blotter. "Seems far-fetched that Dena Miller was lying across a road in the middle of the night and then vanished. But then, the whole story is unusual. You're positive she didn't leave on her own?"

"Not a hundred percent," Stella said. "But it doesn't seem likely."

The chief's fingers drummed.

"Mac Barrett would like to assist in the investigation," Stella said. "The incident bothers him."

"Understandable." The chief rubbed his perfectly smooth chin. "I'll have to check with his superior officer."

Stella cleared her throat. "With all due respect, sir, I had the impression that Mac will be looking for this woman with or without our cooperation. As you remember, the Barretts are a determined lot." And they liked to handle their matters personally, as both Grant and Hannah had demonstrated.

"I remember." Horner's eyes narrowed. "No offense," he glanced at Brody, "but the Barretts are headstrong and difficult."

"No offense taken," Brody said. "That's one stubborn family."

"You." Horner pointed at Stella. "Keep Mac Barrett under control. I don't care who he works for. I won't have another rogue Barrett running around my town."

How was she supposed to keep Mac under control?

The chief folded his hands on his blotter. "What's your next step in the investigation?"

"Retracing Dena's activity yesterday," Stella said. "I'll check in with forensics, too. Adam Miller will get a second round of questions, and his alibi needs to be verified with the country club. I'm running background checks on everyone involved and working my way through the recent calls, texts, and contacts on her phone."

"Sounds like a good start." The phone at the chief's elbow rang. He ignored it. "Pull Lance to help with the investigation. No going off on your own, either one of you."

"Yes, sir." Stella had no desire to play heroine. As she'd learned last fall, a situation could go south in the span of a heartbeat. She shuddered at the memory. Gunfire. Lance going down. Blood. More gunfire.

"Stella?" the chief prompted.

She blinked. "Sorry."

His eyes narrowed with suspicion. "Is everything all right?"

"Fine."

Horner stared for a few seconds, then nodded as if she passed muster. "Now, what's going on with the Green case?"

"Waiting on toxicology reports." Stella summed up the medical examiner's findings. "But she was restrained and tortured. If she overdosed, it seems unlikely she did it herself."

Horner scanned her report. "Maybe she owed a dealer money and he decided to make an example of her. Addicts run with dangerous crowds."

"Ex addict," Stella clarified. "Sir."

"Keep plugging away at it." Chief Horner met her gaze head on. "But I want you to concentrate on the accountant's missing wife. Our citizens can't feel safe if suburban women disappear from their homes without a trace."

"What if the cases are related?"

"Do you have any evidence they're related?" he asked.

"Not yet, but the cases have some similarities," she admitted. Her inexperienced gut wouldn't impress the chief.

"I want you both working the accountant's missing wife. Pull uniforms in to help with the grunt work. We can't help a dead woman, but there's a chance we can save Dena Miller if we find her alive." Horner gave them his dismissive nod. "Dena Miller's husband has already reached out to the media." Horner tugged the wrinkles from his sleeve. "I'll be holding a press conference tomorrow. Give me something intelligent to say, and I want you standing next to me. You did a good job with the reporters on Monday. They love you."

The compliment rubbed Stella the wrong way. She wanted to be a cop, not a politician like the chief. Right now, she needed to get back to work on her cases.

"Is there anything else, sir?" she asked, tight-lipped.

"No." The chief picked up his phone and waved them toward the door. Brody and Stella wasted no time bolting from the office.

Brody pulled the door closed. "Is there anything else you want to tell me about Mac?"

"No."

"Hannah was upset about him last night. I can't believe he didn't call her."

"He didn't want to worry her any more."

Brody's gaze sharpened. "Is everything OK with *you*?"

"Sure." She avoided his gaze.

Brody's eyes doubted her answer. "It's not like you to be late with a form, let alone a qualification. You're usually disgustingly punctual and efficient about these things."

She smiled, but the effort felt weak. "I'm not used to juggling so many cases."

Brody stopped her with a hand on her elbow, turning her to face him. "Do not hesitate to call me if you need help, and I'm not talking about the cases."

"Thanks." She turned her back on Brody's stare and bolted toward her cubicle. She hadn't fooled him. He knew something was wrong. She added a trip to the firing range to her to-do list. She'd have to go at closing, when no one else would be there. Spectators didn't help.

At her desk, she reviewed Dena's cell phone call log. Adam, the spa, the physical therapist's office. Adam again. She highlighted an unidentified number, then continued down the list to the previous day. A few numbers that needed to be traced. More calls to and from the husband. Many more.

Odd.

Making a notation, Stella scanned Dena's contact list. Nothing seemed out of the ordinary, except for her very long list of doctors, but that wasn't unexpected from a person who'd suffered a debilitating injury.

Stella moved on to Missy's phone, which had only a few contacts. Stella matched a few numbers to the short list that had been on Missy's refrigerator. Wait. Stella recognized the next number. She pulled out her own phone to double check.

Gianna Leone was one of Stella's former informants. Gianna had also kicked a drug addiction, which could explain the connection between her and Missy.

Knowing exactly where she could find Gianna later that morning, Stella gathered her files and contemplated snagging a uniformed officer to go with her for her first interview. But a uniform affected the way people reacted during questioning. Some would talk more, others less, but in general, it put them on guard. They never forgot they were talking to a cop. Stella had already found in her six months as a detective that she could get people to say things they never would have blabbed if she was in uniform.

"Detective Dane." An administrative assistant waved a yellow clasp envelope at her. "This came for you."

Stella turned the envelope over in her hands. No return address. Stella's name and rank and the address of the police station had been printed on an adhesive label.

"Thanks." Stella slid a letter opener under the flap and shook out an eight-by-ten photo. It was a picture of Missy's body in the dugout. Taken at night with a flash, the picture highlighted her features. Except the picture didn't portray the body exactly as it had been found. In this shot, Missy's arms were folded over her body, and the needle was under her hands.

Stella's insides went cold.

There was no longer any question that Missy had been murdered. The picture had been taken when Missy was positioned on the bench. By her killer.

Chapter Fourteen

Standing in front of Horner's desk, Stella wiped her palms on her slacks. "The postmark is local."

The chief held the plastic bag containing the photo and envelope by the corner. "This is the downside to all the media attention you've been receiving."

Which hadn't been Stella's idea.

"I don't want this leaked to the media. Keep it quiet." He handed the photo to her over the desk. "Get this to the lab. See if they can pull prints."

"Yes, sir." Stella turned to the door.

"Be extra careful, Detective," Horner said. "I don't like that he's focused on you."

That made two of them.

More jittery than she wanted to admit, Stella dropped the envelope and photo at the forensics lab for fingerprinting. Then she drove to Mrs. Green's house to update Missy's mother. Heading up the walk, she scanned the street and shivered.

The chief was probably right. The killer had seen her on the news, but being watched by a sadistic murderer gave her a cramp between her shoulder blades. She shook it off and knocked on the door. With Horner as her boss, she had no way to avoid media exposure.

Once again, Stella sat in the familiar kitchen. Mrs. Green's face was paler and her eyes more vacant.

She handed Stella a cup of coffee. "I appreciate you taking time to give me an update."

"Have you slept?" Stella asked.

Mrs. Green's gaze flickered over Stella's face. "Not really. Have you?"

"No." Stella sipped. "Did Missy ever talk about cutting?"

"No," Mrs. Green said. "She never mentioned cutting herself."

"She was wearing long sleeves when she was found. Did she ever wear shorts or short-sleeve shirts?"

"Yes. She was wearing a miniskirt last Thursday when I took her to lunch. There weren't any marks on her legs. She never wore short sleeves because of the track marks on her arms." Mrs. Green blew her nose. "There's no way Missy would have given herself more scars. She was self-conscious about the marks she already had." Mrs. Green tossed the tissue in the garbage can. "If you want, you could talk to Missy's psychiatrist at the rehab center." She went to a drawer and rummaged through its contents. "Here it is." She handed Stella a business card that read New Life Center for Hope.

Stella took the card. "Did Missy have a recent boyfriend?"

"No." Mrs. Green's tone was emphatic. "She told me she had no time or energy for another person until she had her life in order."

"How about a past boyfriend?"

"I don't know much about her life in California." Mrs. Green twisted her hands. "Do you know how she died?"

"Not yet." Stella debated how much to reveal to Mrs. Green and as much as she hated to distress her, the woman deserved to hear the truth from Stella—not a news report. "The toxicology reports will take a few weeks." She covered Mrs. Green's hands with her own. "But she didn't do this to herself."

A tear slid down Mrs. Green's cheek and dropped off her chin. "Then someone killed her?"

"Yes."

"I knew it from the beginning." Mrs. Green sniffed and drew in a shaky breath.

"I'm sorry." Stella squeezed her hands. "There's more."

Mrs. Green's eyes cringed.

As much as Stella wanted to spare Mrs. Green, the press would eventually publish all the gory details. Stella could think of no way to soften the truth, so she just said it. "Missy was tortured."

Mrs. Green gasped. Her hands curled into fists. Then her watery eyes turned angry. "Find him."

"I will." Stella let herself out. She heard sobbing as she pulled the front door closed. She would not stop until she found the bastard who hurt Missy.

In her car, she called the rehab center. The earliest the psychiatrist could see her was the next morning.

Her phone rang. The display showed an unknown caller.

"Hello?"

"It's Mac."

"Where are you?"

"I'm at the auto body shop waiting to talk to the mechanic." He sounded depressed. "I found my phone. Where do you want to meet?"

"I'll come there." She wanted to take a quick look at his Jeep, though the chances were slim the vehicle held any clues.

"OK."

Ten minutes later, she parked next to a plain-Jane rental sedan. She scanned the large, weedy lot for Mac but didn't see him. The office was a red brick building that fronted a row of garage bays. She went inside. No one stood behind the counter, but she heard Mac's voice echoing in the main shop. The smell of oil hit her nose as she walked through a doorway and stopped dead.

Mac and a coverall clad mechanic stood next to his Jeep. He was dressed in his usual snug cargos, T-shirt, and hiking boots, but he was clean-shaven, and his blond hair was swept back from his face in a style GQ would approve.

Had she ever seen him clean-shaven? Once, at his brother's funeral. But he'd been subdued and not himself. Stella wasn't sure if she liked him better looking tame or wild, but when his eyes roamed over her, a delicious shiver zinged through her belly. Those eyes . . .

The mechanic walked away, and Mac waited.

Shaking off her shock, Stella crossed the grease-stained concrete and examined the Jeep. *Ouch.* "What's the prognosis?"

The front end bore the brunt of the damage. Crumpled hood and fenders. Broken windshield and windows. She peeked inside. A large branch had punctured the passenger window and speared the headrest. The fact that he'd gotten out with minimal injuries was a miracle. If he'd hit that stand of trees just a little differently, he wouldn't be standing here.

"Totaled," Mac said.

"Sorry."

He shrugged. "Could be worse. Better the Jeep than me."

The thought swept a wave of sadness through her. Too much death had filled her life lately. His, too.

Mac walked around the vehicle to stand next to her. "You're not going to comment on my change of appearance?"

Stella looked him up and down. "You clean up OK."

"OK?" He laughed. "That's it?"

Her gaze lingered on his face. "I kind of miss the scruff."

A quick blast of heat lit his eyes. Then his head tipped back, and he laughed. "Well then, no more shaving for me. Where are we going first?"

"You're sure you want to get involved? Your family doesn't need you?" Stella had a feeling that Mac was in funeral-planning-avoidance mode.

"My day is clear until dinnertime." He turned toward the exit. "As I told you last night, I'm going to look for this woman with or without you." Picking up a backpack from the ground next to the Jeep, he glanced over his shoulder and gave her an *are you coming?* look. "I'd much rather work with you."

Better to keep him in her sights. "Do you promise to stay out of the way and do what I tell you?"

"You're bossy."

"That's not an answer."

"No, it's not."

They walked through the shop. Stella paused next to the rental car. "Do you want to drop this off at your place?"

Mac grinned. "That's not mine." He held out his backpack. "Would you mind taking this?"

"No." Confused, she tossed it into her backseat.

He crossed to a Harley-Davidson parked in the shade of the building. "I told you I had a bike."

Stella hadn't noticed the sleek black vehicle in the shadows.

"That's not what I'd pictured." She'd thought he'd meant a bicycle, but when he slung a leg over the Harley, the image of him on a mountain bike was ridiculous.

"Where are you going?" she asked.

He held his helmet in two hands. "I'm going to talk to Adam Miller about his missing wife."

What the . . . ?

"How did you get his name?" she asked.

"He was on the news about fifteen minutes ago, giving an impassioned plea for his wife's safe return." Mac settled his black helmet on his head and nodded toward the auto shop. "I saw it on the TV in the office."

Damn. That was fast.

With no other options, she said. "Let's drop your bike at your house, and you can ride with me."

His eyes gleamed with victory. "Yes, ma'am."

Stella opened her car door. "Follow me."

But Mac's engine started with a throaty rumble, drowning out her words. He roared out of the parking lot, and Stella rushed to catch up. Driving after him, she sincerely hoped this was not an indication of how well she could keep Mac Barrett under control.

Chapter Fifteen

In the passenger seat of Stella's cruiser, Mac rubbed at his jaw. Shaving off his thick beard had left his face raw.

"I'd like to start at the accident scene," he said.

"Makes sense. We'll be passing it in a minute."

Stella cruised to a stop on the shoulder of the road and they got out. Mac walked to the spot where he'd seen the woman. He closed his eyes. In his imagination, he saw driving rain, darkness, and a lifeless, female body. Cold passed through his bones and he opened his eyes to the sunlight.

Stella touched his arm. "Are you OK?"

He nodded, walking to the shoulder and scanning the roadside. He searched a sizable square of ground around the bend in the road, but saw nothing in the mud or tall weeds growing by the shoulder. "I'm pretty good at tracking. I was hoping to find something to follow."

"Any footprints or tire tracks were washed away by the storm." Stella watched him search the ground. "We issued an updated alert. Local, county, and state officers are looking for Dena Miller."

Fifteen minutes later, he gave up. Back in the car, Mac found her case notes on the floor. He opened the file, appreciating her thoroughness and attention to detail. "How long has Dena Miller been married?"

"Five years, but you shouldn't be reading that file," she said but didn't make a move to take it away from him.

Mac speed-read through her notes. He was of the ask-for-forgiveness-later mindset, and she seemed resigned to his intrusion. "What do you know about the husband?"

"We're still investigating him." Stella's tone was curt.

"You don't like him."

"I don't know enough about him to form an opinion."

Ten minutes later, they stopped at a day spa. Dena's massage therapist, Laura, verified she'd finished Dena's massage around one and stated that Dena had acted normally. She didn't seem to know her client on a personal level and didn't have anything interesting to say. On the way out of the building, the receptionist gave Stella a printout of Dena's receipt showing a one-oh-five p.m. checkout.

Stella parked in front of Active Physical Therapy and Personal Training, and they went inside. A door on the right led to a gym room. Weights clanged as a short, ripped guy grunted his way through a set of bicep curls.

Stella showed her badge at the reception desk and asked for Lyle Jones. They were shown into a small patient room to wait. Mac paced. Small spaces didn't agree with him.

The door opened and a short, jacked dude walked in. His skin bore the deep orange of a bottle tan over a scattering of acne.

"I'm Lyle." He shook their hands. "You want to talk about Dena?"

"Yes." Stella produced her badge.

Lyle barely glanced at it. "I can't give out any medical information, even to the police. We're under strict guidelines about that."

"We know," Stella assured him. "Dena is missing. We're just trying to find her. I know you can't tell me anything about her condition, but we know she was here yesterday." Stella probed. "Did she seem upset or under any unusual stress?"

"Well . . . It's just that . . ." Lyle scratched his shaved head. "Well, her husband calls all the time to check up on her. Yesterday, he called just after she left."

Interest piqued in Stella's eyes. "What did he say?"

"He asked if she was still here." Lyle folded his arms over his chest, disapproval on his face. "Dena always got upset when he called. Once she asked me to please not say anything personal about her to him."

Stella asked, "Did that strike you as strange?"

"Very," Lyle agreed.

"Did you ever meet Adam Miller?" Mac asked.

"Yes. In the beginning of her therapy, Dena couldn't drive, and Adam would bring her to her appointments. He got really annoyed when I told him I couldn't discuss his wife's medical issues with him." Lyle's mouth tightened. "Of course, I could have if Dena had agreed, but I just didn't like the guy."

"Thanks for your help. We'll let you know if we have any additional questions." Stella moved toward the door.

Mac trailed behind them. He stopped and pointed to a picture on the wall. "I see you're a professional bodybuilder."

Lyle stopped. "Yes. I'm also a personal trainer. I'm fascinated by the way a body can be altered, shaped by diet and exercise."

Diet, exercise, and steroids, Mac thought.

They left him in the main lobby. Back in the car, Stella pulled out a notebook and scribbled some notes.

She lifted her pen. "What did you think about Lyle Jones?"

"Besides the fact that he hates Adam Miller?" Mac asked. "Not many people can get that bulky and cut without artificial hormones."

"Do you think he uses steroids?" Stella's brow wrinkled.

"Probably. It's basic biology. I'm not saying it's impossible, but the human body can only get so big. The kind of muscle Lyle was carrying. . ." His acne was another indication he was supplementing with hormones.

Stella closed her notebook. "So what does that have to do with Dena Miller?"

"Probably nothing." Mac pulled Dena's photo from the file and stared at it. No smile for the camera. The woman looked like she was about to get a root canal. "But Lyle likely uses illegal drugs, and he seems to know a lot more about her than the massage therapist did."

"Good point. I'll run a deeper background check on him."

"What now?" he asked.

"I have an idea." She dialed her phone. "Yes, is Laura available? Thank you." She studied her notes while she waited. "Laura? This is Detective Dane. I have a quick question for you. Did Dena's husband ever call to check up on her while she was at the spa? He did? Did he call yesterday?" Stella flashed Mac a predatory smile, thanked the woman, and ended the call.

"I need to talk to Dena's husband." Stella dropped the phone on the console. "I owe him an update on his wife's case, and I need to know why he didn't tell me he already knew his wife had made it to both of her appointments yesterday."

"Lying is never a good sign," Mac said. "Should we go see Mr. Miller now?"

"Not yet." Stella pulled out onto the street. "I have to talk to some-one about another case. Do you mind?"

"No."

Stella turned on the air-conditioner. "An old friend of mine was found dead. She was a former drug addict. She was tortured and killed."

"I'm sorry."

"Thanks." Stella summed up her homicide investigation on Missy Green. "I found a recent call number in Missy's phone that I recog-nized as one of my former informants. Gianna Leone was a prostitute and a heroin addict. She overdosed a year ago. Her customer actually called it in. When I arrived, she was barely breathing. Thank God we're equipped with Narcan."

Naloxone, brand name Narcan, was an opioid antagonist nasal spray used to reverse the effects of an overdose.

"It saved her life, but unfortunately, Gianna was left with irreversible kidney damage from years of heroin abuse." Stella parked in front of a grocery store. "She comes from a very rough background." Grabbing her purse, she got out of the car.

Mac followed her into the store as she grabbed a basket and headed for the dairy aisle. "Errands?"

"Not for me. Gianna is on kidney dialysis and disability now." Stella selected a quart of milk.

Mac took the basket from her. "So you bring her food."

"Occasionally. She's come a long way, and she has no support. No father in the picture ever. Her mother was a prostitute. Gianna started hooking when she was thirteen." Stella added eggs and bread and a few other staples, then crossed to the prepared food section and selected a family-size portion of fettuccine Alfredo and a chocolate cupcake.

Nice mom. "What happened to her mother?"

"She's in prison for cooking meth."

Mac unloaded the items in the checkout lane. "You sure this is enough?"

"She only has a mini fridge." Stella knew this Gianna pretty well.

After checking out of the store, she drove a few miles and parked in front of a dialysis center.

Surprised, Mac scanned the front of the medical building. "We're going to question her here?"

Stella lowered the front door windows and turned off the engine. The air was still. Heat began to build in the car immediately. "No. She should be done in the next few minutes. She doesn't have a car. She lives close and walks to the center, but she's exhausted when she comes out of dialysis."

"So you drive her home?" It didn't surprise him.

Stella squinted through the windshield, her gaze scanning the sidewalk. "If I happen to be nearby."

Mac bet Stella happened to be nearby as often as possible.

The door opened and a coltish, dark-haired girl stepped out. "There she is."

"She looks like a teenager." Mac knew the realities of teens and drug use, and every damaged kid showed him the importance of his reconnaissance in Brazil. Going back to the jungle would be dangerous, but wasn't the outcome worth the risk? Mac didn't have a wife or kids to support. Wasn't it better that *he* take the risk than a man who would leave a family behind?

The girl's pallor was sick-pasty, her skinny jeans could have fit a twelve-year-old, and Mac could see the dark circles under her eyes from twenty feet away.

"Gianna's only eighteen." Stella opened the car door and got out. They greeted each other with a hug. There was nothing *occasional* about their relationship. The girl rested her head on Stella's shoulder, relaxed until she spotted Mac in the car. Then her body jerked straight.

Stella rubbed her arm, leaned close, and spoke in her ear. The girl grinned, and Mac wondered what Stella had said.

As they approached the car, Mac got out and opened the back door for the girl. She gave him a once-over way too mature for her age, then gave Stella an approving nod. "You're right."

About what?

Stella blushed. "This is Mac Barrett. We're working a case together."

"Sure you are." Gianna's tone was amused. "Nice to meet you."

They all climbed into the vehicle. Mac angled his body to look over the seat. Up close, the kid looked even worse.

"Appreciate the ride," Gianna said from the backseat.

"Rough today?" Stella started the engine. Cool air blasted from the dashboard vents.

Gianna lifted a bony shoulder in a shrug, then, shivering, she zipped her sweat jacket all the way to her chin. "It is what it is."

Stella glanced in the rearview mirror. "Any word on the transplant?"

Gianna's mouth tightened. "Nope. Long list, ya know?"

Mac suspected a former prostitute and heroin addict didn't exactly soar to the top. People tended to make judgments, and there was no escaping the stigma.

A few minutes later, Stella pulled into the parking lot of a low-income apartment complex. Three utilitarian brick buildings squatted around a weedy patch of grass. Mac opened the car door for Gianna. The girl stepped out, but her legs buckled as she stood. Mac took her elbow. Humiliation and frustration hardened her features as her legs steadied.

"Thanks." She forced a tough smile on her face. Pulling her arm from his grasp, she walked toward the closest building in a pained gait, as if her entire body hurt.

Mac nodded, shutting the door and then sticking close enough to catch her if her balance gave out again. Stella followed with the groceries.

Gianna's apartment was partially below ground. The entire unit was the size of a two-car garage and just as damp. They stepped directly into the kitchenette. A window over the sink looked out on the street. A card table and two folding chairs crowded the tiny space. A lopsided sofa, a milk-crate coffee table, and a TV took up most of the living room. A door behind the kitchen likely led to the bedroom and bathroom.

Stella put the milk and eggs in the pint-size fridge, which was jammed under three feet of counter.

Gianna sank onto the couch. Exhaustion lined her face, aging her ten years in the span of two seconds. "Thanks, Stella. I don't know what I'd do without you."

"Hungry?" Stella held up the plastic container of pasta. "I brought your favorite."

"Yeah." Gianna smiled, her eyes looking watery. With a sniff, she rubbed a knuckle under her eye and lifted her chin. "That'd be great."

Tough kid.

Stella warmed the pasta in the countertop microwave and delivered it to the girl. She took the food and ate a few bites without speaking.

Mac moved the two folding chairs into the living area and opened them in front of the sofa. A dog-eared book on the floor caught his eye: *GED Practice and Review.* A single framed snapshot decorated the table: a selfie of Stella and Gianna against a clear, blue sky.

Stella dropped into a chair and leaned forward to face Gianna. "I need to ask you a couple of questions."

Gianna's face snapped up. "You know I've been clean all year. I ain't had nothin' to do with my old life."

"I know." Stella held up a hand. "It's not about you. It's about someone else."

The girl settled again, twirling a forkful of noodles. "OK. Anything for you, Stella."

"Do you know Missy Green?" Stella asked.

Gianna's fork stilled. "I know *a* Missy."

Stella leaned forward, resting her clasped hands on her knees. "But you don't know her last name?"

"No." Gianna chewed. It looked like effort, as if she was too tired to eat. She swallowed. "Why?"

"Because your cell number was in her phone contacts," Stella said.

Mac asked, "Is it because you know her from NA?"

"Yes." Gianna grinned at Stella and jerked a thumb at Mac. "Guess he's not just your arm candy?"

Stella didn't bother to cover her grin. Instead, she played along, waggling her eyebrows until the girl laughed out loud. "When did you last see her?"

"Wait." Gianna's body jerked straight, as if she just realized a cop was questioning her about her friend. "Did something happen to Missy?"

Stella hesitated, no doubt deciding how much information to reveal about the case in order to gather more. "She was murdered."

"No." Gianna dropped her fork and set the dish on the crate.

"How well did you know her?" Stella asked.

Gianna lifted a bony shoulder. "She was nice. She gave me a ride sometimes. I know she worked a lot, but I don't know much about her personal life."

Stella pressed. "Did she seem upset lately or show any signs of relapsing?"

"No." Gianna's hair swayed as she shook her head. "Missy seemed pretty solid."

"How often do you go to NA meetings?" Mac asked.

"I try to go a couple of times a week, depending on how tired I am or if I feel like walking. Otherwise I have to get a ride, and a lot of members don't like to give out their cell phone numbers. Missy did, though. She was sweet."

"We're doing everything we can to find out who killed her." Stella stood and picked up Gianna's pasta. "I'll put this in the fridge for you to heat up later. You know you can always call me for a ride."

"Thanks." The girl's eyelids drooped. "You do enough for me."

Mac jotted his cell number on the back of an envelope on Gianna's table. "You shouldn't be walking around alone in the dark. Call me if you ever need to go and don't have a ride."

She smiled, but her eyes were sad. She turned to Stella. "You have hit the mother lode, girlfriend. He is definitely not just a pretty face."

Mac laughed. "I only have my Harley right now. So you'd have to ride on the back of that."

"Seriously?" Her eyes brightened. "That'd be so awesome."

"Anytime." Mac wondered what would have become of him if Lee hadn't straightened his ass out. Would he be dead or homeless?

"I wish I wasn't so . . ." Gianna's fist curled around the edge of the blanket. "Helpless."

"Everybody needs help now and then. There's no honor in going it alone." A lesson Mac had learned the hard way. He pushed the piece of paper toward her. "Put my number in your phone. No more walking alone at night."

She took the number, picked up her cell, and input his number with her thumbs. "Thank you."

His phone chimed with a text. Mac's screen read: Gianna :)

"We need to go. Lock up behind us before you fall asleep." Stella led the way outside. They waited to hear the deadbolt turn in the lock before walking back to the car.

"How long has she been waiting for a kidney?" he asked.

"Probably only six months, but to her it seems like forever. Dialysis is miserable." Stella glanced back at the apartment building.

"Can we go interrogate Adam Miller now?" Mac wanted to see this guy, badly.

"Oh, yes." Stella slid behind the wheel and turned the key in the ignition. "It's time."

Mac opened the file on Dena Miller and checked Stella's notes. "If he had something to do with his wife's disappearance, why would he call the police?"

"Hard to explain his wife's sudden absence." Stella pulled out onto the street.

Mac looked up from the file and caught Stella's glare. "Or he wants you to find her for him."

Her brows shot toward her hairline. "That would be particularly devious."

"It would," Mac agreed. "No chance she ran?"

"Naked?" Stella's brows rose again.

Melinda Leigh

"Maybe they fought and she didn't have time to grab clothes." Mac scanned her perfect penmanship. "Your notes from his interview say Dena has no close friends or family."

"*According to her husband,* she has no close friends or family." Stella made a right turn and the car leaped forward. "But maybe Dena kept secrets from Adam. What time is it?"

"Just after one."

Stella pointed at the case file. "Can you call the clubhouse restaurant and find out what time he paid his check? They were closed yesterday when I called."

"On it." Mac made the call. The hostess had heard about Dena Miller's disappearance and cooperated. "She says he paid the bill with a corporate credit card at twelve thirty p.m."

She banged a fist on the steering wheel. "That's two hours before he said he left."

Her phone rang. She answered on speaker. "Detective Dane."

"Have you made any progress on finding my wife?" A man's tinny voice emanated from the cell's small speaker.

Stella lifted the phone toward her mouth. "Hello, Mr. Miller. Are you at home?"

"Yes."

"I'm on my way to your house right now to give you an update." Stella ended the call and glanced at Mac. "He's already lied to me twice, so let's go see what Adam Miller is hiding."

Chapter Sixteen

Stella parked the car at the curb in front of the Miller's house. "You need to keep a low profile. My boss specifically doesn't want you going all rogue."

"Rogue?" In the passenger seat, Mac lifted his sunglasses. Humor glinted in his eyes.

"His word, not mine. Please, just don't do anything that will get me fired." Exasperated, both with his smart-assery and her attraction to it, Stella got out of the car. "How should I introduce you?"

"However you want. Just don't call me agent anything."

She looked at him over the roof. "If you're worried about your cover, you probably shouldn't be with me."

"Probably not." Another evasive answer.

Which she wasn't going to accept. "Is this dangerous for you?"

He considered her question for a few seconds. "I'm not particularly worried about my cover in Brazil. But years ago, I was tight with a pretty nasty gang. They might consider my association with a cop as a betrayal."

A real answer. She was making progress. "And if they found out you were DEA?"

"They'd kill me," he said with complete certainty before walking off.

Stella rushed to keep up with his long strides. "Do you want to elaborate on that?"

"Not now." Mac walked off, circling the house.

Stella swallowed her frustration. He'd opened up more than she'd expected. From the regretful frown on his face, maybe he'd shared more than he'd intended. She'd try for more information later. She'd need to be patient. Maybe sneaky.

They made a complete circuit and ended up on the front walk.

He scanned the ground and the exterior. "Any sign of forced entry?"

"No." Stella studied the tall hedges that lined the property lines. "But the landscaping was designed for privacy. Once he pulled his car into the driveway, he'd be shielded from view."

"Carrying a woman out of her house in broad daylight is still bold."

"Yes," she said. "Disturbingly so."

Mac hung his sunglasses on the front of his T-shirt. The corners of his eyes crinkled as he assessed the scene. "He feels like he can't be caught. Is he arrogant or self-righteous?"

"Maybe both."

Adam answered on the first knock. His face was puffy, his eyes bagged, and his breath smelled as if he'd drank whiskey for breakfast then gargled with coffee. Wrinkles creased the front of his tan slacks, and his hair was mussed.

Stella would have pitied him if he weren't a liar.

"Come in." He gave Mac a questioning look.

"This is Mr. Barrett. He's offered his assistance. He helped me find several people last fall." That was close enough to the truth that saying it didn't give Stella hives.

Adam shook Mac's hand and led them back to the kitchen.

Stella stood at the counter in front of a stack of posters emblazoned with "Missing" and Dena's photo.

Scanning the rooms, Mac wandered into the adjoining living room. He stopped in front the shelving unit full of pictures and studied at each photo.

"Have you found any sign of my wife?" Adam asked, keeping one suspicious eye on Mac.

"Not yet," Stella answered. "We're retracing her movements yesterday. Her photo has been distributed in a statewide bulletin. Every state, county, and local law enforcement officer on duty is on the lookout for her."

"I put up fliers all over town this morning." Adam spun. His lips flattened into a white line. "What about forensics?"

Everybody was an expert on police work. *Damn CSI.*

"Our techs are still sorting through the evidence," Stella said.

Adam's frown deepened as he continued to pace back and forth across the tile floor. "You don't have any clue where Dena is, do you?"

"Not yet," Stella admitted. "But I have a few follow-up questions for you."

He paused, turning to face her again. "Of course. I'd do anything to find her." But his shuttered eyes contradicted his offer.

"You kept very close tabs on your wife." Stella leaned a hip on the counter and relaxed her posture. She didn't want Adam on the defensive. "We've talked to a few people who commented that you frequently checked up on your wife's whereabouts."

"I love my wife." He smoothed his disheveled hair. "Since her fall, I worry about her constantly."

Stella zeroed in on his guilt. "Did you call the spa yesterday while your wife was there?"

He glanced away. "I might have. I don't remember."

"How about her physical therapy office?" Stella pressed.

"I did call *them*," he admitted. "But they wouldn't tell me if she'd been there, so it hardly matters." Anger tightened his eyes before he reined it in. He smoothed a wrinkle from the front of his slacks.

"Except that you lied in your statement," Stella pointed out.

"I was upset when I spoke with you yesterday." He enunciated each word distinctly. "I didn't lie. I forgot."

Stella did not buy that for one second. "How closely did you monitor Dena's activities?"

"I like to know where she is." Adam's eyes narrowed with suspicion and his upper body tilted toward Stella. "What are you implying, Detective?"

He was playing the devoted spouse well, but Adam Miller set off Stella's creep alarm. There was something about him that just wasn't right, as if he straddled the line between love and obsession.

Stella met his aggressive posture with a small step forward. "Did you get angry with her? Did you hit her?"

Tension sharpened his tone. "Why would I hurt the woman I love?"

Not quite a denial. It happened all the time.

Stella watched his eyes as she delivered the next statement. "You said you left the restaurant at two-thirty yesterday, but the club says you paid your bill two hours before that."

"I walked my client to his car. We talked for a while in the parking lot." He waved off her comment as trivial, but his gaze held hers. Behind his anger, Stella saw arrogance.

"Can you give me your client's name and number?" Stella asked.

"No." Adam's face darkened. At his side, his right hand curled into a tight fist. The knuckles whitened. "I won't have you ruining my career. I didn't have anything to do with my wife's disappearance. I'm the one who called you to find her." The veins in his neck protruded and his mouth went tight with fury. "What is wrong with you? Why don't you understand how much I love my wife?"

Just how violent was Adam Miller? There was one way to find out. Stella let her voice rise. "You're missing two hours yesterday afternoon. Did you and Dena have a fight? Did you hurt her and call us to cover your tracks?"

"How dare you!" Adam exploded. Two rapid strides brought him across the six feet of space that separated them.

Balanced on the balls of her feet, Stella prepared to counter if he actually struck out at her. But a fast-moving body collided with Adam and knocked him out of the way. Adam careened sideways and landed in a sprawl on the tile. Mac had been so quiet, she'd forgotten he was in the next room, but obviously he'd been paying close attention. He'd knocked Adam on his butt.

"What the fuck?" Rolling onto his back, Adam rubbed his hip.

Stella tugged on Mac's arm, but she might as well have been trying to move an oak tree. He glared down at Adam. "I could ask you the same thing. Assaulting an officer will get you arrested."

"I didn't touch her." Adam scrambled to his feet. Leaning around Mac, he jabbed a finger at Stella. "I'm calling my lawyer. Your boss is going to hear about this. Next time you want to interrogate me, make an appointment."

Stella ignored the threat. With Mac impossible to budge, she walked around him to confront Adam. "You came right home after you left the golf course yesterday?"

Fuming, Adam leaned closer. Then with a quick glance at Mac, he backed off. "You're wasting your time questioning me while my wife is in danger."

"In that case, the faster I rule you out as a suspect, the faster I can pursue other lines of investigation," Stella said in a quiet voice. "Lying to me complicates the process."

"My wife is missing, and you're fucking around investigating me instead of looking for her." Despite his protest, Adam scrawled the name and number of his client on a business card. "Find my wife." He thrust it into Stella's hand as she and Mac turned toward the door.

"Why didn't you bring him in?" Mac asked when they were settled in the car. "Questioning him at the station might take away his arrogance."

"Because thanks to you, he's already screaming for his lawyer." Stella turned to face him. "I don't have any evidence that he had anything to do with his wife's disappearance."

"He's lying." Mac's voice flattened.

"The two discrepancies in his original statement are explicable," Stella reasoned. "Or at least that is what an attorney will say."

Mac snorted. "He's hiding something."

"Thanks to your reflexes, I can't arrest him for assaulting an officer. You body-blocked him before he touched me."

"Sorry." But Mac's tone didn't sound apologetic. "Instinct."

"I appreciate the gesture, but you can't feel as if you have to protect me. I provoked him intentionally. I wanted to see if he's a violent man. If he had taken a swing at me with you standing a few feet away, that would have told me he was impulsive and doesn't have a good handle on his temper. I would have known he was capable of hitting a woman. I would have taken him to the station. A possible assault charge would have given me leverage."

"I didn't want him to hit you."

"I understand that, but you have to trust me to do my job. I was ready for him. If he'd tried to strike me, he would have found himself facedown and in handcuffs before he could blink." But frankly, Stella would have taken the blow if it helped her find Dena Miller.

"Antagonizing him wasn't necessary."

Anger heated Stella's face. "Adam Miller is controlling and arrogant, and I know he's hiding something. But I'm not concerned with him. *I* want to find Dena. She's been missing twenty-four hours. Time is running out. I need to know if Adam hurt her or some other man took her." Stella jammed the key into the ignition. "Every minute that passes decreases the chances of finding her alive."

Mac rubbed his face. "I'm sorry."

Stella turned to face him. "Look, if we're going to continue this . . ." she gestured between them, "arrangement, then you have to trust my training. Just because I'm a woman doesn't mean I'm defenseless."

"I grew up with Hannah." Mac snorted. "I have the utmost respect for a woman's ability to kick ass. Trust me. I don't think of women as defenseless."

"I guess not." Stella pulled away from the curb. She had nothing but respect for Mac's sister, who really could kick butt.

Mac rubbed his chin. "Did you notice anything strange about the pictures in the Miller's house?"

"Like what?"

"There are no other people in them. Not a single friend. No one. Every picture in that house is of Dena and/or Adam."

"He said they don't have any close family or friends."

Mac shook his head. "She didn't have a single family member? I'm not saying it's not possible, just not probable. People who don't have much family tend to have a few close friends."

"Maybe she's an introvert."

"Maybe." Mac nodded. "I also noticed from the photos that she's an experienced hiker."

"Adam says her neck injury kept her to short distances."

Mac shrugged. "We've already established that they were less than honest with each other. She could be in better shape than he knows."

"True." Stella turned out of the development. "But you saw a naked woman four miles from her house in a storm. That seems quite a distance. And if Dena left her husband, wouldn't she have gotten dressed first?"

Mac considered her argument. "Unless she was desperate and didn't have time to grab clothes."

"In which case, she wasn't walking. She was running away. But that seems like a stretch." Stella's gut insisted that Dena had been violently taken from her home. But Mac was forcing her to see other possibilities.

"What now?" Mac asked.

"Now I go back to the station and fill out some paperwork." Stella texted Brody the information on Adam's alibi.

"Fun," Mac teased.

"It's exactly as exciting as it sounds." She needed to update her files with today's interviews, and she and Brody needed to compare notes. "Do you want me to drop you home?"

"Please. I need to head over to my brother's house, where I will be tormented for shaving."

"Siblings." Stella grinned.

"Exactly." Mac squinted out the window.

She drove out to Mac's house.

"See you tomorrow." His gaze dropped to her lips for a split second before he reached for the door handle, and she wondered if he wanted to kiss her.

Not professional.

But Mac seemed to bring out every inappropriate thought she could possibly have.

"Yes. Good night." After he'd gotten out of the vehicle and disappeared inside his cabin, Stella turned the air-conditioning vents toward her face. She was halfway back to the police station when her cell buzzed. She picked it up. Gianna's phone number was displayed on the screen.

"Hello," Stella answered the call.

Gianna didn't bother with niceties. "I was getting ready to go to my NA meeting tonight, and I remembered something I should have told you this morning. I saw this guy hanging around outside when I went into the last meeting"

Stella grabbed for her notebook and pen. "Can you describe him?"

"About six feet tall," Gianna said. "Thin, short hair."

"Where did you see him?" Stella asked, excitement humming in her blood.

"Thursday night at the Catholic church."

"Was he at any of the other meetings?"

"Not that I noticed."

"Do you have a meeting schedule?" Stella asked.

"It's posted on the local NA group website." Gianna rattled off a web address.

Stella put the call on speaker and accessed the site on her smart phone. There were multiple meetings listed every day in the region, which covered the tri-county area. A recovering addict with a car could find a meeting every single day if that's what he needed.

Scrolling down the list, Stella spotted the meeting at Our Lady of Sorrows at nine o'clock that night.

"Was Missy at the meeting last Thursday night?" Excitement buzzed in Stella's veins. Missy hadn't shown up for work on Friday. The NA meeting could be the last place she was seen alive.

"Yeah. Missy was there."

"Was the guy outside when the meeting was over?" Stella asked.

Gianna's face scrunched in concentration. "Yes. I remember because he creeped me out, and I had to walk home alone."

"Missy didn't offer you a ride?"

"She wanted to stay for the coffee hour. Sometimes, you feel so much support during the meeting, you're not ready to let it go when the hour's over. But I was too tired."

"Thanks, Gianna. I really appreciate this information." Stella ended the call energized by the new lead. Her paperwork could wait.

Tonight, Stella was going to stake out that meeting.

Chapter Seventeen

Mac steered his Harley onto the main road. A few minutes later, the space between his shoulder blades itched. He glanced in his mirror. The mammoth SUV far behind him set off an internal alarm and Mac made a sudden left. The SUV lumbered through the turn and settled into place the exact same distance behind him. Mac's gut twitched. At the next intersection he turned left and rode away from his brother's place.

The SUV followed.

Mac eased off the throttle, but the truck stayed a stubborn distance behind him, just far enough that he couldn't see the driver clearly or read the license plate.

Like a professional.

He drove to the grocery store in town, parked, and went inside. He watched through the plate glass window as the SUV continued past the store. He went out and fired up the bike again, leaving the lot through a different exit and heading in the opposite direction. Ten minutes later, when there was no sign of the truck, Mac headed for Grant's house.

Had that been coincidence or had the old gang spotted him? If he stayed in town long enough, they'd catch up with him. But for now, Mac hoped he was being paranoid.

Knowing he'd be on his bike, Grant had left the detached garage open. Afternoon storms had been hitting the region daily. Mac parked and walked to the front door.

Grant answered the first knock. "Mac?"

He stepped into his brother's house.

Grant was staring at his face. "I hardly recognize you."

"I shaved. No big deal."

"You don't have to knock. You're always welcome here."

"Thanks."

"Down!" A toddler's scream sounded from the back of the house.

"Come on back." Grant led the way down the hall to the kitchen. The house had been a project when they'd bought it, but Grant and Ellie had transformed it into a home. The kitchen was Mac's favorite room. Done in earth tones, with hardwood floors and bronze granite, it boasted a huge picture window that framed a view of the woods out back.

"Faith, hold still." Grant's fiancée, Ellie, struggled to unclip the high chair straps while his nineteen-month-old niece squirmed.

"Down!" Faith wailed, flinging her body sideways in an Oscar-worthy dramatic gesture. She grabbed Ellie's dark ponytail, and Grant hurried across the kitchen to pry her fingers free.

Ellie straightened her ponytail, lifted the child out of the chair, and set her on the floor. "Let me wipe your hands."

But Faith bolted toward Mac like a mini missile. He swooped her up and carried her to the aproned sink at arms' length while she babbled. Kicking a stool into place, he set her down on top and turned on the water. "Can you wash your hands like a big girl?"

By the time she was done, water was spattered over both of them, but her hands were free of whatever orange substance she'd been coated in.

"Sorry. We're working on spoon use, but you know Faith. She's very tactile." Ellie used a towel to wipe her ponytail.

Mac grinned as the toddler turned to face him. She smacked his face between her pudgy hands and rubbed. Her tiny forehead wrinkled with a frown. "No wike."

Ellie laughed. "I don't think she approves of the shave, but I think you're handsome."

He leaned over and kissed Ellie on the cheek.

Grant crossed his arms over his wide chest. "The last time you were clean-shaven was for Lee's funeral. What's up?"

"Thought it was time for a change," Mac said.

Grant nodded in approval. He still wore his blond hair in an army-buzz. "Hannah's on her way."

The back door flew open, and seven-year-old Carson ran into the house at full speed, directly into Mac's legs. His golden retriever barked behind him as he flung both arms around Mac's thighs. Mac shifted Faith to one hip to hug his nephew. The toddler kicked his gunshot wound, and he sucked wind. That local anesthetic could only do so much.

"Let me take her." Grant held out his arms, and Faith tried to leap to him. "That's my girl." Mac was still amazed by Grant. Not that his tough, career-soldier brother had given up his military future with no regrets to raise his niece and nephew, but that he was so good at parenting and clearly happier than Mac had ever seen him.

Grant put Faith on his hip. "You all right?" he asked Mac. "She didn't do any damage?"

"I'm fine, just thankful she hates shoes." Mac put a hand on his side. He set the other on Carson's shoulder. "What have you been doing?"

"Me and AnnaBelle are catching frogs in the creek." Carson's blond hair was too long, sun-streaked, and speckled with mud. More mud coated his bare feet and legs, and he'd left a grimy trail on the hardwood.

"Sounds like fun." Mac meant it.

"It is." The little boy pushed away, grabbed Mac's hand, and tugged. "Wanna come?"

Mac would much rather play in the mud than talk about their father's funeral. He glanced at Grant.

A smile spread across his brother's face. "Go ahead. I'll let you know when Hannah gets here."

Carson sprinted for the back door, leaving more smears across the hardwood and a few flecks on the walls.

"Me." Faith pushed away from Grant's chest and reached for Mac.

"I don't know." Grant frowned. "She's liable to eat the frogs."

She turned sad baby blues on Mac, betrayal and hurt quivering her upper lip and misting her eyes. "Wanna go."

"She's going to win an Oscar someday." Mac hesitated. The enthusiasm from the kids was overwhelming, and the ache in his gut was nowhere near his injury.

Grant rubbed her back. "The kids miss you."

And Mac couldn't say no. He took the toddler. "A little extra protein won't hurt her."

Ellie stopped them on the way out the back door, offering Mac a pair of tiny white sandals.

He laughed. "We both know she won't keep them on, so why ruin them?"

"Watch her feet, then. Rocks and sticks can be sharp. And she will put anything—and I mean *anything*—into her mouth," Ellie said. "Maybe I should come with you. A toddler can drown in two inches of water."

Faith blinked innocent, pleading, blue eyes at Mac.

"We won't be out too long, and I promise not to take my eyes off her for a second."

How hard could this be?

Twenty minutes later, all three of them were soaked, creek slime coated Faith from her wispy blonde hair to the soles of her tiny feet, and Mac was in awe of his brother and Ellie. How did they manage these kids all day, every day? Twenty minutes of keeping rocks and bugs out of Faith's mouth had been exhausting. He grabbed his boots from the bank and herded the kids out of the shallow water. They trooped back to the house, content and filthy.

"Sorry." Mac turned on the hose. "We really don't have any other options. We are disgusting."

"Yay." Faith raced through the spray.

"You have mud on your eyebrow, Uncle Mac." Carson broad jumped into a puddle on the grass.

Mac sprayed his calves and feet and rolled down the cuffs of his cargo pants. Hosing down the kids was like trying to hit metal ducks in a carnival game. He shut off the faucet. "I guess that's as clean as you're going to get."

Laughter erupted from the back porch. Carrying two beach towels, Grant met them at the bottom of the steps. He tossed one to Carson and spread the other wide between his arms. Faith raced into it, giggling. Grant's face lit up.

"How much mud did she eat?" Grant cocooned Faith in a towel and scooped her into his arms. Tossing her over his shoulder, he turned toward the house. High-pitched, happy baby squeals pierced the evening.

Mac rubbed Carson down to make sure he didn't drip in the house. "Not enough to ruin her dinner."

Carson gave his legs an ineffectual swipe with the towel. "Uncle Mac says there are poisonous frogs in South America. They're only this big." He held his forefinger and thumb close together. "And they have enough poison in them to kill *ten* men." His eyes widened.

Grant whistled. "Those are deadly frogs."

"I know." Carson nodded. "Hunters put the poison on darts and shoot them through a blowgun." He mimicked the act by blowing through his closed fist. "But we don't have that kind of frog here." He gave the wet grass a disappointed kick.

"What a shame." Grant jostled Faith until she exploded into another fit of giggles.

Carson raised three fingers. "But we do have three kinds of venomous snakes," he said with enthusiasm, as if that made up for the lack of toxic frogs. "We found a snake skin. Do you think it might be from a venomous one, Uncle Mac?"

"Sorry, buddy. Looked like the skin from a milk snake to me." Mac was impressed. The boy had memorized Mac's answers to his rapid-fire questions. "I'll show you a picture of one inside so you can keep an eye out for it."

Grant chuckled. "They really do miss you, Mac. You're the only adult who actually enjoys playing in the mud."

"I miss them, too. More than I realized." Longing filled Mac. He was sick of solitude, something he never thought would happen to him.

"Do you have to leave again?" Grant asked.

"I don't know. I have some decisions to make."

"You know I'm around if you need to talk. I've been where you are." Grant opened the door and ushered them into the kitchen.

Ellie plucked a limp weed from Faith's head. "I'm impressed. You got her filthier than she's ever been, and that's saying a lot."

"It was my pleasure." Mac grinned, carrying his boots into the house.

"Dinner's in a half hour. Hannah called. She'll be here in a few minutes," Ellie said. She and her teenage daughter took charge of bath time, while her grandmother set the table.

Ellie walked away, smiling at Grant over the baby's shoulder. Though in her midthirties, she looked younger, with her freckles and makeup-free face.

Grant's eyes brightened. "I never thought I'd have this kind of life."

"You are one lucky SOB," Mac said. His brother had found a beautiful woman, inside and out. She'd taken on a soldier with post-traumatic stress and two grieving children, and she still had time to worry about Mac's sorry ass.

Grant led the way to his office. Mac stepped over the threshold and froze. The Colonel's dress uniform hung on the back of the closet door. Pressed and stiff, it looked as if it could stand up on its own.

Mac shuffled closer, stopping a few feet away. He wanted to reach out and touch the shiny medals and ribbons pinned to the chest. But just like when he was a boy, he didn't want to mar it with his touch. "I'd forgotten how big the Colonel was when he was younger. I don't remember ever seeing him stand up."

"You were pretty young when he was injured, and he shrunk over the years." Grant stopped next to him. "I have something for you." He opened the closet and took a box from the top shelf. Opening it, he handed a black bundle of neoprene to Mac.

"The Colonel's KA-BAR." Grief constricted Mac's throat. He slid the knife from the sheath. The Colonel had carried it when he'd been a Ranger.

"You gave it to me after Lee died. I noticed you had a knife at your place. I thought you should have this one back. I don't have a need for it, and you still do."

"Thanks." He rolled up his pant leg and strapped the sheath to his calf.

The door opened, and Hannah came in. Her eyes widened with shock as she stared at Mac's face. "You shaved. All. The. Way. To. Skin." She patted his cheek. "I had no idea my baby brother was so handsome."

She wrapped an arm around him and focused on the hanging uniform. "How can it be that intimidating? He's not even in it."

"Because it's part of him." Grant said. "It represents what he wanted to be. Where he wanted to be. And what he was in his heart."

"The last two and a half decades must have been a nightmare for him." Hannah's grip tightened around Mac's bicep.

"Trapped in a body that could no longer serve or obey his commands." Mac's voice turned rough. "All he ever wanted was to be a general."

Grant put a hand on Mac's free shoulder, the grip heavy and firm. "He had choices. He had four kids who wanted nothing more than to please him, and it wasn't enough. *We* weren't enough for him."

"We tried." Hannah sniffed and wiped a hand under her eyes. "God knows we tried."

Grant would never treat Carson and Faith the way the Colonel had treated his children. Grant would go to his grave cherishing those kids, and they weren't even his.

"Some people aren't cut out for family life," Mac said. "The Colonel was one of them. He didn't do it to be mean. I think he honestly thought he was doing us a favor by toughening us up."

"He suffered from post-traumatic stress disorder and depression," Grant said. "But he was old school. Military men of his era didn't address mental health issues. They soldiered on."

Their father's depression had been so deep and dark that it had sucked up all the light in their home.

"I'm glad he's finally at peace," Hannah lowered her arm and crossed to the desk to pluck a tissue from its box. She wiped her eyes, crumpled the tissue, and tossed it into the trashcan. "What do we need to do? I assume he *clearly* spelled out his burial wishes."

"You know it." Grant smiled. He moved behind his desk and picked up a yellow envelope marked "Do not open until death" in their father's shaky scrawl. "I thought he wanted to be buried in the

National Cemetery, but he updated his will after Mom died. He wanted to be with her."

Mac's eyes and throat burned. They'd buried Lee near their mom, too.

Grant cleared his throat. "He'll have a military honor guard ceremony, of course. And the chaplain from the base agreed to drive up. I'll take care of the details. Hannah, I'll leave the rest of the will in your hands."

She nodded. "I'll do whatever you need."

"If it's OK with you both, we'll have a reception here after the service," Grant said. "Ellie and her grandmother have that under control. Do either of you want to say anything at the service?"

"No," Mac and Hannah said in unison.

Grant nodded. "Then you want me to give the eulogy?"

"Definitely." Mac didn't even know how *he* felt about his father or his father's death. There was no way he was ready to speak about the topic to a hundred people.

"Yes." Hannah agreed. "And thanks. I don't know if I could sort out my thoughts enough to be coherent."

"Let me know if either of you change your mind," Grant said.

"What can I do?" Mac asked.

"Well," Grant said. "Carson wants to attend the funeral."

The kid could have Mac's chair.

"Since I'll be speaking," Grant continued. "I'll need you two to stick close to Carson. The service is bound to remind him of Lee and Kate's deaths. I don't know how he'll handle it. He might want to leave in the middle."

Mac suspected *he* might want to leave in the middle. "Whatever he wants."

A small knock sounded on the door. "Uncle Grant?"

"Come on in, Carson," Grant called out. "The door's not locked."

Carson slipped in. He was clean, his hair damp, and he smelled like soap. His pale blue pajamas were covered in tiny red race cars. He walked up to the closet and stared up at the uniform. "Is that Grandpa's?"

Grant lifted him into his arms. "It is. See the eagle? That means he was a colonel."

Carson turned his head to the Colonel's uniform. "Grandpa had a lot of ribbons." He reached toward them, then pulled his hand away.

"It's OK, Carson. You can touch them." Grant moved the boy closer.

Carson traced the ribbons on the chest of the uniform then dropped his hand. "Can I see yours, too?"

"Sure you can." Grant lowered him to the floor. "I'll be getting it out tonight."

"I had fun today." Carson walked to Mac and leaned on his thigh. "Can you come over and play tomorrow?"

"Maybe." Mac rubbed Carson's head.

"Uncle Grant says Grandpa is going to be with Daddy and Mommy now," Carson blurted out. "Is that right?"

Eyes blurring, Mac squatted to the boy's level. "You bet. He's with Grandma, too."

Carson nodded, then rested his head on Mac's shoulder. "I miss them."

"We all do." Mac's throat constricted until it felt as if a noose was wrapped around it, choking him.

Carson lifted his head and turned his face toward Grant. "Can I have ice cream after dinner?"

Grant laughed. "Definitely. Ellie bought your favorite."

"Cookies and cream?" Carson's eyes brightened. "Awesome."

He squirmed away from Mac and bolted for the door. "I forgot. Ellie said to tell you dinner was ready. Nan made macaroni and cheese."

"Then we'd better go eat." Grant followed Carson. "We can't let macaroni and cheese get cold."

And Mac knew exactly how he and Ellie managed the kids. They enjoyed every exhausting minute. Unbelievably, Mac was a little jealous.

Which was ridiculous and selfish. He was the one who kept leaving. He was the one who took off for South America every time he felt like the kids were getting attached to him. The last thing they needed was more grief.

Who was he kidding? It was *his* heart he was guarding.

What was he going to do? He'd committed himself to stopping drugs, to protecting kids like Carson and Faith from the poison entering the country every day. But the thought of leaving his family again left him empty, just as the idea of committing to being a permanent part of their lives terrified him.

"Are you all right?" Hannah asked from the doorway.

Mac shook off his mood. "Yes. Just thinking."

"Need to talk about it?"

"Not yet." Mac joined her in the hall. "I'll let you know."

"Don't shut us out again, Mac. We need you."

"I know. I'm trying." Mac rubbed the ache in the center of his chest.

Hannah leaned her head on his shoulder. "You can let us all in. We don't bite."

"Faith might."

She laughed. "Seriously, Mac. I was always chasing something. Success. Independence. Approval. I struggled when every milestone felt so . . ." Hannah paused. "Empty. What's the point if there's no one to share those moments?"

"My job is dangerous, and sometimes it feels like I can't possibly make a difference. No matter what I do, the drugs keep flowing." Frustration filled Mac. "As long as there's a demand for drugs, some scumbag will be willing to fill it. On the other hand, how can I refuse to do what I can? I know better than anyone that drugs can ruin a life. A whole family."

Hannah turned him to face her. "You didn't ruin anything. We love you. You had a perfectly legitimate problem as a teenager. The stress we all lived with was soul smashing. No wonder the three of us ran as far as we could from it."

"Only Lee was strong enough to stay, and we abandoned him."

Hannah nodded. "The best we can do is learn from our mistakes and not repeat them, because Lee was the one who had it right. This is what counts, Mac. These kids. This family. This is for keeps. Sure, it's a commitment, and an intimidating one, but I promise, you won't regret it."

His siblings had managed to sort out their problems and find peace. Why couldn't he?

Chapter Eighteen

Stella parked her unmarked car half a block from Our Lady of Sorrows Catholic Church. Lance rode shotgun. She rolled down the window and let the evening breeze into the vehicle. The scent of freshly cut grass lingered in the humid night air. Lightning bugs blinked neon green over the lawn.

"Do we have a picture of this creeper?" Lance asked.

"No. No name either."

"But you think this guy might be stalking women from this Narcotics Anonymous group?"

"Gianna saw a tall, thin man lingering outside the meetings. This might be the last place Missy Green was seen alive." Stella stretched her neck and checked her watch. "Today is Thursday. The meeting is over at ten. It'll be dark enough for a stalker to follow the women undetected."

"It's a good start anyway." Lance shrugged. "Some people can be followed in broad daylight. You'd be surprised how little people pay attention to their surroundings. Everyone's totally focused on their phone."

Stella slid down in the seat and stared through the windshield. Our Lady was an old stone structure. An attached parochial school formed one wing of the campus, while church offices comprised the other. Narrow and tall, the sanctuary's spire towered over the neighboring buildings.

She scanned the sidewalk and the parking lot on the other side of the street. A woman got out of a blue Prius and hurried to the crosswalk, her heels clicking on the pavement. She jogged up the steps and disappeared inside the office wing.

"The meeting is in the basement below the offices," Stella said. "The church donates the space several nights a week."

While she watched the church, Stella played with a spare hair elastic on her wrist.

Bored, Lance slid his straw in and out of his Coke. "So how's your grandfather?"

"Busy as ever." Stella smiled. "I'm glad Morgan and the kids are living with us. It takes all of us to keep him occupied and out of trouble."

"He's a character." Lance spun the straw. "How's your sister?" he asked in a fake casual voice.

Stella took her eyes off the street for a few seconds to study his profile. He and Morgan had dated in high school, but Stella couldn't remember which one of them had done the breaking up. She directed her gaze back to the church. "John's death was hard on her."

"How many kids does she have?"

"Three girls." Who seemed to be coping better than their mother was.

"That's tough." Lance straightened and nodded toward the building. "Do you see that? There's a person in front of the school office."

Stella's eyes pierced the shadow under the roof overhang. Something shifted. A faint orange light glowed brighter and then faded. "Gotta love smokers. Let's see if he goes inside when he's finished with his cigarette."

Instead, he lit another. Stella gave him another ten minutes, but he didn't move.

She reached for her door handle. "Let's go have a talk with him."

"Give me five minutes to circle around behind him in case he decides to bolt." Lance opened his car door and slipped out into the dark, shutting his door gently. He disappeared into the shadows alongside the church buildings.

Stella checked her watch. When five minutes had passed, she started the engine and drove down the street, passing the suspect and making a U-turn. She pulled to the curb just as he lit another match. Under the hood of a sweat jacket, the flare highlighted sharp cheekbones over a gaunt face and scruffy beard.

Stella spotted Lance twenty feet away, hugging the side of the building. Flashlight in hand, she got out of the car and approached the loiterer. "Excuse me, sir. I'd like to talk to you for a minute."

The man startled. He backed up two steps. Behind him, Lance's shoe scraped on the pavement. The suspect's head swiveled and he bolted straight between them, tearing off across the street directly into the path of a minivan. A horn blared. The van bumped his legs as he slid to a stop. He spun, slapping the van's hood with both palms, and scrambling around the vehicle.

"Stop! Police!" Lance sprinted after him.

Stella was right behind them. The suspect hit the back edge of the parking lot and made a sharp left, skidding into an alley. Lance's shoes slid on a patch of loose sand as he followed. He cursed and went down on one knee. Lunging to his feet, he ran, limping, toward the corner.

Stella gained ground on Lance, passing him and rounding the brick building. She spotted the suspect in the light of a streetlamp at the other end of the alley and willed her legs to move faster. Her thighs and lungs burned as she cranked up her speed. The suspect slowed, glancing over his shoulder.

She wanted to yell "stop" again but saved her breath for running. The suspect's strides shortened, and he cut right and disappeared. Stella slowed, her hand hovering near her sidearm as she emerged from the alley into the next street.

Where is he?

She waited, listening, as her pulse thundered in her ears. A movement to her left startled her. Crouching, she flattened herself against the bricks.

The suspect bolted from a dark patch next to a Dumpster, and adrenaline sent Stella's heart rate into hyperdrive as she went after him. He skidded around another corner with Stella right on his heels. She was close enough to hear his labored breathing over her own.

Stella made the turn into the rear yard of an auto body shop. A six-feet-tall chain-link fence blocked the rear exit. The suspect ran between rows of cars and leaped for the fence.

"Oh, no you don't." She closed in, grabbing him by the leg of his jeans. The baggy pants slid down until the waistband encircled his thighs.

Afraid his pants would slide right off and he'd slip away, Stella shifted her grip to his ankles and pulled hard. He fell off the fence onto his back, taking her to the ground with him, right into a pile of garbage. The fall knocked the wind from her lungs. Stella gasped for air.

He tried to scramble to his feet, but the jeans around his knees tripped him. He fell face-first onto the pavement.

Stella flipped onto her belly, got a leg under her body, and launched herself forward. "Get back here."

He rolled and swung a wild haymaker at Stella's head. She ducked, but the blow glanced off her jaw. Bright spots flashed in her vision.

She shook her head to clear it as a backhand flew at her face. She blocked the strike with two open palms and grabbed his wrist. Pressing the bone of her forearm into the hollow of his elbow, she arm-barred him to the ground.

He wriggled. "You bitch."

Placing a knee on his spine to pin him to the ground, she wrestled his hands behind his back and cuffed him. A pat down for weapons yielded a wallet, a pack of cigarettes, matches, a small knife, and an oval medallion on a chain.

She collapsed onto the ground next to him and sucked in oxygen.

Lance limped into the alley. "Are you all right?"

Huffing, Stella nodded, rubbing her jaw. "You?"

"Fine." But his face was lined with pain. "Just took a wrong step back there."

She hoped he hadn't hurt his bad leg on his first week back on duty. "I'm sorry I couldn't keep up."

Stella sat up and forced three deep breaths in and out of her lungs. "I got him."

"You did." But the frown on Lance's face told her he was unhappy with his own performance. He held out a hand.

Taking it, she let him help her stand. "Seriously, stuff happens, Lance. I could have tripped just as easily as you did."

"But you didn't." Self-reproach flashed in Lance's eyes as he grabbed the suspect by the bicep and hauled him to his feet.

Stella cupped her aching face.

Lance's frowned deepened. He swung the suspect around. His hands were cuffed behind his back, and his face slammed into the brick exterior of the building.

"This is police brutality. I didn't do anything," the man screamed.

The hood had fallen off his head during the chase. In the light of the streetlamp, Stella got her first full look at the man she'd pursued. He was about thirty and as thin as an aging rock star.

"You assaulted a police officer." Lance jerked the suspect's arms high up his back.

The suspect rose onto his toes and screamed, "You're gonna break my arm."

Lance's body tensed even more.

Stella grabbed him by the shoulder. "Back off, Lance. We got him."

"I'm gonna sue your asses," the suspect screamed into the bricks.

Lance spun the man to face him and leaned closer to his face. The cords of his neck went as taut as steel cables.

"Lance!" Stella grabbed Lance's arm, her effort barely budging him. His chest heaved, and his jaw muscles twitched. He wanted to hurt the man. Stella could see it in his eyes. He wouldn't take his eyes off the suspect's. Stella forced her body between them, pushing on Lance's chest with both hands. "I'll take him from here."

Lance jerked his gaze from the suspect's face to Stella's. He blinked and took a step backward, frowning as if the level of his own aggression surprised him.

"I'm gonna sue this whole city." The suspect licked his bleeding lip. A small cut on the side of his mouth dripped blood, as did an abrasion on his cheek. Rotten lettuce from a broken-open garbage bag hung from the shoulder of his hoodie. "I did nothing to warrant this treatment."

"Then why did you run?" Lance picked up the wallet from the asphalt and opened it. "Noah Spivak." Lance thumbed through the contents. "This is impressive. He has six hundred dollars in his wallet. That's a lot of cash, Spivak."

Spivak's arrogant glare set off a warning in Stella's head.

"Let's take Mr. Spivak down to the station for questioning." Stella steered him toward the street.

Lance was still limping as they escorted the suspect to the car and put him in the backseat. Stella turned around in the parking lot. She stopped the car and stared through the windshield. An older model blue Toyota Corolla sat in the light-puddle of a streetlamp. Stella used her computer to run the license plate. "That Toyota is registered to Missy Green."

They got out of the car and walked around Missy's Toyota. The doors were locked. Stella doubted there was any evidence in the car. Missy obviously hadn't made it back to her vehicle after the meeting. "This is where she was abducted."

Lance pulled out his phone. "We'll get forensics out here to check the vehicle and have it towed to the impound lot."

Sliding back into the vehicle, Stella looked over the seat at Spivak. "Does that car look familiar?"

He shot her a *fuck-you* smile but didn't answer.

At the station, they secured Spivak in an interview room and posted a uniform to keep an eye on him. While Lance searched for his criminal history, Stella spot cleaned some oily substance from her jacket and pants. From the Italian spice smell, she guessed it was salad dressing.

She met Lance in the hallway. His face still looked pained, his lips pressed white. His gait was stiff, as if he was making a great effort not to limp.

"You OK?" she asked.

He nodded and opened a file folder in his hand. "Spivak isn't our typical scumbag. He has a degree in chemistry. After college, he moved to Albany, where he was brought up on charges three different times: once for assault, once for domestic violence, and once for statutory rape. The assault charge went away when the victim refused to testify. The domestic violence case was dropped when his girlfriend disappeared— she's never resurfaced. The Albany detectives think he did her, but they weren't able to prove anything, which means he's no dummy. He did serve eighteen months in the state prison for the rape. He returned to Scarlet Falls to live with his parents after his release from prison."

"Lucky us." Stella reached for the doorknob.

Spivak had been sitting in the cramped, windowless space for thirty minutes, stewing. His cuffed hands were fastened to the back of the metal chair. His hoodie had been taken with his personal effects, and sweat had soaked through the armpits of his T-shirt.

With an exaggerated sniff, Lance pulled out a metal chair and sat. "The smell of fear in the air."

Belligerence—and intelligence—shone from Spivak's eyes.

"If I take the cuffs off, you're going to behave, right?" Stella wanted his cooperation. Most criminals were smart enough to restrain themselves while being videotaped by a ceiling-mounted camera.

The look Spivak shot Lance could have burned brick. Spivak nodded, and Stella circled behind him to release his hands. He rubbed his wrists, and Stella spotted scars in the crook of his elbow. Track marks?

She sat in the chair across from him, read him his Miranda rights, and slid an acknowledgment across the table for him to sign.

"I know my rights." Ego lifted his jaw, but a line of sweat trickled down his temple. "I'm not signing anything."

They'd intentionally shut off the air-conditioning vent in the room. Discomfort could loosen a tongue.

Stella pushed the paper aside. She raised her voice and spoke to the camera. "Let the record show that Mr. Spivak was read his rights and stated verbally that he understands them."

Spivak's mouth flattened as he realized his mistake. His eyes flickered to the camera.

Stella slid the file in front of her and opened it. "You have quite the record. You've been charged with assault, domestic violence, and statutory rape."

"I was never convicted of anything except the rape, and I was railroaded on that."

"You like little girls, Noah?" Lance cocked his head.

"She told me she was eighteen." His face went smug.

Stella checked the file. "She was thirteen."

"She looked mature for her age." Spivak clasped his hands. "Must be the hormones in our food."

"Where do you live, Mr. Spivak?" Stella asked.

With one blink, his eyes went dark. "With my parents."

Stella leaned forward, interlocking her fingers and resting her forearms on the table. "Why were you outside the church tonight?"

"Contemplating God's grand plan." His eyes shrank to mean slits. "Why did he put us in the same place tonight, Detective?"

Stella ignored the question. "Who were you waiting for?"

"I was waiting for you." Excitement drew him forward and glittered in his eyes. "Women aren't meant to be in positions of power. Fate put us together tonight. I'm supposed to teach you to be a properly submissive female. I'd handcuff you, bend you over this table, and give you a lesson in a woman's true purpose."

"You little—" Lance said, his teeth bared.

Stella put a *cool-it* hand on his forearm to ward off the pending explosion. She glanced sideways at him. One more sign of aggression and she was kicking him out. He eased back a scant inch, but the muscles under her palm were rigid as stone.

Spivak's eyes laughed at them. He was enjoying Lance's reaction.

"If we drug tested you right now, would you be clean?" Stella gave his arms a pointed look.

"Yes." He bent his arms to conceal the scars. "Those are from prison. I've been clean since I got out."

"Isn't that backward?" Lance asked.

"You try serving time," Spivak shot back. "Many things happen in prison that aren't optional."

"You were forced to use heroin?" Lance asked in a skeptical tone.

"I was forced to do a lot of things," Spivak said without breaking eye contact.

Hostility rose between the two men like heat waves off hot blacktop.

Time to change tactics.

Stella set a picture of Missy Green on the table. "Do you know this woman?"

Spivak glanced at it. Recognition lit his eyes, then pure spite twisted his mouth. "I've never seen her before."

"Fucking liar." Lance slammed a fist onto the table.

"He's out of control. I'm not answering any questions without a lawyer." This wasn't Spivak's first trip to the police interview room. He leaned back and crossed his arms over his chest, his nasty gaze landing on Stella's chest. "Unless she strips down and gives me a look at her tits."

And that was the end of the interview. Stella got up and opened the door for the uniform standing outside the door. "Put Mr. Spivak in holding."

"I won't be in here long, not once my lawyer gets a look at this." Spivak pointed to his abraded cheek and split lip. "And when I get out, I'll be keeping an eye out for you around town." He pointed at Stella and licked his lips. "I want to bite into you like a ripe peach."

He was looking for a response, so Stella didn't give it to him. She gathered her papers into her folder. But inside, her stomach protested the images his words put in her head. Plenty of criminals tried to intimidate her with sexual insults and comments. It was one thing about being a female cop that she couldn't get used to no matter how hard she tried. But this was somehow worse. Spivak wasn't some idiot loser spewing empty threats. This man was cunning, cruel.

Based on the disgusting visual he'd given her earlier, he liked handcuffs.

Had he sent her the photo of Missy's body? He was definitely the type who would enjoy tormenting a woman. Despite the heat in the room, goose bumps rose on Stella's arms.

The uniform spun Spivak around with unnecessary force, snapped the cuffs on his wrists, and marched him down the hall.

Below the general sense of disgust, anger rumbled in Stella's throat. She tapped Lance on the chest and pointed to the door. He followed her into the hall, where the camera on the ceiling didn't record audio.

She leaned close and whispered, "What was all that?"

"He's a lying scumbag," Lance's voice was low, but the rage on his face startled her. "I should have put his head through the wall. He's a waste of oxygen."

"He was goading you, and you let him."

He studied his Frankenstein cop shoes. His shoulders slumped.

"Are you all right? This behavior isn't like you."

"I'm working on it." He ran his hand through his buzz cut. "I'm sorry. I fucked up. It won't happen again."

Stella exhaled. "You want to talk about it?"

Lance clamped his teeth together. "I'm not real happy with psycho druggies right now."

Like the one who'd shot him.

Lance punched his palm with his fist. "And the thought of that guy stalking you makes me want to snap his neck."

"Spivak is going to jail, so neither of us has to worry about him," Stella said. "Deal with this now. Don't let it build." As if she should give advice.

His head dropped in a single, curt nod.

He went into the conference room. Stella followed him, watching as he updated the whiteboard with Noah Spivak's information. He pinned a mug shot of Spivak under "suspects." His posture relaxed. "I'm sorry about the interview. And the alley."

They both knew there would be repercussions from Lance's aggression. Spivak had been around the legal block a few times. He'd play the abuse-of-force card for all it was worth.

"Yeah." He sighed. "I came around the corner just as he hit you. I kind of lost my shit for a few minutes."

"I know, and I appreciate your concern."

"I'm just so fed up with everything. Everywhere I look in this town, I see drugs and crime. We catch the criminals, and the system lets them out. What's the fucking point?" Lance pressed a hand to his thigh. "My leg won't ever be the same."

"I'm sorry," Stella said quietly.

"What now?" Lance picked up a marker and listed Spivak's arrest record under his picture. Frustration pressured his strokes, and the letters he wrote were sharp and dark. "He recognized Missy's picture."

"I know. Let's see if we can get more information on Spivak. For now, we can hold him for assaulting an officer and illegal weapon possession." Stella rubbed a sore spot on her butt. Her skid in the alley had likely left a few marks. "If my witness IDs him, we can apply some additional pressure."

"When can you get your witness here?" he asked.

She'd called Gianna's cell earlier, but the phone had gone to voice mail. "If she doesn't call me back by morning, I'll stop at her place tomorrow. We can't talk to Spivak again without a lawyer. That's not going to happen tonight." She glanced at the clock. "It's way past shift change. You should go home."

Lance draped an arm over her shoulders. "You, too. Get some sleep." He sniffed her hair. "And take a shower. You rolled in garbage."

"A shower would be great." Stella planned to spray her car with disinfectant, too. The interior smelled like a Caesar salad.

"I'm serious. Don't do anything else tonight. Go home and ice your face."

"I'll leave soon. I want to update my notes from tonight's arrest while the details are still fresh."

"You and your paperwork fetish." Lance stalked away. Though obviously making a great effort, he couldn't completely conceal his limp. But it wasn't his physical injury that bothered Stella the most. It was the murderous look on his face when he'd slammed Spivak into the bricks. If she hadn't been there, how far would Lance have gone?

"Stella."

She turned to see Brody leaning into the doorway. He dropped into a chair and stared at the whiteboard. "What's happening?"

145

She gave him a rundown on Noah Spivak's arrest. "Did you verify Adam Miller's alibi?"

"Sort of." Brody frowned. "His client verified that they talked in the parking lot before leaving the club. He refused to sign an official statement because he isn't sure of the amount of time involved."

"So Adam has a weak alibi."

"The client was nervous. I'm going to keep working on it. I'm still working my way through interviewing the waitstaff, valets, and caddies at the golf course. A background check on the client is pending."

Stella made a note on the board. "Unless you break Adam's alibi, Spivak is our only suspect. For now. We really need a search warrant for his parents' house and his car. To get that, we have to establish a link between him and our victims." Being at the church wasn't enough.

"But there's something that bothers you about him as a suspect."

"Missy wasn't sexually assaulted. If Spivak tortured and killed her, there would have been a sexual component to the murder."

"Then we keep looking for other suspects," Brody said. "I found something interesting in Lyle Jones's background check."

"Dena's physical therapist?" Stella asked. "I thought we checked his record."

"He's clean in New York," Brody nodded. "But he has two old assault charges on his record in New Jersey from four and five years ago."

Stella found Lyle's picture and pinned it to the bottom of the board. "He's a long shot, but maybe we should take a closer look at him."

Brody leaned forward. "When were you going to tell me about the photo you received this morning?"

"I haven't seen you all day, and the chief wants it kept quiet."

"You should have told me immediately," Brody said.

"I told Horner."

Brody huffed.

"I know. I'm sorry. I should have called you," she admitted. He was right. She'd gotten caught up in the investigation, but her own safety had to be a priority, whether or not she liked it.

Brody pointed. "Promise me you won't let it happen again."

"All right." Stella moved to stand in front of the two photos of the Green crime scene where they hung on the board, side by side. "Why would Missy's killer want me to see the scene? Forensics couldn't lift any prints from the envelope or photo."

Brody's gaze fixed on the pictures. "He posed her carefully, and he wanted you to see that. She wasn't discovered for a day and a half. Her body position changed, either from the wind or animals. But what bothers me is that he sent it directly to you."

Stella lifted a shoulder. "He probably saw me on the news."

"I don't like it."

"I don't like it either, but there isn't anything I can do about it." Though Stella wished she could avoid the media, dealing with them was part of the job, especially when her boss kept shoving her in front of the cameras to prove he was an equal opportunity employer.

"I'm following you home."

"I was going to finish my notes first."

"Well, now you're not." Brody stood, his posture stiff.

"You're right." Stella packed up her briefcase. "I can finish at home. And thank you."

"I'm saying this both as your superior and your friend." Brody escorted her to her car. "You are to take backup with you everywhere. Me, Lance, Mac, someone. I don't even want you walking to your mailbox alone. You are to take zero chances. Whoever killed Missy Green has singled you out for special attention."

Chapter Nineteen

The air was sticky and hot as Mac climbed into Stella's cruiser late Friday morning. Her charcoal slacks and white blouse were all business, as was the weapon at her hip. But she'd have to wear a Sumo wrestler costume to cover those curves.

She turned to hand him a take-out cup of coffee.

"Thanks." He fastened his seat belt and took a long sip. Sleep hadn't come easily the night before. The insomnia had nothing to do with his wound. As the ER doc had promised, pain wasn't keeping him up at night. At worst, his stitches itched. It was thoughts of death that invaded Mac's dreams. A woman lying on a dark road. Cheryl, Lee, and the Colonel all made special appearances until Mac woke sad and frustrated. He couldn't even escape his grief in sleep.

Stella's gaze lingered on his face. "No time to shave?"

"Rough night." He reached up to feel his jaw. Stubble rasped under his fingers. "I thought you liked the scruff."

"I do." The blush on her fair cheeks sent a warm wave of pleasure through him. Why didn't he dream of *her* last night? His imagination did a fine job of conjuring the feel of her skin under his hands, the taste of her . . ."

Yeah. Those images would keep the nightmares away. He made a mental note to think of her the next time he closed his eyes. A vision of Stella, naked in his bed, flashed into his mind.

Not now.

He refocused on the conservatively dressed woman next to him, *dressed* being the key element. Her hair was wound into its usual tight bun, exposing the delicate line of her jaw and the column of her throat. Her cotton blouse was buttoned up far too high. *What was that?* A purple shadow outlined the left side of her jaw. He reached out and turned her face to catch the light. "Is that a bruise?"

She pulled her face out of his gentle grip. "It's nothing."

Anger surged.

"Who put it there?" Mac barely recognized his voice.

"A suspect."

"When?"

"Last night." Stella turned the car around and drove away from his cabin. "It's not a big deal. Gianna called me to say she'd seen a strange man creeping around her NA meetings."

"So you went and staked it out?" While Mac had been hanging out with the family, she'd been working the case. Alone.

"I took a uniform with me, and we caught him. Getting him into the handcuffs was a challenge." She frowned.

"Do you think he had something to do with Dena's disappearance?" Whoever he was, Mac wanted to smash his face.

"No. He's a suspect in Missy Green's murder." She checked her phone. "I'm waiting for Gianna to return my call so I can get her to ID him."

"Have you found anything to connect the cases?"

"No. Maybe I'm wrong and they're not related." She turned the rearview mirror to examine her face.

As much as Mac hated to see that mark on her face, he said, "Gives you street cred."

She smiled, then winced as if the motion hurt. "Always good."

"Where are we going?" He gulped coffee.

"The drug treatment center Missy used. The New Life Center for Hope." She glanced at him. "Like I told you on the phone. You don't have to come with me. This might not be related to Dena's case."

"Then again, maybe it is," Mac said. "I read the case files. Both women are about the same age. They both have dark hair. Both the murder and the abduction were violent crimes, and they occurred within days of each other." He paused. "Besides, I trust your instincts even if you don't."

Blushing, Stella settled into her seat, her fine-boned hands low on the steering wheel.

"What do you know about the center?"

"It's run by a Dr. Randolph. He has no pending malpractice suits and no criminal record." Stella tucked a stray hair back into her bun. "His center is supposed to be the best. People come from quite a distance to get treated there."

"The Who's Who of rehab?"

"Something like that."

"Do you always wear your hair all coiled up like that?" He regretted the question as it left his lips.

"Our chief takes the dress code very seriously." Stella sighed. "My other option is to buzz it above my ears."

He pictured the way her hair had looked tousled and damp the night he'd crashed his Jeep. "The bun is awesome."

"I think so, too." Her grin eased the pressure in his chest. The more time he spent around Stella, the more interest he had in his hometown. He enjoyed the kids, too, and Hannah and Grant when they weren't too pushy. Was it possible that the good memories would eventually outweigh the bad?

"I'm taking you with me, but you have to behave." She shot him a bossy look, which was just plain hot. *Stella* could push him around anytime. Hell, she could handcuff him and—"I'd like to get on the doctor's good side, so please don't body slam anyone," she said with a direct gaze that made his blood hum.

"Yes, ma'am." Might be interesting to see those handcuffs on her wrists, too. Padded of course. Mac would never leave a mark on her perfect skin. He stared out the windshield. "I've been thinking about Missy's case. Heroin as a weapon seems odd if she was tortured."

"Why do you say that?"

"Why inflict pain on someone and then give them a painless death?"

"Good question." Her gaze darted to his arms.

"I never did heroin, if that's what you're curious about."

"No?"

"No. My drug of choice was oxy. I had this buddy in high school who introduced me to it. His father dealt the stuff in a major way. Looking back with the hindsight of an adult, I realize that I was pretty depressed and frustrated. I was the only kid left at home by that point, and my Mom wasn't well. We didn't know at the time she had cancer. I thought she was worn out from taking care of my dad and didn't have any energy left for me. No one was really on top of things at that point."

"So you were alone with two very sick parents. How old were you?"

"Sixteen."

"I'm sorry that happened to you." Her voice held too much sympathy for his comfort.

"I didn't mean to unload on you."

"That's what real friends are for."

Mac did not want to be *friends* with Stella.

She slid her hands to the top of the steering wheel and drummed her fingers. "Did you belong to NA?"

Mac watched the blur of trees pass by. "I tried it, but sharing my problems with strangers never appealed to me. My brother, Lee, the one who was killed last year, dragged me to my mother's deathbed and made me swear to her that I'd straighten out. Later, anytime I felt tempted, I'd visit her grave."

Grief bloomed in Mac's chest. His mom's illness and death had torn him apart. Except for Lee's funeral last year, he hadn't been to the cemetery in years. Because he hadn't needed to be reminded of his promise? Or because he couldn't bear to be reminded of her death? He was dreading the Colonel's funeral.

"Are you sure you want to go out here with me?" Stella's concerned gaze felt like a touch. Or perhaps that was wishful thinking on his part.

"I'll be fine." He certainly didn't want her going alone. His memory of Adam Miller reacting to her questions was too fresh, as was the bruise on her face.

For a guy who never had much of a temper, Mac was feeling uncharacteristically violent. Stella brought out his uncivilized side, not that it was buried all that deep.

He was sure Stella was trained in hand-to-hand, and in no way did Mac think women were weak. His sister was one of the toughest people he knew. But he couldn't control the urge to protect Stella. The emotions stirring in his chest worried him. He could get attached to her. He had enough commitment issues with his family, and Scarlet Falls was a huge pot of bad luck for him. Did she feel something for him? And if she did, how could he walk away from the potential?

The highway narrowed to two lanes. They passed meadows and patches of woods. Ten minutes later, Stella turned down a forest-lined gravel lane. They passed a lake and an old stone barn set back off the road.

The lane ended in a tight clearing. A split rail fence defined the parking area. The main lodge was a two-story cedar rectangle with a deep, covered porch. Appropriately, Adirondack chairs were grouped around low tables. Two men playing chess looked up as Mac and Stella got out of the car. The New Life Center for Hope looked more like a resort than a rehab facility.

They went up the steps and crossed the porch. Mac held the door for Stella. In the reception area, a thirty-year-old man typed on a computer. A folder lay open on the desk.

"Can I help you?" He said in a southern accent as he closed the folder. A brass plaque on the front of his desk read *Reilly Warren*.

Stella showed her badge. "Detective Dane. I have an appointment to see Dr. Randolph."

Reilly glanced at his phone. A red light blinked. "He's on a call, but he should be done in a few minutes."

Stella ignored the row of chairs in the lobby. "How long have you worked here?"

"Three years." Reilly folded his hands on his blotter.

"You don't sound like you're from around here." Mac picked up a pamphlet from a wall rack.

Reilly straightened his row of office supplies. "I'm from Atlanta."

Stella flashed him a warm smile. "Do you like working for Dr. Randolph?"

He adjusted the position of his stapler a millimeter. "Yes."

"The center is highly recommended." Mac tucked the brochure back into its slot.

"Josh is good at what he does," Reilly said.

"But patients relapse, right?" Stella sounded innocent as she pried information out of the admin.

Reilly straightened a stack of Post-it packs. "Josh can only do so much." He glanced at the phone. The red light had gone out. "He's done." Reilly slid out of his chair. Then he carefully lined up the armrests with his keyboard tray before straightening. "Follow me."

He led them down a carpeted hall, then knocked and opened a door. "Detective Dane is here to see you, Josh."

"Thanks, Reilly," a male voice responded. "Please show her in."

Mac followed Stella into the office. Behind a mahogany desk, a leather chair faced a sleek laptop. A tall, lean man rose. About forty and fit, he wore jeans, an Earth Day T-shirt, and trail running shoes. His dark hair was a half inch past needing a cut, and wire-rimmed glasses gave him a nerdy look. He rounded the desk.

Stella introduced Mac. "Mr. Barrett is assisting with my investigation." Her tone warmed. "I must say, Dr. Randolph, you're not exactly what I expected. I was expecting someone more . . . formal."

Was it wrong for Mac to be instantly jealous over the smile Stella gave the doc?

"Formal doesn't help people relax." The doctor gestured to a circle of leather chairs in the corner. "Please, call me Josh."

"The center looks like a mountain lodge." Mac eased his body into a low-slung seat. He wasn't sure if fancy digs would have helped or hindered his own recovery. The utilitarian decor of the center he'd attended had made the process feel serious. Rehab was not a vacation.

"I don't see any reason for people to be uncomfortable while they recover." Josh removed his glasses and polished the lenses on the hem of his shirt. "People come here voluntarily. They should feel good about their decision to make their lives whole again."

Mac took in the expensive-looking, modern furniture. "You don't take insurance, do you?"

Josh shook his head. "No. All my clients pay privately. This is a small facility. I prefer to keep it that way."

So what motivated the doctor? Money?

"Why do you do this?" Mac asked.

Josh sighed. "When I was a teenager, my older brother died of an overdose. He'd suffered from depression all his life. Drugs were his escape."

"I can understand that." The words slipped out of Mac's mouth before he could stop them, but the doctor's words had struck a nerve.

The doctor's gaze was too sharp. Too understanding.

Mac shifted his position in the chair. "You want to prevent others from the same fate."

"That's the idea." Josh smiled.

Stella leaned forward, clasped her hands, and rested her forearms on her knees. "I want to talk to you about Missy Green. She was a patient of yours?"

"Yes. I was sorry to hear of her death." Josh replaced his glasses. "How can I help you?"

Stella tilted her head. "You treated Missy for addiction, but she was recovered, right?"

"Yes, but addiction doesn't end when someone checks out of this facility," Josh said. "The first step toward recovery is committing to a life-long treatment plan."

"Did Missy ever relapse?" Stella asked.

"A few times." Josh crossed his ankle over his knee. "But most patients will relapse at some point. Recovery tends to be a forward-and-back process. There are inevitable stumbling blocks on every patient's road."

Stella's lips thinned. "That doesn't sound promising."

"It's important that the patient not view a relapse as failure but as an experience he or she can learn and grow from." Josh rested his hand on his calf. "Building self-esteem is an important part of controlling addiction."

She leaned forward. "Most people would say why not let them destroy themselves."

"That's not an option. Addiction doesn't only hurt the user," Josh said.

Which was why Mac had devoted his life to stopping drugs before they hit US soil.

"When was the last time you saw Missy?" Stella asked.

"I saw Missy just a few weeks ago, and she seemed to be using her coping mechanisms well. She'd borrowed money for her treatment. During our last session, she decided that once she finished paying her debt, she was going to attend community college. This was the first time she'd looked that far ahead in her life. I thought the new direction was promising."

"What about cutting?" Stella asked.

"Missy had a period of self-harm when she first came home from California. We dealt with it during her stay. As far as I know, she hadn't done it since."

Stella took a small tablet from her purse and made a note. "You saw Missy here after her inpatient program was finished?"

"No. Missy didn't want to borrow more money, I run a few therapy groups for local charities." Josh glanced at Mac. "I'm not completely materialistic."

A knock sounded on his door, and Reilly opened it. "Your next patient is here."

"Thanks, Reilly." Josh got to his feet.

"Thank you so much for your help with this case." Stella stood and offered him her hand.

Josh held it too long for Mac's liking, and the doctor's eyes showed definite interest. Mac got up and stuck his hand out. Josh released Stella, but reluctance was clear on his face.

Stella and Mac returned to the car.

"What did you think of Randolph?" Climbing into the passenger seat, Mac shook his coffee cup. Empty.

"I appreciated his candor." She turned the wheel. Gravel crunched under the tires as the car circled the parking area and nosed onto the long driveway.

"He appreciated you, that's for sure," Mac grumbled.

Stella lifted her brows in surprise. "Did that bother you?"

"Maybe."

She grinned. "Not that it's any of your business, but I was just trying to butter him up. He's not my type."

"Really?" Mac perked up.

"Really." She glanced over at him. "Why?"

Mac caught her gaze and held it. "Maybe I want it to be my business."

"Josh Randolph is intelligent and good-looking, but he's too passive for me. I come from three generations of cops. Men I date tend to be less . . . beta." She brought the car to a stop at the intersection with the main road. "Not that I've dated anyone recently."

Blood warming, Mac reached over the computer mounted on the dashboard. He hooked a hand behind her neck and pulled her closer. Their lips met, but a quick taste of her wasn't enough. Not nearly enough. He tightened his grip, cupping the back of her head and tilting it for a better angle. Her mouth opened, and her tongue played with his. The soft moan in her throat made him want to drag her over the console and into his lap.

There was nothing passive about Stella. She met him quip for quip, heat for heat. When she lifted her hand and rested it on the center of his chest, right over his thudding heart, desire speared him to his core.

He wanted her.

Mac eased his mouth off hers. She licked her lips, and he wanted to do the same. The intensity of his desire for her sent a wave of uncertainty through him. His longing for Stella wasn't just sex. He liked talking to her. He liked sitting in comfortable silence with her. Simply being in her presence soothed him.

He'd never imagined having what Grant had with Ellie. Mac had always assumed he'd be a lifelong bachelor. Being part of a couple required trust, a give-and-take he'd never considered possible.

Now he wondered.

But would it be fair to Stella? He was a work-in-progress who was supposed to be heading back to a job in Brazil.

Stella's phone buzzed, breaking the connection between them. Clearing her throat, she answered the call, "Detective Dane."

Her hand curled into a fist and thudded on the steering wheel. "Where? OK. I'm on my way. ETA fifteen minutes."

She turned to Mac; anger, frustration, and tears shone in her eyes. "A dog walker just found Dena Miller in Bridge Park. She's dead."

Chapter Twenty

Stella drove past the public library and over a rise. As her cruiser topped the hill, the park came into view. From the top of the hill, a stone bridge arched high over the rushing water. Recent heavy rains had left the river deep and the current swift. Nestled at the base of the bridge, a bronze monument depicted three Revolutionary War soldiers firing muskets. On the near side, three wooden benches faced the water. A dozen wild geese waddled across the grass. On the opposite bank, woods provided a deep green backdrop.

Except for the geese and a pair of ducks cooling off in the shallows, the park was empty and quiet on a hot summer day.

Flashing strobe lights on three patrol vehicles parked at the curb destroyed the tranquility.

Stella drove down the embankment and parked behind the patrol vehicles. Three uniforms and an elderly man waited in the shade of a lone oak tree. A yellow lab was stretched out at the man's feet. A hot wind blew across the field as she and Mac got out of the car.

Fifty feet beyond the police cruisers, a woman appeared to be sitting on the center bench, her head tipped to one side as if she were dozing. The seat and back of the bench were solid wood. Below it, Stella could see two bare feet. The back of the woman's bare shoulders and a curly head of dark hair were visible above.

From a distance, the woman could have been watching the birds, but Stella already knew she was dead.

Lance approached. His limp was barely noticeable, but he was clearly working to keep it to a minimum. "The old man and his dog found her."

"Have you called the ME?" Stella's eyes strayed to the bench. The detective in her was anxious to see the body, but her human side recoiled at the thought.

"Yes." Lance nodded. "He'll be here any minute, and I see the forensics teams pulling in now. Brody's coming, too."

"It's that bad?"

He paled. "You'll see."

Apprehension coiled in Stella's belly. Banishing it, she took a pair of gloves from her pocket. "Did you touch her?"

His face went greener. "No. I could see that she was dead from ten feet away. I didn't want to compromise the scene."

"Is that the man who found her?" Stella nodded toward the old man.

"Yes."

"Did he touch her?"

"He said no." Lance squinted at Mac, who stood behind Stella. "Do I know you?"

Mac introduced himself. "We might have met last year."

"Barrett. Your brother was murdered. I'm sorry." Lance's voice went tight.

Stella turned to Mac as she opened the trunk and exchanged her shoes for boots. "You might want to stay behind the tape. Any closer and you'll be listed on the crime scene log."

"Then I'll wait here." He leaned on the car, and crossed his arms over his chest. He might have to stay away from the body, but she had no doubt he'd notice everything about the scene.

Stella took a few minutes to verify the dog walker's story before getting his contact information and releasing him. He didn't look as shaken as the man who'd found Missy Green.

She spotted a long rut in the mud leading from the parking area toward the bench. Strange, flat footprints followed the line. The impressions had been marked off with orange cones and crime scene tape.

"What do you think left that?" she asked Lance. "It's too wide for a regular bicycle tire. Some sort of off-road bike?"

He shook his head. "Wheelbarrow. He put her in a wheelbarrow and walked her down to the bench."

She shielded her eyes from the sun and stared toward the bench. "Because of the way the hill lays out, you can't see the park until you drive over the hill. This isn't a through street. There's no reason to drive over the hill unless you're coming to the park. No one would see him unless they were coming here." The park was a seemingly isolated spot right behind town.

"Even if he did it in the dark, it's still a ballsy move," Lance said.

"No bolder than abducting her from her house in broad daylight."

"The footprints have no tread."

"He covered them." Stella stared at the tracks. "We'll still get them cast. At least we can get his shoe size."

A minivan emblazoned with the county medical examiner logo pulled into the lot. A few minutes later, a coverall-clad Frank walked to her side.

The ground was soft from recent rains. Water squished under Stella's boots as she walked toward the bench. She tracked the long, single furrow that ran from the street, down the hill, to the bench.

Keeping clear of the rut, she and Frank walked toward the bench and circled around to get a full, frontal view of the body.

Frank whistled. "Fuck. Me."

Dena Miller sat upright, her head lolling to one side. Nylon rope had been used to secure her shoulders to the bench. Her legs were crossed and tied together. Around her neck was a pale blue scarf. Below it, in the center of her nude belly, he'd carved the number 2.

Stella pictured Missy's body on the autopsy table. "That single cut in Missy's stomach was a number *1*."

Frank nodded. "Looks like."

The sun beat down on the top of Stella's head, but the pit of her belly went ice cold. Her gaze skimmed over the body, stopping on the hands folded in the victim's lap. They were mangled. "Her fingers."

Frank exhaled sharply. "All broken."

That wasn't the kind of injury that could happen by accident. Dena had been tortured.

Poor Dena.

A black satchel-type purse sat on the bench next to her. Just like Missy, bruises colored the left side of Dena's face. More purple marks were visible on the pale, pale skin of her body. She sat upright, but the skin along her back was stained purple. Before being positioned on the bench, she'd laid on her back long enough for lividity to set in. "She didn't die here."

She'd been positioned after death, just like Missy.

Frank moved closer. He pointed to her wrists. Under the nylon rope, bruises darkened her skin. "She was restrained." He bent low to squint at her battered hands. "Do we know who she is?"

"Her name is Dena Miller." Stella's gaze traveled from Dena's smashed fingers to the rope burns on her ankles and wrists. "She's been missing since Wednesday afternoon." Stella stared at the silk scarf. She kept her voice low. "This whole scene was carefully staged."

"Yes." Frank propped one hand on his hip and the other on the back of his head as he glared at the body. "Fuck. Fuck. *Fuck*."

Stella stepped up to stand next to him. "This is exactly like Missy Green's death."

"Don't say it." Frank looked over his shoulder.

Stella followed his gaze to a news crew climbing out of their van. She signaled a uniform to keep them far away from the scene. He nodded and moved in, hands spread and palms out. A lollypop-thin brunette newswoman cocked a hip in irritation.

"Do not imply these two cases are related," Frank warned. "The media will broadcast that Scarlet Falls has a you-know-what."

Stella nodded, but anger surged in her veins. The news media shouldn't dictate her discussion with the medical examiner. But Frank was absolutely right. If the press got any wind of any possible similarities between the deaths, the words *serial killer* would be scrolling across the next special bulletin. The chief would have a coronary, the mayor would implode, and Stella would be writing parking tickets for the rest of her career.

"The deaths have commonalities." Frank prodded her with an elbow. "But let's not jump to conclusions."

Stella tilted her head and raised a disbelieving eyebrow.

Frank raised a palm. "I know. We know the truth, but we can't tell everybody. Not yet."

She stared at Dena. "The way he left her . . ." The careful planning, the positioning, the scarf. This hadn't been a dump and run. "It took some time."

Just like Missy's body had originally been staged.

"More than the first, as if he didn't get enough attention with the other." Frank rubbed a hand across his head. "Christ, now you have me jumping to conclusions." He frowned. "Let's get her bagged and out of sight before the press gets a look at her fingers or that scarf. We don't need any public speculation. I'll move her autopsy to the top of my list. I'll call you as soon as it's done."

"Can you give me any idea how long she's been dead?" Stella asked.

Frank moved Dena's arm, testing for the telltale stiffness that would indicate rigor mortis had set in. "Six to eighteen hours. I'll be able to give you a tighter window when I get her on the table."

Stella glanced at her watch. It was just past noon. If Frank was right about the time since death, then she'd died in the twelve hours between six p.m. Thursday night and six o'clock this morning. They'd picked up Spivak around nine o'clock the previous night. The window of opportunity for him to have killed her had just narrowed to the unlikely three-hour slice of daylight between six and nine p.m. Thursday night.

A brown mark on the inside of Dena's forearm caught Stella's attention. "What's that?"

Frank rotated the arm, revealing more faint marks. "I'd say they're track marks."

"Like Missy's." Stella rocked back on her heels. Adam hadn't mentioned that his wife had a drug habit. But if Dena had injected drugs, that gave her and Missy a real connection before they died. Was this the work of a serial killer or were the women murdered for personal reasons?

A door slammed. Carrying cameras and plastic field kits, three coverall-clad forensics techs followed the same path toward the pond.

Stella used a gloved finger to open the clasp on the purse. Inside, on top of Dena's wallet and assorted female paraphernalia, a syringe rested on a bed of cotton batting. A pale blue ribbon was tied around the needle.

The same person had killed Dena Miller and Missy Green. His ritual was getting more complex, his staging more elaborate. Thoughts whirled in Stella's head. She needed to talk to the chief and Brody, and she needed to question Adam Miller again.

Stella straightened, moving out of the way to give the forensic team room to work. Side by side, she and Frank watched the photographer capture the body from all angles and distances. When he'd finished, he stepped back and let the morgue attendants bring the gurney in.

Brody arrived. He was quiet as he surveyed the scene, but his grim expression agreed with Stella. "Mac wants to talk to you."

He was still waiting by the car, leaning on the front fender, arms crossed over his chest.

She walked over. "I'm sorry. I'm going to be tied up, probably for a while."

His gaze drifted over her shoulder to where the black-bagged body was being loaded into the medical examiner's van. "It's Dena?"

She nodded.

"Can you tell me anything?"

She glanced toward the news van. "Not here. Later."

"All right. I wish I could help, but since there's nothing I can do here, do you mind if I take off?"

Stella wished he could help, too. Only a short time had passed since he'd kissed her, but it felt like days.

"Not at all." She didn't move closer, but she wanted to. The news media was too present, too interested in her. Mac wouldn't want to be caught in a sensationalized story.

"Do you need a ride?" she asked.

"No. I called Grant a few minutes ago. There he is." He pushed off the vehicle.

Stella turned her head to see an oversize pickup truck parked on the road just beyond the cluster of emergency vehicles.

"Please call me later."

"I will."

With a regretful glance, he turned and walked away.

"Detective Dane!"

Stella turned to face a dozen reporters. The afternoon heat wilted her, but she sucked it up and braced for the media onslaught.

Six microphones were in her face in seconds.

"Is this case related to the woman who was found on Monday?"

Damn. Stella was too tired to think of a noncommittal response. She leveled the press with a serious look. "I can't comment on an ongoing investigation."

"Two women were found dead in the same week. Does Scarlet Falls have a serial killer on the loose?"

The chief was going to have a fit.

"Speculation at this point is pointless and irresponsible." Unable to summon a drop of politeness, she shot the offender a glare. "If you'll excuse me, I'm going to go earn my salary."

Stella broke away. The forensics team was still crawling over the crime scene, but they'd be occupied for the rest of the afternoon.

She went back to Brody, grateful for his experience as they reviewed the scene with the forensic team. Typically a death warranted more than a few off-color remarks. But the gallows humor they used to cope with the horrors of their jobs was absent, and the team worked with an uncharacteristic gravity as they laid out a grid and began collecting evidence.

"This is not your average dead body, boys and girls," Frank said in a low voice as he slipped paper bags over Dena's mangled hands. "I know you always do your best work, but let's take extra care with dotting *i*'s and crossing *t*'s. I have a bad feeling about this one."

The same creepy-crawling sensation drifted over Stella's skin.

This wasn't just a dead body. It was a message.

Chapter Twenty-One

Mac paced his cabin. When had it seemed so small and isolated? Never. Before this week, he'd craved solitude like a drug. Now, the silence around him sounded dead. He pivoted, took three strides, and crossed the living room again.

No matter what he did, he couldn't get Stella out of his head. The defeated look in her eyes at the crime scene was permanently etched in his brain. He viewed Dena Miller's death as a personal failure, and he knew that Stella did, too. But unlike him, Stella couldn't escape the sight. She'd spend the afternoon studying the body and the scene. Even from a distance, the sight of Dena Miller posed on that bench had brought back images of Cheryl that left him shaken. Close up, the sight must've been horrifying, and Stella would see it for the rest of her life.

Enough.

Mac strode for the front door. Grabbing his sunglasses and helmet from the counter, he retrieved his bike from the shed. The throaty rumble of the engine drowned out the quiet. He navigated the rutted lane that led to the main road. As soon as his tires hit blacktop, he opened up the throttle. The wind whipped at his clothes, and the vibrations under his body hummed in his bones, mirroring the fury coursing through his veins.

A prickly sensation drew his gaze to the mirror. He wasn't surprised to see a black SUV hovering ten car lengths behind him.

He was being followed.

Son-of-a . . . He was not in the mood for this. Or maybe he was.

He turned off onto a narrow road that snaked through the woods to the Scarlet River. Two wooden tables occupied a picnic area near the water. A trail opened off the clearing. Mac parked his bike in plain sight and jogged twenty feet down the trail. Then he looped around through the underbrush and picked a spot at the bend in the road, right where a driver would see his parked Harley.

Mac waited behind the fat trunk of an oak tree.

The SUV came around the bend and slowed to a crawl, as if the driver was deciding whether or not to follow. If he was smart, he'd turn around.

The vehicle stopped exactly where Mac predicted. Only one figure was visible through the windshield. The man got out. As soon as he closed the vehicle door, Mac launched himself at his midsection and tackled him. They rolled in the damp earth. The man was thin and wiry and squirmed out from under Mac. Jumping to his feet with the speed of youth, the man whipped out a switchblade.

"Oh, you want to play with knives?" Mac pulled his father's KA-BAR from its sheath on his ankle. The KA-BAR was more than a knife. It was a jungle survival tool that could chop wood, slash through foliage, and still maintain an edge sharp enough to slice ripe tomatoes. That flimsy, folding blade was a butter knife in comparison.

Mac lifted his gaze from the weapon to the man's face and got his first good look at him. The man was just a kid.

He was beyond thin, nearly gaunt. The sallowness of his skin and the hollows in his cheeks marked a lifetime of poor nutrition. Silver hoops pierced his ears, nose, and one eyebrow. Shaggy jet-black hair hung in points across his forehead like a Japanese anime character. From behind the thick fringe, insolence shone from stubborn dark eyes. His gaze dropped to the KA-BAR. He licked his lips and shifted his weight, uncertainty crossing his face.

"Drop the knife. I don't want to kill you."

"Can't do that." The kid adjusted his grip.

"Who told you to follow me?" Mac asked. "Freddie?"

The kid didn't respond, but Mac could see the affirmation in the surprise on his face.

"I know Freddie a hell of a lot better than you," Mac said.

Silver rings swayed as the kid shook his head. "Then you know I can't cross him."

Mac sighed. This kid could be the Christmas Past version of him. But damn it, he didn't want to hurt him.

With a stubborn sneer, the kid lunged. The awkwardness of the movement suggested he hadn't trained with Freddie very long.

Mac stepped aside, out of the path of the knife, and brought the hilt of the KA-BAR down on the kid's wrist. The knife fell to the dirt.

"Ow." The kid clutched his wrist and turned to run away.

In one motion, Mac kicked the switchblade away and grabbed the kid by the neck of his shirt. He hauled him against the side of the SUV. Pinning him, Mac searched his pockets for weapons but found only a bag of weed and a cell phone. "What's your name?"

"Rabbit."

"OK, Rabbit, here's what's going to happen." Mac guided the kid toward his bike. "You're going to leave town."

The kid spun and jabbed a finger at Mac's nose. "If you know Freddie, you know why I can't do that."

Mac had been close with Freddie's son Rafe in high school. At the time, Mac imagined that they'd folded him into their family right when he'd felt very much alone. But the reality was a far cry from his teenage impression. Freddie used Mac for all sorts of duties.

"What were you going to do if you caught up with me?" Mac asked, staring pointedly at the kid's finger.

Rabbit dropped his hand. "I wasn't supposed to catch you. Just watch you."

This was just the kind of task Freddie used to assign to Mac. He watched people and buildings, delivered messages, and ran back and forth between Freddie's camps. Freddie's attention hadn't been free. Mac had paid a high price for that "friendship," and it was still costing him.

"How long have you been working for him?"

The kid blew long bangs out of his eyes. "Couple of weeks."

"I'm going to give you a piece of advice. Get out now, kid, while you still can." Mac released the teen. "Once Freddie sets his hook, you're on the line forever."

"I don't have anywhere to go."

The kid's simple statement hit home.

"Parents?"

The kid didn't hesitate. "Dad's in jail. Mom's dead."

"How old are you?"

"Eighteen."

Could have passed for much younger. That was what a life of chronic malnutrition did to a growing body. Mac might have lacked emotional support, but he'd always had a roof over his head and food in his belly.

"So you aged out of foster care." What the hell was Mac going to do with him? "What about other family?"

"Got an aunt in Jersey I haven't seen in ten years."

Mac held up the kid's cell phone. "Did Freddie give you this?"

Rabbit nodded.

Mac took the battery and memory card and ground them both under the heel of his boot. Then he tossed the phone into the woods and handed the kid his helmet. "We both know the only way you're going to get away from Freddie is to leave town. I'll give you two options: jail or Jersey?"

Rabbit took the helmet.

"Good choice." Mac straddled his bike. The kid climbed on the back. The train station was a twenty-minute ride. They used Mac's smartphone to look up Rabbit's aunt's address. Inside the small lobby, Mac studied the schedule and route maps, then he bought a ticket and handed it to Rabbit. "This will take you to Penn Station. From there, you'll have to grab a local train into Jersey." He handed the kid fifty dollars for food and sat with him until the train arrived. Mac didn't leave until the train pulled out of the station. Then he climbed back on his bike and headed back to Scarlet Falls.

The kid should be safe.

But Mac couldn't say the same about himself. No good could come of being on Freddie's radar.

———

The man replayed the news footage he'd taped earlier. Detective Dane strode across the grass in front of the park. Weariness slowed her long lean legs, and with her hair contained in its usual tidy bun, there was no softening the exhaustion lines on her face.

Lovely. Wholesome. Strong. The women he'd kept in his basement prison were nothing compared to that stunning creature.

Detective Stella Dane was perfection.

But why was she working so hard against him? He didn't think she fully understood his mission. The fallen were a waste of her precious time. That was the whole point. The women he'd killed hadn't been worthy of her efforts. They hadn't deserved the air they'd breathed.

Perhaps he'd better send her another message. The police seemed to be missing the meaning of his work. How could he get his point across?

He had to make Detective Dane understand that they were on the same side.

Chapter Twenty-Two

Finished with the scene, Stella practically ran for her car.

Brody caught up with her. His own vehicle was parked on the road. "Where are you going now?"

Sweat dripped down her back. She swigged from a bottle of lukewarm water. A dull ache throbbed at the base of her skull. She'd missed lunch, but there was no way she'd be able to stomach food for a long time.

"I have to go tell Adam Miller his wife is dead and hope he doesn't already know." Leaning into the sweltering vehicle, she shoved the keys into the ignition and started the engine. Hot air blasted from the dashboard vents. "I need to call the chief and give him an update."

"I'll follow you. Let's hope no one leaked the victim's identity."

"Miller shouldn't find out about his wife's death from a news report." Stella shot an angry glare at the news vans crowding the parking area. On the blacktop in front of the fluttering yellow crime scene tape, the brunette spoke into a microphone.

"Murder is big news in Scarlet Falls," Brody said, turning toward his own vehicle. "I'll be right behind you."

Stella jammed the car into drive. Her fingers clenched the steering wheel all the way to the Miller house. En route, she called Chief Horner and gave him a brief update on what they'd found at the scene. Then she parked at the curb, and Brody pulled in behind her. As they got out of their cars, the door burst open. A wild-eyed Adam stood on the front porch. "Was it her?"

Brody stayed close as Stella approached him.

"Was it my wife they found at the park?" Adam demanded, moving closer.

"Let's go inside." Thinking he might want privacy, Stella gestured toward the door. Her hand accidentally brushed his arm.

Adam jerked it away. "Don't fucking touch me."

"Mr. Miller—" Stella soothed.

"Fuck you. Fuck your whole police department." He cut her off, leaning in. Sweat coated his skin, moisture brightened his eyes, and the vein on the side of his neck bulged. "My wife was being murdered by a madman while you investigated me."

"We need to ask you more questions," Stella said. "I'd like you to come down to the police station."

"I can't believe this. My wife was kidnapped from our home and killed and you still want to question me? You are fucking unbelievable." Adam shook his head. His fist curled at his side. He wanted to hit her. She could see his barely contained rage rimming his eyes with white.

Apparently so could Brody. He inched forward.

But Stella didn't budge. "Mr. Miller. I want to find out who killed your wife. You didn't tell us she had a drug problem."

Adam ground his molars. "That was two years ago."

"It might be a factor in her death." Stella gestured toward the street. Hedges might block the neighbors' view, but sound traveled. "Are you sure you want to discuss this out here?"

Red-faced, Adam spun and strode into his house, leaving the front door open. Stella and Brody followed him into his kitchen.

Adam poured himself a generous two fingers of whiskey from a bottle on the counter and dropped into a kitchen chair. "As I told you before, she fell down the stairs four years ago and broke a bone in her neck. Even after surgery and rehab, she was in constant pain. The doctor prescribed oxycodone. I knew she was taking too many, but what could I say? She was hurting all the time, and the doctors didn't have any options for her." He set his glass down. "I knew she was in trouble when I found a needle in the back of her car."

Stella took the chair facing Adam. Brody backed up and leaned on the counter.

"She said she went to heroin because oxy wasn't enough for her pain. She'd built up a tolerance." Adam took a deep swallow of liquor. "The second I found out, I got her into rehab." Was he trying to convince Stella or himself that he'd done his best?

"Was it an inpatient rehab center?" Stella asked.

"Yes." He nodded.

"Where?"

He frowned. "It's been years. It had a long name. New Life something."

"The New Life Center for Hope?"

"That sounds right. Dena did well there. Everything seemed to be working out for us. She found her new physical therapist, who seemed to help her get some relief from the pain with diet, exercise, and meditation. She joined Narcotics Anonymous. She still goes to a meeting almost every night."

"Do you know where she attended meetings?" Stella held her breath.

"The Catholic church. Our Lady of Sorrows." He sipped his drink. "I can't believe she went back to using, if that's what you're suggesting."

"I'm not suggesting anything."

"Dena was moving forward. She didn't have any interest in going back to being an addict. She told me once that she never wanted to feel that out of control again. It had been terrifying for her." Adam wiped his mouth with the back of his hand.

"Had your wife been tested for drug use lately?" Stella asked.

He hesitated. "Not officially."

"What do you mean, officially?"

Staring at his glass, Adam spun the tumbler on the tabletop. "I administered tests to her here at home."

"At home?"

"Yes. You can buy the kits at the drug store. It's a simple urine test. Gives you the results in minutes." He tossed back the remaining whiskey and slammed the glass onto the table. "I did it randomly for her own good. I had to make sure she stayed clean."

"Did she ever test positive?" Stella couldn't imagine her significant other forcing her to pee in a cup.

"I feel responsible for not getting her help sooner. How did I not know she was using heroin? What kind of husband pays that little attention to his wife? I couldn't allow her to fail again."

Stella shifted her weight forward. "Why didn't you mention your wife's former addiction before?"

Adam stiffened. "That was years ago. I doubt it's relevant. *I* wanted to find my wife while she was still alive. But you let her die." He pointed at Stella's nose, his finger inches from her face.

Guilt was an anvil on Stella's shoulders. He was right. She hadn't found Dena and now the woman was dead.

"You need to back off, Mr. Miller," Brody said quietly.

Adam dropped his hand, but his focus remained fixed on Stella. "Listen up, bitch. I'm through with you. Either arrest me or get the fuck out of my house. If you want to question me again, make an appointment to talk to me through my lawyer. I'll have him call your boss." He jumped to his feet and gestured to the hall. Brody and Stella left the house. The door slammed shut behind them, and the deadbolt shot home.

Stella stared at the house. Frustration pounded in her temple.

Brody steered her back into the car. "None of this is your fault. We'll get him to the police station for an interview. It will just take a little longer than we'd planned."

"What if he's right?" Stella asked. "What if I've been wasting time investigating him when a stranger took his wife?"

"His behavior has been suspicious since the beginning," Brody assured her. "And you haven't neglected looking for other suspects. You even arrested one, but Adam's name keeps coming up."

"He has an alibi." She moved toward the car, her stomach twisted and sick.

"His alibi is weak." Brody's voice rose. "Dena Miller's death is not your fault."

If she'd been a better detective, she could have saved Dena's life. And if her aim had been truer last November, she could have prevented the deaths of two cops. But she'd come up short both times, and that knowledge would weigh on her forever.

But Stella didn't admit that to Brody. "I guess I can't get a roster of everyone in that NA group."

"I think they take the anonymous seriously," Brody said.

"Dena and Missy were also admitted to the same rehab center, although their stays were a year apart." Stella reached for her car door handle. "I already ran background checks on Dr. Randolph and his assistant, Reilly Warren. They were both clean. Maybe I should dig deeper. I wish privacy laws didn't prevent us from getting the medical records of the other patients."

"I'll check out the staff at Our Lady of Sorrows." Brody got into his car. "Again."

She drove back to the station while she checked her messages. Still no response from Gianna. Stella tried to call Mac, but the call went directly to voice mail. She headed to the chief's office.

Horner stood in front of his open closet, straightening his uniform in the mirror that hung on the back of the door. His eyes met hers in the mirror. Frowning, he turned. "You snapped at a reporter this afternoon. That isn't acceptable. The media can be your ally or your enemy. Trust me. You don't want them as an enemy."

"Yes, sir." Stella shoved a stray hair behind her ear. "I want to bring Adam Miller in for more questioning."

"No. Adam Miller's attorney was on the news claiming we're to blame for his wife's death because we focused on him as a suspect while she was being murdered." Horner tugged the creases from his sleeve. "You are to leave Mr. Miller alone."

"But Brody thinks his alibi is weak." Stella protested. "And he lied to us."

"When I give an order, I expect you to follow it. Adam Miller is a publicity nightmare. Let it go. We have a perfectly good suspect. Prove he did it."

"But what if he didn't?" Stella wanted to reel her words in as they left her lips.

"That's an order, Detective." The chief stared. "You'll be joining me at a press conference in thirty minutes. I expect you to be gracious. The media has been on your side since that shooting back in November. They love you. I want to keep it that way. We'll focus on the fact that we have a person of interest, which refutes Mr. Miller's claim, and that we're pulling out all the stops on this investigation."

"But we now know that Dena Miller had a drug addiction. She attended the same Narcotics Anonymous meetings as Missy Green."

"All the better. Noah Spivak was seen outside those meetings. That places him in proximity to both victims. He's our man. There will be no mention of serial killers running around town."

"But it's possible we have one."

"Spivak is in custody. You should be proud. You caught the killer. Now you have to tighten the noose tightly around his neck. Build your case before the judge grants bail."

"Yes, sir." Stella's teeth hurt from clenching her jaw.

Studying her, the chief wrinkled his nose. "Get cleaned up. Fix your hair. Put on some makeup, and give your jacket to my secretary to steam. And for God's sake, put on your poker face. You look as if you want to strangle someone."

She did.

Stella exited the office, anger a red haze in her vision. Handing her blazer over to the polished blond, Stella retreated to the ladies' room. Humiliation burned the back of her neck. Two women were dead, and the chief wanted her to look pretty for TV. Arguing with Horner was no use. He wanted to use her as a PR tool for the department, and there wasn't a damned thing she could do about it. She wanted to be a detective. Unfortunately, this was part of the deal.

Frustrated, she jammed her hair back into place.

The chief's secretary, Cecily, entered the bathroom and handed Stella her jacket. She also held out a small container of makeup. "Concealer. The chief wants you to cover up that bruise on your jaw."

Stella sighed.

"I know." Cecily smoothed her perfect blond chignon. "It seems ridiculous. But if you want to work for him, you must understand that your personal appearance matters."

Stella dabbed concealer on her bruise.

With a frown, Cecily took over, her movements deft and efficient. She opened a compact. "The powder will make the concealer last longer."

"Horner doesn't care if Brody is wrinkled." Stella winced as Cecily pressed the applicator on the bruise.

"Brody's a man." Cecily stood back, assessing her work. "Wrinkles make Brody appear to be working around the clock. They make you look sloppy." She slid the cap off her lipstick with a pissy snap. "Don't give me that look. It's not my opinion. I'm just laying it out for you. If you want to get promoted, you'd better get with the chief's program."

She smoothed her expression back into what Stella now recognized as a mask.

Stella looked in the mirror. The bruise had vanished. "Thanks for the makeup. And the advice."

"You're welcome." Cecily gave her a nod of approval. "Now break a leg."

Thirty minutes later, Stella stood next to the chief on the front steps of the station.

Horner tilted the microphone toward his face. "Two women were killed this week. We are conducting a thorough investigation into the deaths of Missy Green and Dena Miller."

"Is there a serial killer loose in Scarlet Falls?" a reporter called out.

Horner shook his head. "No. Miss Green and Mrs. Miller were acquainted, so their cases are linked."

"Should women be afraid, Chief?"

He gave the questioner a solemn nod. "Women should always be careful, but we don't feel there's any special danger because of these murders. Dena Miller and Missy Green did know each other. Their deaths weren't random acts."

"What are you doing to catch the killer?"

"We have several of our detectives working the case, including Detective Dane." The chief gestured to Stella. "We would also like to ask the public for any help. We're setting up a tip hotline. If anyone has any information regarding the murders of Missy Green or Dena Miller, they can call the number on the bottom of the screen. A one thousand dollar reward is being offered for any valid tip that results in an arrest."

"Does this mean you aren't close to solving the cases?"

The chief answered, "As always, we appreciate any help the public can provide, but we have several leads, including one person of interest, and we expect to solve these murders quickly."

"Detective Dane, is it true that both victims were drug addicts?"

Chief Horner stepped aside so Stella could access the mic. His gestures were polite, but she caught the warning in his eyes.

She lowered the mic a few inches. "I can't divulge details in an ongoing investigation, but this case is my number one priority."

"But we heard both women died of heroin overdoses."

"The medical examiner hasn't issued a cause of death in either case," Stella said, working hard to keep her voice level.

Horner brushed her aside. "As Detective Dane said, we can't discuss the details of the investigation. Once again, the hotline number is at the bottom of the screen. I believe photos of both victims are being shown on the screen right now. If you know anything about the deaths of either of these women, please call the hotline. An officer will be standing by to receive your calls."

Horner herded Stella away from the press. "You need to work on politics, Detective. Next time tell them less in more words, and try not to look angry."

"Yes, sir."

Horner scrutinized her face. "You look tired. Make sure you're taking care of yourself and not letting the case exhaust you."

"Yes, sir." Stella followed Cecily's example and schooled her face until she was out of Horner's view. Did the chief ever tell Brody to make sure he got enough rest? No. But what could Stella complain about? Being promoted? Having a concerned boss? Her boss was superficial, but he'd made her a detective. And that was all Stella had ever wanted.

Wasn't it?

Back at her desk, Stella checked her messages. Finally, Gianna had returned her call. Stella dialed her number. "Can I stop by and show you something?"

Gianna chuckled. "If it's that hottie you brought the other day, sure thing."

"Sorry. That's not it." Stella grabbed her briefcase and headed for the door.

"I guess you can still come." Gianna sighed.

"I'll bring ice cream." Stella ended the call. A quick stop at the convenience store yielded a container of vanilla fudge swirl, Gianna's favorite.

If the girl picked Spivak out of the photo lineup, Stella's life would get much easier. He was a scumbag. He had a record that included assault. But she had her doubts about his ability to have dumped the body. If the ME was right, and Dena had been dead for no more than eighteen hours before she was found, then Spivak would have had to dump her body before sunset last night. Stella had arrested him at nine-thirty the previous night. Dena couldn't have been dumped before six p.m.

If he'd also been outside the church the night Missy disappeared, Stella would feel better about building a case with him as her killer.

The sun was setting as Stella parked outside Gianna's apartment. The girl must have been watching for her because she opened the door before Stella knocked. As usual, the apartment was hot as a sauna. Stella stripped off her jacket and tossed it over the back of a chair.

Gianna walked into the kitchen and took a bowl from the microwave. The aroma of warm fettuccine Alfredo drifted into the room. Stella's appetite stirred to life, but Gianna needed every calorie.

"Do you want some? I'm not really hungry, but I have to eat." Gianna put the bowl on the tiny table. Even though she'd clearly been crying, the girl's color was pinker, her eyes brighter, and her step quicker. The TV was set to a local newscast. She picked up the remote control and muted the volume.

"Go ahead. Please." Stella dropped into a folding chair. "You look better today."

A bony shoulder poked out from the neck of Gianna's oversize T-shirt. "Not a dialysis day."

Ironically, the treatments that kept her alive also drained her energy. Stella reached into her pocket and removed the photo of Dena Miller. "Do you recognize this woman?"

Gianna leaned forward. "Yes. That's Dena."

"Was she friendly with Missy?"

"Yeah. Sometimes they'd talk during the refreshment hour after the meeting or go out for a late dinner."

"Did you ever go with them?" Stella's mind whirled. Not only were the victims members of the same group, they were friends.

"You know I can't afford dinners out. I can't even afford dinners in." Gianna snorted. "Wait. Why are you asking me about Dena?"

Stella put a hand on her forearm. "I'm sorry. She's dead."

"No!" Gianna covered her mouth with her hand. "Not her, too."

Stella gave her arm a gentle squeeze. "I'm sorry. How well did you know her?"

"We talked a little. It's the part of the whole NA deal." Her mouth set in an angry scowl. "If I were you, I'd be looking at the son-of-a-bitch she was married to."

"Why do you say that?" Stella asked.

"He creeped me out." Gianna pushed her food away. "It was normal for him to call her during the meetings. She wouldn't turn off the phone. It was almost as if she was afraid not to answer. Anyway, at the last meeting, I was sitting next to Dena. The prick called her wanting to know where she was, who she was with, and what time she'd be home. I could hear him. His tone was all nasty. She was shaking by the time she grabbed her bag and took the phone out in the hall to talk to him in private. I was gonna ask her to be my sponsor, but I figured she had enough problems of her own."

"You're sure he wasn't just concerned?"

Gianna's eyes were weary. "I know all about nasty-tempered men."

Stella sat back, linking her fingers and digesting the information. What good was knowing Adam Miller was mean to his wife? The chief had ordered her to leave him alone and build her case against Spivak.

As much as Stella hated to admit it, the chief had a point. Spivak was an excellent suspect.

Stella took out six photos. She dealt them out onto the table like a hand of solitaire. "Is the man you saw outside the NA meetings one of these men?"

Gianna scanned the pictures. She studied each one carefully, then shook her head. "I don't think so."

Stella pushed the picture of Spivak in front of Gianna. "Have you ever seen this man before?"

"No. That's not the creepy guy," Gianna said. "Well, he's *a* creepy guy, but he's not *the* creepy guy I saw outside the NA meeting Thursday night."

Disappointment slumped Stella's shoulders.

"Wait." Gianna rose from her chair and walked into the living area. She pointed the remote at the TV. The volume increased. Outside Adam Miller's house, a news crew followed him to his car. Bright lights illuminated his driveway as the reporters shouted his name and asked if he knew anything about his wife's death. The caption on the bottom of the screen read: Local Accountant Suspected in Wife's Murder.

Adam shoved the microphones away from his face, picked up his pace, and got into his car. A photo of Dena appeared in the upper left corner of the screen as a newscaster's voice read, "Dena Miller's body was found at a local park this afternoon. A source in the Scarlet Falls Police Department says Adam Miller is a suspect in the murder of his wife."

Gianna lowered the volume again. "That's the man I saw."

"You saw Adam Miller outside the church Thursday night?"

"Yep." Gianna gave up on the pasta and returned it to the fridge. She took the ice cream from the freezer. "Are you having some?"

"No thanks. I'm not hungry," Stella said. Gianna's recognition of Adam had wiped out Stella's appetite. If the man outside the NA meeting was Adam, then Stella had nothing on Spivak.

Brody had to break Adam's alibi or she had no case against anyone.

"You have dialysis in the morning, right?"

Gianna scooped ice cream into a bowl. "I do."

"If I pick you up afterward, would you come to the station and make a formal statement?"

Gianna lowered her spoon. "There isn't enough ice cream in the world to get me to the police station."

"Missy's car was found in the church parking lot. I think she was abducted there. Do you have any idea why Adam Miller would have killed Missy?"

Gianna shrugged. "No, but he's creepy, and he didn't like anyone hanging around Dena. Maybe he was jealous of their friendship."

That *was* creepy. Stella crossed her fingers that Brody could break Adam's alibi. "If Dena's husband killed her, I want to put him away."

"And if you don't, he'll come after me." Gianna set the bowl on the coffee table. "I make it a rule not to get involved in other people's shit. It never works out for me. No offense or anything, but cops usually treat me like dirt."

"No one will hassle you. I promise."

"I'm tired after dialysis."

"I'll bring you right back here. It'll take fifteen minutes, tops."

"I don't need any reminders of the life I left behind." Gianna's body slouched, defeated and depressed in a way Stella hadn't seen in months.

"I know." Guilt simmered in Stella's belly. Had she set Gianna back? Would formally dragging Gianna into the case put her in danger? Stella believed the same person had killed Missy and Dena. If Adam was willing to kill Missy just for getting too close to his wife, Gianna testifying against him would definitely make her a target.

"I'll do it for you."

"Thanks. I appreciate it." Stella gave her a one-armed hug. "I'll see you tomorrow. I'll bring you something special for lunch."

"You don't have to do that. You already do too much for me. You saved my life. That doesn't make you responsible for the rest of it."

Stella rubbed her shoulder. "I like you, so you'll have to deal with the attention."

Gianna smiled, but her eyes were troubled. She refused to meet Stella's gaze. No doubt being taken to the police station tomorrow would stir old memories she'd rather not relive.

"Lock the door behind me." Stella stood.

"Yes, Mom." Gianna mocked as she let Stella out.

Stella stood on the cement for a few minutes, the wind outside was hot and thick, but at least it was fresher than the stuffy air inside Gianna's apartment.

What now?

It was nine o'clock on a Friday night. Stella hadn't eaten since breakfast. She was so tired that her eyelids felt like sandpaper. As much as she wanted to work the case until it broke, she needed to eat and sleep. Silly as it was, it annoyed her that Horner was right.

But as she drove home, impulse turned her wheel. She called dispatch and asked for backup from patrol. A few minutes later, she was parked in front of Missy's apartment.

She still had the key the landlady had given her. As soon as the patrol car pulled into the driveway, she let herself into the apartment, tugged on gloves, and began another, thorough search. Maybe there was something she'd missed the first time around.

She started in the living room, where the sparse furnishings afforded a quick search. She moved into the kitchen. Not bothering with the obvious places she'd already checked, she lifted drawers from their runners and checked the spaces between appliances and cabinets. She turned toward the bedroom and rolled her head on her shoulders. Most people hid highly personal items in their most intimate space.

In the closet, she slid hangers to check the wallboard behind Missy's clothes. Then Stella knelt and ran her fingers around the edges of the carpet. The corner lifted. She pulled it back. A square had been cut into the floorboard. She pried it up with her fingertips to find a shoebox in the small hole. Inside the box, Stella found a fat envelope. Cash. Lots of cash. She thumbed through the bills. Mostly tens and twenties, the sum totaled at least two thousand dollars.

Where had Missy gotten that much cash?

Chapter Twenty-Three

What an arrogant prick.

He got up from his chair and paced in front of the television, where his recording of the press conference played.

So Police Chief Horner thought he'd solve these murders quickly, and they already had a person of interest that they were investigating.

How were the police possibly going to catch him when they were too incompetent to decipher his simple message? Rage seethed in his chest. Its warmth spread through him like rocket fuel.

Pivoting, he crossed the room again. His basement was empty, and he needed to fill it. He was anxious to get back to work.

But the police needed to be taught a lesson.

He turned and stared at the TV screen. On the steps of the police station, Chief Horner puffed out his chest and postured for the cameras. What a blowhard. With his perfect hair and whitened teeth, the Scarlet Falls police chief didn't look like he'd ever gotten his hands dirty. Had he really walked a beat or driven a patrol shift? Didn't seem likely.

The man was a well-groomed windbag who needed the air taken from his sails. But how?

Pictures of Dena Miller and Missy Green popped onto the left side of the screen. Across the chief's uniformed chest, a phone number was displayed.

"We're setting up a tip hotline," Chief Horner said. "If anyone has any information regarding the murders of Missy Green or Dena Miller, they can call the number on the bottom of the screen."

A hotline? How perfect. The hotline was going to get a tip they'd have to follow. He booted up his computer and began looking for the perfect location. He called up Google Maps and considered rural locations on the outskirts of town. There were plenty of abandoned buildings. But the police would be wary, and he wanted them more comfortable.

It had to be somewhere innocuous. Somewhere they'd never see him coming. Right in the middle of town should work. But how to find an empty house? Houses for sale or rent? Many would be empty.

He searched a real estate website for properties in the area and found several possibilities. He printed off a short list. Several might work for his *fuck-off* gesture to Chief Horner.

Tomorrow, he'd make time for a quick reconnoiter of the locations. Then he could set his trap. He didn't have time to make an elaborate plan. Simplicity often was the best option.

Now it was time to get back to business. He'd already chosen Number Three, and he didn't want to keep her waiting.

The empty cell called. He was bored. He needed her tonight.

A short time later, he cruised down the street, following her slender figure as she disappeared into the apartment. Now that was a strong woman. Not physically. Her body was slim. But there was nothing weak about her spirit. She didn't let stumbling blocks hold her back. She would continue to push forward until she'd reached her objective.

Beauty only got a woman so far in life. He admired her determination. He designed each test to suit the individual. This one would take some extra consideration.

Dena had been a disappointment. She'd snapped even faster than Missy. Instead of proving her resilience, she'd caved immediately. After all she'd been through, he'd expected so much more from her.

How could he have judged her so poorly? She'd rallied from a physical challenge in the past, and it hadn't been the torture that had broken her. With Dena, the game had been mental.

She'd had plans. She'd had hope. Once he'd taken that away, she'd wilted like a thirsty daisy.

Dena had proven that mental and emotional strength were as important as physical resilience. He needed someone who had faced life-long challenges and had overcome them.

A light in the apartment turned on. Through the window, he watched her rummage through a kitchen drawer.

Someone like her. Yes. She would be next.

Turning off the dome light, he got out of the car. The street was empty and dark in both directions. His shoes scraped on the concrete steps. He peered through the kitchen window but couldn't see her.

Where was she?

His fingers closed on the hypodermic needle in his pocket. He'd slipped roofies into Missy's coffee when she'd set it on a table to use the ladies' room. Then he'd followed her at a discreet distance through the church parking lot. She'd collapsed, and he'd been right there. He'd put her in the passenger seat of his car as if she were sleeping. The drugs had worked well. She'd remained unconscious through the drive back to his place. But he didn't have that opportunity this time.

His initial success had made him cocky. He'd surprised Dena in her shower. He'd punched her in the head and tossed her into his trunk. Considering that she'd escaped, and he'd had to track her through the woods in the rain for hours, that hadn't been the best method. As much fun as it had been to see her terror, he didn't intend to repeat himself.

What would have happened if she'd escaped? She would have been able to identify him. That couldn't happen again.

But this one would be easier. He would keep it simple. A paralytic would keep her immobile long enough for him to transport her to his facility. He moved to the door and inserted his lock-picking tools. The mechanism gave after less than a minute. His practice was paying off.

He opened the door and slipped inside, then tugged the mask over his face. The small kitchen and living room were empty. He could hear someone in the bedroom, opening and closing drawers. He pulled the syringe from his pocket.

His blood hummed as he approached the bedroom door. Her footsteps sounded on the carpet. With two fingers, he eased the door open a few more inches and peered through the crack at the hinges.

She was searching through a dresser drawer, totally focused on her task. Rather than rush her, he waited.

Patience was important when hunting. A crocodile would lie submerged in the reeds for hours waiting for a gazelle to lower its head to the water for a drink.

She closed the drawer and turned away from the door. He held his breath, his thumb on the plunger. Pushing the door open, he pounced, sliding a hand around her face to cover her mouth and jabbing the needle into her thigh. Flailing, she reached for the lamp on the dresser. He depressed the plunger, then wrapped his other arm around her body to control her limbs. She froze, her body slowly going limp and collapsing to the floor. The lamp shattered on the thin carpet. A framed picture slid from the wall to the floor. Her fingers curled in the cord.

Success sent adrenaline coursing hot through his veins. He bound her hands and ankles with zip ties in case the drug wore off while she was in the trunk.

That had been almost too easy. The lack of challenge was almost disappointing. But he had to keep his eye on the prize. This was all just a means to an end.

He smoothed a piece of duct tape across her mouth. Rushing back to his car, he hefted the steamer trunk and hand truck from his trunk.

The street was still empty. Returning to the apartment, he shoved her into the box, tucking her arms and legs in fetal-style. He turned off the lights and locked the door behind him. Everything must appear normal. Then he used the hand truck to cart her out to the car and hoisted the heavy chest into the trunk.

His baggy hoodie hid his face, and he'd obscured his license plate with mud in case anyone saw him. But no one would pay attention to a man loading a box into his car. The apartment buildings were surrounded by commercial properties, which were closed at this late hour, and the people who lived in her complex were the sort who minded their own business.

He slammed the trunk. Getting behind the wheel, he started the engine and drove toward home. Excitement buzzed though his whole body, almost like a mild version of the shock he'd given her.

She was going to be The One. He could feel the anticipation humming through his bones.

He could hardly wait to get started.

Chapter Twenty-Four

After dropping the envelope of cash at the forensics lab, Stella drove toward home but didn't make the turn onto her street. Restlessness made her drive past. Despite her lack of sleep and skipped meals, frustrated energy buzzed under her skin. There was only one person she wanted to see.

Mac's cabin's lights blazed as she parked in front of his porch.

This was a terrible idea. He'd acted strangely at the crime scene. They'd found Dena Miller. Maybe he had no more interest in Stella. She should go home. Exhaustion and lack of food were impairing her judgment.

She reached for the gearshift, but he walked out onto his porch. His hair had reverted to its untamed state, making her want to run her hands through it, and the way his snug T-shirt hugged his lean torso stirred a hunger deep in her belly. She was not going home tonight. She wanted those strong arms around her. He could make her forget one of the worst days of her life.

Stella got out of the car.

Mac met her at the bottom of the steps. He didn't say a word, just drew her to his chest and held her close. She leaned on him.

He rubbed her back.

Stella lifted her head and met his eyes. Her hands shook as she raised them to splay on his chest. He covered her fingers with his, his hands warming hers. The night was hot and humid. A storm lingered in the air but refused to break the heat wave. Atmospheric tension buzzed as loudly as the symphony of insects in the surrounding forest. It had to be eighty-five degrees. How could she be cold?

"Come inside." He tucked her under one arm and guided her into his kitchen. "Have you eaten?"

Turmoil churned in her stomach. She shook her head. "I'm not hungry."

"No wonder you look sick." He filled a mug with water and put it in the microwave. Opening a cabinet, he took down a can, opened it, and poured the contents into a saucepan.

"He put her on display." She wandered into his living room. The night air blowing through the screens chilled her skin. She didn't see the cozy cabin in front of her. Her mind was replaying every detail of the horrifying scene she'd analyzed that afternoon.

He lit the burner under the pan. "I'm sorry you had to see that."

"It's my job." She walked back into the kitchen. Her hands gripped the back of a chair, as if the weight of it would ground her.

"I know. But it's still awful, and you're human."

Anger and frustration burned in her chest, and tears threatened. She blinked them back. "I have to find him."

"I couldn't see much from the parking area, but today's scene sounds more elaborate than the first."

"Yes. His ritual is getting more complicated." She shivered.

"Why?" Mac pulled out a chair and guided her into it.

She rested her chin in her hand. "I don't know yet. Spivak has a record of sexual assault. A perv doesn't need a reason that you and I would understand. He just wants who he wants, whether she's someone who looks like his mom or the first girl who spurned him. But the fact that Missy wasn't raped nags at me. From the way he acted in the interview, my gut says Spivak would have sexually assaulted her."

"You already said motivation is hard to predict. Maybe the torture is what drives him." He set a bowl of soup in front of her. "Sorry. This is all I have on hand. I haven't been grocery shopping."

She ate without tasting, her mind occupied with the case.

She told him about Adam's reaction, the press conference, and the cash she'd found in Missy's apartment. "Everyone said Missy was broke. Where did she get over two thousand dollars? And why was it stashed under her floorboard? She had a bank account."

"Are you sure the money is hers?"

"I'll have our fingerprint examiner see if she can pull any prints tomorrow." Stella's first stop of the morning would be the county forensics lab.

Mac set a cup of tea on the table. Leaning over her shoulder, he reached for her bowl. He smelled like the forest. She turned her face to his body and inhaled. "Were you outside?"

"For a while."

"You smell like pine trees."

His breath quickened, and he froze. "Is that good?"

Standing, she placed both hands on Mac's arms. His biceps were hard under her touch. The wind blew across his kitchen, bringing the scent of trees and earth into the room.

"Very." She rested her forehead on his chest and closed her eyes. "I don't want to think about the case anymore tonight."

"I don't blame you." His hand settled between her shoulder blades. "You've had a hell of a day. You need to take a break, even if it's just a short one."

Images of Dena's body flashed in her head. She raised her eyelids. Mac's bright-blue eyes studied her. Much better.

Something unfurled inside her. Want. Like a young moth testing new wings, desire opened and closed, indecisive. What did she want? She hadn't had so much as a date since the shooting the previous November. Her focus had been on her career, and she hadn't met a man who warranted her attention.

Or once she'd met Mac, she hadn't met anyone as interesting. He was more than he appeared. Mac was layers of kindness and humor, intelligence and determination, vulnerability and courage. And he sparked a need inside her that could only be described as primitive. With him, she didn't have to be perfect. She didn't have to contain anything. She could let go.

Her fingers tightened on the solid flesh under them. "Will I scare you off if I say that I really want you right now?"

Mac coughed. "Sorry. You surprised me."

She'd surprised herself. She took his hand in hers, turned, and tugged him toward his bedroom. He followed, then paused at the threshold. Her fingers found the top button of her blouse while her eyes roamed over him.

He crossed his arms and leaned on the doorjamb. Worn and soft, his T-shirt and cargos molded to his body. He was lean and hard without an ounce of bulk. She had no doubt he'd earned his body through hiking, climbing, and basic survival in the jungle, not pumping iron at a gym on his lunch hour. Underneath the subtle woodsy cologne, his scent was all male.

"You know I like talking to you. I'm in no rush to sleep with you." He flushed. "Not that I don't want you. I do." His eyes brightened as her fingers lingered on the button. "I really do." He licked his lips. "But you've had a horrific day. If you just need to talk, I can do that."

His gaze was as hungry as his words were polite. This man was such a study in self-control. Stella suddenly wanted to break it, to make him lose his fist-tight grip on his emotions, to lose himself in her.

She flicked open the button. "I'm finished talking."

Chapter Twenty-Five

"Are you sure?" Mac couldn't believe he asked the question. The woman of his dreams was getting naked in his bedroom and he was practically telling her she should reconsider her decision. He was a moron.

"I'm sure." Stella shook out her hair. It fell around her shoulders in a dark, tousled wave. Hairpins dropped to the floor.

"You're positive I'm not just a distraction?" Damn his conscience. And ego.

In the past, he wouldn't have cared. He would have been happy to provide the release of her pent-up frustration. If she hadn't wanted to see him again, he wouldn't have cared.

But this was Stella, literally the woman of his dreams. The first woman he craved conversation with as much as sex.

Who would have thought *that* would ever happen? Not him.

It was a freaking miracle.

And yet it wasn't enough. He wasn't satisfied being with her simply because his body ached for her. This thing between them had to be equal. He wanted Stella to need him just as much as he needed her. If he was going to let himself be vulnerable, to give her power over him, then she had to do the same.

He wanted her pulse to thud in her ears like a bass drum. Her blood to rush as hot as lava through her veins. For every cell in her body to yearn for him. He wanted to be the man she chose above all others.

She opened the second button on her blouse.

Enough with the biology lesson, Mac. Woman getting naked here.

Mesmerized, Mac stared as she flicked a third button, then a fourth. The fabric parted, revealing the swell of her breasts. He licked his lips, dying for a taste of that smooth skin.

Button number five.

White satin and lace. That's what she'd been hiding under that up-tight, mannish blouse. All. Day. Long. Hell, she probably wore sexy, feminine silk against her skin all the time.

Any blood remaining in Mac's brain flowed south with the power of the Amazon.

She stood for a minute, letting him look. Breasts swelled over white lace. Flat abs tempted him to lick his way . . .

She moved on to her cuffs, seemingly content to continue her strip-tease, but Mac couldn't wait any longer. He was going to implode if he didn't get his hands on her. In two steps, he was standing in front of her, their bodies inches apart. The animal in him wanted to strip off her pants, hoist her legs around his waist, and take her against the wall right that second.

Finesse.

He wasn't one of the beasts he studied in the jungle, but his desire for Stella stripped him raw. Still, the woman deserved a little consideration.

"Let me help." He slid the cotton off her shoulders, putting his lips to the creamy white skin of her collarbone. She arched back, her head lolling to the side as he brushed his lips up the side of her neck.

A taste of her wasn't enough. The need to explore every inch of her roared through him. He tugged the shirt sleeves to her elbows, his mouth hungry.

She groaned as his lips cruised down to the swell of her breast. He traced the lace edge of her bra with his tongue. Her full-body shudder sent a knee-buckling wave of anticipation rushing through his blood.

"I can't move." She wiggled, trying to free her arms, but they were trapped by the sleeves of her blouse.

Mac gathered the fabric tighter. "I know. I kind of like it."

That sexy, skeptical brow shot upward.

"I can have my way with you." He gave her earlobe a playful, gentle nip.

Irritation wrinkled her brow. "You can have your way with me because I *want* you to have your way with me."

"I know." Mac laughed, tugged the sleeves behind her, and held them against the small of her back with one hand. With the other, he stroked her waist, his fingers playing across her abdomen. "Just give me a minute or so to indulge myself. My hidden caveman has needs."

"Hidden? You don't hide him very well." Her eyes darkened as he flicked open the front clasp of her bra.

"Trust me," he said.

Her head tilted. "I do."

Her statement, and the sight of her bare skin, nearly brought him to his knees. In fact, it did. He dropped to one knee in front of her.

He let his gaze roam over her, suddenly in no rush at all, taking in each lovely curve. "You're perfect."

Her blush spread to the pale skin of her breasts. "You're a tease."

"Me?" He laughed. "I just want to look at you for a minute. Indulge me."

"It's been a minute." She tugged at her sleeves.

"Don't rush me." Grinning, he closed his mouth over a nipple.

She stopped struggling. Her head fell back. Her body relaxed, and a sweet moan purred from her throat.

He lifted his head to watch pleasure drift lazily over her face. "See?"

"I see." She smiled down at him. Her voice shifted into a command. "More."

"Yes, ma'am. You're hot when you're bossy." He cruised across her chest and down her belly, letting her response guide his attentions. Nibbling, kissing, tasting. His tongue delved into her belly button and just below the waistband of her slacks. He wanted more. Much more.

"Mac." Her tone sharpened, but her eyes begged. "Please."

He released her sleeves and undid the button of her slacks. The silky fabric slid off her hips and pooled at her feet. But she made no effort to slide her hands free.

Hot damn.

Her panties were white and lacy and covered just enough to stir his imagination—and whet his appetite. He leaned forward to kiss her through the lace. He caught a hint of her taste through the fabric. Sweetness. Utter sweetness. She was more addictive than any drug, and he had to have more. He'd never have enough.

He hooked his thumbs in the fabric over her hips and drew them down her legs.

Rocking back, he took a long look. "God, you're beautiful."

"Why am I naked, and you're still dressed?"

"Because I love to look at you." He slid a hand down her long, long leg. Wrapping a hand around her ankle, he lifted her foot, kissed it, and drew off her panties and slacks. She stood in front of him, wearing only her white shirt drawn down around her biceps and her bra hanging open.

He'd never seen anything so lovely.

He leaned forward and pressed his mouth to her core. The taste of her on his lips wasn't enough. His tongue delved in. And her body went taut as a bow.

She pulled her arms free of her sleeves. A button popped. Fabric ripped. Then her hands were on his head, her fingers twined in his hair, her moans driving him faster.

"Now." She tugged on his hair.

Mac climbed to his feet. Unlike him, she didn't take her time. *Thank God.*

She grabbed his shirt by the hem and ripped it over his head. Her eyes cooled as she touched the edge of his bandage. "Oh, lord. I didn't think. I don't want to hurt you."

"You won't." He slipped a hand between her legs and watched her face heat again. *Better.* The truth was, he couldn't care less about his stitches.

"I'll be gentle." Tossing his shirt over her shoulder, she attacked the button of his pants. She had them down to his knees in two seconds. When her hand curled around him, he almost lost it.

"Hold on." He reached for his pocket. "There's a condom in the back of my wallet."

"Already got one." She held a foil packet in her other hand. *Where did she get that?* Ripping it open, she covered him.

"I like a woman who knows what she wants."

"I want you." She pushed him backward onto the bed. "Now."

Mac bounced on the mattress, kicking off his pants as she climbed on top of him.

"I've been very patient." She straddled his thighs, careful not to touch his bandage.

His hand stroked up her arm and wrapped around a lock of her hair. Her eyes. Yeah. He could stare at those all day, too. And the focused, hungry look on her face. "You have, and I appreciate it."

"You'd better let me do all the work." In one smooth motion, she rose and took him into her body. Goddamn. She was tight and wet and hot. Buried inside her, he decided this moment could go on for the rest of his life.

But she moved. His hands slid down to her hips, his fingers grasping to slow her down.

"Easy."

"Need. To. Move." Her head tipped back, her expression total bliss. Her breasts thrust forward. Mac reached up and cupped one, his thumb stroking her nipple.

On one hand, he was dying to make this last as long as possible. On the other, the thought that he'd driven her senseless almost ended the moment. His senses sharpened, and his heartbeat echoed from the soles of his feet to the top of his head. Every molecule in his body was tuned, as if his nervous system was cranked into overdrive.

She moved faster. Pleasure spiraled through him. He wrapped his arms around her and flipped them over. Tugging her legs up around his waist, he took control. Slow, even, long thrusts that made him forget they were two bodies instead of one.

Her body bowed, her back arched, and all of her muscles went taut. Mac felt her pulse around him. He held out as long as he could, drawing out her orgasm, experiencing every second of bliss.

When he finally let go, the release made him lightheaded. He collapsed on top of her, chest heaving, heart aching. He was sure he'd never experienced anything like making love to Stella. She fit him in every way, like a lock to a key, and being inside her was like being home.

Her fingers toyed with his hair.

"Why did we wait so long to do that?" she asked.

"I have no idea." With great regret, he slid from her body and levered up on one of his elbows. He liked the way she felt underneath him, all soft, smooth skin. He ran a hand along her hip. Her body was fit and athletic, with enough flesh under his hand that he didn't feel like he would break her if things got energetic. Which they had. He kissed her mouth. Slow and deep, as if he wanted to make love to her again. Which he did.

2

All dark eyes and disheveled hair, she cupped his jaw. "I wish this moment could last forever."

"Me, too." He nibbled his way to her neck. "The best I can do is make it last a while longer."

They both knew in the morning they'd have to face reality. But for the next few hours, the real world could wait.

"I'll take every minute I can get." How did her hand get down there?

"I like it that you're greedy." He got up to deal with the condom and find another. "I'll be right back. Don't move."

She fluffed her pillow and got comfortable. "I'll be here."

But for how long?

Mac had spent his entire adult life running from personal responsibility. Fleeing connections. Running from his emotions. Now, for the first time, he wanted something to be permanent.

The ache in his chest was an acute reminder that his growing attachment to Stella made him vulnerable. If he let himself fall for her, it would be like stepping off a cliff. There'd be no going back.

She appeared in the mirror behind him. "Do you think you should check your stitches? I'd feel awful if I hurt you."

He turned and kissed her. "I was careful. The wound is fine."

Tonight, it was his heart at risk.

Chapter Twenty-Six

Thunder boomed. Stella opened her eyes. She oriented herself as she recognized Mac's bedroom in the dark. Erotic images played in her mind.

What a night.

Lightning flashed, illuminating Mac sprawled next to her. The room had been warm—and so had their bodies—when they'd finally fallen asleep. The sheet draped across his waist, leaving his torso bare. Her gaze roamed the lean muscle of his arms and chest. She thought about following her eyes with her hands, but it wasn't even light yet. Why should they both be awake?

Rain burst from the sky and drummed on the roof. Leaves rustled as the wind whipped at the trees. Cool, moist air blew through the open windows, a welcome chill. Another clap of thunder boomed, closer this time. The loud crack brought back the memory of her nightmare. Gunshots and an endless stream of blood. In her dreams, it flowed until it formed a slick, red lake in the grass.

Nausea welled. Moving away from Mac so as not to disturb him, she curled into a ball.

But he stirred, rolling toward her. His hand settled on her hip. "What's wrong?"

"Just a bad dream." She balled up tighter.

He stroked a hand down her back, as soothing as the patter of rain.

"Shouldn't you close the windows?"

He shook his head, scooting closer and pulling her to him until his body spooned hers. "The roof was designed to protect the windows. The rain won't get in."

The wind blew the cool scent of wet pine and earth into the room. Stella shivered, and Mac drew the sheet up over her shoulders.

He pressed his lips to her temple. "Do you want to talk about it?"

She sighed, wiggling her butt closer. She loved the feel of his body pressed against hers. He was solid and real and warm. "Just a nightmare."

"Do you have them often?"

Her shoulders rose and fell with a deep breath. "They started back in November."

"After the shooting?"

"Yes." She rolled onto her back, flung an arm over her head, and stared up at the ceiling. "They'd been fading, slowly, over the months, but seeing two dead bodies this week seems to have brought them back."

He stroked the underside of her arm. Last night, he'd found places on her body she hadn't known were erogenous. Or was it his touch, pretty much anywhere, that stirred desire until it simmered in her veins, thick and hot and as sweet as syrup?

"Have you seen anyone?" he asked.

"You mean a shrink?" She rolled to face him.

He nodded. "Yeah. I'm considering it." He slid his hand to her hip. "I never really dealt with Lee's death."

"And now your father . . ." She cupped his jaw. "Your family has been through so much."

"Yeah. Putting the issue on my backburner hasn't worked out for me. I don't recommend it." Grief welled into Mac's eyes. "You should deal with the problem now, instead of letting it grow."

Like he obviously had.

Stella nestled her head deeper into the pillow. "I don't have anything against therapy. My required sessions with the department shrink were important after the shooting, but I thought I was getting over it. Looks like I was wrong. I'm not worried about the actual nightmares. I'm pretty sure they'll fade when this is over. The doctor said they could come and go, depending on triggers." But as long as she was a cop, her life would never be free of triggers.

"Then what's bothering you?"

She tucked the sheet over her breasts. "I blew off my pistol qualification last week."

Mac waited, patient as always, making her feel like one of the wild animals he studied.

"Every time I pull the trigger, I flinch." Stella flung a hand over her head. "You know about the shooting back in November?"

"Not all the details."

"The suspect fled, and I shot him. The bullet struck him in the arm, but it didn't stop him. He went on to do terrible things. He killed two cops. Your sister and Brody almost died." She smoothed the edge of the sheet against her skin. "If I had stopped him, none of that would have happened. Those two cops would still be alive."

"You cannot possibly think any of that was your fault." Mac shifted closer and took her hand. "There is only one person responsible for their deaths: the shooter."

"My brain knows this, but my heart sees the police chaplain on the doorstep." A tear slipped from her eye. "Just like when my dad died."

Mac pulled her into his arms. Holding her against his chest, he stroked her hair. "You know you're being completely unreasonable. The mayor gave you a medal for your performance in the shootout."

"How do you know about that?" Stella lifted her head.

"I might have been keeping tabs on you."

"From the jungle?"

"I didn't say it was easy." He brushed the tear from her cheek. "But you're worth it. I ran all the way to South America, but I couldn't get you out of my head."

She rested her head on his chest. Just being in his arms helped. "I'll see the shrink, but I still have to get through my qualification."

"Have you been to the range?"

"Not lately. The cop crowd there makes me nervous. I feel like everyone is staring at me, even though they're not," Stella said. "I know this is all in my head."

Mac glanced at the clock. He stood, taking Stella's hand and dragging her to her feet. "It's five o'clock. Grab a shower. I'll make coffee."

"Where are we going?" Still groggy, Stella headed for the bathroom. She turned on the spray to let the water warm up.

Mac was sending a text. "Firing range."

"Who are you texting?"

"Hannah. No one makes shooting more fun than she does."

"It's not even light out."

"She gets up early." His gaze darkened as he scanned her from head to toe. "It's a real shame, but I guess you'll need clothes."

"I keep a bag in the trunk of my car." Crime scenes were rough on her wardrobe.

Forty-five minutes later, they pulled into the dirt and gravel parking area. Hannah was waiting.

Stella eyed the building. Nerves swam through the coffee in her belly.

"Trust me." Mac got out of the car to greet his sister.

Dressed in jeans, boots, and a Syracuse University T-shirt, Hannah didn't look like a hotshot lawyer. She opened her trunk and unlocked a portable gun safe. She palmed a handgun, and handed Mac one.

Stella looked over Mac's shoulder. The box contained additional handguns and rifles. "What is this?"

"The Barrett family arsenal." Mac picked up a magazine and a box of bullets. "The Colonel took his weapons very seriously."

"He must have." Stella faced the concrete bunker-type structure. No signs gave away the building's purpose.

Mac opened the door. "This is a very private club. Mostly former military types. For the retired set, it's half firing range, half social club."

Fluorescent lights brightened the reception area.

"Mac! Hannah!" A giant, ridiculously fit man of about sixty vaulted over the counter. The overhead lighting gleamed off his bald head. He slapped Mac on the shoulder. "Hannah practices regularly. Where the hell have you been?"

"Around," Mac said. "You know I prefer a blade."

Craig lifted Hannah off her feet with a hug. A wide grin split her face as she returned the embrace.

Mac gestured to Stella. "Craig, this is Stella." He didn't provide her last name or occupation, which she appreciated. She wanted to remain low profile.

Her slim hand disappeared in Craig's as they shook, and she didn't miss the older man's quick, approving wink.

Mac put a hand on her back. "Craig served with the Colonel. We've been shooting here since we could walk."

"Maybe before," Craig said. "I heard the Colonel passed. I'm sorry."

"Thanks." Mac studied the cinderblock wall for a few seconds before gesturing with his handgun. "I need to figure out if I can still shoot this thing."

"I'm sure you can." Craig crossed his arms. "Not as well as Hannah, but then, she was always my star pupil. If you'd only apply yourself a little more."

"Story of my life." Mac laughed.

"Go to it." Craig waved them toward the door and stepped back. "You have the place to yourselves for now."

Mac guided Stella into the range. The big room was bare bones: concrete floor, cinderblock walls, wooden partitions.

Craig followed them in, doubled up on ear protection, and leaned against the far wall.

Entering the indoor range, Stella tensed.

Mac put a hand on her arm and leaned close. "None of your cop friends are here. You can relax. Why don't we hang out and watch Hannah for a while? It's usually pretty entertaining." He steered her toward the back wall.

Hannah handed out earplugs, loaded her weapon, and lined up in front of a target. She pulled the trigger. Hannah fired away, emptying her magazine into the paper target. She pressed a button and brought her target in. Seven shots, dead center. She replaced the target and sent it back. "You're up, Mac."

Mac gave Stella a questioning look. She nodded.

"Want to make it interesting?" Hannah stepped back. "Maybe a little wager?"

Mac snorted. "Not even tempted. You'll have to hustle someone else." He took his time with his shots, and his cluster was more than respectable, but Hannah could practically draw a smiley face.

Several men wandered in. Some lined up at stalls and practiced. Others hung back to watch Hannah, who moved her target back farther and farther. In the next thirty minutes, she accumulated a crowd of admirers, some of whom were now placing side bets or bringing alternative guns for her to try. Hannah kicked butt with everything she touched.

Mac gestured for Stella to take his place.

Though she'd relaxed while watching Hannah, sweat broke out under Stella's arms and her heart kicked into gear as she stepped toward the stall. She wiped her hands on her jeans, and then unholstered her weapon. She took her stance. Her body stiffened, her arm feeling wooden as she aimed and fired.

"Your hand is drifting as you shoot." He stepped up behind her, lined his body against hers, and slid one hand along her left arm. His other hand strayed to her hip.

OK. So that was distracting.

Stella glanced back at him. Mac nodded to the target. With his hand steadying her arm, she squeezed the trigger. The air stank of gunpowder, and shots rang on cinderblock as she emptied the magazine. Four shots later, she pulled her target in. The first few shots were left of the human outline, but one by one, each shot moved a few inches to the right.

Mac pointed to two shots in the target's chest. "Those'll do."

Her first decent shots in months! Pleasure flooded her chest as she reloaded and emptied another magazine into the target. Even better. She could do this. Her career wasn't over.

She flung her arms around Mac's neck. "Thank you."

He smiled down at her. "Before today, this wouldn't have occurred to me as the perfect date."

"Well, it was. You have no idea how relieved I am."

A half hour later, Mac, Stella, and Hannah went out into the parking lot. The rain had stopped, but moisture hung in the air.

"I can't believe it's actually more humid than before the rain. Thunderstorms are supposed to relieve a heat wave." Hannah opened her trunk and put her weapon in the gun safe. "That was fun. Thanks for calling me."

Mac tucked his gun at the small of his back. "I'm going to hold on to mine for a while."

Hannah kissed his cheek. She tapped her hand on his jaw. "You need to shave."

Mac laughed. "I shaved once this year. That was more than enough."

With a roll of her eyes, Hannah left.

"Thank you again. I needed that." Stella slid her arms around Mac's neck and kissed him. Mac tapped his temple. "It's all a head game. All the crazy drills my father made us perform—and the sheer insanity of some of them would make you squirm—did one thing for all of us. They gave us confidence. He taught us that we could do things we never believed possible. He pushed us so far out of our comfort zones, we needed GPS to find our way back." He reached over and rubbed her shoulder. "You can do it. I just saw you. When do you have to test?"

"Soon." Relief faded to worry.

"Just remember, when you watch all those guys at the range, that my sister can outshoot all of them. And don't think she can't fire in a live action scenario. The Colonel did plenty of live-fire drills with us."

Stella was horrified. Military recruits died in live-fire drills. Mac and his siblings had been children.

"Oh, yes he did." Mac nodded.

"That's crazy." She shook her head. "They should call Hannah The Gun Whisperer. She's amazing."

"She was always that way. We all had our special skills. Grant was our strategist; Hannah the marksman."

"What about you?"

"I can find my way anywhere." He scanned the woods around them. "It's like I have a built-in compass. I can't explain it."

"Raised by wolves?" she joked.

"Practically."

"And Lee?" she asked softly.

Mac sighed. "Lee was awful at everything physical. He was a scholar. The Colonel had no business sending him into survival training drills."

"How did he get through them?" She imagined a skinny boy, suffering through tasks when his siblings all excelled.

"The rest of us carried him. Lee more than made up for it in adulthood," Mac said. "He was the touchstone while the rest of us wandered as far away from Scarlet Falls as possible."

"Sounds like he was lucky to have the three of you."

"I never really thought about it quite like that, but I guess he was." Mac was quiet for a few seconds, as if this was a new thought. Then he smiled. "I'm hungry. What do you have planned for the morning?"

"I have to see if forensics could pull prints from that envelope I found under Missy's closet." Stella couldn't imagine the money was Missy's. So who was she hiding it for?

"Then what?"

"I'm not sure." She checked the time. Seven-thirty. "I'm supposed to catch up with Brody and Lance at lunchtime. We have to review tips that come in on the hotline. I also have to pick up Gianna from dialysis and take her to the station to sign a statement. What about you?"

"I have an old contact that is very in tune with the local criminal scene," Mac said.

"And?"

Mac shrugged. "I could take pictures of your suspects and see if anyone in his gang recognizes them. Plus, Freddie knows things."

"A gang? That doesn't sound safe."

He lifted a palm. "Safe is relative. He already knows I'm in town."

"These are those dangerous associates you talked about before." Stella poked a finger in his chest. "Don't think I'm letting you go there alone."

"I can't take Grant. He's too important to the kids. They already lost one father. I won't put him at risk."

Discomfort stirred in Stella. "You aren't any more expendable than your brother."

"Maybe."

Did he really think he was less valuable than his siblings?

She propped a hand on her hip. Under her irritation, fear slithered. She felt more for this man than she'd planned, knowing he was likely not going to stick around Scarlet Falls. Mac spent more time in South

America than the US. If—when—he left, she would be heartbroken. But she couldn't bear losing him to a drug dealer's bullet. He'd gotten lucky in Brazil. How long could his good fortune hold out? "There's no *maybe* about it. Your family needs you."

I need you.

The words in her head stayed there. She wouldn't guilt him into staying. It had to be his decision, but she wanted him to choose Scarlet Falls.

To choose her.

He stepped back, out of reach. "I'm used to working alone."

"Get unused to it." Stella headed for the car. "I'm going with you."

Chapter Twenty-Seven

"Like hell." Mac grabbed Stella's shoulder and spun her around. He would not put her at risk. "Freddie will smell cop on you in a second."

Her chin went up and her eyes blazed. "I'm dressed down."

He skimmed her jeans, T-shirt, and running shoes. Her black hair fell in waves past her shoulders. She didn't need the pistol, badge, or handcuffs. She wore cop like a uniform. "It's not the clothes." It was her eyes. They were flat and sharp, not missing a thing. "It's too dangerous."

"You're kidding, right." She folded her arms over her chest.

"No." Mac swallowed. "I don't want anything to happen to you."

"I appreciate the chivalry, but it's not necessary."

"This has nothing to do with chivalry." He closed the gap between them. "I've been attracted to you since the first second we met, but what I'm feeling for you now is more than I'd expected. This wasn't what I planned." The deep connection he felt with Stella both excited and scared him.

He kissed her hard on the mouth, and the stunned expression on her face said she hadn't expected what was developing between them either.

She blinked, surprise shifting to stubbornness. "I feel the same way, which is why I won't let you go alone."

He put a hand to the back of his skull where tension throbbed.

She cupped his cheek. "This isn't a one-way street. You don't get to care about other people and not let them feel the same about you."

"But—"

She pressed her fingertips to his lips. "Either you let me go with you, or I'll call your brother. Putting yourself into an unnecessarily dangerous position isn't fair to me or to Grant or Hannah. *You* matter."

"Grant isn't getting dragged into this." Mac wouldn't allow any danger to touch his family.

"I wasn't suggesting Grant take my place. But he'd be able to talk you out of whatever you're planning." Her eyes locked on his. "I'm going with you."

Mac had a choice. He could skip the whole visit with Freddie. He and Stella could continue to follow leads through official channels. But if he had the chance to prevent another girl from being hurt, how could he not try? Once he learned Rabbit had bolted, Freddie would pay Mac a visit. Next time maybe he wouldn't spot the tail. Maybe he wouldn't be prepared. The thought of Freddie's gang showing up at his cabin—or worse, at Grant's house—gave him the shakes. A confrontation was inevitable, and Mac would rather be the initiator.

He could lie to Stella and go alone anyway. But that felt wrong in a thousand ways.

"You'll stay in the car." He glanced at her cruiser. "Not that car. We'll have to rent one."

"We can use my Honda."

"All right." Mac raised his hand to his face and covered her fingers. "But you have to promise to do what I say."

The cocky lift to her brow shouldn't have turned him on, but then everything about this woman cranked his testosterone into overdrive.

"Unless you're in danger," she said.

"That's not an answer."

"No, it isn't."

"OK." But Mac wasn't happy with her refusal to commit. "Where is this friend of yours?"

"He used to operate out of the rail yard, but that location got too popular with the homeless. He's under the power lines by Hidden Lake."

"I've never been there." Stella opened her phone and pulled up a map of the area.

Mac manipulated the image and pointed at a patch of green. "It's here."

"Where?" Stella squinted at the display.

"It's called Hidden Lake for a reason."

Stella opened her car door. "Let's change cars and get out there. I want to be back by lunchtime."

In the driveway, they parked her police vehicle, and Stella locked her purse and badge in the trunk. She transferred her AR-15 to the Accord. "Just in case."

"Don't let anyone see that." Mac wasn't planning for Freddie to ever set eyes on her. "It will only cause trouble. There's no shooting your way out of that gang. You'll be ridiculously outgunned, and they have enough ammunition to turn your car into a colander." Tension clamped down on the nape of his neck. "Maybe we should forget this whole plan."

Stella tucked her long hair behind her ear. "I need some evidence to tie Noah Spivak to the murders, or he's going to get bail. I'm not entirely convinced he killed Missy and Dena, but I don't want him on the street."

"All right." He held out a hand. "Why don't you let me drive? I know where we're going."

She handed him the keys, and Mac got behind the wheel. He shifted to grab the seat belt. Something poked him in the leg. He reached under and found one of Stella's hairpins. "Do you shed these things?"

"Sorry. They're always falling out."

She reached for it, but he closed his fist around it. "I'll hold on to it. For good luck." He tucked it into his pocket.

"You're weird."

"No doubt." But the pin reminded him of their night together, and what Stella looked like when she let her hair down.

A half hour later they bounced along a dirt road. Mac hadn't been out to Hidden Lake in years, but he remembered the basic terrain. He stopped the car next to a fire tower, nosing the vehicle behind a patch of shrubs for concealment. Fifty feet ahead, a metal gate blocked the road. An electrified fence prevented him from walking around. "You can wait here. There's a clearing around the bend. I'll walk into camp."

Overhead, the sky teemed with heavy clouds, and the wind whipped with an approaching storm.

Stella scanned the area. Her lips pursed. "I can't see anything, and cell coverage is weak out here. How will I know if you need me?"

"If I'm not back in thirty minutes, call for backup." He kissed her and got out of the vehicle. "It'll be fine. I know Freddie."

But Mac didn't feel as confident as his words sounded as he slipped through the gate and set off down the dirt road. The gate was probably rigged with an alarm that went off in the camp. They would know someone was coming.

Usually being in the woods calmed him. But electricity hummed in the air, and adrenaline buzzed in Mac's veins. He'd left Stella at the fire tower because he wasn't sure how Freddie was going to receive him. The last time they'd connected, Freddie had owed him. But that debt had been paid. Now they were even.

He paused at the edge of the clearing. This early in the morning, most of Freddie's men would be sleeping. Their clients tended to be night people. But Mac had no doubt guards were on duty. His shoulder blades itched. Eyes were on him. No question.

A sturdy cabin and several sheds occupied the clearing. Behind the buildings, the approaching storm whipped the lake's surface into tiny whitecaps. Three mammoth SUVs were lined up in front of the cabin. All looked suspiciously like the one that had followed him.

Mac stepped out of the shadows.

"Stop." A man in cargo pants and a muscle tank looked comfortable with the assault rifle pointed at Mac's chest.

He raised his hands. "I'm not armed. I know Freddie."

The man jerked the barrel toward the cabin. "We'll see about that."

A second man stepped out from behind a huge oak tree. He gave Mac a cursory pat down. Mac knew better than to bring a handgun into the camp, but he'd hidden the Colonel's KA-BAR in his boot. It wasn't as accessible as he'd like, but they'd have to look hard to find it.

A half dozen men emerged from the cabin and sheds to congregate on the pine needle carpet. Freddie's son, Rafe, stood a head taller than the others. Despite the heat, he was dressed in slim, European-cut jeans and a tailored black shirt. His blond hair was tied off his chiseled face.

Mac caught his gaze. Once, Rafe had been his closest friend. "I see you're still dressing like a fancy-pants."

"And I see you still need a new wardrobe." Rafe took two steps and gave Mac a shoulder-slapping hug. Rafe's face went serious. "What brings you here, Mac?"

"I came to ask you a favor."

Looping an arm over Mac's shoulders, Rafe steered him away from the other men. He lowered his voice. "What do you need?"

Mac pointed to his pocket, then slowly withdrew the two pictures. "Do either of these men look familiar?"

Rafe barely looked at Adam Miller's photo. "Never seen him before." He touched Noah Spivak's mug shot with the tip of his finger. "This one is a crazy motherfucker. He's with that white supremacy militia group, WSA."

"WSA?"

"White Survival Alliance. They're preparing for an invasion or some shit."

"Do you know where they are?"

"They spread themselves out over a bunch of locations. Dad probably knows more."

As if on cue, the front door opened, and Freddie stepped out onto the porch. At six feet six, he bore an uncanny resemblance to Hulk Hogan, from his long blond and gray hair to the matching beard. He crossed the distance between them with rapid, anger-driven strides. Stopping in front of Mac, he glared. "What are you doing here?"

"I was just talking to Rafe," Mac said. His body went tense as aggression radiated from the big man.

Freddie's weathered face turned grim. "You shouldn't have come here, Mac."

"That's not the welcome I expected." Sweat broke out at the base of Mac's spine. Something was wrong.

"I don't owe you anything." Freddie leaned over and spat tobacco juice into the dirt.

"What's wrong, Freddie?" Mac cut to the chase.

Freddie drew a knife from the sheath at his waist. "Rumor has it that you're a cop."

"Really?" Mac held his gaze and prayed the river of sweat sliding down his back would be attributed to the heat.

"You were spotted riding along with a woman cop." Freddie's eyes dared him to deny it. "Where is she?"

"I came alone." Mac would die before he led an angry Freddie to Stella.

"What's the deal with the cop?" Freddie asked.

Mac considered a lie, but Freddie's bullshit meter was prime. "Two women were abducted, tortured, and killed. I want to find the bastard who did it."

Freddie tapped the flat side of his knife on his palm. "Wasn't anyone here."

"I didn't think that for a minute." Mac nodded. "But you know what goes on in this town. This killer is using heroin as his murder weapon."

"I don't work with cops. You're awfully cozy with them lately." Freddie's thumb slid along the edge of his blade. "You're right. I do know what goes on in this town."

"Dad, this is Mac." Rafe stepped forward. "He's not a cop."

Mac swallowed, his throat arid.

But Freddie didn't take his gaze off Mac. "Do we look like fucking police informants?" Freddie gestured with the knife. "Why are you really here? Are you setting us up?"

Rafe put a hand on his father's shoulder. "Mac wouldn't do that."

Rafe's faith in him stirred up old feelings. They'd been close. They'd been arrested together, and Lee had gotten them off without charges. Mac had once saved Rafe's life. But Freddie would make no exceptions. None. Sure, Mac had run with Rafe in his youth, but Freddie was a hard man. Anyone who crossed him ended up at the bottom of a lake tied to cinderblocks.

That's how he kept a tight rein on the violent men he led.

"People change, Rafe," Freddie said.

They did indeed.

Did Freddie know that Rabbit was gone? If he didn't, Mac certainly wasn't going to bring up the subject.

"I'm sorry I bothered you." Mac eased backward.

Freddie flipped the knife into a reverse grip. Mac used his peripheral vision to track the other men in the group. He didn't recognize any of them. But working for Freddie warranted hazardous duty pay. Membership turned over frequently.

The knife rose into a pre-strike position in front of Mac's chest.

How long had he been gone?

If he didn't turn up, Stella would go for help. But what did it matter? By the time she returned with backup, Mac would be dead.

There was no way he was going to talk his way out of this. Nor could he possibly fight off a dozen well-trained, heavily armed men. His heart stammered. A few years ago, the prospect of dying wouldn't have bothered him that much, but now everything was different. Grant, Hannah, the kids . . .

Stella.

A red dot appeared in the center of Freddie's chest. He froze. "Looks like you didn't come alone after all."

All eyes tracked the laser scope's trajectory. Something glinted at the top of the fire tower.

Stella?

"You'll be the first man down," Mac said to Freddie. Smart girl. She'd picked out the leader from a hundred yards away.

Freddie lowered his knife and took a step back. The red dot followed him. "I suggest you leave town." Or Freddie's men would find him, and they would kill him. "You have family here. I'd hate for anything to happen to them."

The threat to Mac's family turned fear to fury. This wasn't over. He backed out of the clearing. Thunder cracked, and lightning streaked across the sky as the storm broke. Once he was out of sight, he turned and sprinted for the car. The downpour soaked his clothes in seconds. Stella was climbing down the tower, her rifle slung across her back. She slipped on a wet rung, recovered, and finished her descent. He jumped into the car and started the engine. As soon as she slid into the passenger seat, he sped away as fast as the rutted lane would allow.

"That was quick thinking." He steered the sedan around a deep hole in the road. "I'm impressed." Stella was awesome.

"I added the laser scope after the last shooting, and I told you I wasn't letting you go in there alone." She brushed water from her eyes and pulled out her phone. Her hair was plastered to her head. "No signal."

"You know what?" He couldn't control the crazy grin that spread across his face. "My father would have loved you."

Rain poured onto the windshield as Mac gave her a brief summary of his conversation with Freddie. The tires slid on a patch of mud, and Mac slowed the car.

"What will you do?" Stella asked. "Leave town?" Even though Mac hadn't intended to stay, he certainly wasn't leaving Scarlet Falls with his family on Freddie's radar. Having that knife in his face had given him a crash course in what was important in his life. Grant, Hannah, the kids . . .

Stella.

Freddie's quick turn on Mac had also taught him that the loyalty between them only went one way, and was therefore, null and void. Freddie hadn't been there for Mac as a teen, he'd used him. Whatever bond had existed between Mac and Rafe was just as twisted. After all, Mac owed his time in rehab to Rafe.

"No. I'm not running. I'll have to deal with the gang. I should have done it years ago, but it was easier to go fight drugs in a different country than face a hard decision at home." But no more. Freddie's operation was going down.

He turned onto the paved road. The car rocked in a gust of wind, and the windshield wipers couldn't keep up with the deluge.

Stella turned and peered behind them. "I see headlights."

Real terror streaked up Mac's spine. He couldn't let Freddie and his crew get their hands on Stella. She was a cop, and they'd know it in seconds. He pressed harder on the gas pedal, but off-road, the Honda couldn't outpace one of the gang's monster SUVs, especially not in this storm.

Stella squinted through the windshield. "I don't know how you can see the road."

He could see well enough to know that water was rising under the car.

"The road is flooding. We need to find higher ground." His gaze went to the rearview mirror. "I can't see if that's one of Freddie's SUVs behind us, but I can't take the chance." He glanced at her. "If they catch us, we're dead."

A bridge loomed ahead. On the other side, the road inclined, but water covered the surface. Could they make it? He glanced in the side mirror. The headlights were closer. They had to try. Mac gunned the engine.

The car was halfway across the bridge when the vehicle began to drift sideways.

Chapter Twenty-Eight

"Hold on!" The wheel was loose in Mac's hands. He held his breath. The tires of the Honda gripped the road again, and the car chugged onto the road on the other side. Behind them, water washed over the bridge.

Stella pressed a hand to the center of her chest. "That was close."

"We made it." Mac checked the rearview mirror. The river undulated behind them like a fat greedy snake. "There's no way Freddie's men got across. I think we're safe."

For now.

Mac checked his phone. Still no cell reception. Grant and Hannah had to be warned, and Mac would have to deal with Freddie.

Stella bent forward and put her head between her knees.

"Are you all right?"

"Yes. Sometimes an adrenaline crash makes me throw up. You might need to pull over. Thankfully, I usually wait until after a high stress situation is over to get sick." Stella's voice was tight.

"Better than during," Mac said. "Seriously, you were great. You really saved my butt back there. You can watch my six anytime."

She pressed a hand to her mouth. "Even if I throw up afterward?"

"Breathe through it. You'll be all right." Mac reached over and rubbed her back. She needed a distraction. "I've hurled a time or two. Have I ever told you about my childhood?"

She shook her head. "Not much."

"The Colonel put us through training exercises." Mac slowed the car now that the bridge was behind them. "We learned hand-to-hand, how to handle weapons, and advanced survival training."

Stella's next breath was a slow, audible inhalation through her nose. She blew the air out through her clenched teeth.

He opened the dashboard vents, directed the air toward her face, and continued, "There was this one time when we practiced water rescue drills."

As he told the story, the memory was so clear, he could feel the cold of the water on his skin, the weight of his wet clothes dragging him down . . .

He barely heard his father's speech. Treading water in jeans, boots, and a backpack took all his concentration. When he tried to look up at the Colonel, the spotlight shining off the back of the house caught him in the eyes.

The Colonel's super-light wheelchair rolled past. "Time."

Mac swam for the edge of the pool. Grant hauled him out as easily as if he were a puppy that had fallen in.

"Well done," the Colonel said. "Catch your breath, Mac."

Mac's shoulder muscles quivered under his wet T-shirt as he took his place in line. As the youngest of the Barrett siblings, he was the last to participate in every drill.

The Colonel spun his chair to the edge. Except for the spotlight, the water rippled dark in the September night. The pool was a standard thirty-six-by-eighteen backyard size, built long before the Colonel's injury, when backyard parties were part of summer vacation. Now the pool was used for conditioning and for the Colonel's aquatic physical therapy sessions. In the winter, he used an indoor hydrotherapy.

Mac shivered. Hannah stood next to him, and he could hear her teeth chattering. At the end of the week, the pool would be closed for the winter. The weather had just turned, and though the water remained in the seventies, the air was much cooler.

"Next up, rescue drills. Grant, you're first. Lee, you're timekeeper." Before any of the four kids could blink, the Colonel tossed a stopwatch to Lee then used his jacked arms and shoulders to push himself from the chair over the edge. His body hit the water like a bag of powdered cement. From the waist down, his body was sheer deadweight. Instead of attempting to keep himself afloat, the Colonel hugged his torso, expelled the air from his lungs with a trail of bubbles, and let himself sink.

Grant jumped in the water before their father hit the bottom. Using brute strength, he hauled him up with little difficulty. They broke the surface and gasped for air. Grant towed the Colonel to the side.

"Hannah, you're up," the Colonel said. "Push me back out to the middle, Grant."

No. The Colonel couldn't expect Mac to do this drill. That was insane.

Hannah took her turn. No fear crossed her face, only a little disappointment when her time was seconds slower than Grant's. Lee, whose swimming was significantly better than his wilderness survival skills, managed to beat Hannah, something that didn't happen very often. Lee's arms trembled as he guided the Colonel to the edge.

Mac's entire frame shook; his muscles went slack with exhaustion and terror. His heart flailed in his chest. Grant and Lee were both well over six feet tall. Even Hannah, at fourteen, had reached five-ten. But at twelve, Mac hadn't experienced his promised growth spurt yet. He was short and scrawny, and the Colonel, even after his legs had atrophied, was still a large man. With a full meal in his belly and pockets full of rocks, Mac might be half his father's weight.

How could he possibly pull the Colonel from the water before he drowned? How could he not? Grant moved toward the water, ready to assist.

The Colonel raised a hand. "Stand back. Mac can do this. Lee, out of the water. Get some towels.

Mac swallowed. The cold air vanished as fear heated his body. Clammy sweat broke out under his arms.

"Ready?" Holding his head up with one arm on the side of the pool, complete confidence shone from the Colonel's eyes. "Remember, being smart is just as important as being strong. Stay calm and think. Panic is your worst enemy, especially in the water. Panic will get you killed."

Mesmerized by the piercing blue of his father's eyes, Mac nodded.

The Colonel pushed away from the edge and began to sink.

Mac jumped into the water, the cold not even registering on his skin. He dove to intercept the Colonel before he hit bottom. Water closed over his head and filled his ears, deafening him. He grabbed the back of his father's shirt and pulled, kicking with his feet and paddling with his free hand. But they didn't move. Mac couldn't propel them both toward the surface. His lungs burned. His brain scrambled. His mouth opened, emitting a stream of air and filling with water.

He couldn't do it. They were both going to drown. He was a split second away from letting go and summoning Grant when his father tugged on his arm. His eyes were open and still full of confidence, even though his lungs must have been screaming. Mac's were. The Colonel pointed toward the shallow end of the pool.

And Mac understood. Renewed purpose lent him strength.

He planted his boots on the concrete bottom and walked up the incline, using the muscles of his legs to pull his father behind him. The entire incident took less than ninety seconds, but Mac felt as if he'd aged ten years when their heads broke the surface. The cold air that filled his lungs felt like a thousand needle pricks. Lightheaded, Mac rolled the Colonel onto his back and pulled him toward the steps. Grant and Lee waded into the water and helped lift the Colonel out onto the concrete. They wrapped him in a blanket. Hannah grabbed Mac's hand and guided him up the steps. She wrapped a thick towel around his shoulders and patted him on the back, her best effort at comforting him.

Numb and weak-legged with relief, Mac sank onto the patio. The adrenaline that had fueled the rescue drill left him high and dry. Nausea flooded him. He scrambled for the flowerbed and hurled pool water into the shrubs.

"I knew you could do it," the Colonel said. "There's no shame in puking after you get the job done." The Colonel laughed and reached over to slap him on the shoulder.

"My father was a crazy bastard," Mac said.

He could still picture the Colonel's face, his raw determination, his complete confidence in Mac. As a kid he didn't realize what was happening, how the Colonel had been manipulating his emotions. But now Mac understood how the Colonel had led his troops. His sheer force of will had been contagious, and just as his soldiers had followed his orders in battle without question, his children had followed his lead into insanity.

But he'd taught Mac a few things about determination and faith.

"No kidding," Stella agreed.

"The next day he shoved us into a pool, blindfolded and with our hands bound."

"What?" Stella stared at him. "That's crazy."

"It was OK. We lived. He taught us not to panic."

"Sounds like your father took his water drills seriously."

"The Colonel took everything seriously."

Chapter Twenty-Nine

Two hours later, Stella climbed out of the car in front of her house. Local flooding had forced them to take a long detour. Her still-damp clothes clung to her body. She couldn't wait to shower and change. "We can lock the rifle in the trunk."

"Without cleaning it?" Mac's tone disapproved.

"You're right. I'm sure there's moisture in the barrel."

The storm had passed, and the yard smelled wet and fresh. Still carrying the rifle, Mac followed her up the walk. "Big house."

"After my dad was killed, Mom couldn't wait to get us all out of the city." She led him toward the front door. "She was tired of being crammed in a tiny house with four kids." And her husband's memory.

"I couldn't live in the city," Mac said. "Too many people. Not enough trees. It always feels like it's short on oxygen."

The door wasn't locked. She opened it and walked into the empty kitchen. Stella scanned the family room. Where was everyone? "My mother did everything she could to get us out of the city and away from the police force. She didn't want any more Danes in law enforcement."

"Since you're a cop, I assume that didn't work out for her."

"Not at all. My brother is NYPD SWAT. My sister, Peyton, is a forensic psychiatrist. She's been working in California for the past couple of years. Morgan lives here with her kids. She was an assistant prosecutor in Albany before her husband died in Iraq."

"What does she do now?"

"Not much, if you don't count arts-and-crafts projects with the girls. "The first year after John's death was awful. Morgan quit her job and moved in here with her girls. But lately, the local district attorney has been cozying up to her. He wants her to work for him." Stella hoped Morgan was ready to work or date again, or take up a hobby—anything to get her out of the house.

"Morgan is the one you asked to pick up Gianna?"

"Yes." Knowing she wouldn't get to the dialysis center in time, Stella had called her sister as soon as her phone had picked up service. Gianna would never get into a cop car, so she couldn't send a uniformed officer, but the girl had met Morgan a couple of times when Stella had brought her back to the house for dinner. Gianna would go to the station with Morgan.

"Is that you, Stella?" Grandpa's voice came from the back of the house. "I have the kids outside. They've been cooped up too much with all this rain."

She went onto the deck, motioning Mac to follow. Snoozer's high-pitched, raspy bark sounded from the yard. A deck spanned the rear of the house. Below it, a long expanse of Ireland-green lawn sloped toward the water. A hundred feet away, the current rushed high and swift from the heavy rains. Just on the other side of the deck, Morgan's three girls and Snoozer chased bubbles. A picket fence surrounded the play area, keeping the kids and dog away from the water.

Stella shielded her eyes. The girls ran in circles, oblivious to their arrival.

Grandpa leaned on the railing and gave Mac a careful dose of scrutiny. Grandpa was critical of any male in Stella's presence, but considering she hadn't come home the night before, his attention would be dialed to high.

"Grandpa, this is Mac Barrett." She gestured between them. "Mac, Art Dane."

Mac held out his hand. "Nice to meet you, Mr. Dane."

"Call me Art." Grandpa angled his body to keep the kids and Mac all in his line of sight. He took supervision of Morgan's little girls very seriously. His gaze darted to Stella. His lips pursed with concern. "You're all right?"

"Fine. Just wet," Stella said. "I'm going inside to shower and change."

"Give me your handgun. I'll clean it and your rifle while you shower." Mac held out his hand, and Stella handed him her weapon.

"I'll make sure he does it right." Grandpa crossed his arms over his chest.

She smiled at him. "Be nice. No interrogating."

Grandpa smiled back, but she could see his teeth as he turned to Mac. "What is Mac short for?"

"I'll be right back. I promise." Stella hurried to her room. Grandpa looked sweet and innocent, but she knew better. Once a cop, always a cop. The same went for being a grandfather.

She stripped down and showered. Twisting a towel around her hair, she stepped into a clean pair of black slacks and a white button-down. She glanced in the full-length mirror on the back of her closet door. Maybe she should pick a different colored blouse. She looked like a waiter or a *Men in Black* extra.

Who cares? This was work, not a date. She didn't have to impress him.

But she wanted to.

Gah.

This was why she didn't date much. There was too much effort required when involved with a member of the opposite sex, energy she could funnel more productively into her career, which balanced on a precarious brink. Had she let her emotions rule this case? God knew she didn't have much control where Mac was concerned. Maybe her impulsiveness had spilled over.

A vision of Dena Miller's body flashed into her head. Then Missy's. Her duty was to them, not Horner.

"So who's the hottie out back with Grandpa?" Morgan stood in the hall. A red power suit hugged her tall frame. Totally put together, from her nude pumps to her pearl necklace, her older sister always made Stella feel like the tomboy she'd been in grammar school. While Morgan had jumped rope and practiced her cheers, Stella had played kickball in the street.

"Mac Barrett. I'm sort of working with him." Stella shook her hair out. "Did you get Gianna to the station?"

"No. She wasn't at the dialysis center when I got there." Morgan leaned on the doorframe.

Alarmed, Stella froze. "She's always there."

"I was there early and I waited outside until fifteen minutes after you said she'd be done. I went inside. The waiting area was empty, and the nurse behind the counter refused to talk to me."

"Damn it." Stella moved faster now, maneuvering around Morgan and speeding to the bathroom. She coiled her damp hair in front of the mirror. "She was hesitant last night when I asked her. I should have known she'd be skittish."

"You could hardly plan for a flood. Let me do that." Morgan took over the bun-making. They were polar opposites. Morgan, with her refined silks and polished locks, had always known how to wear a scarf and which earrings complemented each outfit, while Stella was far happier in jeans.

"I'll swing by her apartment on my way to the station." Stella reached for her toothbrush.

Morgan did some twisty thing and pinned it into place.

"What did you do?"

"Nothing fancy. A simple chignon." Morgan tucked a lock into place. "It's no harder than that same old bun you wear every day."

"I'm a detective, not a cover model. No one, including me, cares how my hair looks, only that it's neat and out of my way."

Morgan's exhale was filled with disgust. "But honey, that man is really hot."

"I've been working with him for days. He knows what I look like." After last night, he knew every inch of her.

Morgan sighed. "You're hopeless."

"You're bossy." Stella echoed their childhood.

"I'm the older sister. I'm supposed to be bossy." Morgan flashed a quick grin.

Since her husband died, Morgan's smiles were rare.

"How was the job interview?" Stella waited for an answer. Swigging some mouthwash, Stella studied her sister in the mirror.

"This is Saturday. It wasn't an interview. It was lunch." Morgan shrugged.

Stella spit in the sink. "With a guy who wants to hire you. You're not exactly dressed for running errands."

"It was a nice restaurant." Morgan said, but her voice lacked conviction. "And I'm not even sure I want the job. He kept talking about his win of the Simmons case."

"The news anchor who killed a family of six while he was under the influence?" Stella remembered the case. Simmons had been a local celebrity. The accident had closed down the highway that led into Scarlet Falls for half a day. She'd been off duty, but two of the responding officers had taken several weeks off afterward. Four small children had been in the car. Simmons had battled addiction for years.

"I guess he finally lost the fight." Morgan sighed, moving from behind Stella to stand next to her. "I don't know if I can handle cases like that anymore, Stella. That's why I left the DA's office in Albany."

"Putting Simmons away might prevent more senseless deaths." Stella rubbed her sister's shoulder.

"But it won't bring that family back to life." Grief filled Morgan's eyes.

"No it won't." Stella caught her sister's eye in the mirror, hating the doubt and sadness she saw there. "Addicts don't just hurt themselves."

Morgan's smile was sad but she swallowed. "Now that I've played Debbie Downer, let's go see your hottie."

Stella stopped in her bedroom and put on a thin blazer to conceal her weapon.

Morgan lifted the hem. "Your gun is wearing a hole in the fabric. My seamstress can reinforce the inside panel of your blazers so that won't happen."

Leave it to Morgan to think of her clothing.

They walked down the hall to the family room. They could see Mac and Grandpa cleaning guns on the patio table.

"Holy hell. He looks even better up close." Morgan sucked in a breath and leaned close to Stella. "I assume that is what kept you out all night."

"Yes."

"What's your relationship with the hunk?"

"I don't know," Stella said.

"Well if you don't want him . . ." Despite her teasing, the interest in Morgan's eyes was mild. She wasn't even ready for a job yet, let alone a man.

"Dibs." Stella played along. Her sister wasn't anywhere near ready to date, but humor was a big step forward. When she'd first moved back home, she'd spent too many nights sitting on the deck alone in the dark, crying.

"That's what I thought." Morgan steered Stella out onto the deck. Then her sister went down the steps to the yard to hug her girls.

At the table, Mac was reassembling her AR-15 with practiced movements.

"You should see how fast he fieldstrips a weapon." Grandpa tossed the gun oil into the cleaning kit. "Where did you learn how to do that?"

Mac wiped the exterior of the gun with a clean rag. "My father was an army colonel. Other families had family game night. We field-stripped weapons." He handed her the rifle. "Ready?"

"Yes, thank you." Stella took it. "Do you want me to clean your wound? Your shirt was soaked."

"It's fine," Mac said. "What does the rest of your day look like?"

"I need to stop at Gianna's on the way to the station." Stella picked up her clean Glock from the table and put it in her holster. "I have to call the ME." She took out her phone and called. Frank wasn't available. Instead of leaving a message, Stella chose to be connected with his secretary, who told her that Dena's autopsy was finished. She ended the call. "I have to go to the medical examiner's office."

"Do you want me to find Gianna?" Mac offered.

"Would you?"

"Sure."

"Do you want to borrow my car?" Stella asked.

"No. I don't want it recognized. I can take my bike."

"What if it rains again?"

"I'll survive." Mac was definitely a survivor.

"He can borrow my car." Grandpa offered Mac a set of keys. "You might not mind a motorcycle in the rain, but that sick girl would."

Mac took the keys. "Thank you."

Morgan came back up the steps. "Stella, is this yours?"

Stella's gaze dropped to her sister's hands. The pale blue scarf sent fear rippling cold across her skin. "Where did you get that?"

He knew where she lived. He'd been to her home.

Near her family.

Morgan held it out. "The girls found it outside tied to a tree."

"What's wrong?" Grandpa stepped forward, his eyes sharpening.

Stella lowered her voice. "We've held back this fact from the media, but both dead women wore pale blue scarves."

"No." Morgan's gaze darted between the scarf and her girls.

"I'm getting my gun," Grandpa said.

Panic bloomed hot in Stella's chest as she took the scarf and held it by the corner. She reached for her phone to call the chief and Brody. "It looks like you're going to get that surveillance camera."

———

Fighting the urge to stay and protect her family, Stella drove to the ME's office. She'd left forensics at her house, but they wouldn't be there long. The scarf had been left outside so it was unlikely that fingerprints, tracks, or trace evidence had survived the storm. The chief had sent a patrol car to sit in the driveway. Still, Stella didn't want to leave, but she knew the only way to neutralize the threat was to find the killer.

She wavered between terror and fury. How dare this creep violate her home, threaten her family. She wasn't going to rest until she'd stopped him.

She went inside the ME's office. At the secretary's direction, she headed for the locker room. She checked her phone for messages even though she knew it was too soon for Mac to have found Gianna. Shoving her purse into a locker, she donned a protective gown, booties, and face shield and pushed through the doors into the autopsy suite.

Dena Miller was on the table, her nude body icy white against the stainless steel. Large ugly stitches across her torso said Frank had been busy.

He motioned Stella to the lightboard and pointed at rows of X-rays. "This is the victim's right hand. As you saw at the scene, all of her fingers were broken. With the damage to the skin and the way the bone is impacted, I suspect he used a hammer."

Stella felt sick.

The next X-ray showed Dena's skull and neck. "I found the vertebrae fracture her husband told you about." He waved at the board, where images of Dena's bones were displayed. "I found four more recently broken and healed bones: one wrist, an elbow, and several ribs. The Scarlet Falls hospital only has records showing Dena's neck injury, so I had my assistant check with the three other hospitals in the area. Dena had records at all of them. Each emergency room treated her once. Each time she claimed to have fallen down the stairs."

"Classic abuse history."

"Repeat visits to the same ER would spark suspicion," Frank agreed. "She was careful not to use hospitals in the same network to avoid the possibility of digital records automatically cross-referencing."

Poor Dena.

Stella put aside her anger and sadness. Justice was all she could offer Dena now. "What else did you find?"

"She'd been recently washed and her fingernails were clipped." Frank tossed the file back on his desk. "There was no sign of sexual assault. Tox screens are being rushed. The lab has promised to get Missy Green's done by Monday morning as well."

Stella left the medical examiner and hurried across the lot to the forensics lab. She still didn't have enough to convince anyone that Adam Miller was a killer. The fact that his wife had multiple broken bones didn't *prove* he murdered her.

Darcy Stevens, the county latent fingerprint analyst, leaned over her desk. Her coffee-colored skin looked too smooth for her to be a grandmother.

"How's your grandson?" Stella picked up a framed snapshot of a two-toothed baby.

"Perfect." Darcy smiled, then sobered. "I have something for you."

"Is it going to make me happy?"

"I think so," Darcy said in her rich, deep voice.

Stella dropped into a chair facing her desk.

"I found several sets of fingerprints on the envelope of cash you found in Missy Green's apartment." Darcy opened a file on her computer. She pointed to the envelope, encased in a protective plastic sleeve. "Missy Green's matched right away. That was easy. But then I had an idea, and I pulled Dena Miller's prints. Perfect match."

"You matched prints from Dena Miller *and* Missy Green?"

"I did."

"You are a genius."

Darcy rubbed her fingernails on her black suit jacket. "I know."

Dena was keeping cash at Missy's house.

"Do you know if Vinnie's in?" Stella asked.

"He was. I saw him at the coffeepot an hour ago." Crime didn't adhere to a weekday schedule, and Saturday was often a time for playing catch-up.

Stella's steps were quick as she went down the hall to Vinnie's office. The swarthy forensic tech looked like a *Godfather* extra.

Vinnie was holding a paper evidence envelope. "You're just in time. The tech just came back from your house."

"Did he find anything besides the scarf?"

"Nothing interesting. The rain destroyed the scene." With gloved hands Vinnie opened the envelope and looked inside. "This scarf looks like the ones found on the dead girls."

"What do you know about them?"

"Polyester. The tags were removed."

"Not Hermes?" Something high end would be easier to trace.

"No. Sorry. These are fairly generic." Vinnie set the envelope on the desk. "I don't like that he left this at your house."

"That makes all of us," Stella said. "What about Dena Miller's crime scene?"

"Opposite problem. The scope of the scene gave us a lot of evidence to sort through. My team barely got the evidence bagged, tagged, and locked up yesterday. I called in two techs to work overtime, but it's still going to take a while."

"Thanks, Vinnie."

Spivak was in jail, but Stella had no idea when the scarf had been tied to the tree, so that didn't eliminate him. The tree wasn't visible from the driveway, mailbox, or front windows. It could have been there for a few days. Could everyone else be right and Spivak be the killer? It felt too easy, and Frank's suspicion that Dena Miller was a victim of domestic abuse made Stella doubt Adam Miller's alibi further. She knew he was violent—and lying.

Chapter Thirty

Mac parked Art's silver Lincoln Town Car in front of Gianna's apartment, then he banged on her door. No one answered. The windows were dark. He cupped his hands over his eyes and peered into the kitchen. No Gianna. Mac knocked on the doors to the left and right of Gianna's. Silence was his answer.

Where was she?

Except for the apartment complex, the neighborhood was mostly businesses. No nosy old women sitting on porches or watchful young mothers pushing strollers.

Mac leaned close to the lock. Tiny scratches marred the brass, but the lock was old. Hard to say which scratches were new.

A neighbor came out of the apartment next door. A brittle blond, she was probably in her forties but a deep tan had aged her skin twenty years. She sucked deeply on a cigarette, giving Mac a serious once over. Her eyes lit with appreciation. "Never mind. You can bang on anything you like."

Mac grinned wide and stepped out into the light. If a little charm got him answers, he saw no harm in trying. "I'm looking for Gianna. Have you seen her?"

She shook her head. "Not since yesterday."

"You wouldn't by any chance have a key to her apartment?" he asked.

"No, sorry." She stepped back into her own unit. "This isn't that kind of neighborhood."

The door closed before he could ask any other questions.

Mac sized up the entry. He didn't want to pick the lock in case the police needed to dust it for prints. He went to the kitchen window. Pulling out his knife, he popped the window lock and slid open the sash.

The apartment complex clearly didn't spend much on security.

He sheathed his knife and hoisted himself through the window. He swung his legs around and slid off the tiny kitchen counter next to the sink.

The apartment looked much the same as when they'd visited on Thursday. One glance verified that the kitchen and adjoining living area were empty. He headed for the short hall that led to the bedroom and bath.

He stopped in the middle of the corridor. A ceramic lamp lay in broken pieces on the carpet, and a framed poster had been knocked from the wall. Under the fractured glass, script over a photo of a mountain read: *Dream. Believe. Hope.* Mac's gaze tracked to six spots of red that dotted the beige carpet. Blood.

No.

Being careful not to step on any evidence, he quickly checked the bedroom and bath. Empty. There were no signs of a disturbance anywhere else in the apartment. Standing in the hallway, he imagined a man watching Gianna through the kitchen window, then picking the lock while she was in the bedroom. Whoever had taken her had waited in the hall for her to emerge from the bedroom, then overpowered her. It wouldn't have been hard. The girl was sick and weak.

And in the hands of a killer.

He opened his phone and called Stella to give her the bad news.

"Oh no." She quickly masked the distress in her voice. "I'll send a forensic team to her apartment. Maybe they'll turn up some prints."

But they both knew they wouldn't find any.

"The kitchen window was locked when I got here," Mac said. "I'm going to the dialysis center to see if I can sweet talk any information out of them."

"I'll trace Gianna's phone, and we'll put out an alert on her," Stella said.

But who would see the girl if she was being held by a madman?

Mac picked up a picture of Stella and Gianna from the table. "I'm stealing that photo of you and her to show around."

"Good idea. Would you bring it to the station?" Her voice caught. "I remember that day. I brought Gianna back to the house for a barbecue for her birthday. She loved hanging out with my family. Why didn't I do that more often?"

Mac tucked the photo into his pocket. "We'll find her."

"We'd better. If she didn't make it to dialysis today, she's going to get sick fast. He won't have to kill her. Without treatment, she's just days from death."

"I'll start looking for her in the neighborhood." He ended the call, left the apartment, and drove the few blocks to the dialysis center.

He walked into the dialysis center and flashed a wide smile at the woman in her fifties wearing maroon scrubs behind the reception desk. "I'm looking for Gianna Leone."

She gave him a tired stare. "Privacy regulations prevent me from giving you any information."

Mac sobered. "Gianna is missing. I need to know if she showed up for dialysis today, and if she didn't, then how quickly she's going to deteriorate."

"Hold on." The woman disappeared for a few seconds. When she returned, she showed him to a private office.

A tall woman in gray slacks and a white blouse rose behind the desk. "You said Gianna is missing?"

"Yes. Did she show up for dialysis today or not?" Mac couldn't get the images of dead bodies out of his head. He couldn't let that happen to Gianna. He had to find her. "I don't want to look at her medical files, I just need to know how long she's been gone and how much time we have to find her."

"I could lose my job for this, but I'm worried about her, too." The woman sighed. "She didn't come today. We called her, but she didn't answer her phone."

The anxiety in Mac's belly flip-flopped. "How much time does she have?"

"Some of our patients have partial kidney function, but not Gianna. She has practically no kidney function at all. Her last treatment was Thursday. Without dialysis to filter the toxins and fluid from her body, she won't last long."

Chapter Thirty-One

At the station, Stella slipped into the conference room. On the other side of the table, Lance stood, studying the crime scene photos, notes, and pictures of evidence that were tacked to their murder board. Stella's case notes were spread out on the table. Pinned to the left side of the board were pictures of Dena and Missy before and after death. On the opposite side, photos of Adam Miller and Noah Spivak stared back at Stella.

"I've heard you've been busy." Lance turned and regarded her with serious eyes. "Are you all right?"

"Yes." Stella sank into a chair, fear for Gianna a cold, queasy lump in her belly. Where was she? Stella's trace on her phone had turned up nothing. Her phone was either off or the battery was dead.

"Is your house secure?"

"There's a unit there, and Grandpa and Morgan are both armed." Her sister might be depressed, but she was a soldier's wife, a cop's daughter, and a very protective mother.

"Let me know if you want me to spend the night there for a while." Lance said. "I live alone. It's not like anyone will miss me."

Stella smiled. "Thanks."

The conference room door opened and Chief Horner strode in. He picked up a remote control, turned on the TV that sat on a side table, and tuned to a local news station. On the screen, Adam Miller sat in a newsroom. "Detective Dane focused her investigation into my wife's disappearance on me, while my wife was being murdered."

The picture shifted to the interviewer. "Two women have been found dead this week in Scarlet Falls. Is a serial killer stalking women in the New York suburbs?"

Stella winced.

"I read your report." Chief Horner pointed the remote control again, muting the TV. "You should have come to me or Brody instead of letting this investigation get out of hand. What the hell were you doing meeting with a drug dealer this morning?"

"I didn't meet with him. I was purely there for backup. Mac has connections—"

"I don't want to hear another word about Mac Barrett." Horner pointed a rigid finger at her. "You've been spending too much time with him. The Barretts' rogue tendencies are rubbing off on you."

Angry thoughts popped into Stella's head like cartoon captions. She bit the inside of her mouth to keep them from slipping out, but worry about Gianna and her family taxed her control. Mouthing off to Horner would get her suspended. All she'd wanted was to be a detective. She wasn't a political person. She didn't want to deal with Horner or the media. She wanted to solve two murders and find Gianna.

Horner dropped his hand and paced between the table and the wall. "Do you know how this looks? You're the only female in the department. It's going to appear as if I promoted you because you're female even though you're incompetent. You've devoted half of this investigation to investigating Miller when he has an alibi."

Stella kept her voice level. She would not let him get to her. "Sir, we have two dead women who knew each other, and now another girl is missing. Adam's alibi is weak; his associate refuses to give a specific time he left the club."

"He was being honest. He didn't know the exact time." Horner huffed, then shook his head. "Wait. What do you mean another girl is missing?"

"Gianna Leone. Another member of the same Narcotics Anonymous group that Missy and Dena belonged to." Stella's spine snapped straight. "She was supposed to come in this morning and sign a statement that she saw Adam Miller outside the church the night Missy disappeared. Adam Miller hasn't been straight with us since the very beginning of this investigation."

"Why would Adam report his wife missing and call us to find her if he killed her?" Horner paced the room.

"The ME suspects Dena was a victim of domestic abuse." Stella filled him in on the ME's findings.

Horner shook his head. "There's no way to prove that Adam inflicted that damage on his wife. I still like Noah Spivak for the murders. He was hanging out at the church, and he has priors. Adam Miller's record is clean."

"But Gianna saw Adam outside the church the night Missy disappeared," Stella insisted.

Horner's face reddened. "The word of a junkie doesn't mean much. You and Lance saw Spivak outside a meeting. That's a better link."

"Gianna Leone is a *former* addict," Stella said.

"She was a drug addict and prostitute. A jury wouldn't take her word over Adam Miller's." Horner didn't care, but Stella knew he was right. No one would believe Gianna.

"I want to bring Adam Miller in for questioning."

"No." Horner straightened his tie.

"But I have another member of his wife's Narcotics Anonymous group who says she saw him hanging around outside the meetings, and two additional people claimed he constantly checked up on his wife. I think he was stalking her."

"Why would he have to stalk his own wife? They lived together."

"Because he was controlling," Stella reasoned. "He checked her phone. Called her dozens of times a day. He made her submit to home urine tests for drug use, and it's likely he beat her as well. He didn't like her to have friends. Maybe he saw her with Gianna and Missy and got jealous."

"Adam Miller's attorney isn't going to let him be dragged in here repeatedly." Horner jabbed a finger in the air at Stella. "You have no actual evidence he did anything to his wife. I want you to focus on building a case against Spivak. We need a search warrant for his vehicle and parents' house. That is your job today. We have a few hundred tips that came in on the hotline. Maybe one of Spivak's low-life friends will turn on him for the cash."

"But if Gianna was kidnapped this morning, Spivak couldn't have done it. He's in custody," Stella said. "And Dena wasn't killed until six p.m. at the earliest on Thursday. Spivak was in custody a little after nine. That leaves six to nine p.m. as the window of time for him to have placed her body in the park. It wouldn't have been dark yet."

"It's still possible. Kidnapping her in broad daylight was bold, too." Horner's phone rang. He answered it, his face darkening as he listened. Hanging up, he stood. "Spivak is out on bail."

"What?"

"Apparently the judge granted him bail late yesterday. A high-powered attorney showed up and convinced the judge we didn't have enough to deny bail. He's filing a counter suit for excessive force, claiming he was pursued for no reason and had his face slammed into a brick wall."

Stella winced. *That* actually did happen.

"Excessive force won't be tolerated," Horner said. "We're lucky no one recorded the incident for YouTube."

"This morning Mac and I learned that Spivak is a member of the White Survival Alliance. Let's see if we can find other members. He might be hiding with them." Stella's phone buzzed. She glanced at the display. "It's Mrs. Green. I have to take this." Grateful for the moment to regroup, she stepped out of the conference room and answered the call.

"Stella?"

"Yes, ma'am." Stella put her finger in her other ear to block out the hum of voices. She ducked into an empty interview room and closed the door. "What can I do for you?"

"This is going to sound silly, and I hate to bother you . . ."

"You're not bothering me."

"I went to the medical examiner's office today." Mrs. Green's breath hitched then steadied. "I signed papers to have Missy picked up by a funeral home, and I picked up her things."

Sorrow enveloped Stella. *That poor woman.* No one should have to bury her child. "I'm sorry you had to do that. I would have gone with you."

"My sister is here. She took me." Mrs. Green sniffed. "But they didn't have Missy's patron saint medal. She never took it off. I gave it to her the day she came out of rehab. St. Maximilian Kolbe is the patron saint of drug addicts. I was wondering if you had it."

Stella froze, remembering the pendant in Spivak's pocket. "Can you describe it?"

"I have a picture of Missy wearing it on my phone. I'll text it to you."

"I'll check the evidence log." Stella ended the call. She opened the message when it came in. In the photo, Missy was sitting in a restaurant wearing a smile that didn't quite reach her eyes, as if she pasted it on to make her mother happy. An oval pendant rested in the V of her white blouse. Stella enlarged the picture with her fingertips. It looked like the same medal they'd found in Spivak's pocket.

She hurried back to the conference room and leafed through her reports.

"What is it?" Horner asked.

She pulled out her copy of Spivak's arrest report and skimmed the list of personal effects: One patron saint medallion of St. Maximilian Kolbe. "Mrs. Green says Missy had one of these and it's missing."

"I knew it." With a satisfied smirk, Horner folded his arms. "Spivak is our man. Get a warrant and search his room. Talk to his parents. Find a friend who will squeal on him. And find Spivak! I've assigned two uniforms to the investigation. Get one of them to research this White Survival Alliance."

Horner turned to Lance. "Put out an alert. I want him back in custody before dark. Also, get a warrant to impound his vehicle and have the forensic team fine-tooth it. This guy is a registered sex offender. They always have high recidivism rates." Horner's eyes sparked with near glee. "All focus is on Spivak. Are my instructions clear?" He focused on Stella.

"Yes, sir," she said. "What about the missing girl?"

"If we find Spivak, we'll likely find her." Horner blinked. "But let's get a picture of her distributed to all local law enforcement."

Brody walked into the room. Horner brought him up to speed.

"You're not going to like what I found." Brody leaned both palms on the table. "The business associate who alibied Adam Miller is his old fraternity friend. And while they were active members, someone at a frat party slipped a girl Rohypnol and she died."

"Were any charges filed?" Horner asked.

Brody shook his head. "No. I checked with the police who handled the case. There was no evidence against any of the fraternity brothers. The boys stuck together."

Horner clasped his hands behind his back and turned to Stella. "Then we proceed on the plan to get Noah Spivak back into custody before he kills your witness."

"I have one more thing for you to consider." Brody tossed a paper onto the table. "Remember Dena's physical therapist, Lyle Jones? His ex-wife just filed for a restraining order. He's been following her for weeks. Last night he showed up outside a restaurant as she was leaving with a date and busted her windshield with a baseball bat."

Stella shuffled through the papers in his file and pulled up Lyle's arrest report. "He had those two assault charges in Jersey, too. But assault and torture are two different things. Lyle's problems are more likely attributed to 'roid rage."

"Do we have anything to tie him to Missy Green?" Horner asked.

Brody shook his head. "No."

"Then we go after Spivak." Horner enunciated each word. "We can't expect help from the county or state. Major flooding throughout the county has caused road and bridge closures."

A uniform popped his head into the room. "Detective Dane, there's a Mac Barrett here to see you."

Stella went to the reception area. Mac held Gianna's picture. The desire to walk into his arms and let him hold her nearly overwhelmed her. She held back. The two feet of space between them felt like twenty. "Thank you. I'll be right back."

She made a stack of copies and brought a few back to him.

Mac put the photos in his pocket. "I'm going to knock on doors in her neighborhood. Someone saw something. I just have to get them to talk."

"I'd love to send an officer to do that," Stella said. "But we don't have enough uniformed bodies."

"I think I have a better chance of getting information. Uniforms aren't welcome in that area."

"Probably." Worry rose into her throat like a bobber on a pond. "Be careful. That's not the best neighborhood."

"I've seen worse," he said. His hand curled at his side, the fist bumping his thigh. "We'll find her. She'll be all right."

Stella didn't respond. No one could make that claim. "I have to go. We have a couple of leads."

"*You* be careful." He lowered his voice, his gaze turning fierce. "Please."

"I'm with Brody today." But she wished she could be with Mac. The possession that rolled off his body was both intimidating and reassuring. No lover had ever made her feel as if he'd lay down his life for her in a heartbeat.

But he would. She knew that without a doubt. She was more worried that *he'd* take chances. He seemed to view himself as more dispensable than other people.

"It's you I'm worried about," she said. "You'll be alone."

"No need. I'm durable." With a quick glance to make sure no one was in sight, he gave her a quick kiss. "I'll call you." Mac turned and left.

Stella returned to the conference room.

Lance was on his way out. "Come with me. We have a woman filing a missing persons report for her teenage daughter. The missing girl's name is Janelle Hall."

He led the way to an interview room. The woman was slumped at the table and didn't look old enough to have a teenager. As they walked in, she jumped to her feet. Sniffing, she wiped bloodshot eyes and shook her red bob out of her face. "Do you know where she is?"

"Mrs. Hall?" Stella held out her hand. "I'm Detective Dane. How can I help?"

"I'm not married. You can call me Tonya," the woman said. "My daughter is missing. She's seventeen. She's run off before, but she always comes back."

Stella steered her back to a chair. "Has she ever been in trouble?"

Tonya sniffed. "Yeah. She got picked up for smoking pot in school before she dropped out. The judge let her off with some community service."

A drug user. *Strike one.*

"What does Janelle look like?"

Tonya fished a photo out of her purse and handed it to Stella. Janelle was a slim girl with dark hair that fell to her shoulders.

Both Dena and Missy had dark hair. *Strike two.*

"When was the last time you saw her?" Stella asked.

"We had a fight Friday night. She walked out. I haven't seen her since." She patted her pockets as if looking for a pack of cigarettes. "She always comes back in the morning."

Friday night. *Strike three.*

Stella softened her voice. "What did you fight about?"

"She's dating another loser," Tonya sniffed. "I don't want her to end up like me. I had her at fifteen."

"We're going to take all your personal information and get copies of this picture out to our officers on patrol. We'll need names and numbers of Janelle's friends, places she likes to hang out, that sort of thing." Stella rose. "I'll get you some paper."

Nodding, Tonya wiped her red nose on her sleeve.

Stella and Lance retreated to the hallway. Stella paced the length of the corridor and back. "Hopefully this kid hasn't returned because she's angry, but Janelle went missing the night after we found Dena."

"You know how many people go missing," Lance said. "Chances are, this kid's case isn't related. She's probably pissed at her mother."

"You're right." But Stella hated to think of another young girl out on the street while a predator hunted.

"Same thing with your informant. Are you sure Gianna is missing?" Lance asked. "Maybe she knocked over a lamp by accident. Maybe she's avoiding you."

Stella chewed on her lip "But not showing up for dialysis would be suicide."

"You've said before that the kid has it rough."

Stella didn't doubt that Gianna was depressed. Her life was out of her control and full of physical misery. As much as she hated to admit it, she couldn't rule out the possibility that Gianna was suicidal. They didn't even know for certain that the killer had taken another woman.

"I have to catch up with Brody."

Lance nodded. "I'll get the paperwork started with Ms. Hall."

"Thanks," Stella headed for her cubicle where her blazer lay draped over the back of her chair. A yellow clasp envelope sat in her inbox. Her name and the station's address were printed on the front.

She knew it was from him. Donning gloves, she used a letter opener to slit the top.

A sheet of paper slid out. A single sentence was typed in the center of the eight by ten white sheet.

I HAVE NUMBER 3.

Chapter Thirty-Two

"What is the purpose of the notes?" Stella climbed the Spivaks' front stoop.

Next to her, Brody scanned the street. "He's taunting you like he did in the interview."

She pictured Spivak's smug leer and shivered.

"God, I hope they know where to find him." Stella rang the doorbell. Another girl's life depended on it. But did he have Gianna or Janelle?

"Even if they do, they might not be willing to share." Brody said. "We're trying to put their son in prison."

The senior Mr. Spivak was a tall and tidy man. He wore his plaid, short-sleeved shirt tucked in, and a sharp crease bisected the exact center of his jeans. The shriveled woman who stood next to him was colorless, gray from her hair to her eyes to her washed-out housedress.

Stella and Brody showed their badges.

"We already said we're not talking to the police." Mrs. Spivak clenched her fingers in front of her sternum. The only parts of her body that moved were her fingers, which worked in a nervous repetition from church to steeple and back again. "Noah's a grown man. He's not our responsibility anymore. You can't hold us accountable for his doings."

"No one is holding you responsible, ma'am." Stella peered around their bodies but saw no one behind them. "We just want to ask you a few questions. Are you aware that we're looking for Noah?"

Mrs. Spivak's frown sank into the folds of her neck. "I thought you had him in custody?"

"We did," Stella said. "Someone bailed him out."

Mrs. Spivak's open palm pressed just below the hollow of her throat. "Wasn't us. He belongs in jail. We kicked him out because he threatened to kill us when we wouldn't give him money to support his cause. We don't have much. We barely get by, but Noah is obsessed."

"Does Noah have any other friends who would have bail money?" Stella asked.

Mr. Spivak folded his arms across his chest and ground his molars. "All his friends are crazy bastards with shaved heads and Nazi tattoos."

"It would help if you could give us a list," Brody added. "The sooner we get him off the street, the safer you'll be."

"I guess you're right. We're just afraid he'll come after us if we turn him in, but I guess he's probably going to come after us anyway." Mrs. Spivak moved back, clearing the threshold. "Come in."

Her husband ushered them into a paneled living room. The decor was stark. No family pictures adorned the walls. No knickknacks cluttered the surfaces. No shoes lined up at the door. Decades of regimented cleaning had scrubbed the house of all signs of life.

Mr. Spivak took a piece of paper from a desk drawer and started writing.

"Did your son leave anything behind in his room?" Stella asked the missus.

"Not really, but you're welcome to have a look." Mr. Spivak handed her a list of six names. Three only had first names. "The first few he went to high school with. The others he picked up since. They're all just as crazy as he is."

"Thank you. We have a search warrant for his room. Did you want to see it?" Brody reached for the folded paper in his suit jacket.

Mr. Spivak waved the offer away. "No need. If there's any evidence in his room, you're welcome to it. I'm sorry to say we'd feel safer if Noah was behind bars."

Stella and Brody went down the hall and took a quick turn around Noah's room. The twin bed, dresser, and desk in heavy grained oak were likely the same he used in childhood. A braided rug occupied the center of the oak floor.

Stella put on gloves and checked the drawers. All empty. Then she pulled each one out and inspected the outside and bottom. Nothing. "He cleaned this place out pretty well."

Brody opened the closet door and took down a box of trophies. "Everything he left behind is from his childhood. Nothing current."

"He wasn't always a bad kid, but he always took up with the wrong sort." Mr. Spivak hunched in the doorway. His gaze settled on the box, his frown turning bittersweet. "He was a smart kid in high school. Went away to college on a scholarship. Then he hooked up with these skinhead types. Nothing but trouble since."

"Is there anything else you can tell us?" Brody returned the box to the closet.

"No." Mr. Spivak exhaled, and his body deflated. "I know we seem harsh, but we're at our wits' end. Noah is out of control. The best thing for everyone is if he gets put away where he can't hurt anyone."

Stella scanned the room one last time but saw nothing left to search.

"I think we're done here," she said. "Thank you for your coopera-tion, Mr. Spivak."

He walked them to the door and let them out. "I hope you find him before he hurts someone."

"So do we." Stella followed Brody out to the car. Her stomach churned. "How many hotline tips do we have?"

"There were eighty-seven calls to the hotline, but most were useless." Brody pulled out a sheet of paper. "We have six."

"Six?" Stella climbed into the car, numb. "This will take all afternoon. He killed Dena within the first day. We don't even know how long he's had the new girl or whether it's Gianna or Janelle or someone else. All we know is that he has a girl and she doesn't have long to live."

Brody and Stella spent a fruitless afternoon hoping for a break, but as the afternoon stretched into evening and the whereabouts of Gianna and Janelle remained a mystery, Stella's patience frayed.

"Brody, what if we don't find them?" Stella's voice cracked.

"We can't think like that. We just have to keep going. What's the next address?" Brody slowed the car while Stella read the list under the dome light.

"Forty-two Sycamore Street."

The two drove in silence until Brody turned onto Sycamore.

She focused on a passing mailbox. "There's thirty-six."

Brody eased off the gas as they passed three more houses in the encroaching gloom. The lots and houses were large in this section of Scarlet Falls.

Stella searched for house numbers in the dimness. "Here it is." She pointed to a yellow Victorian across the street from a pharmacy. "Big houses like this must cost a fortune to maintain."

Brody owned an old beauty near the center of town. "They do, which is why so many of them get broken down into smaller units like this one."

He parked at the curb. Originally a large house, the home had been divided into four smaller apartments. White gingerbread trim cried for repairs and a fresh coat of paint. Overgrown shrubs brushed the faded asbestos siding. From the street, the backyard looked like a rhododendron jungle.

"Your house is gorgeous," Stella said. This one was decidedly not. She tugged her blazer over her handgun and stared at the building.

Brody got out of the driver's seat. "Is this the right address?"

"Yes." She checked her list. "We're looking for Jim Crawley in apartment four."

"What does Mr. Crawley claim to know?" Brody straightened his tie. He'd loosened the knot in the car.

"He claims to have seen a woman taken from the church parking lot last Thursday night. Says she appeared to be incapacitated. He thought her male companion was helping her, but now he thinks maybe he got that wrong."

"So he might have seen Missy's abduction?" Brody asked.

"Right." Stella pulled a piece of hair off her sweaty neck and tucked it into her bun. "Let's see what he has to say."

A porch covered the entire front facade of the house. Two doors, marked *One* and *Two* in black script letters, stood side-by-side in the center. A "For Rent" sign hung in the front window of number two. An exterior wooden staircase ran up each side of the house to the second floor units.

"It's the one on the right." Brody pointed.

Pea gravel crunched under their shoes as they walked across the parking area toward an exterior staircase. Stella glanced at the windows. No curtains moved. She surveyed the neighboring houses and lots, but there was no one in sight.

"Do you feel like you're being watched?" she asked Brody.

"I definitely feel eyes on us." Brody scanned the house. "It's a residential neighborhood. I'm sure there are people around."

Wood creaked as they climbed to a second-floor landing.

They split up, each standing to one side of the white metal door.

"Mr. Crawley?" Brody rapped his knuckles below the peephole. The door swung open an inch.

The hair on the back of Stella's neck twitched, and a bead of sweat trickled between her breasts. Her hand went to her sidearm. Tilting her head, she listened. The apartment was quiet. Voices floated on the breeze. Stella glanced at the street below. A young family was passing the house in the glow of a streetlight. The man walked a black lab while the woman pushed a toddler in an umbrella stroller.

Brody pushed the door with two fingers and peered through the opening. "Mr. Crawley? This is Detective McNamara of the Scarlet Falls PD. We're responding to your call to the hotline."

Silence.

Stella drew her weapon. Brody led with his gun. In unspoken agreement, he aimed high. Stella crouched as he pushed the door with a shoulder. An overhead light glowed a sickly yellow. Stained beige carpet silenced their steps as they went through the doorway.

Stella swept the living room on the right. She glanced behind a brown vinyl couch. The room wasn't big enough to hide anywhere else, even in the shadows. "Clear."

Brody turned left into the kitchen. "Clear."

The floor squeaked as they went down a short hallway. Brody flipped a switch on the wall to illuminate a black and white bathroom. The shower curtain was drawn over an old cast-iron tub. Stella stood in the doorway and covered the hall while Brody pulled the curtain aside. Nothing but mold and rust inside.

Two more doors opened off the corridor. The first stood open. Boxes and plastic totes were piled from floor to ceiling along one wall.

Stella checked the two-by-two closet. Empty. "Clear."

She rejoined Brody in the hall. The final door was closed. Brody opened it and they went in, a table lamp lighting their way. The room was empty. Stella checked under the bed. Brody headed toward the closet. "We're all clear."

Relief tried to slip through her, but her instincts were still on alert. Post-traumatic stress or real threat? That was always the question these days.

"I guess Mr. Crawley isn't that anxious to talk to us." Brody holstered his weapon.

But Stella still had the creeps. She put her Glock away. "I don't like this."

"Stella." Brody was staring at the opposite wall. Stella turned. Over the bed, bright red letters spelled *BOO*.

Fear prickled hot on Stella's back. Unfortunately, it wasn't her PTSD.

"Let's get out of here." Brody prodded her with a hand to the arm.

Crack. Something struck the ceiling above her head. Bits of ceiling rained down on her. Gunshot?

Confusion and fear jolted Stella.

"What was that?" She ran to the hall with Brody shoving her from behind.

"Gunshot."

With his gaze on the floor, Brody steered her to the edge of the corridor. The floor squeaked underfoot.

Crack.

"Shit. He's shooting at us from the apartment below." Brody's hand dropped off Stella's shoulder. She turned. He was down on one knee. Blood seeped through his gray slacks. He waved her away and yelled, "Go! Get out of here."

Not going to happen.

Drawing her weapon, she fired three shots through the floor, aiming at the bullet holes. Then she turned back to Brody, grabbed his wrist, and ducked under his arm. She half-dragged him to the door, staying off the direct path. Another shot came though the floor inches from her foot. Wood splintered. Something stung her ankle.

Stella yanked the door open, and they staggered onto the wooden landing of the staircase. Brody's weight sagged on Stella's frame, and she was forced to holster her gun and wrap her right arm around his waist to keep him upright as they hobbled down the steps. Stella's ears rang as they made it to the walkway.

A door slammed and footsteps on concrete faded.

The shooter was getting away. Stella wanted to chase him. Brody went down, and Stella stumbled. Recovering, she turned to look back in the direction of the gunman.

But Brody was on the ground, pale and bleeding.

She'd have to let the shooter go. Again.

Chapter Thirty-Three

"Have you seen this girl?" Mac held up the picture of Gianna.

A man in jeans and a T-shirt bearing the logo of a local bar emerged from his apartment, closed the door behind him, and locked it. He squinted at the photo. "I think she lives around here."

"She lives in the next building," Mac said. This apartment had a good view of the parking area. "She disappeared sometime last night."

"Sorry. I'm a bartender. I work nights." He took a step toward the lot.

"Have you seen any weird activity around here lately?" Mac asked.

"Nothing any weirder than usual. I gotta go. Hope you find your friend."

"Thanks." Mac tucked the picture into his back pocket. He'd knocked on every door in Gianna's building, and every door with a view of her apartment or the parking area. Now what?

He walked back to stand in front of Gianna's unit, facing the rows of cars. A strip mall lined the road on the other side of the cracked asphalt. Tattoo parlor, Laundromat, check cashing. He walked across. Cool moisture in the wind promised another storm.

He stepped onto the curb on the other side. The streetlight was out, and darkness smothered the sidewalk. A shoe scraped on cement. Mac froze, his instincts on alert.

In the storefront window, he caught the reflection of two figures moving in the shadows behind him. Mac ducked into an alley between the buildings. The narrow space would force the men to attack him one at a time, if that was their intent.

Since they followed him into the alley, he assumed it was.

A hulk of a man rushed him, his beefy arm looping over his head. Mac whirled and focused on his attacker's hand. A knife. The blade ice-picked toward Mac's head. He side stepped out of the weapon's path and caught the man by the wrist with both hands. Redirecting his assailant's momentum, Mac guided the weapon down. Following the natural arc of motion, the point slid into the man's thigh.

He howled. A second man rushed at Mac from behind the first. Small, lighter, more nimble. Ripping the knife free, Mac swept the first man's leg out from under him and shoved him at the second. Number two tripped over his pal and went face-first into the cement. He got a knee under his body and turned back, blood streamed from his nose and triangled over his chin. With a roar, he scooped a broken bottle from the ground and charged.

Mac ducked the first wild swing. The bottle came back at his head, number two's eyes were white-rimmed and wild. He slashed back and forth, the jagged edged of glass sweeping the air in front of Mac's face.

Mac plucked the KA-BAR from his boot and reverse-gripped his knife.

Hands in front of his face, he dodged the swings and waited. Number two backslashed. Mac leaped forward and blocked the back-swing with an upward sweep of the knife. The blade sliced number two's forearm to the bone. Mac hooked the point of the knife over the man's wrist, slammed a palm into the back of the man's elbow, and armbarred him to the ground. Mac pulled the arm, stretching the man out on his belly and pinning him to the pavement.

Still the guy struggled, his feet running in place, the toes of his black trainers scraping for purchase on the blacktop.

Mac checked the status of number one. No worries. The guy was busy trying to plug the gusher in his thigh with both hands.

"Looks like a bleeder," Mac shouted at him. "If I were you, I'd want to get to a doctor ASAP."

The big guy's glare was wide with fear and pain. The man under Mac continued to kick his feet. Mac added a knee in the small of his back. The air rushed out of number two's lungs and he went still.

"What. Do. You. Want?" Mac enunciated carefully.

"You," Number two hissed. "You're worth five grand to Freddie, and he don't care if you come in a box or a bag."

Freddie had put out a contract on Mac. He shouldn't be surprised, but damn, he really hadn't expected Freddie to go this far.

He called 911. Five minutes later, a patrol vehicle arrived, then an EMT vehicle. The paramedics bandaged the bleeder. The cop handed out handcuffs and took Mac's statement. A steady stream of quiet radio chatter flowed from the open police car. An ambulance arrived and the thugs were loaded into the back.

The cop's head swiveled toward his vehicle. "Hold on."

He ran back and grabbed the mic. Snippets of the quiet conversation made Mac's belly ice up.

"Shooting in progress. Officer down."

Stella knelt next to Brody and wrapped her arm around his waist.

"Just go!" He waved.

"No." Hauling him to his feet, Stella staggered under his weight.

A man in a white coat ran toward them from the pharmacy. "I called nine-one-one."

He went to Brody's other side and helped Stella carry him across the street and into the building, where they eased him down on the floor in front of the register. Sirens approached. "I told them you needed an ambulance."

Weapon in hand, Brody tried to sit up.

Stella shoved him down. "Hold still. You're leaking."

Brody stopped fighting her and lay still.

"Did you get a look at him?" Stella kept one eye on the yellow house through the plate glass windows. She suspected their shooter was long gone, but she wasn't taking chances.

"No." Pain glazed Brody's eyes. Blood soaked his pant leg and puddled on the gray linoleum.

Dropping to her knees beside him, she tore open his pant leg. "Can you get me some gauze?" she asked the man.

"Yes." The man disappeared into an aisle. He returned a few seconds later with boxes of first aid supplies.

"I'm the pharmacist." He opened a box of gauze pads and tore a package. "Bill."

"Nice to meet you, Bill. I'm Detective Dane and this is Detective McNamara." Stella exposed a nasty wound on Brody's leg. A bullet had struck the meaty part of his calf. Covering the wound, she said, "We're going to need more of these."

"Try this." Bill handed her a roll of gauze and an ace bandage.

"That should work." She wrapped the wound, pulling the bandage snug but not too tight. "Are you hit anywhere else?" she asked Brody.

He didn't answer, and his eyes were closed.

"Brody!" Stella felt for his pulse. It beat rapidly against her fingertips, but his face had gone dead-white. His leg wound hadn't bled *that* much. "He must have another wound." She ran her hands up his arms and legs.

"Here." Bill moved aside Brody's jacket. Blood soaked his dress shirt. "He must have been hit under the arm. How the hell did that happen?"

"He was below us." Stella pulled at Brody's jacket. "Do you have scissors?"

Bill ran to the counter and returned with them. She cut away Brody's suit and shirt. Lifting his arm, she stacked gauze and applied pressure to the wound. The hole was smaller but more dangerous than the one on his leg.

Two patrol cars parked in front of the pharmacy. Bill went out to signal for the ambulance. Stella leaned into Brody. Blood welled between her fingers.

The next few minutes seemed like an eternity. Finally, two EMTs nudged her aside. Stella stepped back. They took vitals, started an IV, and applied a pressure bandage. By the time they loaded Brody onto a gurney and wheeled him into the ambulance, Stella's legs were trembling and queasiness stirred in her belly like a toxic brew.

Lance rushed into the store, and Stella gave him a quick summary. Then she stumbled to the back of the store, went into the restroom, and heaved her afternoon snack.

She added Ring Dings to her list of foods never to be eaten again. Last time it had been apple cider donuts. At this rate, all her favorite sweets were going to be off-limits.

After washing her face with cold water, she opened the door. Bill the pharmacist was standing outside. He handed her a bottle of mouthwash. "Thought you might need this."

"Thanks." She went back into the bathroom and swigged a capful.

Second shooting of her career. Second after-shooting hurl. At least she consistently got the job done before letting adrenaline take over.

"Thank you. For everything." She handed Bill the bottle and went outside. Three SFPD cars lined the street. Forensic techs crawled over the lawns under portable floodlights, and a mixed crowd of gawkers and reporters gathered behind sawhorses.

Lance led an elderly man with a cane to Stella. "This is Mr. Kiel. He's the owner of the property. Lives in apartment one."

Skinny, stooped, and sweatered, despite the blistering heat, Mr. Kiel could have been anywhere from seventy-five to a hundred years old. He squinted at Stella through Mr. Magoo glasses.

"Do you know where Mr. Crawley is?" Stella asked.

"Hold on." He reached to his ear. A tinny sound, like feedback on a microphone, came from his head. "Sorry. I turned off my hearing aid to take a nap."

"Where is the tenant for unit four?" Stella repeated.

He leaned both hands on the top of his cane. "Jim died of a massive heart attack last week. His kids live in Florida. They took his personal stuff with them, but they arranged to have the furniture donated. Someone is supposed to pick it up by the end of the month."

"What about the unit below his?"

Mr. Kiel sighed. "That's been empty for two months. With two empty units, I don't know how I'm going to pay my bills."

"Did anyone inquire about the empty unit recently?"

He nodded. "Got a call this afternoon. First bite in weeks."

"Can you tell me anything about the voice?" she asked.

"Sounded like a man."

"Do you have Caller-ID?"

"No," Mr. Kiel said.

She'd have to request his phone records. Stella realized the sheer ridiculousness of her next question as she asked it. "Did you see or hear anything earlier today?"

He laughed. "I can barely see and hear you, darling, and you're standing right in front of me."

"Thank you," Stella said. "We'll be in touch if we have any more questions."

The old man tottered away.

"Let's get some uniforms knocking on doors." Stella eyed the maze of juniper bushes and rhododendrons that covered the landscaping. The chances that the neighbors saw the suspect were slim. The shooter had plenty of time to walk away while Stella was busy keeping Brody alive. But she spent the next hour interviewing the residents of the surrounding houses anyway. No one saw the shooter. The uniforms were still canvasing the rest of the neighborhood when she gave up and found Lance in the street.

"I'm going to the hospital," she said.

"Any word on Brody?" Lance asked.

"No. I'll text you when I have news."

Church bells rang as Stella walked to the car. As she turned toward her vehicle, her eyes drifted toward the sound. A few blocks away, a church spire towered over the neighborhood. She hadn't realized Our Lady of Sorrows was this close.

A reporter broke through the line, jamming his microphone in Stella's face. "Detective Dane, can you identify the officer who was shot? Was it Detective McNamara? Is that his blood?"

Her hand rose in front of her face in reflex. She glanced down, her stomach recoiling at the splotches of red soaking her clothes.

A large body blocked him. Lance. Before Stella could blink, he sent the reporter sprawling with a shove to the chest. The jerk landed on his back in the street. His microphone flew from his hand and skidded across the pavement.

Stella stepped in front of Lance. She put two hands on his chest, but he plowed forward. Her shoes slid on the blacktop. "Lance. Stop. Please."

Rage widened his eyes. Breathing hard, he stepped backward. His fists opened and closed at his sides.

Stella signaled for a pair of sheriff's deputies to take over crowd management. When she turned back, Lance was walking away. He climbed into his cruiser and drove off. Stella made a mental note to check in with him later. Maybe he'd returned to work too soon.

She got in her car, numb, and headed for the hospital, praying that Brody hadn't lost too much blood.

Chapter Thirty-Four

He locked his gun in his glove box.

Now back to his original agenda.

We now return to your regular programming.

He felt so much better after letting the police know just what he thought of them. They'd be running from their own shadows. He'd need a cool head to ensure tonight's mission went according to schedule. He had something special planned. He was pretty sure he'd found The One.

And if not, another judgment and more punishment would be delivered.

Back home, he checked the camera feed of the girl's cell. She was curled up in a ball, unmoving. He should be anxious to get started. He should be preparing her challenge. Instead, he was filled with nothing but apathy. What was wrong with him?

He'd slapped the police. He should be focusing.

Pacing his control room, he reconsidered his plan. He glanced back at the monitor. She looked pathetic and weak. In choosing her, he'd wanted to test the will to survive against physical strength. Missy had been healthy. Physically, she should have had more stamina, but she'd failed. Dena had been accustomed to pain. He'd thought that would give her an edge. It hadn't.

But this girl was a survivor. Pain and impending death were part of her daily life. She should have great resilience. But looking at her now, all he saw was frailty. He could do nothing and she'd die.

Hardly a challenge at all. In fact, he already felt like he was wasting his time. What had he been thinking?

What he needed was to be truly challenged. But who would give him what he needed? It would have to be someone who was both physically and emotionally strong. Someone intelligent.

Wait.

He didn't know why he hadn't thought of it before.

He'd been selecting victims when he should have been seeking heroes.

Detective Dane was in for a big surprise.

Chapter Thirty-Five

Mac sat in the waiting room, his hand linked with Hannah's. Grant sat on her other side, his arm wrapped around her shoulders. Mac's eyes kept straying to the open doorway of the surgical waiting room. Stella had called to say that she was all right, but until he saw her, touched her, he couldn't believe it. He needed to put his hands on her body and feel her alive and warm.

A green-scrubbed surgeon stepped into the doorway, his mask pulled down around his neck. Sweat beaded his brow below his green surgical cap. He scanned the room. "Who's here for Detective McNamara?"

Hannah stood. Her hand trembled in Mac's. He squeezed her fingers as the doctor approached.

"He's going to be OK," the doctor said. "He lost a lot of blood, but he got lucky. The bullet missed the brachial artery. He's asking for Hannah. Is that you?"

"Yes." Hannah's voice was weak and shaky. This was the second time in his life that Mac had seen her truly terrified.

The doctor pulled the cap from his head. "I'll have a nurse come for you as soon as he's settled in recovery."

Hannah dropped into the chair as if her legs gave out. Tears poured down her white face. Mac gently pushed her head toward her knees. "Breathe."

"He's OK, Hannah." Grant rubbed her back.

She sat up and wiped the tears from her face with both hands. "I'm sorry."

"Nothing to be sorry about. I'd be in the same shape if something ever happened to Ellie," Grant said. "You too, Mac. I know you feel like you owe us—and the world—a debt of some sort, but we feel the same way about you. We abandoned you. Mom and Dad were both sick. You had no one, and we were both so caught up in getting the hell out of Scarlet Falls that we didn't see that."

"We didn't want to see it," Hannah added. "We failed you, and we're sorry."

"What?" Mac was incredulous. "I'm pretty sure I'm the one who failed."

Hannah shook her head. "You were a kid. We went off on our merry way, all full of the conquer-the-world Barrett ambition."

"I know I should have been worrying about you, instead of single-mindedly concentrating on my military career." Grant shook his head. "Dad gave us a lot of good qualities. We're determined. We don't believe in failure."

"We're honest and honorable to a fault." Hannah added. "We know how to work together as a team."

"But he never taught us unconditional love." Grant put a hand on Mac's shoulder. "That's what raising Carson and Faith has taught me. You love your family without judging them for their faults."

And Mac realized that Grant was right. The only person Mac judged was himself. He would do anything for his Carson and Faith. Nothing they could ever do could diminish his love for them.

Footsteps in the hall approached. Stella appeared in the doorway. Rusty red-brown stains streaked her white blouse and black slacks. Dried blood spotted her face and crusted in her hair. Mac jumped to his feet, fear sprinting through him.

He crossed the room in two steps. His eyes traveled over her body, looking for injury. "Are you hurt?"

She shook her head. Her face was too white and her eyes too dark. "I don't think so. How's Brody?"

Think?

He steered her to a seat. "The doctor was just in. Brody's going to be fine."

"Thank God." Relief seemed to weaken her. She rested her head against the back of the chair.

"How about letting the ER docs have a look at you?" Mac didn't like the shiver that passed through her body or the stunned look in her eyes.

She shook her head. "I want a hot shower."

Grant nudged him. "Why don't you take Stella home? I'll stay here with Hannah."

"Are you sure?" Mac asked.

"Go." Hannah nodded. An exhausted smile lifted the corners of her mouth. "She needs you."

Did she? Mac turned back to Stella. She looked totally beaten. She definitely needed someone.

Her eyes opened and locked on his. "I'll be all right if you need to be with your family."

There was no way he was letting her drive home alone, covered in her partner's blood. He didn't want anyone else to comfort her. He wanted her to need *him*, for the bone-deep connection between them to go both ways.

He stood and tugged Stella to her feet. In the hallway, he turned her to face him. Cupping her face in both hands, he kissed her on the mouth. "You scared the hell out of me."

"That makes two of us," she said. "Did you think I wouldn't hear about the incident in the alley near Gianna's apartment?"

"It was nothing."

"It was two armed men trying to kill you." The no bullshit expression in her eyes demanded the truth.

"Freddie has put a bounty on me." He kissed her again. "I'm going to deal with it."

"How?"

"I've already called the local DEA office." Wrapping an arm around her waist, he steered her toward the elevator. "All I have to do is stay alive until they raid the compound."

"Is that all?"

The door opened and they stepped in.

Stella turned to face him. "You are not expendable."

"OK."

"I mean it, Mac." She splayed a hand in the center of his chest. "I care about you. You have to promise me to use the same caution that you expect from me."

She cared about him.

"All right. I promise."

The tension left her body in one exhalation. "No more skulking around dark alleys alone?"

"No."

The doors opened. She leaned on his shoulder as they walked arm in arm to the exit. Despite her clear exhaustion, her pallor, her distress, he absorbed strength from her embrace.

Outside, they walked to her vehicle. Mac took her keys and then drove out of the parking lot. "Do you want to go home?"

Stella held her hands out and looked down at her clothes as if just realizing she was covered in dried blood. "Not like this. I'll scare the kids. Where's your bike?"

"I came with Grant." Mac drove to his cabin, where he took her into the bedroom. Piling clean towels next to the sink, he began undressing her with efficiency. No pausing to enjoy the show this time. He wanted to inspect every inch of her skin for wounds. Adrenaline was almost as good as lidocaine for numbing injuries.

She stared at the opposite wall, her eyes vacant as he peeled off her blouse. Red patches blooming on her skin would probably be bruises tomorrow. But no bullet holes. Unzipping her slacks, he slid them down her legs. A trickle of red ran from her ankle into her shoe. "You're bleeding."

"I didn't feel that." Her brow knitted.

Mac knelt to inspect her foot. An inch long splinter of wood was embedded in the soft skin just above her ankle. "This is going to hurt if I pull it out. Do you want me to run you back to the hospital?"

"No. Just do it."

"You'd better sit down." Guiding her to the edge of the tub, he reached under the sink for his first aid kit. The wound was shallow but it was going to bleed when he removed the chunk of wood. He guided her foot over the edge of the tub and put on the surgical gloves from the kit. "Are you sure?"

She nodded.

Mac gripped the edge of the splinter and tugged it free in one pull. Breath hissed from Stella's lips and her face went as white as the porcelain sink. "Now it hurts."

He'd rather have a hundred chunks of wood dug out of his own skin than ever see her in pain again. Blood rushed from the wound. Mac let it flow for a minute to flush any dirt from the wound.

"If the bleeding doesn't stop, we might have to get it closed with a stitch." He started the water in the tub. When it ran warm, he guided her foot under the stream and cleaned the injury with soap and water.

"Can I just get in the shower?"

"Of course." Mac yanked the curtain across and switched the water to the overhead spray.

Stella unsnapped her bra, shimmied out of her panties, and with Mac's help, stepped into the shower.

"Do you need help?"

"No."

Mac peered around the edge of the curtain. She stood with her back to the spray, head tipped back, water sluicing over her long limbs. Pink ran from her body into the tub. She opened her eyes and caught his gaze, as if just noticing he was watching her. "What?"

"I was afraid you would fall down."

"Me, too." Stella reached for the shampoo. "But I'm all right."

"You and Brody weren't wearing your vests."

"We were just going to interview an old man." Stella rinsed her hair.

Mac handed her the soap. She scrubbed her entire body twice. She started lathering for a third round, and he took it away. "You're not going to have any skin left."

By the time he helped her from the tub, the bleeding on her leg had slowed. Mac wrapped her in a thick towel. Drying the wound, he closed it with a butterfly bandage, applied antibacterial ointment, and wrapped her ankle in gauze.

"I'm impressed. Let me guess, the Colonel trained you as a medic."

"Basic emergency first aid is crucial for any survival training." Mac closed the first aid kit. "How does that feel?"

"It hurts, but I'll live."

Mac scooped her into his arms.

"I can walk."

"I know." He carried her to the bed. Laying her down, he stretched out next to her.

"I have to go back to the station." She nestled her head onto his shoulder. "Chief Horner will be freaking out."

"He can freak out for a few minutes." He wrapped his arm around her body and pulled her close. He wanted full body contact, to feel the beat of her heart, the rise and fall of her chest, to know that she was alive. "I need to hold you. Is that OK?"

She draped her arm across his chest and wiggled closer, her legs moving as if restless.

Mac stroked her arm. "Is something wrong?"

"You confuse me." She lifted her head.

Mac's blue eyes worried. "In what way?"

"I'm an independent woman. I'm a police detective raised by a police detective. I'm trained in hand-to-hand and weapons. But when I lay here with you I feel safe, and I like it."

"That works for me." A slow smile spread across his face. He thumped the center of his chest. "Because Me Tarzan."

"I'm serious." She rolled onto her side and rested her chin on his belly. "What is wrong with me?"

Mac's face went serious. "It's eleven-thirty at night. You've had a hell of a day. You shouldn't be going back to work. You should be on admin leave until you've had a nice long session with the department shrink and a few weeks to decompress."

"I have to find Gianna. I have to stop him from hurting another girl."

"I know." He stroked her hair. "You're tired, and maybe deep down you know I'd keep you safe while you slept." He lifted her hand and kissed her knuckles. "I would. I'd watch over you. I'd kill for you." His pulse thickened. "I'd die for you."

Especially kill. Mac wanted to find the man who'd shot at her and slowly squeeze the breath from his throat.

She slid up on the bed until their faces were inches apart. "I'd do the same for you. It's a little scary."

No kidding. "For me, too."

"I've never felt this way about anyone before, except for my family."

Mac nodded. "Same here."

276

"So what do we do about it?" she asked.

Mac leaned forward and kissed her, a gentle and tender caress of his mouth on hers. His lips brushed her cheek. "I don't know. First time for me."

"Me, too." Stella's phone rang from the kitchen. Hooking her towel around her breasts, she went to get it and brought it back into the bedroom.

Mac could hear a male voice. "We narrowed the list of Spivak's pals down to the most likely candidate. Cyrus O'Neil. He lives on a farm on County Line Road, and he's also a member of the White Survival Alliance. We've had some complaints over noise and odors on the property, and one of the neighbors says they saw Spivak on the property. I'm going over there to see what's what as soon as the search warrant is signed. You want to come?"

Stella straightened. "I'm in."

"Meet me at the station in thirty."

"OK." She turned to Mac. "Did you hear all that?"

"I did." And he'd hated every word. Mac wanted to be the one raiding a farmhouse instead of Stella. But he respected her enough to let her do her job. "Maybe Gianna will be there."

"Maybe."

"No chance I could go with you?"

"None. Sorry." She was off the bed and looking for clothes.

He took a clean T-shirt from his drawer. "You don't want to put the blood-stained shirt back on."

She tugged the T-shirt over her head, then went into the bathroom where her slacks were still puddled on the tile.

Mac caught her around the waist. He drew her close, pressing his body to hers from thigh to chest. She was warm and soft. He wanted to tug her back to bed and keep her there all night. "Back to what we were talking about before your call." He tucked a long hair behind her ear. "The first thing we have to do is stay safe."

She placed a hand over the center of his heart. Seemed appropriate. She owned it. He knew that now. There was no point in analyzing anything. He was a hundred feet over his head in love with her. But now wasn't the time to profess anything. He didn't want Stella distracted tonight. He held her face and kissed her hard. "Be careful."

"I will." She cupped his cheek and touched her mouth tenderly to his lips. Pressing her forehead to his, she said, "I'm not concerned about me."

"I know. That's why I'm worried."

Stella would do whatever it took to rescue her friend. "Gianna's in the hands of a killer. She doesn't have much time. I have to find her."

He kissed her again, just a slow press of his lips. When he lifted his head, fear tumbled through him like a boulder down a slope. "Be careful. Wear your vest."

"I need to ask you a favor."

"Anything."

"Would you go to my house and stay there? We'll be shorthanded tonight. If the uniform on duty gets a call, they'll be alone. I'd feel much better if you were there to protect my family."

"I need to return your grandfather's car anyway," Mac said, though he'd rather be with her than babysitting her family. "I'll drop you at the hospital to get your vehicle. We can call Art on the way."

His heart clenched. As much as he respected her abilities, he'd never adjust to watching her walk into dangerous situations.

Chapter Thirty-Six

The farm was in the middle of nowhere, the closest neighbor two miles down the road. A woman could scream her lungs out and no one would hear her.

A driving sheet of rain hit the windshield as they parked. Sweat dripped under Stella's body armor and rain jacket.

Stella said a silent prayer that Gianna or Janelle or whomever had been abducted was still alive, and that they'd find her before it was too late. Darkness shrouded the O'Neil farm. The driveway was a lopsided spot of mud. She parked next to two black-and-whites.

Patrol Officer Carl Ripton greeted her. Rain poured off the brim of his campaign hat.

"Where's Lance?" Stella looked over his shoulder at the small group of officers behind him.

"Quit."

"What?"

"He walked into the chief's office and quit." Carl checked his weapon.

"Damn." Even though she knew Lance had been having trouble adjusting to his return to work, she'd never expected him to quit when she needed him. He had the case in his head. With him gone and Brody wounded, that left Stella and Horner.

"Yeah. Bad timing." Carl waved toward the house. "Shall we?"

She breathed and scanned the surroundings. The house sat on the right, with a large barn and several smaller outbuildings scattered around the yard. Junk, including the carcass of a rusting convertible and a rotted mattress, dotted the weedy grounds.

"More of a junkyard than a farm," she said.

Carl tugged the brim of his hat lower. "Ready?"

"Ready." Nerves dried her mouth, and when she swallowed, it felt like burrs moving down her throat.

They crossed the yard. Her SFPD cap shielded her eyes from the downpour as she crept up the wooden porch steps. They approached the front door, the buzz of adrenaline deafening. The house was two stories of peeling white paint. She glanced at Carl. His hand was poised next to his weapon as he motioned two uniforms around the house to cover the rear exit in case anyone inside decided to bolt. The situation was eerily like the one in November. And with the shooting of Brody so fresh, visions of Brody and Lance, bleeding and pale, flashed through Stella's mind.

She shook the images away. Lance and Brody were both alive. No uniformed chaplains had visited their loved ones.

"Stella?" Carl stopped her with a hand on her wrist. "You were just in a shooting this afternoon. Are you all right?"

She wouldn't be sidelined in the search for Gianna. "I'm fine."

Stella shook off the mental slide show. No one was going to get shot tonight. They weren't going to be surprised.

Carl took one side of the doorway. Stella stood on the other. The third uniform crouched behind them. She wiped water from her forehead and knocked on the door. No one answered. She rapped again. "Mr. O'Neil? This is the police. We have a warrant."

The only answer was the sound of rain beating on the porch roof.

Stella gave knocking one more try. "Mr. O'Neil, open the door."

Next to her, Carl drew his weapon.

Stella shielded her eyes and tried to peer through the glass panes in the door. "I can't see much. It's dark in there."

Carl walked to the end of the porch and looked in another window. "Same here."

"Are you ready?" Stella asked.

Carl nodded. The uniform brought the battering ram and swung the heavy black rod by the handles. It hit the door next to the lock. The door burst in. Carl and Stella led the entry. The uniforms followed. They swept the house, clearing each room floor by floor. When the entire house was declared empty, they met on the front porch again.

"There's a vehicle parked in front of the barn. Let's check it out." Stella moved off the porch. Their warrant included outbuildings. The rain beat on her shoulders and dripped down the back of her neck as she skirted a mud puddle. The barn doors were closed. The windows were high and boarded over. The two uniforms jogged across the yard.

Stella sniffed. Over the wash of rain, a faint but caustic odor lingered.

"Doesn't smell like a body. Smells like cat piss." One of the uniforms wiped his face.

Stella scanned the front of the building. High windows were covered with plywood. "Can you boost me up to the window? Maybe I can see through those boards."

"Careful," Carl warned as he moved under the opening.

But they both knew going in blind was dangerous. It was better to know what they were facing than to rush in.

Stella put a hand on his shoulder and stepped into his locked fingers. He boosted her a few feet into the air. She grabbed the sill and got a toehold on a loose board. She put her eye to the space between the boards. A distinct odor wafted through the tiny slit. She recognized the smell with one sniff. Ammonia.

"Can you see anyone?" Carl asked.

"Give me a minute." She squinted into the dim, but all she could see was piles of junk and shadows. "It's too dark inside."

"I'm sorry." He reached for her hand to help her down, then scanned the front of the barn.

"Can you see anything between the board over the other window?" Stella gestured to the other side of the door.

"Let's just open the damned door." Carl reached for the long, metal handle on the sliding door. "There's probably nothing inside but fertilizer and old junk." He pointed to the rusted hinges of the barn door. "This barn doesn't see much action."

His fingers closed around the handle.

Turning, Stella saw a thin metal wire running along the doorframe.

"Don't!" Stella shouted.

But it was too late. He was already pulling.

"Get down!" Stella dove at him, looping an arm over his chest and taking him to the ground with her just as the front of the barn exploded.

Mac drove toward Stella's house. His phone chimed with a text message. Stopping at an intersection, he checked the screen. It was from Gianna.

He pulled over to the shoulder and opened the message.

can't find stella. can u pick me up?

Stella would have her phone off.

Mac typed back, yes. where r u?

Bridge Park.

Why would Gianna be sitting at the park where Dena Miller's body had been found? As if she knew what he was asking, she texted, was thinking about jumping. Changed my mind. :)

Shit. He pictured her standing on the bridge in the rain, looking over the edge, the water rushing and swirling in the dark below. Gianna was depressed, sick, and suicidal. As Stella had pointed out, without constant intervention, the girl was always a few days from death.

He tried to call her, but she didn't answer.

On my way, he answered, then he sent Stella a quick text. Gianna texted me. I'm going to pick her up at Bridge Park.

She'd want to know Gianna was alive the second she finished her op and turned on her phone. Should he call the station and have them call off the search for the girl? No. Not until he had eyes on her. If she was a no-show, Mac wanted the cops looking for her.

How the hell did she get out to the park? That was a long walk in the rain, but desperation could provide plenty of fuel.

The storm picked up as he stopped before the bridge. Mac squinted through the windshield. His headlights gleamed on wet pavement and driving rain. Gianna wasn't on the bridge. Where was she? Her text had specified the park. He backed up and turned into the park entrance, drove down the embankment, and parked near the monument. Thunder cracked, and lightning slashed across the sky as the drizzle became a downpour. He didn't see her, but the rain had increased considerably from when she'd texted him. She must have sought cover under the bridge. He parked the car as close to the stone foundation as possible.

Mac searched in the backseat of the sedan and found a jacket. Wind whipped the rain sideways. He tucked the jacket under his arm. Leaving his phone in the car, he found a flashlight in the glove box and stepped out into the rain. Water drenched his clothes in seconds. He splashed through a puddle, his mind conjuring images of the pale, thin girl under a heap of blankets in her sauna of an apartment. The night was muggy and warm, but if Gianna were wet, she would be freezing.

"Gianna!" he shouted over the storm and jogged toward the bridge. Through the downpour, he saw a figure lean out of the shadow and wave, then duck back under. *Thank God.*

Hunching against the wind, Mac ran under the stone arch. Something hit him in the shoulder. A slice of pain, then a paralyzing jolt, rammed through his body. His muscles seized. He saw the ground coming toward his face but was unable to move a hand to catch himself. He hit the dirt like an oak struck by lightning. The flashlight landed next to him, its beam moving as it rolled down the slope toward the river.

Had he been struck by lightning?

The pain eased. Mac twitched. The figure stepped out of the dark.

Up close and out of the driving rain, he could see the person was too big to be Gianna.

Warning blasted through him. Not lightning. Taser.

Mac shook off his paralysis and planted a hand on the ground. He needed to get up. The muscles of his arms trembled as he forced his torso off the packed earth. A second jolt ripped through him. His body went stiff as stone, and his face smacked into the dirt.

A boot landed in the center of Mac's spine. He struggled, his limbs still twitching, as his hands were yanked behind his back. A third jolt slammed his teeth together. But the most frightening sight was the needle aimed at Mac's neck. The second his muscles relaxed, the needle bit into his flesh. His muscles went lax in an instant. He blinked. He could feel every inch of his body, but his muscles did not respond to commands. He wanted to protest, but he couldn't make a sound.

Fear raced through his blood. His heart sprinted inside his chest.

A hood was drawn over his head. Blind and paralyzed, Mac felt his limbs being moved, his wrists and ankles bound. His body was rolled onto a tarp and dragged across the ground. Mac was rolled down the hill and into something metal and concave. His legs flopped uselessly over the edge.

He was in a fucking wheelbarrow.

Probably the same wheelbarrow that had been used to dispose of Dena Miller's body.

"You have quite the tolerance for pain. We're going to have an interesting night."

Chapter Thirty-Seven

Stella was airborne for a few long seconds then landed facedown in the mud, one arm still looped over Carl. The impact with the ground slammed her teeth together and knocked the breath from her lungs.

Ears ringing, she lifted her head. Carl lay on his back. His eyes were closed, and he wasn't moving. Blood trickled from a gash on his temple.

No!

A second blast blew the top of the barn into the sky. Stella belly crawled on top of him. Putting her arms over her head, she used her upper body to shield his face and head. Fire roared behind them. She put her fingers to his throat. Relief washed through her as she felt the steady throb of his pulse.

"Detective Dane!"

She turned. Twenty feet away, one of the uniforms lurched to his feet. His body swayed for a second before he ran toward his partner. The second uniform stirred in the center of the space, flat on his back. The blast had thrown him fifteen feet straight backward. He rolled over and crawled away from the blaze.

Stella got her feet under her body. Her legs trembled then steadied. She grabbed Carl by the ankles and leaned into the pull, but she couldn't budge him. The two uniforms helped her drag him away from the fire and called for backup, fire trucks, and an ambulance.

Stella glanced at the uniforms. "Are you both all right?"

"Fine," one coughed.

Carl stirred and pressed a hand to his head.

"Hold still." Stella put a hand on his shoulder. "I don't know how badly you're hurt."

He moved his arms and legs. "Just cracked my head."

"Detective, the fire is spreading."

Stella followed the uniform's finger to an outbuilding behind the barn. Embers drifted through the air. Despite the rain, the barn was burning at flash speed.

"That's one hell of a fire." Carl nodded toward a nearby shed. "We'd better start clearing outbuildings."

She lurched to her feet and ran toward the shed. Carl staggered behind her. They cleared the property shed by shed but found no one.

Fifteen minutes later, Stella sat on the bumper of her vehicle staring at the inferno of a barn. Where was Gianna? If she'd been inside the barn . . .

Stella refused to believe Gianna was dead. Needing to hear Mac's voice, she turned on her cell phone to call him and saw that he'd sent her a text. As she read the message, she was lightheaded with relief. Gianna hadn't been in the barn. Mac was picking her up at Bridge Park. Stella called him. The line rang five times before switching to voice mail. Stella left a message and then tried texting him. He didn't respond.

Where was he?

A prickly sensation crawled up the back of her neck and choked her. She tried Gianna's number, but the call went immediately to voice mail. Gianna's phone was off again. Stella ran over to Carl, who was talking to the fire chief. Carl met her halfway across the barnyard.

Soot streaked his face. "The fire chief thinks the barn was full of fertilizer and other explosive materials. The door was booby-trapped. They won't be able to look for remains until tomorrow, but it seems Spivak and his pal were making explosives."

She quickly explained Mac's text. "I can't get either one of them on the phone. I have to find them. Can you handle things here?"

He glanced back at the barn. Fire hoses rained water on the blaze. The scene crawled with emergency responders. "We're shorthanded. Do you need company?"

"Not necessary. I'm just driving out to Mac's house. If I don't find them there, I'll head over to Gianna's apartment." But considering Gianna's odd behavior, she doubted he'd take her home and leave her. No, Mac would stick with the girl. He'd make sure she got whatever help she needed.

He was a good man. The kind of man she wanted.

She climbed into her car and sped toward his house. Pulling into the clearing, she looked up at the dark cabin. Not here. Just to be sure, she jogged onto the porch and rapped on the door. When he didn't answer, she returned to her car and tried his cell phone again. Still no answer.

Could he have taken her to the hospital? He would have called Stella. Maybe his phone was dead. She drove to Gianna's apartment, but it was also dark and empty.

She called Mac's sister.

Hannah answered. "Stella?"

"Have you heard from Mac?" Stella asked.

"No." Hannah's voice hesitated. "What's wrong?"

"Maybe nothing. I'll try your brother."

"Grant is here at the hospital with me. He hasn't heard from Mac either," Hannah said.

"This is Grant. Tell me what's going on," a deep male voice said.

"Mac messaged me earlier that he'd heard from Gianna and was going to get her," Stella explained. "Now he's not answering his phone."

Grant was quiet for a few seconds. "Don't panic. He's not good about keeping his cell charged." Chair legs scraped. "But I'll start looking for him."

"I've already been out to his cabin. He's not there," Stella said. "I'm going to check Bridge Park. I'll let you know if I find him. Please let me know if you hear anything."

"Will do." Grant ended the call.

Stella called for a backup unit and drove toward the park. On the way, she called Lance's cell. He answered on the first ring.

"Are you all right?" she asked.

"I'm at your house," Lance said. "I thought, since I didn't have anything else to do, that I'd hang out here and make sure everything was OK. The patrol car got called away to the explosion."

"Thanks, Lance."

"I'm sorry. I—I just didn't trust myself to keep my shit together tonight."

"Carl said you quit."

"Stella, don't worry about me or your family. I have them covered. Focus on the task. Keep safe, Stella." Lance ended the call.

Stella put Lance's emotional state out of her mind. Rain poured onto Stella's windshield, and the bridge loomed dark. She checked the surface, but there was no one on the bridge. Turning into the entrance, Stella reported her location to dispatch. Six inches of water flooded the grass around the memorial. The river churned well above its normal level. Her high beams swept across her grandfather's Lincoln parked next to the bridge supports, and ice balled up in her belly.

Where was Mac?

She pulled up next to the Town Car and scanned the area, but the torrential rain limited her visibility. Headlights swept down the entrance ramp, but they were too high to be another SFPD cruiser.

A pickup truck parked next to her, and Grant Barrett got out. He walked to the side of her vehicle. Stella stepped out of her car. Grant didn't seem to notice the rain soaking his cargo shorts and T-shirt. Within seconds water plastered his short, blond hair to his head. His only response was to blink.

"A backup unit is on the way." Stella wiped water from her forehead. "He was driving my grandfather's car." Stella turned toward her grandfather's vehicle.

She took a pair of gloves from her pocket and put them on before opening the Lincoln's door. Mac's cell phone sat on the console. She grabbed the phone and slid it into her pocket under her jacket.

Grant was headed toward the bridge support. Stella ran to catch up. She grabbed his arm. "Be careful where you step. This could be a crime scene."

Please let me be wrong.

He nodded grimly, stopping as soon as they were under the protection of the stone arch. The dirt was disturbed.

"Here are footprints." Grant crouched and pointed to the ground. "Stella . . ."

She bent low. Scattered in the dirt were tiny colored discs the size of confetti. "Taser confetti."

Her vision fuzzed as the implication settled in. "He was lured here with a message from Gianna's phone. Then someone tased him."

Grant's face went hard. "And took him."

She nodded, emptiness sliding through her body as if her blood was thinned with anesthetic.

The killer had Mac.

The best man she'd ever known. The man who made her heart thump and her pulse thicken with one blink of his clear blue eyes. The man who would kill or die for her.

"I have to call this in. We can trace the serial numbers on the Taser confetti."

As she ran for the car, she saw another equally frightening sight on the muddy edges of the dried earth under the bridge: wheelbarrow tracks.

———⌣———

He had to work quickly. Etomidate was a fast-acting sedative commonly used for emergency intubation. The injection would only last fifteen minutes, and he most definitely did not want Mac Barrett able to fight back.

Which was why he'd used the Taser.

He wouldn't stand a chance if the fight was fair. Cheating was his only option.

Getting a full-grown man in and out of the trunk proved challenging, and one of the reasons he'd limited his subjects to women until this point.

But this would be worth the effort.

Mac was The One.

Not a victim, but a deeply flawed hero.

He could feel it in his bones. He sped toward his house and opened the bulkhead doors. The specially built ramp led straight down to the basement. He pushed the wheelbarrow through a growing puddle past the heavy wooden door. He didn't have time to put Mac in the cell. No, he'd have to go straight to the reception room. Mac had to be restrained by the time the drug wore off. Pushing the wheelbarrow through the doorway, he lowered the treatment table and transferred Mac to it, sliding his upper body across the gap first, and then following with his legs. He carefully secured his wrists to the handrails with handcuffs. He didn't trust simple rope with a strong, healthy man. Leather medical restraint straps buckled across Mac's hips and around his ankles.

The Hulk couldn't break those binds.

Melinda Leigh

Satisfied, he stepped back and mopped the sweat from his forehead. The cool of the basement was a welcome reprieve from the muggy summer temperature above ground.

Now to prepare for the first stage. He wheeled the rolling tray to the side of the bed. Mac's fingers twitched.

"Oh good. You're waking up." He mopped his forehead with a cloth. "Got you here just in time."

He took a pair of scissors from the blue sterile cloth and cut Mac's T-shirt up the center to reveal a square bandage taped to his ribs. "What's this?"

Mac grunted. He'd be able to talk soon.

He peeled back the medical tape and exposed a long, stitched wound that wrapped round Mac's side. "What happened?"

No answer, but Mac's eyes were angry.

Anger was new. He'd never had a victim get mad. It was a very good sign that he'd finally made the right choice.

"Where should we start?"

Chapter Thirty-Eight

Stella paced the conference room in front of the murder board. Grant was in his truck making a phone call, probably to his sister. Horner was gathering more forces while Stella desperately tried to eliminate possible locations where two victims could be held prisoner.

He had Mac.

He had Gianna.

Visions of the two tortured victims assaulted her mind. She tried to push them away, but every time she pivoted, autopsy photos pinned to the board pummeled her: fresh, full-color reminders of what had happened to his previous victims. Terror scraped through her, its icy talons tearing at the hope inside her chest. What was he doing to them right now? Were they even still alive?

Chief Horner walked into the room, his impassive face showing unusual signs of fatigue and frustration. "Noah Spivak and his buddy were picked up in the woods not far from the farm, and a unit stopped by Adam Miller's house. A friend was pouring him out of his car, nearly passed-out drunk. The friend said they'd been drinking together all evening and the bartender over at The Pub verified his statement."

"Then we have no idea who has them." Head spinning, Stella closed her eyes. Was Mac or Gianna being tortured right now? Having their fingers smashed with a hammer or their flesh cut with a knife?

But there was no way to compartmentalize this horror. If she wanted to save them, she would have to face it.

She turned and gave the board her full attention. Horner walked around the table and stood next to her. They faced the case board side by side. The answer had to be here somewhere.

"What do all the victims have in common?" Horner asked. "Why would he take Mac when his previous victims were all women with former drug addiction problems?"

"They all have a history of drug abuse." Stella stopped, nearly tripping over her own momentum as the pieces fit into place. She'd been so afraid for Mac and Gianna that she hadn't questioned the killer's motivation in taking him.

"But what about Mac? Did he find something?"

"No." She whirled. "He's one of them."

"Seriously?" Horner's brows stretched upward.

"When he was a teenager," she explained.

"Who would know that?"

"I don't know." What other suspects did they have? Her eyes went back to the board.

"What about Lyle Jones?" Horner asked. "He has a record."

"Domestic squabble. It sounded personal." Stella shook her head. "Plus, he was Dena's physical therapist. He has no connection to Missy or Gianna."

"Both Dena and Missy were treated at the New Life Center," Horner said.

Stella thumbed through her file. "I already cleared Dr. Randolph of any criminal record. I wanted to check the story about his brother dying of an overdose."

"What was his name?" Horner opened the laptop on the table.

Stella scanned her report. "Lucas Randolph. It happened approximately fifteen years ago."

Horner scrolled. "Did he live in this area?"

She flipped to Josh's background report. "He's from Manchester, New Hampshire."

He typed.

"Josh said his brother was mentally ill," Stella continued.

"Here's the story." Horner turned the screen. "Lucas Randolph, age nineteen, died of a heroin overdose."

She skimmed the text. "Everything is exactly as he said."

Horner flipped through one of Stella's detailed reports. "What about his assistant, Reilly Warren?"

"I was waiting for the report on his assistant. Let me see if it's in." Stella hurried to her cubicle, grabbed the report from her inbox, and returned to the conference room. She flipped through the pages. "No criminal record here or in Atlanta."

Horner typed Reilly's name into the Google search bar and scrolled through the list of hits. "Here's something." Horner paused. "Three years ago in Atlanta, a Reilly Warren was the victim of a brutal beating, sexual assault, and robbery. The perpetrator was caught and convicted." Horner looked up. "His attacker was a crack addict and was later found to be HIV positive."

"That would certainly give Reilly motivation to kill some drug addicts."

"How did he know Gianna Leone?" Horner asked.

"I don't know. But if he's targeting drug addicts, he could very well have staked out the NA meetings. We did."

"Let's get an address and a warrant on Reilly Warren."

Stella read the address. "He lives at the center."

"You realize this lead is thin," Horner said. "If you're wrong, we'll be raiding a medical facility for no reason."

Stella was well aware that they were acting on a hunch, but the possibility of the department getting egg on its reputation didn't factor into her decision.

If she was wrong, then Mac and Gianna were both going to die.

Brave Gianna had been through so much already. And Mac . . . At the thought of losing him, pressure built in Stella's chest until she could barely breathe. *No!* Mac was going to be all right. She had to believe that. Otherwise, fear would cripple her, and then she'd be useless.

She forced a deep breath into her lungs. "It's the best—and only—lead we have."

Horner nodded. "Then let's follow it. It'll be daylight in an hour."

"We can't wait."

"Sir, you can't go in there." Cecily's shout came through the open door.

"Like hell." A deep male voice boomed in the hallway.

Stella turned to see Grant in the doorway, his wide shoulders filling the space.

Horner rounded the table and confronted Grant.

Good luck stopping him, Horner.

Grant might be retired from the military, but he still wore battle-fit like a uniform. Horner rode a desk, not a tank.

As predicted, Grant plowed past him. He turned laser focus on Stella. "So you think he's at the center. What's the plan to get him out?"

Grant must have overheard their conversation.

"Grant, you're a civilian. I can't let you participate. This is going to be dangerous."

"You need all the help you can get," Grant said. "And I'm going in, with or without you. So don't shoot me. FYI, my sister will probably be there, too."

Frustration filled Stella's throat. "Grant . . ."

He crossed his arms. "I can be in and out of there before you even get your official operation underway."

Stella thought back to Mac helping her with a search the previous November. The Barretts had specialized skills that had proved useful in the past. And the only way to ensure Grant stayed out of the way was to keep him with her. Grant had been an infantry officer. His military experience could be invaluable.

"With Chief Horner's permission, I'd love to have your input. There isn't any time for elaborate planning."

Horner threw his hands into the air. "Why the hell not? We don't have enough bodies for the op anyway. Let's get a map."

In the next twenty minutes, Grant proved to be the master strategist Mac had claimed. Horner called for assistance from the state police and county sheriff's office. The rehab property backed onto a national park. Horner called in every officer that wasn't already on duty handling the fire and the flood issues.

"I can't imagine him keeping a woman prison at the center. There are people there all the time. He'd have to be very concerned with screaming." Especially while he tortured them. Picturing Gianna or Mac being cut made Stella lightheaded. She put a hand on the tabletop to steady her legs.

"Basement?" Horner suggested.

Stella straightened, an image popping into her head. "There was an old barn a short distance from the main building."

"We'll go in quiet," Grant said.

"I'd rather wait until we can get state and county assistance." Horner frowned at the map.

Grant shook his head. "I'm not waiting."

"Sir, there isn't time." Stella wasn't waiting either. She'd throw down her badge and go in as a civilian if necessary.

"All right." Horner tried to look authoritative, but it was hard to pull off next to a former combat officer. "But you will follow my orders and stay out of the way."

Grant didn't answer.

"See if we have a vest that will fit him." Horner walked out of the room.

They finished their prep in the station's parking lot. Stella briefed the small team.

Carl joined them, fresh from the fire scene. "I don't believe it."

Stella followed his gaze. Chief Horner was suited up for the op, complete with body armor and an AR-15.

Carl leaned close. "Do you think he knows how to shoot that?"

"I hope so."

Horner tugged his dark blue cap low on his brow. He nodded to Carl. "Let's go."

"Yes, sir." Carl got into his car.

"You can ride with me," Stella said to Grant as she donned her Kevlar vest.

Grant shook his head. A car pulled into the lot and Hannah got out. Dressed in black cargos and a T-shirt, she tugged a black knit cap over her bright blonde hair.

"Hannah and I will follow," Grant said.

Stella put her foot down. "I won't let your vehicle anywhere near the property. If you're going, you're going with me."

She could not have the Barretts going rogue on her out in the woods and possibly being shot by law enforcement. "You both must stay at the command post. That's not negotiable."

She knew the Barretts well enough to predict they were going to ignore her instructions.

"Of course," Hannah said, bumping Grant with her elbow. "We don't want to get in the way."

Grant's expression said he very much wanted to do just that.

A rumble of distant thunder foreshadowed the stutter of lightning on the horizon. Another storm was rolling in.

"Let's go." She gestured to her car. Hannah slid into the back-seat. Grant rode shotgun. And as much as Stella worried about their presence, something about having the two of them in her car bolstered her confidence. She drove out of the lot as the storm burst from the sky.

She no longer cared if she was fired. The only thing that mattered was finding Mac and Gianna.

If they were still alive.

Thirty minutes later, they gathered outside their dark vehicles near the old stone barn. Stella tugged her cap over her brow to keep the rain out of her eyes. Horner went around the back side of the barn with two uniforms. Drawing her weapon and flashlight, she instructed Grant and Hannah to stay in the car. Then she led Carl and two more officers toward the front door.

At the entrance, she hesitated. The last time she'd faced a dark barn, it had blown up in front of her. She checked the doorframe for wires but found nothing.

The door wasn't locked. She pulled it open and went in, sweeping the space with her weapon and flashlight. Something rustled to her left. Stella spun. A raccoon scurried out the door.

The building was empty.

They took a few minutes to check the floor for trapdoors.

"No one has been in here for a long time." Horner lowered his light. "Let's go check the rehab center."

They returned to their vehicles and drove to the center. Repeating the procedure, Horner covered the back while Stella and Carl banged on the door. They heard footsteps on the other side of the door. Stella held her weapon ready as the door opened.

Reilly stood in the lobby in a pair of cotton pajamas. The front was buttoned all the way to his chin, and they appeared as if they'd been ironed. But his hair was rumpled, as if he'd just gotten out of bed. A sinking feeling settled in Stella's belly.

They'd gotten it wrong.

"What's going on?" he stepped back.

Stella and Carl pushed past him. "Is anyone else here?"

"The patients are all sleeping in their rooms. I did bed check a half hour ago." Reilly scratched his forehead.

"Can you get everyone out here, please?"

"I demand to know what's going on." He propped a hand on his hip.

"Two people have been abducted."

Reilly's eyes opened wide. "And you think they're here?"

"We need to check." Doubt crept around Stella's gut as she showed him the search warrant.

"All right." He rousted the patients. They gathered in the lobby while the police did a quick sweep of all the rooms. The basement was full of boxes and junk. No people.

"Are there any outbuildings?" Stella asked Reilly.

"No." Reilly shook his head. "Everything is kept in the basement. Why did you think they were here?"

"Someone is abducting and killing drug addicts. We know about what happened to you in Atlanta."

"You thought it was me?" Reilly reeled. He backed up to the wall. "I could never hurt anyone. Not after what I've been through. I came all the way up here to get away from those violent memories."

Which Stella had just handed back to him. "I'm sorry."

She paced the lobby, panic overriding her pity. If it wasn't Reilly, then who?

Her gaze landed on a bulletin board. A notice on yellow paper read, "Free Group Session, Thursday night, 10 p.m., Our Lady of Sorrows."

And suddenly she knew. All the pieces fell into place. "Where does Dr. Randolph live?"

"Why?" Horner asked.

"Because it's him. Missy and Dena were his patients. He knew everything about them." Stella walked to the bulletin board and put a fist on the yellow notice. "And if he offered free counseling to NA members after their meetings, he could have worked with Gianna as well."

Horner's gaze landed on the flyer. "But why?"

"It has to be connected to his brother." Stella turned away from the bulletin board. Everything in her gut said she was right. But Randolph wasn't holding Gianna and Mac prisoner at the center, so where were they? "Reilly, where is Randolph's house?"

"Across the lake." Reilly said. "The access road is just past the driveway for the center. You can't miss it."

"You two stay here and keep an eye on him, just in case." Stella pointed to two officers. "Everyone else, let's go."

Racing for her car, she said a quick and silent prayer.

Please let them be alive.

⌣

Panic slammed inside Mac's throat, a blind, feral animal seeking to escape. He moved his fingers, but his muscle control hadn't returned quickly enough. He was immobilized. He yanked at the handcuffs that attached his wrists to the rails on either side of the gurney. His ankles were tied down with leather straps that looked like they'd come out of a horror movie set in a psychiatric hospital.

That wasn't too far off.

"How are you feeling?"

Mac turned his head and shock numbed him for a few seconds.

Josh Randolph walked around a growing puddle to stand a few feet from the gurney, as if he was afraid to come closer.

Smart man.

Mac let anger kill his shock and fear. His rage roiled, wild and snapping as a caged beast. He was going to kill Josh. He didn't know how, but it was going to happen. If necessary, he'd rip the man's throat out with his teeth.

"I think we'd better work on your attitude." Josh raised the Taser and fired.

The prongs hit Mac dead center in the chest. Electricity ripped through him and tore him apart. His body seized, the muscles simultaneously frozen and on fire. It eased off, and Mac's muscles were left twitching.

He gritted his teeth and forced words through his shaking lips. "Fuck you."

Josh's frown was uncertain. "You *are* resilient."

He squeezed the trigger again. The current made Mac's body jump to artificial life, as if Dr. Frankenstein had thrown the switch. Mac's body jolted on the gurney. When Josh lowered the Taser, Mac's body convulsed with the remnants of its charge.

A minute passed before he unclenched his molars. "I'm going to kill you."

Josh smiled. "I knew you were The One."

What. The. Hell?

Mac swallowed. It felt like broken glass moved down the inside of his throat. "What are you talking about?"

"You are The One. Truly redeemed." He set down the Taser and clasped his hands together. "We have a few more tests, but I knew you were special."

"You're crazy."

Josh grabbed his tray and rolled it toward the gurney. Water splashed around the wheels. The puddle had grown, covering most of the floor several inches deep.

"Your basement is flooding." Mac lifted his head. His neck muscles protested. "The lake is rising."

But Josh's eyes were glazed, as if he were lost in his own imagination.

He lifted a scalpel from the tray, his eyes hyper-focused on Mac. "We'll start with the physical test. It's redundant based on the fact that you've been walking around with a bullet wound, but I have to keep my experiments consistent. The physical pain test is first. I've designed each subject's test for their specific background. Missy cut herself, so I used a knife on her. Dena let her husband break her bones, so breaking her fingers seemed appropriate. You are a bit more complicated. I'll have to try both."

Mac tried to slide away from the blade, but the restraints held him fast.

Josh drew the blade over the skin on Mac's arm. With his adrenaline running on high, Mac barely felt the slice. A quick burn, then nothing. Blood flowed over his skin in a thin river.

"No screaming?" Josh all but clapped with glee as he picked up a hammer.

Knowing what was coming, Mac clenched his fist, but Josh hit him with another short Taser jolt. Mac's hands tightened until his fingers dug into his palms. The electricity abandoned him, and his muscles went involuntarily lax.

Josh stretched out his fingers and brought the hammer down. This was no clean sharp blade, and pain exploded through Mac's hand. His jaw clamped, his molars coming together with a brain-rattling *snap* of teeth that caught his tongue. Blood flooded his mouth.

Josh held up a syringe. "I can end all that pain right now."

"What is that?"

"Heroin." Josh said it like he was offering candy to a child. "No more pain, Mac."

Real terror spread like a brushfire through Mac's body. Injuries to his body would heal. But addiction never ended. He couldn't go down that road again. He'd rather die.

"Fuck you." Blood flew from his mouth as he spat out the words.

A crazy-ass grin spread across Josh's face. "I knew it. I can't believe it took me this long to figure out what I was doing wrong."

"What are you talking about? Is this about your brother?"

"I've been studying addiction for years, and every single person I've treated has had a relapse at some point. Take Gary Simmons. We talked about him, remember?"

"The news anchor?"

Josh smiled as if he was a teacher and Mac his star pupil. "Yes. My brother only killed himself, but Gary killed a whole family of innocents. Addiction is a time bomb. Eventually every addict is going to blow up. I've been looking for The One person who has truly beaten addiction. So far, every subject I've tested has failed."

He set the syringe on the tray. Relief spread through Mac at an embarrassing rate. His hand throbbed, every beat of his heart slamming him with a bolt of pain. Relaxing, he breathed and let the pain flow, accepting it. The heat spread up his arm and invaded his shoulder.

"But there's one more test." Josh swiped his fingers across an electronic tablet. He held it out so Mac could see the screen.

Gianna.

And Mac knew exactly what Josh was planning: a no-win situation for Mac. Josh didn't want to find The One person who had beaten addiction. He wanted to kill.

Josh shook his head. "She's not doing very well. I expect the toxins are building up in her bloodstream."

The girl's body was tinted green with a night vision light. She stood in front of the door, her fists raised as she beat on the wood. Water lapped around her knees. The part of the basement in which she was being held prisoner must be lower than the room Mac was in. As he watched, the water rose past her knees. God, it was pouring in. How quickly would the room fill?

"Let her go," Mac tried. "She hasn't done anything. She's sick."

"Maybe we can come to an agreement." Josh raised the syringe. "You take this, and I'll leave her outside the ER. She hasn't seen my face. She doesn't know who I am."

Mac felt defeat flowing over him. The pain in his hand slipped away. "How do I know you'll actually do it?"

Josh looked offended. "I *always* keep my word. Why would you even question my offer?"

"Because you're a psycho killer?"

"I assure you," Josh gave him a condescending, *fuck you* smile, "There's a method to what seems like madness."

"Let me guess. That's a fatal dose of heroin."

"It is," Josh said as if the conclusion was inevitable.

"Why go to all this trouble?"

"The fallen have to be punished," Josh said simply. "They have to be stopped. We both know there's no such thing as a recovered addict. Sobriety is a temporary status. I used to be optimistic. I thought I could save people from themselves. But Gary's relapse made me realize how dangerous addicts are. Anyone who fails my test needs to be culled from society like a diseased animal. Sooner or later, you'll all relapse, and when you do, you'll hurt someone else. The decision is yours."

"But you're not giving me a choice." Mac argued in an attempt to stall for time.

"There's always a choice." Josh's attitude turned pissy, as if he was tired of explaining himself to an intellectual inferior.

"My choice is to sacrifice an innocent girl to save myself. Hardly heroic," Mac pointed out.

"Your integrity should trump all." Josh lifted both hands. "She isn't worth your life. She's one of the fallen. Her life is misery, hardly worth sacrificing yours to preserve."

"Says you." Mac turned the discussion around. "Is this about your brother?"

Josh's eyes went icicle. "My brother was perfect until she cast him in her spell. Sex and drugs were his end. She was supposed to be recovered, but obviously she wasn't. There's no such thing."

"She?" Mac slipped his first two fingers into his front pants' pocket. Did he have one of Stella's hairpins? Please. Please. *Please.*

"Lucas's girlfriend." Josh spit out the words like venom. "She dragged him into her sordid life. She ruined him. My brother was weak, and he followed that whore right into hell." Josh reached for the needle again. Victory shone like insanity in his eyes.

Mac's fingers closed on a thin slip of metal. He drew it out slowly, holding it between the pads of his fingertips. Carefully he drew it onto the gurney at his side.

Josh was focused on the tablet. "Just like this piece of trash."

Mac knew Josh wasn't seeing Gianna. He was envisioning his brother's girlfriend standing thigh-deep in the flooded cell. Josh was beyond reason. Mac inserted the hairpin into the handcuff lock. The angle was tricky, and he had to pick the lock blind and one-handed. If he moved his gaze, Josh might notice.

This was Mac's sole chance of escape.

His only hope to save Gianna.

The lock gave with a thin click.

Josh froze. His head cocked and turned slowly toward Mac.

Oh shit.

Mac yanked his hand free. He snatched the knife from the rolling table and cut the leather straps around his ankles, but the blade was useless on the handcuffs. Josh dropped the tablet and lunged toward him. Grabbing Josh's shirtfront with his freed hand, Mac slammed his forehead against the bridge of Josh's nose. Bone crunched and blood flowed. Josh stumbled back, both hands covering his face.

The remaining cuff rattled on his wrist. He'd dropped the hairpin. Mac searched the bedding, but it was gone.

Josh staggered across the room and reached for the Taser.

He was going to kill Mac and let Gianna drown.

Mac yanked on the handcuffs. He searched the gurney but couldn't find the hairpin.

Shit. Shit. *Shit.*

Josh had the Taser. Mac stretched out an arm, snatched the knife from the rolling tray, and threw it at Josh. The point struck him in the bicep. The Taser fell from his hand and hit the water with a splash.

Mac grabbed the handrail of the gurney. Dragging it behind him, he plowed toward Josh. The doctor turned and fled toward a rear doorway.

The water rose above Mac's knees. How deep was the flood in Gianna's cell? He didn't have much time. He couldn't let her drown, trapped. He pictured her tilting her head to the ceiling for a last breath of air, imagined the panic whirling in her chest as water closed over her head, her eyes shining with terror.

No!

He plunged his free hand into the water, the futility of finding a hairpin in two feet of water sent fear surging cold into his throat.

Leaning on the door, Gianna shivered. Her hands ached from banging on the wood, and she could feel the bruises forming all over her body. He hadn't touched her since bringing her here and locking her in. He hadn't had to. Zapping her with that Taser had pretty much tapped her strength.

"Let me out of here you sick son-of-a-bitch." She pounded on the door, her face turned toward the ceiling-mounted camera.

He was watching.

Watching the water rise.

Letting her drown.

Nausea rose in her throat. Dena and Missy had both been murdered, and she was the next victim. If the water kept rising at this rate, her cell would be full in minutes.

Frustration burned in her chest. It wasn't fair. Not after all she'd been through. Two years ago she hadn't cared if she lived or died. Now that she actually had a will to live, some bastard wanted to kill her.

She drew her hands back and threw them at the door again, then collapsed against the rough, wet wood. It was no use. No one was coming to save her.

Why did she care?

Her life was miserable. She had no money. No family. Her mother was in prison. Her father was dead. She was too sick to work. Her days revolved around her high-maintenance medical schedule. But being near death once before had taught her a valuable lesson.

She didn't want to die.

Chapter Thirty-Nine

Water ran off the windshield of Stella's car in a solid wall. A deep puddle ran across the road. Water parted and the car hydroplaned as she pushed on the gas pedal. The tires slid sideways.

Grant held the hand strap and slid his hand toward the windshield. *"Hold steady!"*

Stella held the wheel steady and prayed. She felt the tires gain purchase and accelerated out of the floodwater.

Two patrol cars followed in her wake. Minutes later, she turned off her headlights and parked just shy of the driveway that led to Josh's house. Two patrol cars parked behind her. They'd gone in dark and quiet. They gathered in the downpour. Rain waterfalled off the brim of her hat, but she slid out of her rain jacket. The nylon was too hot, too noisy, and hindered her movements. She'd rather be wet. Carl shucked his rain gear, too. Grant and Hannah seemed immune to the weather.

The chief checked his radio. He grimaced and gestured to Grant and Hannah. "You two stay with me. The rest of you know what to do."

Stella and Carl led two patrol officers through the rain. Carl carried the battering ram as if he couldn't wait to use it. Josh's house should have stood above the lake, but the water had risen to swirl around the stone foundation. She sloshed through a shin-deep puddle to the rear of the house. Where would they be?

The upper floors had floor-to-ceiling glass overlooking the forest. He wouldn't keep prisoners there. The first floor was a stone foundation. Basement?

Stella chose a side door and gestured to Carl. Two swings of the heavy battering ram and the door burst inward. Stella and her men surged into the house. "Look for a door to the basement," she shouted over the roar of the storm.

With Carl at her side, they cleared room after room.

Stella turned into a home office and drew up short. "Oh my God."

Pictures were tacked on a corkboard: Full color glossies of Missy and Dena. In the first row, they were alive, going about their daily business, and obviously had no idea they were being photographed. In the bottom row, they were carefully posed in death.

He'd stalked them, planned their abductions, and murdered them.

Carl pointed to papers strewn across the desk. "He detailed their torture like professional counseling sessions."

"Here," an officer called. Stella went into a small room. Monitors covered a U-shaped desk. On one, she could see a small body thumping on the door, waist deep in water.

Gianna.

As Stella watched, the water rose around the girl's torso. The lake was flooding right into the basement. They had to find her.

Where was Mac?

She scanned the rest of the monitors. On the last one, Mac fished in the water with one hand. His other was handcuffed to a gurney. Where was Josh?

She bolted for the door. "Find the basement!"

Water swirled around Gianna's body, the chill lowering her body temperature. She shivered against the cold and trembled at the effort to stay on her feet.

"Help!" She raised her fists and hammered at the door. "Help me! The water is rising."

Her legs buckled. She caught herself against the door as the water rose to mid-chest. How long before it was over her head?

Her fists slid down the wood. Terror sheared off her like a glacier, and hopelessness took hold.

This was the end. To think once she'd almost taken her own life, and she'd been healthy then. Now she was fighting to keep her miserable existence.

Truly, she hadn't appreciated life until she was in danger of losing it.

Maybe this was for the best. Was her life even worth living? As much as she wanted to say it wasn't, she couldn't give up. Though, it would be easier to simply let go. Her head would slip under. Her lungs would fill with liquid. How long would it take? A few minutes at best. Then she'd be at peace. So why was she fighting so hard?

Dialysis was awful, but the days in between weren't so bad. And there was always the hope of a transplant on the horizon. Someday, maybe she'd be healthy again.

The water swirled to her neck. She tilted her face to the ceiling and faced the camera.

"Please. Don't let me die."

⌣

Stella took the lead. Gun in hand, she descended the staircase into the basement. At the bottom, she spotted another heavy door. Carl swung the battering ram. Wood splintered as the door burst inward.

Crouching, Stella went through the doorway and ducked right as Carl turned left. She swept the room with her weapon. The twenty-by-twenty room was knee-deep in water.

"Stella!" In the center of the room, Mac was handcuffed to a gurney and dragging it behind him. "He's getting away."

On the other side, a bloody-faced Josh splashed through a doorway and disappeared.

Stella motioned for the uniforms to go after him. She had to find Gianna.

"We have to save Gianna." Mac tugged on the cuffs. "Can you open these?"

Stella waded to Mac. Rain—or tears—were wet on her face. She touched his cheek with one hand. *Thank God.* His skin was warm and alive under her palm. "Where is she?"

He gave her a hard and fast kiss. "Somewhere below here."

"She doesn't have much time. The water is rising." Stella used her handcuff key to free him.

She and Mac sloshed through the water toward the doorway.

The uniforms returned. One said, "There's a bulkhead door that leads outside. He's gone."

"Any sign of the girl?" Stella asked them.

"Not through there." The cop jerked his thumb over his shoulder. His radio squawked as he gave an update on the situation. "The suspect has fled the building. We have Barrett. No sign of the girl yet."

A short burst of static, then the chief answered. "Ambulance is here. Bring Barrett out."

Stella knew that wasn't going to happen. Mac wouldn't leave her side.

She ran back into the hall. Next to her, Mac rubbed his wrists. The hall sloped downward and water filled the corridor.

Stella plunged into it. Gianna had to be down there.

Please let her be alive.

The corridor took a sharp turn. At the end of the hall was a doorway.

"I need that battering ram." Stella yelled behind her. The door was a thick exterior door, the hinges heavily reinforced.

Carl ran into the water, carrying the steel ram. Together they trudged to the door. The water swirled around their chests. Carl and Mac lifted the battering ram above their shoulders and hit the door at the top. Wood splintered but the door held. They swung and slammed it a second time. Boards cracked. Three more hard hits, and the battering ram broke through. Stella looked through the hole. The water was just as deep on the other side, the pressure holding the door closed was more than they could generate with the battering ram. How would they get her out?

"Gianna," she shouted.

No answer.

"I'll go in," Mac volunteered.

But the hole wasn't big enough for him to squeeze through.

But she would fit.

"Boost me in," Stella said.

"No," Mac said.

"We don't have time for this." She grabbed the edges of the hole.

Jaw tight, Mac put his hands in the water, and Stella stepped into the improvised step. He lifted her. She put her arms and head through the hole, then wiggled until her shoulders passed. Then she slipped from Mac's grasp into the cell. She slipped under the water and panicked and flailed for a second before her feet found the floor.

Sputtering, she surfaced, tilting her head back to breathe. The water had risen higher. Her toes stretched for the floor. Behind her, she could hear the battering ram hit the door over and over as the men enlarged the opening.

"Gianna!"

Where was she?

Frantic, Stella swam through the water, feeling for a body, panic and the cold water numbing her.

She spotted a swirl of dark hair and reached for it. Grabbing the girl's shirt, she pulled her above the surface. *No!* Gianna's face was gray, her eyes closed. Stella flipped her onto her back and towed her close. As she moved toward the door, she began mouth-to-mouth.

"I have her." Stella shouted between breaths.

Come on, Gianna.

Stella pushed Gianna through the opening. Mac grabbed her and pulled her through, then passed her to someone behind him.

"Stella, get out of there," he yelled.

The water was barely a foot from the ceiling. Stella dove through the now-larger hole into Mac's waiting arms.

He steered them both out of the flood waters as Stella's lungs bellowed. Ahead, Carl carried Gianna, lifting her out of the water. They went through the torture chamber and up the steps. On the first floor of the house, he set her down on dry ground and began CPR.

Out of breath, he motioned for another cop to take over his resuscitation efforts, but Gianna coughed.

Stella rolled her to her side as water spewed from her mouth. Gianna's eyes opened. Fear rimmed them with white.

Thank God.

"It's all right." Stella's hands trembled as she smoothed the wet hair from the girl's forehead. "We've got you."

Gianna grabbed her hand and pulled her closer to her face. "Did you get him?"

"We will." Stella squeezed her fingers. "They're going to take you to the hospital. I'll come see you later."

Gianna nodded. "Stay safe."

Mac got to his feet. He tapped Carl on the shoulder. "Which way did Josh run?"

"Don't know. Didn't see him." Carl sat back on his heels and spoke into the radio on his shoulder. "I'm taking her to the ambulance." He lifted Gianna and carried her toward the door.

Mac turned toward a set of sliding glass doors at the back of the house. Beyond a short patch of woods, rain beat on the lake. The road was blocked with emergency vehicles.

"Where are you going?" Stella asked.

"I'm going after him." Mac headed for the doors.

"Stop!" Stella followed, determined not to let him out of her sight again. "You can't go after him alone."

But Mac was gone.

Stella ran out the door. She spotted him running toward the woods and bolted into the rain after him. Her steps were slowed by driving rain, slick ground, and uneven footing. But Mac bounded through the forest like a wild creature. He disappeared down a path that led toward the lake below.

Angry and scared for Mac, she moved down the slope too fast. Her feet slid out from under her, and she went down hard on her butt. Wiping the rain from her eyes, she put a hand on the ground to push herself upright. By the time she regained her footing, she couldn't see Mac.

Footsteps slapped wet ground. Stella turned. Grant and Hannah were running toward her.

"Where's Mac?" Grant yelled.

"He ran this way." Stella pointed toward the woods and set off in that direction. Hannah kept pace with her. Grant surged ahead, stopping every few minutes to study the ground before taking off again. His pauses kept him from drawing too far ahead. They entered the trees and ran down a narrow trail.

The rain continued to drown the forest. Thunder boomed and lightning flashed. At an intercession of trails, Grant slid to a stop. He turned in a circle. "They're doubling back toward the lake."

He made a sharp right turn and set off again. Stella struggled to keep up. Her lungs and legs burned. Her head swam with dizziness. Next to her, Hannah wheezed, also working hard to keep up. Grant pulled ahead. They burst from the trees into three inches of water. The lake had flooded the beach.

Grant pointed. "There's Mac."

A football field away, a floating dock extended out over the water. A dark figure sprinted down the length of the boards.

Stella spotted a red canoe slogging through the water. "And there's Josh!"

"Mac. Stop!" shouted Grant.

But she knew Mac wasn't stopping until he had Josh. His motions were too focused, too sure. Mac was going after him.

Fresh fear bubbled into her throat as Mac reached the end of the dock, paused to pull off his boots, and dove into the water.

Chapter Forty

You are not getting away, not after all you've done.

Mac's body sliced through the water. That bastard was going down. Ahead, Josh's canoe moved slowly in the driving rain. The canoe was probably half-filled with water. Mac put his head down and stretched his strokes.

He was going to catch up to Josh. He wasn't going to let that killer escape. His smashed hand throbbed. Each beat of his heart said *getJosh getJosh getJosh*.

The cold water numbed the pain in his hand. Fury fueled his strokes. He gained on the vessel. Josh was looking back, searching the water behind the canoe. Mac dove under the surface. Swimming hard, he came up on the other side of the boat. He put one hand on the aluminum side and tipped it. The canoe capsized. Josh fell into the lake, splashing and sputtering. His oar flew into the air and landed ten feet away.

Mac grabbed the back of his shirt and dragged him back toward the bank. Josh flailed. Mac held him under for a few seconds. Clearly at a disadvantage in the water, Josh came up spewing lake water and curses. Mac dunked him again, and he ceased resisting. Mac towed his deadweight to the shore.

Once his feet were on the ground, Josh came alive. He pulled a knife from his pocket and swung at Mac's face. Mac grabbed his wrist and slammed the back of his elbow with an open palm. The *snap* of bone sang over the lake.

But psycho killer wasn't ready to give in. He dove at Mac, teeth bared.

Mac hooked the back of Josh's head and slammed it downward, meeting his face with a rising knee. And that finally took Josh down. He went limp, folding into the water face-first. Mac was tempted to let him drown. Hell, part of him wanted to hold the bastard's head under for a few minutes.

But he didn't.

He snagged the killer by his unbroken wrist and dragged him out of the water.

Grant, Hannah, and Stella raced from the woods toward him. Mac released Josh, letting him fall onto his face in the wet grass.

Stella didn't break stride. She was on Josh in a second, cuffing his hands behind his back. With Josh restrained, she rolled him onto his back. His face was a bloody mess and Mac still wanted to kill him.

Mac dropped onto his butt. The rain slowed, and the thunder that cracked sounded farther away. The storm was moving on, but not without leaving damage in its wake.

Stella sat next to him. Her bun was drowned, her breaths heaved, and she looked as sopping wet and out of breath as he felt. "I didn't even throw up this time."

"Progress." He bent his head and planted a kiss on her lips. "Let's try and have a regular date, OK?"

She rested her head on his shoulder. Her body shook. "OK."

Grant took charge of Josh, heaving him across his shoulders and carrying him back toward the house. Stella stood. Hannah held her hand down to Mac. He took it and let her pull him to his feet.

"If you ever do anything that stupid again, I'll kick your butt," Hannah said.

"And I'll help," Grant called over his shoulder.

Mac pulled Stella to his side. He couldn't get her close enough.

She leaned close to his ear and whispered, "Me, too."

Mac let Grant and Hannah draw ahead. He pulled Stella under the branches of a mature oak tree. Turning her to face him, he took her hand with his unbroken one. "I'm sorry. I lost it. I couldn't let him get away."

Anger flushed her cheeks. "It was reckless and foolish."

Mac dropped his chin. "I know."

"I could have lost you." She squeezed his fingers. "You have to promise me you'll never do anything like that again.

"Deal."

She cupped his jaw. "I thought you were going to die tonight because I wouldn't find you in time."

"You found me." He covered her hand with his. "I knew you would."

"I've never been that scared in my life."

"You are a damned good cop, Detective Dane." Mac took her hand and held it over his heart. Her grip was warm and solid. "I never doubted you for a second. I knew you'd never give up on me or Gianna. You are solid and smart, stubborn and sexy, dedicated and compassionate. You are the whole package."

Stella rested her forehead against his chest as dawn brightened the horizon. A shudder passed through her. When she lifted her face, her eyes shone with tears. "I love you."

"I love you, too." He kissed her. She tasted of rainwater and hope. "I'm done with being reckless. No more risks for me. I have too much to lose."

Stella balanced her laptop on her knees in the plastic hospital chair. In the bed next to her, Gianna was a slip of pale skin and bones. Her eyes were closed, and thick blankets were drawn up to her chin. One arm protruded, and an IV line snaked from her forearm to a small bag of liquid.

A knock sounded on the doorway.

"Come in," Stella said softly.

Mac walked into the room. A splint immobilized his injured hand. His eyes locked on hers, the intensity in his gaze filling her with warmth.

He eased into the plastic chair next to her "How is she?"

"She's going to be OK. They warmed her up and gave her a dialysis treatment. She's sleeping it off."

He lifted her chin with a fingertip. "You look exhausted."

"I don't want her to wake up alone, not after what she went through."

"What are you doing?"

"Reports." Stella closed her laptop.

"We wouldn't want your paperwork to be late," he teased.

"I like to get the facts down while they're fresh in my head." She stretched her arms over her head. Stiffness gripped her back muscles.

"'What happened to Josh?"

"Treated for a broken nose and arm at the ER." She checked her phone screen. "He's being processed at the jail."

"I wanted to kill him."

"I know." She took his hand. "I'm glad you didn't. Not because I would have thought less of you. Josh deserves to die for what he's done.

But I wouldn't want you to bear that load for the rest of your life. You've carried too much guilt for too long. You are a good man. It's time you saw that in yourself."

"How did I get so lucky that you'll even give me the time of day?" Mac leaned over to kiss her. No quick peck, but a slow and tender gesture that had her heart stuttering. "I love you, Stella Dane. Words can't describe how much."

"I love you, too." She touched his cheek, tears shining in her eyes.

Mac glanced at Gianna.

Her eyes were open. Her mouth curved in a sleepy smile.

Stella reached for her hand, gently covering it. "How do you feel?"

"Alive." Gianna shivered. "More alive with hottie here."

Gianna was a survivor.

Stella stood, unfolded the blanket draped across the bottom of the bed, and drew it up to the girl's chin. "You rest. I'll stay with you tonight."

Gianna shook her head. "Are you freaking kidding me? You should be spending the night with him."

"I can stay tonight, too," Mac said. "I'm not leaving either one of you alone."

"You can both go home." A voice said from the doorway. Stella's sister, Morgan, came in. "I'll stay with Gianna tonight."

"No one needs to stay with me." Gianna waved. "I'm an adult."

They ignored her.

"And when she gets released, we're bringing her home with us." Morgan set a closed umbrella in the corner and unbuttoned her raincoat.

Gianna's mouth dropped open, seemingly unable to come up with a smart-alecky retort.

Morgan moved a chair from the empty side of the room. "Grandpa and I discussed it. She needs to get healthy so she can get that new kidney. Our house is the best place for that to happen." She smiled at the teen. "And I can probably help with the paperwork."

From the fierce gleam in Morgan's eyes, Stella had the feeling she had more planned than helping Gianna with paperwork. Good. Morgan needed something positive to focus on.

A tear dripped down Gianna's cheek.

Mac hauled Stella to her feet. "Thank you, Morgan. As much as I was willing to sleep in that chair, a shower and a bed would be heaven right now."

Stella leaned over Gianna and kissed her forehead. "I'll see you in the morning."

Gianna gripped her hand. "I don't know what to say."

Mac laughed. "You're a smart kid. Say yes."

"OK." Sniffing, Gianna reached for a tissue from the box on her tray.

"Get some sleep." Stella straightened and followed Mac from the room. "Have you decided what you're going to do about Freddie? I assume the contract on your life is still out there."

"No reason to think he's cancelled it, but it won't matter soon. I gave the information about his camp to the local DEA office. They're planning a raid ASAP. They'll move fast on it. That should take care of Freddie."

He wrapped his arm around her waist, and Stella rested her head on his shoulder. She couldn't get enough contact with his body. It was as if her mind needed more reassurance that he was alive.

They turned into the hallway. Lance was sitting in a chair in a waiting area.

"Can you give me one minute?" she asked Mac.

"Sure." He moved toward the elevator.

"Why are you here?" Stella asked Lance.

"I drove Morgan." He crossed his arms over his chest. "I heard Horner got his hair wet."

"He did." Stella noticed her boss also made sure he'd appeared on camera in his body armor, but he'd still surprised her. That night was the first time she'd seen him not behind a desk, mirror, or microphone. "Did you really quit?"

"Look, Stella. I can't control my temper. Physically, I'm not a hundred percent either. I'm a mess. I can't take the risk of another cop getting hurt because of me."

"Go back on disability. Get better." She touched his forearm. "You don't have to quit."

"I really do." He met her eyes. His gaze wandered to the doorway, where Morgan straightened Gianna's blanket. "I need— I don't know what I need, but this is the first step in a long time that has felt right."

Stella glanced back at her sister. "All right, but don't be a stranger."

"I have no intention of doing that." Lance kept his eyes on the doorway. "I promised your grandfather I'd install some security cameras at your house tomorrow. The tech guys came and took theirs back. Art said something about trespassers."

"Did he?" Stella wondered if Grandpa was still determined to catch the errant dog owner or if he wanted Lance around the house for another reason. Like Morgan. Stella wouldn't put it past Grandpa to play matchmaker. He'd do anything to alleviate Morgan's sadness. Stella only hoped Lance didn't get hurt in the process. He had enough of his own troubles. She needed to have a conversation with her grandfather, as if she had any control over him.

"So I'll see you tomorrow, Stella."

"Bye." She returned to Mac.

They went back to his cabin, took a long hot shower, and fell into bed. The storm had broken the heat. Mac closed and locked all the windows and turned on a fan. He tugged her into his arms. "For a guy who once royally messed up his life, I'm feeling pretty lucky."

Stella stroked his bare shoulder. "You should."

He kissed her deeply.

"I'm the one who feels lucky." Stella rolled him onto his back and spent the next hour showing him just how much she loved him.

Chapter Forty-One

Monday

The sun shone with staggering brightness over the cemetery.

Grant, Mac, and four members of the local honor guard carried the flag-draped casket to the grave. Dozens of army officers and servicemen lined up behind the grave. Some had served under Grant. A small, older contingent had served under or with the Colonel. Craig and the crew from the shooting range stood in the back, their mixed bag of dress uniforms starched, their medals shiny. The sea of uniforms extended beyond the graveside rows of folding chairs.

They set the coffin on the platform over the grave. The soldiers saluted. Mac stepped back.

In a tiny navy-blue suit, Carson sat next to Hannah, a crumpled rose clutched in his fist. Ellie and her daughter filled out the rest of the row. Brody hadn't been released from the hospital. A few rows back, Stella sat with some of the SFPD that had come to pay their respects. Mac took the seat on Hannah's other side with the rest of the civilians, while service members stood and saluted.

As the firing party lined up for the twenty-one gun salute, Carson scrambled over Hannah to sit in Mac's lap. When the shots retorted over the quiet span of green, they both jumped three times. "Taps" sounded over the silence, the bugle poignant and stirring.

Mac's eyes blurred as the soldiers folded the flag with precision. Each movement rehearsed and perfect and exactly what the Colonel would have expected.

What he'd deserved.

He'd given himself to his country, body and soul.

The leader presented the tri-folded flag to Hannah. Mac didn't hear the chaplain's speech or Grant's short eulogy. Memories of his childhood flooded him, and he felt strangely calm.

The service ended and he stood. Carson tugged him over to the row of headstones. To the two that read LEE BARRETT and KATE BARRETT. Carson rested the flower on Kate's grave, then turned and leaned against Mac's legs.

Mac's chest went tight and dry until he couldn't swallow. Lee was missing so much. Carson losing his baby teeth. Faith learning to walk. He'd never see a first date or wedding or grandchild. Mac and Grant would fill in, but it wouldn't be the same. On the other side of the Colonel's open grave was Mac's mom. At least they were all together.

Carson tugged on Mac's pants. "Can we go now?"

"Whenever you're ready." Mac was more than ready to leave, but he hadn't wanted to rush Carson.

The boy reached his arms toward Mac. He leaned over and picked him up. Carson's arms tightened and Mac held him close. He'd do anything for the kids. Anything, even stand over Lee's grave and relive all the pain of losing him as many times as Carson needed to visit.

Mac carried him back to the car. Hannah and Grant were waiting at the edge of the grass. Carson jumped from Mac's arms and ran to Grant. Ellie joined them as they went to their car.

Hannah and Stella flanked Mac, each taking an arm.

"We made it." Hannah wiped her eyes. "You all right?"

"I am." Mac had finally made peace with his life. "Our lives were rough, but he prepared us. Got to give him that."

Grant, Hannah, Mac, none of them would be alive without the skills their father had taught them.

Hannah snorted. "He did. If there's ever a zombie apocalypse, we are so ready."

———

One Week Later

Stella parked in front of Grant and Ellie's farmhouse for a Fourth of July barbeque. The past week had her head spinning—in a good way. Sure, she'd had to type a thousand reports, but she'd been able to spend most of her free time with Mac.

In the passenger seat, he gestured toward the house with his splinted hand. "It might be nice to have a place like this someday."

"Are you ready to emerge from the wild?"

He laughed. "Maybe you tamed me."

"I seriously doubt you'll ever be fully domesticated." Stella reached for the door handle. "At least I hope not." Remembering the night before, she glanced back at him, heat and humor filling her with happiness.

Flashing her a wicked grin, Mac opened his car door.

"But it is peaceful here." Stepping out of the car, she breathed in the smell of freshly cut summer grass. The lawn surrounding the house was lush with green from the June rains. They'd just left her house, where Gianna was recuperating under the watchful eyes of Grandpa and Morgan.

"Uncle Mac! Uncle Mac!" Mac's nephew raced around the side of the house and tore across the grass toward them. His large golden retriever loped at his side. The boy almost slammed into Mac's legs. The dog slid to a stop and launched its body at Stella with a happy bark.

"Whoa, AnnaBelle." Holding his splinted hand in the air, Mac caught the dog's collar before she took Stella out at the knees. "Sit."

Stella stroked the dog's soft head. "Such a pretty girl."

Wiry, tan, and covered in grass stains, Carson was a mini-Mac. Mud splattered the bare legs and feet that stuck out from under his black athletic shorts. A dinosaur, and something that might have been ketchup, decorated his T-shirt.

Carson squinted at her. "I know you. You work with Brody. You've been here before, and you were at my grandpa's funeral."

"I was," Stella said.

"Look what I found!" He thrust his hand toward her. A small snake hissed in her face.

"Ah." Stella started, falling backward and landing on her butt in the grass. She pressed a hand to her chest. Her heart protested the shock, and pain shot through her hip where she'd landed on a rock.

Mac extended a hand. She took it and he pulled her to her feet.

"Are you OK?" Concern—and humor—lit his eyes. He was pressing his lips together, as if trying not to laugh.

She rubbed her throbbing hip.

Carson's smile dimmed, his gaze dropped to the ground, and he deflated. "I'm sorry, Uncle Mac. I didn't know she was scared of snakes. Aunt Hannah isn't."

"It's OK, buddy." Mac squatted. "You didn't know."

"I'm fine," Stella reassured him. "I'm not scared at all," she lied. "Just surprised."

"Let's see that snake." Mac reached out and took the creature. It was about two feet long, with a slender body decorated in orange and white stripes.

Instead of hissing at Mac, the snake wrapped its body around his tanned hand and forearm.

Smart snake.

"What a beauty," Mac said.

Carson stroked the snake's head. "He likes you."

"He likes my body heat." Mac held the snake toward Stella. "Want to pet him?"

She didn't. Not. One. Bit. But the pride on Carson's face made her feel like a slug for frightening him. This little boy had lost both his parents the year before. The least she could do was make him happy. And Mac's grin was challenge enough.

"He's not venomous," Carson encouraged. "We only have three kinds of venomous snakes in New York: timber rattlers, copperheads, and the . . . What's the other one, Uncle Mac?"

"Massasauga."

"Right." Carson repeated the name one syllable at a time. "This is a milk snake. He won't bite."

Stella plastered a smile on her face, clamped her teeth together, and lifted her hand. Where to touch it? Venomous or not, she wasn't going anywhere near its mouth. She settled on the tail and touched it with just the tips of her fingers. The skin felt like bumpy plastic. It didn't move, but she thought three strokes were enough to satisfy Carson. The snake hadn't been moist or dirty, but she wiped her hand on her slacks anyway.

Mac grinned, then cleared his throat and worked hard to straighten his face.

"Can I keep him?" Carson gently unwound the animal from Mac's hand. It immediately curled around his arm. "My friend Bobby's dad has a python he keeps in a fish tank."

"Do you really think he'd be happy in a fish tank when he's used to living out here?" Mac gestured to the woods behind the house.

"I guess not." Carson sighed. "I'll put him back in the meadow where I found him *after* I show him to Aunt Hannah." He gave Stella a knowing look that said she hadn't fooled him. "She *likes* snakes."

Mac smiled. "Good decision and definitely what's best for the snake."

"You said we shouldn't disturb the e-co-system if we don't have to." The boy whirled and bolted for the woods. Barking, AnnaBelle raced behind him.

Mac turned and took her hand. "Thanks for touching that snake when you clearly didn't want to."

"Snakes aren't my thing, but I didn't want him to be upset."

"And I appreciate it." Mac stepped closer. "You don't like spiders or snakes. Didn't you spend any time in the woods when you were a kid?"

"No. I grew up in Brooklyn. We didn't move here until I was a teenager."

"I could teach you to love camping." His gaze dropped to her mouth.

God, she wanted him to kiss her. "Maybe you can."

A car door slammed, and Mac moved backward. *Damn.*

She never tired of him kissing her. She might even let him take her camping.

A minivan had parked in the driveway not twenty feet away. How had Stella not noticed? She'd been too focused on Mac, that's how.

Grant's fiancée, Ellie, opened the vehicle's sliding door and lifted a wiggling toddler to the ground. "Ready?" she called to Mac.

Mac crouched and spread his arms wide.

Ellie released the child. Chubby legs churned as she sprinted for him. He scooped her up and gave her a smacking kiss on the cheek. Looping her hands around his neck, she returned the gesture. The front door opened, and Grant stepped out onto the porch.

"Down." Faith wiggled, and Mac set her on the ground. The second her bare feet touched the grass, she shot off for Grant.

"Hi, Mac. Hi, Stella." Ellie closed the van door. She held a reusable grocery bag in one hand. "Come on in."

Mac reached for the bag.

Ellie shook her head and kissed him on the cheek. "I've got it. But if you don't mind, you could round up Carson and hose him off for dinner."

"We're on it." Mac said.

Ellie walked up the steps and disappeared inside.

Mac lowered his head and pressed his lips to Stella's. The kiss was sweet and as warm as the sun on her hair. His hand settled on the small of her back. Gentle pressure urged her hips closer to his.

"Ew." Carson's disgusted voice broke the spell.

Mac lifted his mouth from hers, and the smile that spread across his face was full of promise. "To be continued." He glanced at his nephew. "Without an audience."

"Come *on*, Uncle Mac. Nan made blueberry pie, but we hafta eat dinner first." Carson grabbed Mac's hand and pulled, leaning into the gesture with impatience. "We're going to see the fireworks later."

As Ellie predicted, the boy required a thorough hosing before they went inside.

"I'll take care of this." Mac led the boy to the side of the yard, where the hose lay on the grass.

Stella went up onto the deck.

Brody lay on a chaise, his bandaged leg elevated on a pillow but otherwise looking good. "The case is all tied up?"

Stella sat down facing him. "Pretty much. Forensics found more than enough physical evidence in Josh Randolph's house. Photos of Missy and Dena. Detailed records of his so-called experiments with them. He designed each girl's torture specifically to hone in on her personal weaknesses. He had counseled both of them. He used everything they'd told him against them. He turned Missy's cutting against her, and broke Dena's fingers like Adam broke her bones."

"Too bad New York doesn't have the death penalty." Wincing, Brody pressed a hand to the bandage under his arm and shifted his weight.

"I read his notes. I expect he'll spend the rest of his life in a padded room while doctors stare at him through a tiny window." Stella shivered. "When we originally interviewed him, he said his brother had fought mental illness all his life. That wasn't reality. Lucas was a star athlete and a top student. He had everything going for him. His death was an accidental overdose. Josh, on the other hand, struggled through his teen years. Clearly he was the one with the mental illness."

Josh's interviews had been disturbing.

"We found pictures of his brother and his girlfriend in Josh's office. The girlfriend was wearing a pale blue scarf in many of the photos." Stella tilted her head back. The heat of the sun warmed her face.

"Do they know what sparked his killing spree?" Brody asked. "Why did he kill Missy?"

"It was the Simmons case. That newscaster Gary Simmons had been a patient at New Hope. When he got behind the wheel of his Escapade under the influence and rammed it into that minivan full of children, Josh lost it. He felt guilty for not curing him and angry at Simmons for being weak."

"But he only killed Missy and Dena?" Brody asked. "What happened to Janelle Hall?"

"She came home after a few days. The idea of running away had been more attractive than the reality." Stella watched Mac spray Carson's feet with a hose. "We didn't find any other bodies at Josh's house."

"He didn't hide Missy or Dena." Brody stretched.

"No, he wanted us to know what he had done. Maybe deep down he wanted us to stop him." Stella sighed. "He claims he did it all for the overall good. To find a way to really beat addiction. To stop those he deemed unable to be fully recovered and prevent them from harming others."

Brody snorted. "Or he just lost his shit."

"Or that."

Brody scratched the edge of his bandage. "So Spivak was helping his buddy manufacture explosives. Did he ever say why he was at the church that night?"

"Spivak is not cooperative, but one of the members came forward and said he'd been stalking her. They'd dated a few times and he'd gotten rough. She called it off, but he wouldn't leave her alone."

"What about Adam Miller?" Brody asked.

"He might not have killed his wife, but he wasn't innocent. In the trunk of Missy's car, forensics found a gym bag with several changes of clothes, a disposable cell phone, and a wig. There was also a fake Florida driver's license with Dena's picture on it. She was planning her escape, and Missy was helping her."

"What a shame she didn't leave the week before." Hannah said, rubbing Brody's shoulder.

He took her hand and squeezed it. "What a shame we can't prove anything."

"We'll be watching him. If he sneezes in the wrong place . . ." Stella promised. There was no such thing as a happy ending in a murder case, but she hated having a loose end.

"Did you pass your pistol qualification?" Brody asked.

"Yesterday." Stella was glad to have that behind her. It hadn't been her best performance, but she'd gotten through it.

The hose shut off with a squeak. Dripping, Carson raced across the deck and into the back door. Mac dried his hands on his thighs and sat next to Stella.

Hannah greeted Mac with a kiss on the cheek and hugged Stella. She waggled her eyebrows at her brother.

Mac shook his head. "Don't start."

"Don't start what?" Hannah handed them each a glass of iced tea.

Stella took the drink, condensation coated the outside of the glass. Mac sat next to her and wrapped an arm around her shoulders.

"Dinner!" Ellie called from the doorway.

Mac helped Brody inside. Twenty minutes later, the platters were picked over, and Stella's belly was full. She leaned back, almost appalled at how much she'd eaten.

Mac nudged her elbow. "I'm impressed."

She placed a hand on her belly. "I hadn't eaten all day. I was hungry."

"You must have been." He took their empty plates and carried them to the kitchen. Everyone helped clear the table. Nan brought two blueberry pies and a container of vanilla ice cream to the table.

"Pie!" Carson folded his feet under his butt to get closer.

Faith thumped her fists on the tray of her high chair.

"I hope you're not too full," Mac said.

"There's always room for pie." But Stella couldn't manage the ice cream.

When the coffee and pie were finished, Mac tugged her from her chair. "Let's take a walk." Outside, he inhaled as if he couldn't get enough fresh air.

Mac took Stella's hand and pulled her toward the side yard. The simple, old-fashioned gesture sent a jolt of warmth through her. He made her feel more than heat, whether he was making passionate love to her or simply looking at her.

"How many biology lessons have you given your nephew?" she asked.

"Every visit turns into a thousand questions. The kid remembers everything." His face beamed with pride.

"Do you spend a lot of time with him?"

"Not as much as I should." Mac frowned. "The travel gets in the way, and I was afraid the kids would get too attached and then if something happened to me . . ."

"It would devastate him. He clearly loves you very much." Stella's heart hiccupped. So did she.

"I know. I've been rethinking my career."

"You're not going back to the DEA?" Stopping, she tugged on his hand until he faced her. The thought of another drug trafficker's bullet finding him, of him dying in a far-away jungle, sent a wave of fear careening through her. She didn't want him to leave again. "Carson wouldn't be the only one devastated if anything happened to you."

"Good to know." Pleasure lit his eyes. "In the beginning, it felt like I was doing my share to fight the drug trade. Grant was off fighting the war. I wanted to contribute something."

She squeezed his hand. "There's more than one way to contribute to society. I can think of dozens. Most of them don't even require getting shot at or having people try to lop off your limbs with a machete."

"I'm not going back to Brazil. I'm leaving the DEA."

"Really?" She threw her arms around his neck.

His arms closed around her, holding tight, as if he didn't want to let her go. He whispered into her hair, "Really. I gave them all the information I had on Freddie's gang. The raid went off without a hitch yesterday."

"What about the contract he put on you?" Stella asked. "Can't he still orchestrate that from prison?" Criminals did it all the time.

"There's nothing I can do about that." Mac looked away. "Freddie and Rafe were both taken into custody. Their assets were seized. Hopefully they won't have any funds to pay a would-be assassin. Killers don't work for free."

"That's not the tidy answer I was hoping for."

"Sorry. I promised you no more secrets."

"I know." She held him tighter. "And I appreciate that. I always want the truth, even if it's not the best news."

"I don't expect Freddie to be a problem from prison. He's hardly Al Capone." Mac let his hands slide down her body then wrapped them around her waist. "Your boss called me."

"Horner?" Stella's boss was full of surprises lately.

"Yes. The local search and rescue team needs volunteers. He thinks I'd be an asset."

"There's no doubt you would be. It's a perfect fit for you."

"I think so, too." He linked his arm "And I touched base with the university. They have an opening for a biology professor."

"That's very sexy in an Indiana Jones way."

He laughed. "I'm glad you think so." Mac's face went serious. "I've never loved anyone like I love you."

"I know what you mean." Stella flattened her hands on the hard planes of his chest.

"I worry about you, and I will never get used to you going off to fight crime without me. You bring out the primitive instincts in me. I want to stand in front of you with a knife and kill anyone who so much as looks at you funny. But I also know that you're a cop at heart, and you'd never be happy doing anything else. So I'll deal with it because I not only love you, I respect you, and I want you to be happy."

"You're really staying?" Stella couldn't believe it.

"Yes. I'm going to be there for my family. I'm going to be a part of their lives." He kissed her gently on the lips. He tasted like pie. "I'd like to be a part of your life, too, if you want me."

"I do. I really do. I love you." She wrapped her arms around his neck.

Mac kissed her temple. "That's all I need, for now and forever."

Acknowledgments

As always, credit goes to super-agent Jill Marsal, and to the entire team of Montlake Romance, especially my managing editor Anh Schluep and author herder/tech goddess Jessica Poore. Special thanks to Charlotte Herscher for helping me hone this book.

I'd also like to thank Amelia Elliot and Rayna Vause for their help with details, my Facebook sprint buddies for being my virtual cheerleaders, and Kendra Elliot for daily motivation.

About the Author

Photo © 2014 Marti Corn

Melinda Leigh abandoned her career in banking to raise her kids and never looked back. She started writing as a hobby, but soon she found her true calling creating characters and stories. Her debut novel, *She Can Run*, was a #1 Kindle bestseller in Romantic Suspense, a 2011 Best Book Finalist in *The Romance Reviews*, and a nominee for the 2012 International Thriller Award for Best First Book. She is also a three-time Daphne du Maurier Award finalist and the winner of the Golden Leaf Award. When she isn't writing, Melinda is an avid martial artist: she holds a second-degree black belt in Kenpo karate and teaches women's self-defense. She lives in a messy house with her husband, two teenagers, a couple of dogs, and two rescue cats.